Letters to Luke

from His Fellow Physician,
Joseph of Capernaum

Based on the Gospel of Luke
by

Joe E. Holoubek MD

LITTLE DOVE
PRESS

LITTLE DOVE
PRESS

Graphic design and layout:
MASON Communications
Shreveport, Louisiana
kesm@bellsouth.net
Printing:
Falcon Press
Nashville, Tennessee
Binding:
BindTech, Inc.
Nashville, Tennessee
www.bindtechinc.com

Special thanks to Parrish Gallery in Westlake, Louisiana,
for the graphic use of their stylized Jerusalem cross.
www.parrishgallery.com

For additional copies, visit www.letterstoluke.com
or your local bookstore.

3rd Edition	ISBN-13:	978-0-9753766-2-1
3rd Edition	ISBN-10:	0-9753766-2-4
2nd Edition	ISBN-13:	978-0-9753766-1-4
2nd Edition	ISBN-10:	0-9753766-1-6
1st Edition	ISBN-13:	978-0-9753766-0-7
1st Edition	ISBN-10:	0-9753766-0-8

Library of Congress Control Number: 2004103827
PRINTED IN THE UNITED STATES OF AMERICA

Dedicated
to the memory of
Alice Baker Holoubek MD

God's Gift to Me

Letters to Luke

CONTENTS

Acknowledgments

I would like to thank Robert Clawson Ph.D. and Marilyn Clawson, Rosalind Moss, the Rev. Patrick Madden Ph.D. and Thomas P. Fitzgerald III for their suggestions, encouragement, research assistance and invaluable help through several revisions of this work. I am grateful as well for the friendship and encouragement of John S. and Lois Jackson.

I wish to thank my daughter Martha H. Fitzgerald for her extensive role as editor and her loving commitment as coordinator of publishing. I also appreciate Ky Ellen Mason's dedication as agent, designer and producer of the book and for assistance with editing and research.

This work is the Gospel of Luke as told through letters by Joseph, physician of Capernaum, to his friend and fellow physician Luke of Antioch. It is also the life story of Drs. Alice and Joe Holoubek set in the time of Jesus of Nazareth.

Letters to Luke is the culmination of a lifetime of religious experience, Scripture reading and personal research as well as medical training and patient care. It was started after a severe illness in which I was semiconscious for days. At that time I had a dream that I was with Jesus in Nazareth. I first wrote about this experience in an article titled "When One is Too Ill to Pray," published in the *Linacre Quarterly*, March 4, 1994.

My parents, Mary and Joseph Holoubek of Clarkson, Neb., provided a strong religious background, which sustained me through difficult times in medical school. Dr. Edgar Hull of the LSU School of Medicine in New Orleans, where my wife and I did our fellowships, set us on a course that recognized the spiritual nature of healing and the value of scholarly pursuits. The Rev. Joseph Gremillion, founding pastor of St. Joseph Catholic Church in Shreveport, La., nurtured our growing interest in religion and theology and became our mentor and very dear friend.

My wife, Dr. Alice Baker Holoubek, and I continued to read the Scriptures and attend daily Mass. For more than forty years we gave presentations on the physical sufferings of Christ to churches and medical and academic groups in six states and the District of Columbia. We also made a pilgrimage to the Holy Land as members of the Equestrian Order of the Holy Sepulchre of Jerusalem. To walk in the places where Jesus walked is an unforgettable experience.

For thirty years a group of friends came to our home every other Monday night to study Scripture, listen to religious tapes and discuss what we heard. They included John and Laura Dailey, Robert Clawson Ph.D. and Marilyn Clawson, Wilfred Guerin Ph.D. and Wilda Guerin, Arthur and Joyce Trowbridge, Herbert and Helen Dews, Don and Carrie Baker, John Jackson M.D. and Betty Jackson, Dorothy Richardson, Giffy Marshall, Mary Pickles and Dee Robichaux.

Other major sources of inspiration for this work were Pierre Barbet's pioneering study *A Doctor at Calvary* and the research of John P. Jackson Ph.D. and Rebecca Jackson, co-founders of the Turin Shroud Center of Colorado.

I owe much of my understanding of the Scriptures, theology, Biblical history and early Christianity to instructors with the Greco Institute, a religious education program of the Diocese of Shreveport. Dr. Alice and I took more than forty courses there over a ten-year period. Among the instructors who influenced this work are Jim and Mary McGill, Michael Broussard, Don Emge Ph.D., Sister Eileen McGrory, Sister Carolyn Sur Ph.D., the Rev. Pat Madden Ph.D., the Rev. Andre McGrath OFM Ph.D. and the Rev. James McLelland.

The care of the poor in this book is modeled after the Christian Service Program of Shreveport, founded by Sister Margaret McCaffrey.

The personality and even physical characteristics of Jesus himself, as I see Him, are a compilation of the remarkable qualities of the Most Rev. William B. Friend, Bishop of the Diocese of Shreveport, the Rev. Msgr. Joseph Gremillion, the Rev. Msgr. Murray Clayton, the Rev. Peter Mangum and the Rev. Karl Daigle. I would also like to acknowledge the influence of my friendship with Rabbi David Lefkowitz, Jr.

So many members of the clergy have enriched our lives with love, moral guidance and spiritual insight. I thank them all.

Joe E. Holoubek M.D.
Shreveport, Louisiana
March 2004

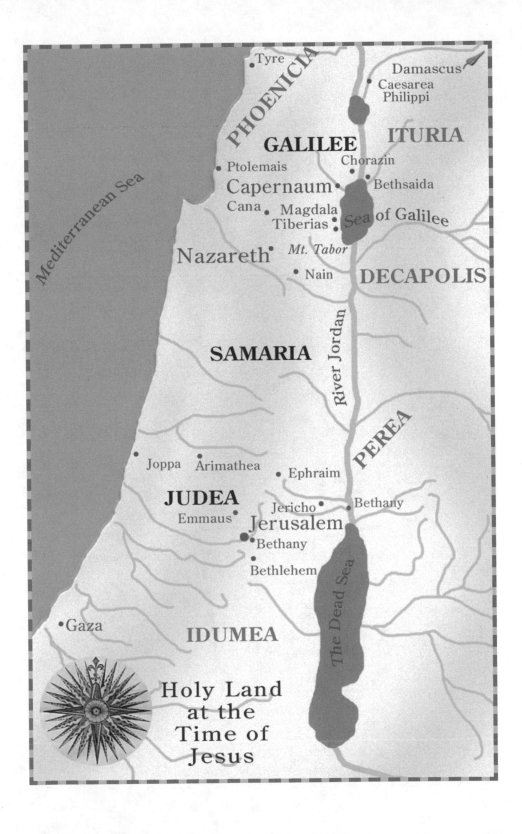

Holy Land
at the
Time of
Jesus

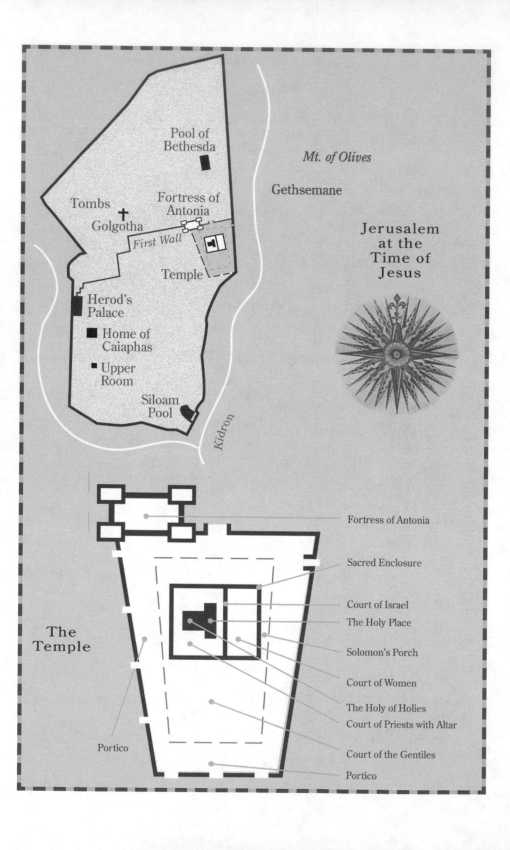

Jerusalem at the Time of Jesus

Pool of
Bethesda

Mt. of Olives

Gethsemane

Tombs
Golgotha

Fortress of
Antonia

First Wall

Temple

Herod's
Palace

Home of
Caiaphas

Upper
Room

Siloam
Pool

Kidron

**The
Temple**

Fortress of Antonia

Sacred Enclosure

Court of Israel

The Holy Place

Solomon's Porch

Court of Women

The Holy of Holies

Court of Priests with Altar

Portico

Court of the Gentiles

Portico

Prologue

I am Joseph, son of Joseph of Capernaum and his wife Mary. My wife is Elisa, daughter of Erasmus, physician of Capernaum, and his wife Sarah. We are physicians after the model of Hippocrates and practice the ancient art of healing with Erasmus. The following are letters I wrote to my friend and fellow physician, Luke of Antioch, who trained with me in Athens. They tell of how we became followers of the man of Nazareth called Jesus.

CAPERNAUM

My ancestors were all tillers of the soil in the fields around Capernaum in the Roman district of Galilee. My father had worked the land since childhood. He was ten years old when his parents died leaving nine children, three to sixteen years of age. They all worked the fields and lived together plowing, planting and cultivating until one by one they married and started homes of their own. My mother's ancestors were also tillers of the soil. She had three sisters and two brothers, all of whom married and continued to grow crops and raise livestock. Altogether I had fifty cousins or brethren.

My father and mother married and worked the fields of large landowners for a share of the crops for fifteen years. When I was eight years old my father became ill and unable to continue the hard labor on the land. He moved our family into Capernaum where he went to work for a caravan outfitter. My mother worked in the home, weaving and knitting handsome garments and selling them. Both of them were accustomed to working hard and saving.

Within a few years they had saved enough that my father was able to start a caravan supply business of his own. His clientele grew because he treated everyone fairly and with excellent service and he always seemed to be laughing. In fact he was known as "Joseph with the hearty laugh."

I grew up working in my father's establishment, like all of the other sons of our tradition. He carefully instructed me in the work in which he was engaged. It was understood that I would take over when he became old. Aside from his responsibilities as supplier to the caravans, he was quite an accomplished carpenter and taught me that trade, too. I was also taught how to be a mason, a builder, a gardener and other vocations. He felt that a man should be able to do many things.

Our entire family attended the synagogue in Capernaum, where the men worshipped in the main area. As I grew into manhood, I was allowed to participate in the service. I had to say the Shema, the basic statement of Jewish Law,[1] three times a day and fast regularly. It was expected that I would soon choose a wife and marry.

My sister, Acida, married at twelve and one-half years of age, as is the tradition. Her husband, Reu, was also a tiller of the soil.

The only employee that my father had at the caravan station was a man named Joshua. He was the oldest of ten children. He did not attend the synagogue or the other activities of the town. Joshua could do the work of a carpenter, a stonemason and a repairman, and he seemed to enjoy working all of the time. My father allowed him to have a small shop in the way station, where the people of Capernaum could bring in their equipment for him to repair.

Our station was the crossroads for caravans as they traveled north from Jerusalem, south from Antioch or Damascus, or east from the sea. We sold supplies and equipment for the journeys and also delivered goods that arrived by caravan to the various shops and homes in the town. Because many of the travelers who came through our city were not of our faith and did not observe the Sabbath as a day of rest, we were forced to provide service on that day. The Pharisees in the local synagogue objected, but they were always eager to use the goods that the caravans brought.

We were familiar with four languages. Aramaic was the common language spoken in Capernaum, and Hebrew was used in the synagogue. The Romans used Latin, so the government edicts were in that language and we were forced to learn to read it. However, the language of the travelers was Greek, and we at the way station had to be able to understand and speak in that tongue as well.

There were long periods of inactivity between the arrivals of caravans at the station. During these times we stayed busy keeping the property clean. We made the property around the station into a flower garden that was the joy of travelers as well as the people of Capernaum.

My mother always wanted to learn all that she could about herbs and the art of healing, and passed that interest on to me. During lulls in the work at my father's business, I would visit the market place and the stall where medicinal herbs were sold and try to learn about them. I obtained some writings on the use of herbs as medicine and shared this knowledge with my mother.

During my visits to the market, I would often see a young woman come in who knew exactly what herbs she needed, would then purchase them and leave. I asked the vendor about her, and he informed me that she was Elisa, the daughter of Erasmus, the only trained physician of Capernaum. Her brother, Samuel, was a physician in Cana. Twenty-seven descendants of her great-grandfather were practitioners of the healing art. Elisa was mixing her father's drugs and potions, as her older sister Rebekah was doing for Samuel. Elisa wanted to become a physician, but no one would accept a woman as an apprentice. Therefore, she was learning medicine from Erasmus, who had, during his younger years, apprenticed with a physician of the Hippocratic tradition.[2] However, most of his knowledge came from observation, examination and careful evaluation of the results of treatment.

I must admit, I thought that only men should become physicians. Still I was eager to learn more about this slender, attractive, rather serious young woman. She was past the usual age for girls to marry and quite independent. I began to time my arrival at the market for when I knew she would be there, and I would listen for the names of the herbs for which she asked. Often she would mention the use that Erasmus was making of them. One day, as she walked by me, I smiled and she smiled back. We had not been formally introduced, and it was not right to speak to her in public.

The vendor had been watching me and he came up and said, "Next time I will introduce you to Elisa." And when the time came, I was momentarily speechless, but she smiled so nicely that I regained my courage. I picked up an herb leaf and asked her how she used it. And she told me all about the uses that her father made of it. I was amazed at her knowledge. I was willing to learn, even from a woman. We began to meet almost daily and my periods of absence from my father's business became longer and longer. As long as no caravan was expected my father did not mind, especially when I told him that I wanted to learn more about herbs. If he needed me he would send a messenger to get me. I also told my parents all about Elisa.

As we talked in the market place, we discussed many things and learned how much we thought alike. We both had hopes to see faraway places and to learn about new discoveries. We each had a deep faith in the God of Israel, although her knowledge of the Scriptures was far greater than mine. I went to the synagogue to read more of the Torah, the Prophets and the Writings, just to be able to understand some of the passages she recited from memory. I soon realized that a woman can be as knowledgeable as a man can be, even more so.

One day, as we were leaving the herb stall, she asked, "What are your plans for the future?" I was surprised that she asked. "I suppose that I will stay here in business with my father." But Elisa had another idea. "With your interest in herbs, why don't you become a physician?" she said. "I couldn't," I said. "My father needs me." But somehow, hearing the idea from her made it seem possible.

During the next few days, my thoughts were of how it would be if I too should become a physician, and if I would be capable, and how my father would feel if I did not follow his trade.

Then came a day when Elisa met me at the market with important news. "Abraham, the leading physician of Jerusalem, has decided to accept two women as apprentices in his training center, a woman named Deborah from Ephraim and me. I will be leaving as soon as I can find a suitable caravan. Would you ask your father to arrange that for me?"

I was so shocked that I stuttered my reply. "I am sure that he can arrange suitable and safe transportation."

On my way back to the business I was in such deep thought that I walked past the place. When I finally returned from the other direction, my father, a keen observer, asked me what was wrong. So I told him of Elisa's request. He replied that he could arrange for safe travel to Jerusalem within a week's time.

The day came, and Elisa arrived at my father's business with her father and mother. We were all so busy that she and I did not have a moment alone together. Soon everything was loaded. As I told her goodbye I heard my father speaking to the caravan leader. "Take good care of the young lady named Elisa." And he replied, "For you, Joseph, I will be like a father to her." And off they went.

My father turned to Erasmus and Sarah. "My friend will see that your daughter is safe. They will take the easier route along the east bank of the Jordan and cross back near Jericho." I saw a great look of relief on the faces of her parents.

After they left, Erasmus spoke to me. "Joseph, your father is a good man." As I nodded he turned to his wife. "Come, Sarah, now you will have to do the work that Elisa did for me." And the two of them walked off rapidly, he with long strides and she, who was a head shorter, with quick steps a short distance behind him.

The remainder of the day I was very quiet, in deep thought. Finally, I decided that I too would attempt to become a physician. That evening, after we had finished our meal and evening prayers, I told my parents of my decision. My mother was very pleased, saying she had hoped I would realize the talents I showed toward healing. My father was obviously disappointed that I would not follow his trade. Still, he did nothing to discourage me. They said they would help as much as they could, but that I would have to work too. I had expected to do that anyway. So it was decided that I would go to study the art of medicine. But where?

In our work, we encountered people from Greece, from Egypt and Macedonia, and I had always longed to see these countries. There were several centers of learning for the art of medicine, but we had no contacts in any of them. However, I had met several physicians as they passed through Capernaum who had trained under Dividimus of Athens. I wrote to him and asked for a position as apprentice.

In time I received a reply stating that he would accept me for three years. I was thrilled to be able to go to a foreign land and especially to Athens, the center of learning. My parents gave me the money that they had saved. I packed my few garments, said farewell to my parents, my mother's widowed mother, my sister and her husband, and set out for Athens.

It was a long walk westward to the sea and the port of Ptolemais. There I was able to obtain a position as an oarsman for my passage. It took three weeks because the winds were variable. It was a very hard journey. I had never been on the sea, let alone rowed a ship. All of my muscles ached constantly.

ATHENS

Finally we arrived at the mainland of Greece. I helped unload the cargo, collected my belongings and started on the two-day walk to Athens. Once I arrived in the city, I went immediately to meet Dividimus. He was the most learned physician in Athens, having taken his apprenticeship under a physician who traced his training to the Father of Medicine, Hippocrates.

Another young man, a Syrian named Luke, was also starting his apprenticeship with Dividimus. He was born in Antioch and had been adopted by a wealthy Roman. He was an excellent writer and well-educated in music, art and history. He was pleasant and seemed interested in how other people lived. We took a liking to each other and found a place to stay together.

I soon learned that my knowledge of Greek was inadequate. The Greek of the traveler that I had learned in Capernaum was different from the

Greek spoken in Athens. I could not read or write it, but Luke taught me, and he was a good teacher.

For three years Luke and I occupied the same room, attended the same patients with Dividimus, and learned all about his methods of treatment. We read the works of Hippocrates and many other writings about medicine. Dividimus had other physicians working in his clinic who had trained in Alexandria, Mesopotamia and other centers of learning, so we were able to get the most current medical knowledge from many regions.

We learned that Hippocrates carefully observed and recorded all of the symptoms and signs of a disease. He taught that disease was caused by defects in the body fluids called humors — phlegm, blood, yellow bile and black bile. We were taught his code of ethics and his use of logic in his approach to a diagnosis.

We did anatomical dissections together, studying from the human dissections done by Herophipus and Erasistratus about three hundred years before. We learned all about the bones, muscles and internal organs.

We cultivated herbs, learning how to recognize plants that had medicinal properties, and how to harvest them and extract the valuable ingredients. We learned how to compound healing potions, ointments and medications. I often thought of Elisa and her great knowledge of herbs.

We observed Dividimus in surgery, and in time we were assisting him. We cleaned debris from wounds, helped saw bones for amputations, sealed bleeding blood vessels, removed tumors from the skin and sutured the remaining healthy tissue. We learned to administer madragora, a plant extract that makes patients drowsy and thereby feel less pain. We learned how to use a trephine to drill a hole in the skull, a drastic procedure to be used only when a patient has received a blow on the temple and later gradually becomes unconscious. Of course, we always had to combat infection, which produced pus, in every surgical procedure.

Throughout our studies, Luke continued to teach me more of the Greek language so that I could read and converse well.

I would go to the synagogue of Athens every Sabbath and on the Feast Days. It was the only place that reminded me of home, so I sometimes went just to sit and listen to the instructions. Luke came from a culture where they worshipped many gods, but he did not seem to bother with any of them. He could not understand just one god and asked me many questions about my faith. Unfortunately, I did not know as much as I wanted to, so I began to visit the synagogue more often to get the proper answer from the learned rabbis.

In the course of time I learned that Luke was a very methodical person, organizing what he learned. He spent much time obtaining a history of the illness from a patient and recorded the details in the order of their occurrence. He kept a record of his studies in Athens, reporting on the different types of treatments, the cultivation of medicinal herbs and the compounding of potions. Since it was a valuable source of information, I copied most of it to use when I returned to Capernaum.

Luke and I were paid occasionally to help serve at the banquets of the wealthy. We learned the techniques of table service. It paid well and we were always allowed to eat after the banquet was over.

During my stay in Athens my parents and I corresponded as we could. I wrote to them every Sabbath, which Dividimus permitted me to take as a day of rest. It took weeks to receive the letters, and sometimes two or three would arrive at one time. After three months, I boldly wrote a letter to Elisa and enclosed it in my letter to my parents. My father was to deliver it to Erasmus in Capernaum, who would send it by caravan to Jerusalem. To my surprise, I received a reply. After that we wrote to each other regularly. In addition to discussing our respective patients and what we were learning, we spoke of our thoughts and dreams and our love of God and family.

Although Elisa's traveling was limited, she was interested in all of my experiences on the way to Athens and about the way of life in Greece. I described the beauty of the Acropolis, which stands high above the city and can be seen from everywhere, and the Parthenon, a temple dedicated to the goddess Athena. The hill is covered with beautiful temples dedicated to various gods.

She, in turn, wrote me all about her education in Jerusalem. Abraham's teachings were more oriented to the theory that disordered organs cause disease rather than disordered humors.

By now I was sure that Elisa was the woman I wished to have as my wife. I told Luke about my plans and his first reaction was "A female in the healing art? Come now, Joseph."

"But this woman is special," I replied. He just shook his head.

Elisa finished her apprenticeship before I did and was asked to stay on as an assistant to Abraham in Jerusalem. That was a distinct honor and I was proud of her, but I was worried that she would not want to marry me.

Some time later as Luke and I finished our three years of apprenticeship, Dividimus called us together and gave us parting advice. "Remember, you will never know all that you want to know about medicine. You must keep your minds open to new methods of healing and to adopt them if they are good." Then he had us swear by the Oath of Hippocrates[3] to do only good for our patients.

I had studied the oath and told Dividimus that I would not swear "by Apollo, the Physician, and Aesclepius,[4] and Health and all Healing and all the Gods and Goddesses." He knew of my strong faith and agreed instead to let me swear by the one true God in whom I believed. Luke, too, seemed to respect me for my decision. Here is the oath as I swore to it.

THE OATH OF HIPPOCRATES

I swear by the one and only true God, that, according to my ability and judgment, I will keep this oath and stipulation.

To reckon him who taught me the art equally dear to me as my parents, to share my substance with him and relieve his necessities if required, to regard his offspring as on the same footing as my own brothers and to teach them this art if they should wish to learn it without fee or stipulation, and that by precept, lecture and every other mode of instruction, I will impart a knowledge of the art to my own sons and to those of my teachers and to disciples bound by a stipulation and oath, according to the law of medicine, but to none others.

I will follow that method of treatment which, according to my ability and judgment, I consider for the benefit of my patients and abstain from whatever is deleterious and mischievous.

I will give no deadly medicine to anyone if asked, nor suggest any such counsel. Furthermore, I will not give to a woman an instrument to produce abortion.

With purity and with holiness of heart I will pass my life and practice my art.

I will not cut a person who is suffering from a stone, but will leave this to be done by practitioners of this work.

Into whatever houses I enter I will go into them for benefit of the sick and I will abstain from every voluntary act of mischief and corruption and further from the seduction of females or males, bond or free.

Whatever, in connection with my professional practice, or not in connection with it, I may see or hear in the lives of men, which ought not to be spoken abroad I will not divulge, as reckoning that all such should be kept secret.

While I continue to keep this oath unviolated may it be granted to me to enjoy life and the practice of the art, respected by all men at all times, but should I trespass and violate this oath, may the reverse be my lot.

Dividimus honored the two of us at a small banquet and there we took the oath. He then gave us a document certifying our training as physicians. I had difficulty realizing that it was true. "If my parents could see this, they would be proud," I thought to myself, and I determined to act always in a manner to make them proud.

As I was preparing to leave Athens, I received a letter from Elisa. She stated that the previous week she had felt a pain in the right upper chest whenever she took a deep breath. Abraham had listened to her chest with his ear and heard the bubbling sounds of phthisis or, as it is commonly called, consumption of the lungs.[5] She had been spending much time with patients dying from the disease.

I read this news with a chill in my heart. This dreaded disease literally consumes the lungs, which are filled with large cavities. The patient coughs up bloody humor, loses weight, runs a fever, becomes weak and slowly wastes away. I could hardly finish reading the letter.

"Abraham is sending me back to my father, Erasmus, to treat me. You know he has had great success with these cases. He says that the lung needs rest in order to recover. I will be in bed for six months." And then she added, "Joseph, do not worry. With the help of God, I will be well."

I sat there as in a trance as I reread the letter. Luke came in and asked, "Joseph, what is the matter?" I translated the letter to him, since it was written in Aramaic. He shook his head.

"Joseph, you know what that means. She may not last until you get home. If she does, and you marry her, the first child will carry her out." Of course I knew that because I had seen many such patients during my training, but I did not want to admit it. I had never seen a patient recover from consumption. Still, her case was diagnosed early. I went outside to be alone and watched the sun set. And then I recalled one of Elisa's letters.

She had written that when she felt depressed she would recite some of the Psalms from the Scriptures. Since I did not know any of them by memory like she did, I went to the synagogue and read and reread them by candlelight. These writings are centuries old and were written by people who were in distress. After telling the Lord their troubles and sufferings, they continued to rely on Him and always ended praising Him.

Then I read the story of Job, a man who had been completely just, yet bad things happened to him, and even though he complained, he continued to acclaim his Creator.

It took me some time to accept that I should rely upon the Lord always and praise Him even when in distress.

"Dear God," I prayed. "I leave Elisa in your loving hands. Take care of her. We praise your name."

I said this over and over again. Soon a calm came over me, and as I left the synagogue and walked back to our room, I felt a great relief. I wrote Elisa an encouraging letter. I told her that I had finished my training and would soon return to Capernaum. I would spend a few weeks with her and visit my family before deciding where and how to begin my new life as a physician.

Several days later Luke and I parted, promising to write to each other. He took passage on a boat to Antioch. I was able to get passage on a boat going to Ptolemais. This time I served as ship's physician and also worked in the kitchen. I sewed a few wounds with the limited material they had on board, since I owned no instruments of my own. The only anesthetic we had was wine, and it was weak. We were stalled for days with no wind. Because of the delay, we were running out of food when the lookout finally sighted the port.

I packed my few belongings, which included the writings on medicine by Luke, and I walked to Capernaum, sleeping under trees at night and purchasing some food with the coins that I had left.

CAPERNAUM

I was so happy to see Capernaum that I ran the last distance to my parents' house. They were visibly older but happy that I was home safely and that I was a physician. And for the first time in three years, I tasted some of my mother's cooking. Then I told them that I wanted Elisa to be my wife. All of this news was too much for my mother, and she cried in happiness.

I hurried to see Elisa, carrying the medical writings of Luke to give to her. Her parents welcomed me and took me to her room. It was a great reunion. She looked so well and she smiled all of the time. I broke with precedent and took her parents aside to ask if I could marry her. In our culture the father of the groom usually makes the initial approach to the father of the bride and bestows on him a gift. "I have nothing to give your daughter but myself," I told Erasmus and Sarah, "but I am qualified to practice medicine as a physician. I will take good care of Elisa."

And they answered, "Have you asked her?" These parents thought so much of their daughter that they wanted her to make up her mind about her future. That, too, was rare in our culture. So I went and knelt by her bed and asked this precious young woman, Elisa, to marry me. She replied, "Oh, Joseph, I want to say yes. But you know that I am ill." My reply was "That makes no difference. You will get well, I know it." And with that our betrothal was decided. My parents seemed as happy about the plans as hers were.

I then made time to visit with my aunts, uncles, cousins and with my sister and her husband, who now had two young children. I enjoyed working in the sun with Reu for two days, tending sheep or cultivating the crops, knowing that soon enough I would begin my own life's work.

A few days later I carried Elisa in my arms to the other part of her parents' house for the betrothal ceremony. This was a joyous occasion with members of both families present. Now we could begin to plan our new lives together. We placed our trust in God that we would have a future together.

For the next few weeks I helped my father when caravans arrived, but spent many pleasant hours helping Erasmus in his work treating patients. I was amazed at his practical knowledge of medicine.

Of course, I visited Elisa every day and it was such a joy to be with her. She was always smiling and encouraging. She had taken up needlework and was making caps and clothing for the poor. We talked for hours about the patients that we had seen and discussed the various methods of treatment.

One day I came in and she was sitting up. "Elisa! Why are you out of bed?" She smiled and said, "Don't worry, Joseph. My father said that he did not hear anything in my chest and that I could resume my activity." That was a blessing and we both thanked God. During the next few days she gradually grew stronger until we could walk a short distance together.

Erasmus kept Abraham informed about Elisa's progress and continued recovery. He knew that she was now planning to marry a practitioner of medicine, trained under Dividimus in Athens. Abraham wrote Elisa asking her to work with him again as his assistant. "Bring Joseph as well," he said, "if you both can live on the pay for a single assistant." The day she received the letter, there was a sparkle in her eyes and joy in her voice as she greeted me. I too was pleased. I would have the opportunity to work under Abraham with Elisa.

Since he wanted us to come soon, our marriage had to take place quickly. Our wedding was typical of those in our faith but a good deal smaller. We did have a great celebration and many of my uncles, aunts and brethren came.

Soon after that, we started to Jerusalem. My father had arranged passage with a trusted caravan leader and Elisa was to ride all the way. We traveled south along the east bank of the river to Bethany on the Jordan and then started the climb west to Jerusalem. It took six days and we were both tired.

We were able to rent a room near where we would work. It was our first home. The next day Elisa took me to meet Abraham. To my surprise he was not an old man like Dividimus. He was short in stature, had a very pleasant smile and welcomed me. He asked me about my work and training in Athens and was interested in the types of cases that we saw there. Elisa had brought the account of our medical training that Luke had written.

Abraham was delighted to receive this and asked permission to have it copied and keep it in the library of his clinic. It was obvious to me that this man was a scholar, eager to learn anything new about medicine no matter where it came from and teach it to his students.

As we left he said, "God bless you." I had never before heard a medical teacher invoke the name of God. Elisa sensed this and remarked as we left, "Abraham always does that in parting."

And so started a new period of our lives.

[1] Deuteronomy 6:4-9

[2] The Greek physician Hippocrates (450-377 B.C.) is known as the father of modern medicine. He taught that man could learn the nature of disease by observation. He applied logic and reason to medical care and showed that diseases had natural causes. He took the treatment of illness out of the hands of religion.

[3] Physicians traditionally took the Hippocratic Oath upon finishing their training.

[4] Aesclepius was deified in Greek mythology as the god of medicine. There are many shrines dedicated to him in Greece.

[5] Tuberculosis, an infection of the lungs, was a leading cause of death. Months of bed rest were the only treatment for centuries. Pneumothorax treatment (collapsing the affected lung by the introduction of air between the lung and the chest wall) was used during the early part of the 20th century. Antibiotics were introduced in the 1940s and have simplified the treatment.

Jerusalem

Letter 1

Dear Luke, so much has happened since I wrote informing you about Elisa's recovery, our marriage and our plans to work as assistants to Abraham, the great physician of Jerusalem.

We have been in Jerusalem for about three months now. Luke, I have married a most wonderful woman. She is a caring wife and a very capable physician. She has a way of explaining a new disease to me so tactfully that I feel as if I knew it all of the time. She has more knowledge of medicine than I have. And Luke, even though she is in a man's profession she retains the graciousness of a woman.

Abraham is a great teacher as well as a learned physician. He insists that all of his assistants wear a white robe, which here in Jerusalem distinguishes us as physicians. It also keeps our other garments clean. We normally wear a long inner tunic, an outer cloak, a belt and sandals, with a headdress to keep the sun off our heads and neck. When we come to the clinic we remove our outer cloak and put on the white robe of a physician. We remove it when we leave.

In Jerusalem we see certain illnesses that you and I did not encounter in Athens. Because of the elevation, many people come here for their health and to escape the heat. We have many cases of a special type of flux where the bowel flows for days.[1] During this time much fluid is lost. The patients lose weight and often die, especially the infants.

There is much dust here and this causes irritation of the eyes. We also have malaria along the River Jordan.

Of course, we have many of the same conditions that we treated in Athens. We have paralysis of one arm, one leg or an entire side of the body.[2] Also we see blindness, deafness, inability to speak and, of course, the hunched back of the aged.[3] We have many wounds to open and drain of yellow pus.[4]

Abraham also believes that some illnesses are due more to the mind than the body. These patients usually do not eat. They just sit and seem to have no energy. We find nothing wrong with them on physical examination. Elisa has a way of talking and listening to these patients and often finds that something has been troubling them, and from that they seem to develop physical symptoms.

We see many patients who suffer from phthisis or consumption. Elisa treats many of them. Most of these cases are so far advanced that they soon die.

I thank God daily for the health that Elisa has now. Abraham checks her regularly and insists that she rest every afternoon. These last months have been very busy, but still she has had no recurrence. Through it all, Elisa keeps up a cheerful spirit.

Luke, I learned a lot in Athens under Dividimus, but Abraham has shown me another aspect of the healing art. He teaches us to treat the patient as well as the disease. He always sits down by patients, holds their hand and makes them feel comfortable. He says a doctor should always touch the patient he is treating. He carefully listens to the patient describe the symptoms and asks questions when necessary. Then he proceeds with a thorough examination, carefully analyzes what he has learned and makes a diagnosis. Following this he sits down with the patient and discusses his findings and his suggested treatment. He insists on a detailed record of the case.

Abraham never discusses a patient's condition with someone else in the presence of the patient. I remember how embarrassed some of the patients were in Athens when they heard their illness being discussed with the physicians and apprentices. Abraham puts humanity into the practice of the medicine. And never does he ask for a fee. If patients can pay, there is a box where they may drop the coins. If they cannot, they receive the same treatment.

Luke, this man is having a great influence not only upon my treatment of patients but upon the way I treat everyone I meet.

Your friend and fellow physician,
Joseph

[1]   Infection of the bowel due to germs or viruses, causing severe diarrhea.

[2]   Poliomyelitis (infantile paralysis) or stroke.

[3]   Osteoporosis (softening of the bones due to age) or Pott's Disease (tuberculosis of the spine) with resulting collapse of the anterior part of the vertebra.

[4]   Pus is secondary to infection.

Letter 2

Dear Luke, your letter of four weeks past has arrived. Elisa and I enjoyed learning about your work. We are pleased that the people of Antioch are recognizing your excellent training and ability. Now I will answer your questions.

Elisa is well-trained and a full member of the medical profession. I know your strong feelings about a woman doing work that traditionally has been done by a man. I had the same feelings before I met her. In our culture there is no place for women in public life. They are not given an opportunity to learn as men are deemed to do. A woman is expected to run the home, bear and raise children, and care for her husband.

Fortunately, Elisa's parents allowed her to learn and Abraham allowed her to train under him, alongside another woman, Deborah. And the patients accept her because they know that she is knowledgeable and competent. She is one of the most intelligent people I have ever known.

To answer your second question, what we will do when she becomes with child ... this we discussed before we married. When the Lord chooses for us to have a child, we will go back to Capernaum and she will stay in bed much of the time so that her consumption will remain inactive. Abraham insists that she rest every day after the noon meal.

Abraham does have other assistants, Reuben and Lemuel, who studied three years with Deborah and Elisa. Deborah has returned to her home in Ephraim, northeast of Jerusalem, to practice medicine. Lemuel and Reuben are both married and we are friends with their wives. They, like Abraham, have accepted me as a colleague. I believe that is because they have such a tremendous respect for Elisa as a physician and as a person.

Abraham has known tragedy in his life. He was married as a young man and he and his wife had a daughter. When the child was one year old, her mother fell down some steps and died. Abraham was deeply hurt but continued to teach. In time he married a woman he had known from childhood. They all have been very happy. In fact, he came in today with a wider smile than usual and announced that his wife is with child. We all rejoiced with him. As you can see, he treats all of his assistants and their families as part of his family.

This is a joyful time as well as a tremendous learning experience.

Joseph

Letter 3

You have asked, Luke, about the medications that we use here. They are much the same as we had in Athens, although Abraham uses dried sap of the poppy a little more than Dividimus did in Athens. We use it to relieve pain when we operate and also as a weak solution to stop the fluids running from the bowels, the condition we call the flux. As we did in Athens, we use mandragora to deaden a patient's consciousness.

Now to tell you more about the city of Jerusalem, where we have worked for several months now. About 100,000 people live here, and there must be thousands more animals — sheep and goats, dogs and chickens, donkeys and camels. Foreign traders, pilgrims and other travelers crowd the narrow streets. And Luke, there is constant noise — baying and barking, the shouts of merchants, the ringing of shepherd's bells. It is very dusty much of the time, even though Jerusalem is much higher than the rest of the country, about 1,625 cubits[1] above the sea, making it cooler than the surrounding area.

Jerusalem is the center of Jewish life because of the Temple. The grounds take up about one-third of the area of the city. King Solomon's temple, built on a hill, was destroyed by the Babylonians. A later temple built on the same hill was made larger and grander by Herod the Great. It took him thirty years to complete. In the center of this magnificent building, concealed by a curtain, is the Holy of Holies, which in Solomon's time contained the Ark of the Covenant. The high priest is allowed to enter the Holy of Holies only once a year at the Feast of Atonement.

Elisa and I go to the Temple to worship regularly. Elisa sits in the Court of Women while I am with the men. This I don't like but Elisa says with a smile, "Be patient, Joseph. It is the custom now."

We all pay tax to support the Temple — half a shekel a year. Hundreds of thousands of pilgrims come here to worship every year. They are devout Jews from all over the known world. They come from Egypt, Libya, Mesopotamia and Rome, from Cappadocia, Pamphlia, Phrygia and distant Asia, and, of course, from Judea, Samaria and Galilee. Some are dressed in silks and travel in splendor. Others are obviously very poor, but they still make the pilgrimage to the Temple in Jerusalem.

Jews are encouraged to make the pilgrimage to Jerusalem every year. Elisa and I both made the journey with our families when we were younger. It is prescribed in the Law that every family take an unblemished lamb or goat, have it approved and sacrificed at the Temple, and roast it on the feast of the Passover.[2]

It is also the law in Judaism that every first-born male be brought to the Temple and consecrated to the Lord,[3] and that the parents offer as sacrifice a lamb, a pair of turtle doves or two young pigeons.

Luke, I do get annoyed now when we enter the Temple grounds. Many of the pilgrims do not bring animals to sacrifice at the Temple and must purchase them at what is called the "Market of the Sons of Annas." Annas is the former high priest and the father-in-law of Caiaphas, the present high priest. His sons own the rights to selling within the Temple grounds, which include several buildings and a market place. As we enter the Temple we have to pass the area of stalls where the animals are tied and doves are caged. There are sellers shouting at everyone to buy their animals. It smells worse than the streets. It is a disgrace to the beautiful Temple.

Luke, until last week Elisa and I had not been out of the city since we arrived. One day she said, "I hear the dome of the Temple glows in the morning sun. Let's go to see this great sight." We left before dawn the next morning. We live in the lower city, where it costs less to lease a couple of rooms but the houses are crowded together. There was a moon out, and most homes leave an oil lamp burning at night, but I carried a torch so that we could make our way easier.

We passed the Pool of Solomon, where there are many fine homes. There were many people and animals awake already.

Soon we passed through the gate and outside the wall. I had hoped that we would leave the smells and the noise of the city behind, but the slope down to the Brook of the Kidron was full of pilgrims with their tents and their animals. I said, "We will have to go farther to escape the animal smell." Elisa did not reply. She seemed intent on the goal.

It is quite a long walk down the valley, steep at times, which required us to walk slowly in the dark. The brook was small and easy to cross. Then there was another steep climb up to an olive grove that is called Gethsemane, from where we could get the best view. As I stopped to catch my breath, I looked back and thought of the long climb back and I wondered if the sunrise was worth this effort. But Elisa kept going, so I followed. Finally she found a place that seemed to have a clear view of the Temple, and we settled down to await the sun.

There was a slight haze in the air as I looked around. There were a few other early risers who had the same idea as Elisa. We all waited. Some were singing the Psalms while others were impatient like I was.

Soon it was dawn and we could hear the call to prayer in the Temple. Then it became lighter and lighter, and streams of golden light were reflected from the dome of the Temple. In moments the entire dome was brilliant in the morning sun. "Oh, Joseph!" Elisa said. She was enchanted with the beauty, as was I. The dome glowed like polished gold. Everyone was amazed at the sight. We were all wishing that the special moment would not end.

Luke, I hope that you can come to Jerusalem to see this great sight and visit our facilities for healing. And, of course, you must meet Abraham. Most of all, you must meet my Elisa.

Joseph

[1] One cubit equals one and one-half feet.

[2] Exodus 12:3-10
Deuteronomy 16:6-8
Exodus 34:25

[3] Exodus 13:11-16

Letter 4

It was so good to receive your letter, Luke. I enjoy learning about your practice in Antioch, which must have about five times as many inhabitants as Jerusalem. I remember Dividimus told us that it takes time to start a practice in a large city. Your hard work will serve you well.

After one year in Jerusalem we have adjusted to our work and now have more time to spend at the great Temple, the center of our faith. With Elisa's help I am learning more and more about the Word of the Lord. We go to the Temple and listen to the priests and rabbis teach, and we also read the Scriptures. Elisa and I are developing a deeper understanding of our faith.

There are always pilgrims from far areas of the known world at the Temple, even though Judea, like Galilee, is now under the domination of Rome. Many are Jews who were dispersed during the numerous conquests of Israel. They have maintained their faith and return to the Temple, particularly during the Passover, the festival that commemorates God delivering the Israelites from slavery in Egypt.

There are four main sects of Judaism, the Sadducees, Pharisees, Zealots and Essenes, all worshipping the same God. The Sadducees are the priestly party and come from the upper class. They believe that the five books of Moses, the Torah, are the only authoritative Scriptures, and they consider oral traditions invalid. They do not believe in resurrection of the body or an afterlife.

The Pharisees accept the entire Scriptures, the Torah, the Prophets and the Writings. They believe in angels and life after death. This sect has a long list of strict rules that they follow. Fasting is an important part of their lives.

The Zealots are political revolutionaries who want primarily to rid Israel of Roman rule.

And finally there are the Essenes, who are the most spiritual. They have withdrawn to a community near Qumran, close to the Dead Sea. They spend much time in prayer, abstain from marriage and lead a communal life. Some of them spend their entire lives writing on scrolls. They are reported to have a great knowledge of herbs. They have a lay order that permits marriage.

In Jerusalem we are exposed to the many Jewish feasts. This is the seventh month of the Jewish year, and on the tenth day is the Feast of the Atonement, when a goat is laden with the nation's sins and expelled into the desert. It is a day of fasting and also one of rest. We also have the Feast of the Tabernacles. It is a joyous feast with both agricultural and historical aspects. It is on the fifteenth day of the seventh month. The people construct booths and live in them for the seven days of the celebration. Torches and lamps illuminate the Temple and people carry fruit as an offering. The horns and trumpets blow frequently.

On the twenty-fifth day of Chislev, we experience the Feast of Hanukkah, often called the Feast of Lights. It commemorates the victories of Judas Maccabeus freeing Judea about one hundred and ninety years ago. Then the worship in the Temple was re-instituted after the exile in Babylon. It is eight days of celebration and a new candle is lighted every day.

The largest and most important feast is that of the Passover, which is celebrated in the spring during Nison/Abib, the first month of the Jewish year. It commemorates the fact that God freed the Jews from their Egyptian slavery and led their flight into the desert. For seven days unleavened bread is eaten to represent the time that they were in such a rush that they did not put leaven into their bread.

Thousands upon thousands of pilgrims come to Jerusalem and stay the duration of this feast. Each family takes a lamb to sacrifice in the Temple. At the evening meal the family listens to the story of the flight from Egypt. Roast lamb, bitter herbs and wine are served with the unleavened bread. Abraham and his wife invited us, as well as Lemuel and Reuben and their families, to celebrate the Passover with them this year. It should be a day of rest, but for us it is not because the many visitors bring with them diseases from afar that spread quickly and require immediate treatment.

Then there is the Feast of Pentecost in the month of Sivan, so named because it is fifty days after the celebration of the Passover. Also called the Feast of Weeks and the Day of Firstfruits, it is really a harvest festival when people bring wheat and barley from the field to offer to God. It is a feast of thanksgiving for the rain and soil that produce the crops.

There are other feasts, including the Feast of the Trumpets, the first day of Tishri/Ethanim, when the ram's horn is blown, and the Feast of Purim, which is celebrated in Adar to commemorate the fact that Esther, queen of Persia, saved the exiled Jewish people from genocide by her appeal to the king, Ahasuerus.

We keep the feasts as well as our practice of medicine allows us to do. However, we always observe Passover.

Luke, as Jews we have various paths of worship to follow. Most of us do not affiliate ourselves with any one group. We attend the Temple services, say our required prayers, read the Scriptures and follow as closely as we can the rules of the faith — the Ten Commandments given by the Lord God to Moses on the mountaintop in the desert.[1]

The Pharisees are the most prominent at worship, but most of us do not have the time or means to follow all of their strict observances.

Those who intentionally disobey the commandments are considered sinners and are to be avoided. Anyone who collects taxes for the Romans, our conquerors, is considered a traitor and thus is treated like a sinner.

Many Jews believe that the Lord God will send a Messiah, a warrior king of the House of David, to free us from our oppressors.

Luke, I do pray that someday you will come to know the one true God.

Joseph

---

[1]   Exodus 20:1-17
       Deuteronomy 5:6-21

Letter 5

Elisa and I are constantly busy, Luke, with the patients who come to Abraham. He has several apprentices in training and we also help in teaching them. It is a new experience, but we promised in the Oath of Hippocrates that we would impart our knowledge to others. Abraham also has us help him in the herb garden, which Elisa loves very much. She records each new herb according to its growth, method of preparation and medicinal use for our future work in Capernaum.

Jerusalem is a crossroads for caravans from Egypt, Greece, Rome, Babylon and elsewhere. Often physicians accompany these caravans and come to visit Abraham, the renowned physician of Jerusalem. In our conversations, we discuss our various methods of treatment and often get some new ideas from them. We feel that this exchange is good.

By tradition, Jews have always been solicitous of the sick and their care, and they hold members of the healing art in great esteem. The Scriptures have many passages that refer to physicians.[1] On the other hand the Romans here do not respect physicians very much. Of course, according to the teachings we follow, the real healing comes from God and the physician is only an instrument in his hands. Therefore, we feel that our vocation has a great spiritual dimension and we ask divine guidance in our work.

We must remember that we are expected to respect ourselves and to act accordingly. We must be neatly clothed and behave properly.

In Athens the physician would set up his shop in the market place. But in Jewish tradition, the physician practices from his home, or if he is in a group as we are here under Abraham, from a clinic. We visit those who cannot come to see us. Abraham insists that we treat every one who comes in whether they can pay or not.

The priests of our faith are in charge of the general health of a community, and it does work well for sanitation and the handling of epidemics. The Essenes, as a sect, do a lot of work with herbs and roots to see if they have healing properties.

You have asked, Luke, about the health practices observed here. As you have heard, many of them are actually prescribed in the book of Leviticus.[2] Erasmus told me that of the six hundred and thirteen laws in the Scriptures, two hundred and thirteen are about medical conditions. Basically these are to help control epidemics, suppress prostitution and prevent venereal disease.

We both have seen the many problems that develop from illicit sexual union and how helpless we are in the treatment of those who develop these conditions. The Commandments explicitly prohibit the coveting of a neighbor's wife. But still it is done. King David coveted Bathsheba,[3] Judah sinned with Tamar[4] and others have sinned in this way throughout our history. The book of Leviticus has many statements prohibiting illicit unions.[5]

The law of stoning a woman caught in the act of adultery, yet allowing the male partner to go free, does not seem fair to Elisa and me. Yes, women are still very subservient to men in our culture.

Our laws reflect what Jews have learned throughout the centuries. Even our ancestors Moses and Aaron and his sons washed their hands and feet before entering the tabernacle or approaching the altar. A cracked earthen vessel must be discarded and a metal one must be scoured and rinsed in running water. Our ancestors who wandered in the desert for forty years followed the laws of the Lord with strict hygiene at every campsite. They always had a place outside of the camp where they disposed of their refuse and buried it.

As you and I know, Luke, five soldiers die of disease for every one who dies of battle wounds. Jewish soldiers carry a shovel to bury their waste.

We are told to wash our hands often so as not to carry any disease. Of course washing of the feet before entering any dwelling is imperative. We wear loose sandals or go barefoot, and the streets and roads are muddy and full of animal and human excrement. It is only sensible not to bring this into the house. We also have laws about caring for the skin. We are told to keep our skin clean, to bathe often and to care for any break in the skin lest it get a condition where it makes pus.

Of course, our dietetic rules are strict. We do not eat unclean meat. We do not eat pork. Indeed, as you know, some illnesses may be due to eating undercooked pork.

We know that a disease may spread by direct contact with the patient suffering from it, from touching his clothing or from using utensils that he has used. The law states that the patient should be isolated, and even contact with the members of the patient's family should be avoided. It further states that an infected garment should be burned. The utensils that were used should be scalded, and the patient's home should be scrubbed. After recovery, the person must be inspected and purified.

At the clinic we wash our hands after seeing each patient and sometimes change our outer garment several times a day.

But, Luke, there must be some other way that diseases spread. I sometimes develop an infection after treating patients who sneeze or cough with an illness of the nose or throat. As it spreads throughout the community, the disease gets much worse, with more coughing, higher fever and longer duration. But then I no longer develop the symptoms myself. Could it be that once we get an illness we develop a resistance to it?

It has been recognized that caravans can carry both human and animal diseases. Of course, the caravans stop at a supply station such as my father operates. He taught me to wash my hands often and also to change my top garment when I left the station.

We are very unsure of the foods that we eat. We know that meat and eggs are very nourishing. But rich foods often seem to be the cause of distress in the abdomen. It seems that older people have more trouble eating than younger ones. Elisa's parents, Erasmus and Sarah, have bloating and rumbling in their stomachs if they eat too much rich food. Erasmus and Abraham taught us that we should encourage all of our patients to eat vegetables several times a day.

We are told that we should drink a large amount of liquid every day. It makes the urine flow from the bladder and also keeps the bowels soft. But some of the water must contain something bad because people get sick after they drink it. Many of them drink wine instead.

Luke, you and I saw the results of too much intake of wine in our patients at Athens. We feel that one glass of wine with a meal is sufficient.

Frequent bathing seems to prevent skin diseases. In some areas, there is hot steam coming out of the ground, and some of our patients tell us that taking baths in these hot waters seems to relieve the stiffness of their joints. This is true of the hot baths that we heard of when we were in our apprenticeship.

Some of the herbs that we use, when dried, ground and mixed with some weak wine, are good to make the bowels move. We have also found that if food is eaten when it is old or has an odor, it seems to cause much sickness.

Recently, Elisa and I joined a guild of Jewish physicians who trained under the precepts of Hippocrates. Our emblem is a branch of the balsam bush. Of course we can still use the emblem of the snake and the knotted stick of Aesclepius, the Greek physician, which is used by all qualified physicians of any culture who have trained in his tradition and taken the Oath of Hippocrates.

I look forward to hearing about the medical knowledge you are gaining in your practice.

Joseph

[1] Genesis 50:2
    Jeremiah 8:22
    2 Chronicles 16:12

[2] Leviticus 11 to19

[3] 2 Samuel 11

[4] Genesis 38:15-19

[5] Leviticus 18:6-30

Letter 6

Luke, your last letters reveal that you are still earnest in your studies. You are fortunate that Antioch, like Athens, has a library where you can read the historical writings.

Much of our extra study is in the Scriptures. Here in Jerusalem, there is plentiful material to read and there are many opportunities to listen to teachers in the Temple. There is a noted teacher called Gamaliel here, and students of the Scriptures flock to the Temple to sit at his feet. Elisa and I have listened to several of his lectures. He is thoroughly versed in his field and has a simple yet complete way of presenting difficult subjects.

At every lecture we attend we notice a short young man sitting at Gamaliel's feet. He is very inquisitive and seems to interrupt often. Once I asked one of the other listeners, "Who is that man?"

"That is Saul of Tarsus."

"He seems very intense."

"Yes. He feels that everything the Pharisees teach is correct and that everyone else is wrong. I have heard him say that everyone should be forced to follow the rules of the Pharisees."

"I think that we had best avoid him."

"That is a good idea. We all try to do that here," he answered.

Elisa has made a rather intensive study of prophecies concerning the Messiah, the long-awaited Savior. Our religion teaches us that the Lord God made all creatures but gave free will only to man. In time, the humans disobeyed God. This offended God, but He promised us a Savior, the Messiah, who would come and free us. Every generation awaits the Messiah, a word that means "The Anointed One."

Perhaps you remember what I explained to you of Hebrew history. Our ancestor Abraham accepted the one and only God, and his descendants were to worship him. God promised them the land where we now live. Later, there was a famine and his descendants went to Egypt to make it their homeland.

The Hebrews became very successful and grew in significant number. Later, the Egyptians became jealous and enslaved the Hebrews. But the Lord heard their cries and sent Moses to free them. He gave Moses the Ten Commandments, our rules of conduct and faith.

After forty years of wandering in the desert, our ancestors crossed the

Jordan River and settled again in the Promised Land. After many wars they conquered all of the territory they had been promised. David became king and expanded their holdings, and Israel became a great nation.

Through the centuries, many of the Israelites adopted the gods of their neighbors and worshipped them instead of the one true God. Therefore, God sent many prophets to call the people back to the God of Israel. Among them: Jeremiah, Hosea, Joel, Amos, Obadiah, Nahum, Zephaniah, Haggai, Zechariah, Malachi and many others. The writings of these prophets say that God promised to send a redeemer or savior, the Messiah who would free the people and many others. A few of the Israelites listened and returned to worship of the one God but many did not.

Eventually, the great nation, made up of the Jewish people and the lands they conquered, divided into two. The northern one, made up of the ten tribes of Jacob, was called Israel, and the southern one, made up of the tribes of Judea and Benjamin, was called Judea. Israel was conquered and the Hebrew race there was eliminated. Judea was conquered too. The inhabitants were exiled to Babylon where they maintained their religious practices and finally were allowed to return. However, the country has since suffered the conquests of one nation after the other. Now we are under Roman rule.

We listen to some of the discussions at the Temple. The learned men believe that the Messiah will inaugurate a kingdom of justice and righteousness. I hope that is true. We need a ruler who will dispense justice fairly, who will end all these wars and conquests.

There are references to God's covenant in Genesis, Exodus, Jeremiah, the book of Samuel, the Psalms and elsewhere in the Scriptures. He will be of the House of David and is to be born in the town of Bethlehem. He will have abilities beyond any known to man, and he will bring peace to Israel. Elisa has found a reference in Hosea that he will come out of Egypt.[1]

In recent times several men have claimed to be the Chosen One, the long-awaited Messiah, but all the claims were false. The Sanhedrin, the great Senate of the Jews here in Jerusalem, considers some who claim to be the Messiah guilty of blasphemy and fit for execution.

Luke, with your desire to understand the truth, you would enjoy learning more about the story of our people and the one true God.

Joseph

[1] Genesis 22:17-18

Exodus 2:24
Exodus 19:3-7
1 Chronicles 17:11-14, 23-27
2 Chronicles 21:7
2 Samuel 7:12-16
Psalms 132:11
Jeremiah 30:9
Jeremiah 33:14-16
Micah 5:1-5
Hosea 11:1

Letter 7

Greetings, dear Luke, from the holy city of Jerusalem, the city of God. Our two years of training here under Abraham are drawing to an end and we look forward to our return to the quiet of Capernaum.

You asked about Elisa's health. Thanks be to God, she is doing well. She has maintained her weight, runs no fever, has no cough and shows abounding vitality. She does the same amount of work that I do except she rests after the noon meal. We have a special cot for her in the clinic.

You asked how we treat consumption here in Jerusalem. As it happens, we just had a conference on that condition. Abraham calls his four assistants together on a regular basis to discuss a disease, and today the topic was phthisis.

Abraham is considered an expert on consumption, yet he asked each of us to tell what we knew about this condition. Three of us had little to offer except observations of the progression of the illness we see in our patients — the fever, a gradual wasting of the tissues of the body, and a cough that develops with bloody sputum coming up from the lungs. The patient becomes emaciated and gradually dies.

When it was Elisa's turn to speak, she discussed a theory about how the illness spreads. "My father, Erasmus, the physician of Capernaum, believes there is something that passes from the ill person that causes the disease in the next person. Also, there are some cases that have come from drinking the milk from an infected cow. We do not have as much of the disease here since we have goat's milk to drink, and goats do not get the disease."

When she finished, Abraham applauded. "All of you remember all that Elisa has said. That is just what we have found here. The disease seems to come from cows that soon die, and also from persons who are sick. We believe Elisa contracted her disease by spending much time caring for a dying consumptive patient.

"Now as for treatment. It seems that living in a dry, cool area helps, but I have had success when I prescribed good food and months of total rest in bed. It seems that the less the lungs are used during the illness, the more likely it will be cured. If caught early, the condition seems to get better, as Elisa's has. But patients must always take better care of themselves or it does come back." He stopped and looked at both of us and added, "Elisa and Joseph, do you hear that?" We both nodded.

Reuben asked, "What about pregnancy in these women?"

"A woman must get more rest during that time, and sometimes, as the abdomen gets larger with the new life, the cough seems to subside."[1]

"But Abraham, we have seen many women get worse after having a baby."

"That is true. The mother becomes very active caring for the baby. She gets little rest and uses much of her energy producing milk for nursing. This causes a sudden aggravation of symptoms of the disease. So, yes, it is hazardous for a woman with consumption to be with child but, with proper care, she can become the mother of several. She must rest in bed at least one month after delivery, and also have help with the care of the child and home."

Elisa and I knew that he was talking to us and about the family we hope to have. But we were not discouraged. As we left, Elisa said, "Did you hear Abraham? We can have several children."

"But you must take more rest at that time."

"I will," she said.

Luke, when that day comes I will see that she does.

Joseph

---

[1] The lung partially collapses due to the pressure from the child in the womb below. This causes less use of the diseased part of the lung, and healing may occur.

Letter 8

Dear Luke, Elisa and I have completed our two years as first assistants under the great Abraham of Jerusalem. Today was our last day. Abraham honored his four assistants with a banquet at his home and presented us with a certificate that read:

> *At this time in the fifteenth year of Tiberius Caesar,*
> *when Pontius Pilate is governor of Judea, Herod,*
> *tetrarch of Galilee, his brother Philip, tetrarch of*
> *Ituria, and Lysanias, tetrarch of Abilene, during the*
> *high priesthood of Annas and Caiaphas, I, Abraham of*
> *Jerusalem, do hereby testify that Elisa and Joseph of*
> *Capernaum served as my first assistants for two years.*

Reuben and Lemuel received similar certificates. Reuben is planning to settle in Joppa, and Lemuel will stay in Jerusalem.

As we were finishing, Abraham called me to one side and said, "Take good care of Elisa. You can do much good practicing the healing art in Capernaum. And the time will come when the two of you can take in apprentices and begin to establish a training center for physicians in Galilee. One is needed there."

As we were thanking Abraham and his wife for the banquet, he said, "You need a few days to yourselves before you begin your new lives in Capernaum. Why don't you stop in Jericho? I have a friend who runs an inn there." Abraham's wife said, "It is a lovely place, quiet, peaceful, cool."

"But be careful on the road there," Abraham said. "There is a narrow place between Jerusalem and Jericho where robbers attack lone travelers. Always travel in a caravan or a large group."

I looked at Elisa and she nodded in approved. "That sounds wonderful. We have enough money for almost a week at Jericho and then a week to travel up the Jordan to Capernaum." Elisa added, "Could we possibly visit the Essene community? I would love to see it."

"Of course," replied Abraham. "My wife and I have been there several times, just to pray with them. My friend Matthias will arrange it."

Tomorrow we will leave Jerusalem, which has been our home for two

---

years. We will rest in Jericho and then continue our travel home to Capernaum.

May the Lord God of Israel guide us and protect us on our journey. And may He continue to bless you, dear Luke.

Joseph

Jericho

Letter 9

Dear Luke, we are at the inn in Jericho. We made the trip safely. We travel lightly since we have few possessions. We own a few scrolls on which are written medical information, and we carry two medical bags. As Dividimus instructed us, I always carry a bag with surgical instruments — a scalpel, needles, sutures, a metal probe, a few clamps and clean cloths for bandages. Elisa's bag is filled with herbs that she mixes into potions and salves, as her father first taught her.

It was easy for us to attach ourselves to a caravan since our skills as physicians are in demand. On the journey I incised two boils and sutured a few wounds. Elisa treated a patient with the flux and used some of Erasmus' healing balm on skin infections. The patients paid well.

It took us two days to travel from Jerusalem to Jericho. It is hilly country and we were particularly vigilant when we came to the narrow passage where Abraham cautioned us that robbers might hide. The first night we stayed at an inn.

On the second day we continued our journey and finally, in midafternoon, approached the top of a hill. There before us was the fertile valley of the Jordan. It was such a contrast from the arid land we had just traversed. It has been written that this valley is well-watered like the garden of the Lord[1] and has been called the Garden of God.

We passed through an area of small farms and watched men, women and children working the fields. This is harvest time, just about six weeks after Passover, and much of the grain is ready for the sickle. It will be gathered and threshed and winnowed on a public floor. I enjoyed explaining all of this to Elisa, since I was raised on the land and she was not.

We saw fields of barley, beans, lentils, wheat and oats. There will be a good crop this year. We saw many sheep and goats grazing. There were a few cattle. Chickens pecked around the farmhouses, and geese and ducks waddled at the edge of a pond.

Soon we passed into an area of olive trees and vineyards and knew that we were near Jericho. There were fruit trees all around — bananas, papayas and oranges.

As we approached the city it was Elisa's turn to talk. Our surroundings brought to mind the history of our people, their slavery in Egypt, their flight to freedom by crossing the Red Sea led by Moses, their forty years of wandering in arid land and finally, under the leadership of Joshua, the dramatic destruction of the walls of Jericho as described in the Scriptures.[2] I had heard the story before, but it was much more vivid now as we approached Jericho. As we saw the many palm trees we knew why it is also called the City of Palms.[3]

"Jericho is an old, old city," Elisa said. "Maybe thousands of years old. Each successive city was built upon the previous one.

"You realize that we are below sea level," she added, "and that the Jordan River empties into a sea that has no outlet. Just south of here is where our ancestors Lot and Abraham went their separate ways." By this time, we were in the city and too busy looking around to talk.

The caravan stopped at its usual place. We gathered our possessions, thanked the caravan leader and headed across the road to the inn of Matthias. The innkeeper made us feel especially welcome since Abraham was a good friend of his. We were hot and tired and dusty from the trip. The inn had a place where we could bathe, and it did feel refreshing!

Our room was spacious and cool. As we lay down to rest, Elisa remarked, "Joseph, have you noticed how quiet it is?" We thanked the Lord for the peace in this time and for all of the blessings that he has bestowed upon us.

Soon it was time for the meal. We dressed and were met by Matthias, who introduced us to the other guests. There were traders from Mesopotamia, one from Egypt, one from Athens, and a group of Pharisees from Jerusalem. We had a lot to talk about. I was able to learn what had happened in Athens during the two years that I had been gone. They were all inquisitive about a woman practitioner of the healing art. But Elisa, in her pleasant way, was able to prevent any slurs that would have angered me.

After the meal, Elisa and I walked in the garden. There are date palms, fig trees and flowers of all types. It is truly peaceful. As we strolled hand in hand, Elisa remarked, "The Lord has been so good to us."

Luke, this will be a new experience. Never have I had a week when I did not have to work. All we have to do is rest and enjoy Jericho.

Joseph

[1]   Genesis 13:10

[2] Joshua 6:20

[3] Deuteronomy 34:3
Judges 1:16
2 Chronicles 28:15

Letter 10

Luke, it was delightful to awaken and hear birds in the garden outside our window. Elisa and I lay there and enjoyed their singing. We were interrupted by a knock at the door and a servant with the morning meal. Elisa and I ate leisurely. As we finished she said, "Now for a quiet walk in the garden."

But there was another knock on the door. As I opened it I was surprised to see the innkeeper standing there. "Joseph and Elisa," he said, "I know that you have worked under my friend Abraham and you are well-trained physicians. Please come to see one of my servants who is desperately ill."

"Of course," I answered. "We will be glad to come." Elisa already was preparing her bag of herbs, as she often had done for her father.

We went to the servant's hut but as we approached the door, we could smell the foul odors of vomitus and excrement. We examined the man, saw that he was breathing heavily, his skin was hot and dry, and his tongue was cracked from dryness. We were told that the illness had started three days ago and he had been unable to retain food or fluids since then. He had eaten at a friend's home the night before he became ill, and the friend was sick also but not this seriously.[1] It was our first case on our own as physicians.

We agreed that he had eaten something that had caused this condition, that he had become dehydrated from loss of fluids and these had to be replaced immediately. Elisa sent for some vinegar wine. When it came she took a small amount and added mandragora to make him drowsy. Then she mixed some salt and the powder used in baking into the wine with extract of the poppy. We tried to get him to swallow this mixture, which Erasmus has used for years in the treatment of flux.

We helped the servants clean the patient. In time the vomiting did cease and he was able to retain more of the salty, sour drink. We knew that the sedative would not only make him drowsy but help stop the bloody flux. And it did. We awakened him frequently and made him drink the salty fluid. Matthias came in to see how we were progressing several times. All we needed was to wash our hands. There was no time to eat.

Finally at about the ninth hour,[2] the patient's breathing slowed and his hot skin became cooler. We sat down and thanked the Lord for the improvement. Soon he was able to retain more liquids and it became clear that he would recover. Elisa fixed liquids for him and instructed him how to take them.

We were not very presentable as we emerged from the hut into the late afternoon sun. I remarked, "And this was to be a restful time."

Elisa smiled. "This is our calling. We go whenever and wherever there is a need." "That sounds like Abraham," I replied. "And Erasmus," she added. I nodded as we saw Matthias coming toward us. We explained the servant's recovery and he was grateful. We asked that everything in the room be thoroughly cleaned and directed that anyone who handles anything the patient touched must wash well. Matthias passed on these instructions to the servant who was to care for the patient. Then he turned to us and said, "Come, I will have your clothes washed." That was a blessing. We bathed with hot water and changed into our only other garments.

Elisa took a short nap and we then went to eat. Matthias had a splendid meal arranged for us in the garden. The cool breeze felt good after our long day in the sick room.

Luke, the meal consisted of delicacies that only the rich can afford. We had goat's milk, eggs and several types of meat, pepper and cinnamon from the East. There were also the usual breads, beans, lentils, onions and artichokes. Then there was a dessert of apricot cake. Wine was served in silver goblets. Finally the servant brought a plate of fruits including melons, figs, mulberries, grapes and blackberries.

After the meal, Matthias again came to express his gratitude for our treating his servant. He told us he had arranged a guide to show us around Jericho and take us to the Essene community at Qumran. Elisa was elated.

We are exhausted and will retire early in anticipation of a great day tomorrow.

Joseph

---

1   Infectious diarrhea secondary to eating spoiled or uncooked food filled with infectious bacteria.

2   The Jewish day is from sunset to sunset. The four night watches, three hours each, begin about 6 p.m. modern time. Daytime is measured by the hour, with the sixth hour being midday and the ninth hour about 3 p.m.

Letter II

Luke, Matthias had a full breakfast for us again this morning. A chariot and driver were waiting. He had arranged provisions for a full day. Before we left we stopped to see the ill servant. He was up, eating and able to retain his food. We were very pleased with his progress. We washed our hands thoroughly after we left the hut.

The horses were fresh and they set a fast pace. This was the first time either of us had ridden in a chariot. It was rough riding at first, but smoother as we got out of the city onto the open sand. Of course it was dusty, but traveling in caravans had accustomed us to that. Soon we were on the hot desert again and we could see the Dead Sea. The driver stopped near the bank to rest the horses and we got out.

The edge of the water was full of all types of formations made up of materials that have been dissolved in the water, which cannot flow into the sea. As the water evaporates, they form various shapes. Elisa put her foot into the water and when she took it out, it was covered with a white substance that looked like salt. Nothing can live in that water. It is a desolate place. In a short time we got back into the chariot and were off to the community of the Essenes.

As we arrived at the gate, a member of the community greeted us. He wore head coverings and full robes to protect him from the sun and the heat. We told him that we wished to visit and he invited us into the settlement, asking us not to disturb anyone in prayer. He arranged for the driver to water and feed our horses.

Elisa and I walked through the open area. Soon another man came to us and offered to guide us through their buildings. We passed a large building made of rough stones. On the north side we could see a defensive tower. Then there was the dining area with kitchen. All of the members live in a community and all eat together. We then passed the pottery workshop, the dyer's shop, the stables where they cared for our horses, and the mill.

There was another huge building that the guide showed us, the scriptorium. We looked inside and there were about twenty members busy at writing tables. Our guide told us that they were preparing scrolls of the Scriptures. These Essenes spend their entire lives in prayer, reading the Word of the Lord and copying the Scriptures.

Then we went to the meeting room where others were in prayer. They were reading and singing from the scrolls. We watched and listened to them for a long time. I find intriguing the sound of male voices singing in prayer without music.

Soon the guide motioned to us that it was time for the midday meal and we were invited to eat in a room separate from the community. The meal consisted of soup made of a variety of vegetables, bread, cheese and wine. He left us to enjoy our meal alone and rejoined us afterward.

He told us that the Essenes are an ascetic sect of Judaism. The members leave their homes and devote their lives to work and prayer. The community is governed by a council of twelve laymen and three priests. A new candidate must live in the community one year before he is allowed to attend some of the communal functions. It takes two years of intensive training and prayer to become a full member. Only then can he join the community at the common meal.

Every third night, after a full day of work, they stay awake to study the Law, read and recite the blessings as a community. Their yearly calendar is different from ours so they celebrate the Jewish feasts on different days than we do.

They emphasize obedience, purity, prayer and a communal life. They baptize with water, pouring over someone or immersing him in water, to signify remission of sins. The guide explained that to be truly cleansed of sin, one must also submit to all the ordinances of God.

Elisa asked about their knowledge of herbs and he took us to the herb gardens. Elisa carefully observed each plant and questioned the caretaker. Luke, she was able to obtain some rare sprouts to plant into her herb garden at home.

Near the tenth hour we bid our guide farewell and thanked him for his courtesy. He arranged that our horses and driver be brought to us and we started back to Jericho. Our horses were now rested and traveling was rapid. It was late when we returned to the inn. Matthias was happy that we had enjoyed the trip.

"Tomorrow," he said, "you will go to Bethany. They tell me that there is a preacher speaking on the banks of the River Jordan who attracts large groups of people.

"Like members of the Essene community, he preaches the repentance of sin and baptism in water." And with a wink he added, "Be careful, he may get you both into the water too."

We were exhausted and sleepy. We were not eager to take another long trip but we could not refuse our host. We dragged ourselves to our room, and as we opened the door we saw that our soiled clothing had been washed clean and returned. Elisa carefully watered her new herb sprouts and set them in the window to get the morning sun.

As we prepared to retire, Elisa spoke thoughtfully. "I can see how someone living in a community like that, away from the cares of the world, could spend time in prayer in adoration of God and really commune with God." I agreed that one is able to focus more on a subject if there is no distraction. And if the subject is God, that is a good way to come closer to Him.

She continued. "Did you notice that they have a council of twelve similar to the twelve tribes of Israel?"

"I never thought of that." By that time we were too tired to talk anymore.

As I fell asleep, the sound of men's voices joined in song resounded in my memory.

Joseph

Letter 12

Dear Luke, this morning after breakfast, a servant brought the midday meals that Matthias had asked be prepared for us. Then he led us to two beautiful horses offered for our disposal. We packed the food on one horse and our medical pouches on the other.

Elisa is far better at horseback riding than I am. Erasmus used to take her on his calls with him and taught her well. Off we went through the fertile land, the watershed of the Jordan. As we passed green fields rich with fruits, Elisa remarked, "I can see why this land was so desired by our ancestors who had spent forty years in the desert when they left Egypt. No wonder they called it 'the land of milk and honey.'"

The air was clear and there was a slight wind. The breeze swept back Elisa's hair as the horses galloped. It didn't take long to get to the banks of the Jordan. Now, Luke, this river is not very wide, just 75 cubits, and varies from ankle-deep to over a man's head. It is formed near the city of Dan from the melting snows of Mount Herman, many days' walk north of Capernaum. It flows to the Sea of Galilee and then follows an irregular course for about six days' journey and finally empties into the Dead Sea. This river is what brings life to what would otherwise be a barren place.

As we approached the river, the vegetation became a massive thicket. We were told that bears, lions, hyenas, foxes and other wild beasts have been reported here but we did not worry. The road was wide and no attacks had been reported lately.

Finally, we got to the river and a settlement they called Bethany on the Jordan. It is not the Bethany that is near Jerusalem.

We found a secluded spot downstream, watered our horses and tied them where they could eat the tall grass. We lay down under a broad blue sky to enjoy the breeze.

"Joseph," Elisa said, "it is so peaceful here that it is hard to realize there is so much violence and cruelty in the world. Wouldn't it be wonderful if everyone could enjoy the beauty of God's creation as we are doing?"

She had expressed my thoughts so beautifully. I said, "I wish that this would never end. I feel so peaceful. I do not want anything to bother us."

We lay there until about the sixth hour. It became a little warmer with the sun nearing its peak, but the breeze kept us cool. Elisa spread out the food — cheese, bread, bananas, grapes, papayas, dried meat and wine —

and we sang, laughed and ate. When we finished, we packed what was left and hung it on a branch in the shade and away from the animals. It was time for Elisa to rest. I soon fell asleep beside her.

Suddenly we were awakened by a loud voice. It seemed to come from downstream. "Who is doing that shouting?" Elisa exclaimed. I checked the horses and they were secure. We took our medical bags from under a bush and started in the direction from which we heard the voice. Elisa found a path to follow through the thicket and along the river. As we neared, we could hear the voice grow louder. Elisa reached a knoll and called down to me. "Come up here, Joseph, we can see well from here."

As I reached her, I could see that a gaunt man of thirty years or more was addressing a crowd of about one hundred people. He was dressed in a garment of camel hair and had a leather belt around his waist and sandals on his feet. His hair was long and unkempt. So was his beard. He was balancing on a rock, steadying himself with a long shepherd's hook. "This must be the preacher that Matthias mentioned," Elisa said. We settled down in the shade of a eucalyptus above the river to listen.

"A voice cries in the wilderness," we heard him say.

"Prepare a way for the Lord. Make his paths straight.

"Every valley will be filled in, every mountain and hill laid low.

"Winding ways will be straightened and rough roads made smooth. And all mankind shall see the salvation of God!"

Elisa whispered, "Those are the words of the prophet Isaiah."[1]

The man continued. "Repent, for the kingdom of heaven is close at hand." He continued to exhort the people gathered to confess their sins and step forward to be baptized.

We could see that most of the crowd was made up of laborers, tillers of the soil and others in plain and worn garments. However, there were some wearing more elaborate garments — two cloaks in many cases — and these we recognized as Pharisees and Sadducees from Jerusalem. He turned to them and said sharply, "Brood of vipers! Who warned you to flee from the retribution that is coming? But if you are repentant, produce the appropriate fruits.

"And do not think of telling yourselves, 'We have Abraham as our father.' Because, I tell you, God can raise children for Abraham from these stones. Yes, even now, the axe is laid to the roots of the trees so that any tree that fails to produce good fruit will be cut down and thrown into the fire."

"What is it we must do then?" they asked. He answered swiftly. "If anyone has two tunics, he must share with the man who has none. And the one with something to eat must do the same." The Pharisees and Sadducees stepped back, murmuring among themselves.

I recognized a few tax collectors in the crowd. One asked, "Master, what must we do?" And the man replied, "Exact no more than your rate." There were some soldiers also and they asked, "What must we do?" And the man replied to them, "No intimidation, no extorts. Be content with your pay."

Then a spokesman of the priests and their assistants, the Levites, stepped forward boldly. "Who are you?" he demanded.

The preacher raised his voice so that everyone could hear. "I am not the Messiah."

"Well, then," several in the group asked. "Are you Elijah?"

"I am not."

"Are you the prophet?"

"No."

"Who are you? We must take back an answer to those who sent us from Jerusalem. What do you have to say for yourself?"

The man's voice rang in our ears as he again echoed the words of the prophet. "I am, as Isaiah prophesied, a voice that cries in the wilderness, 'Make a straight way for the Lord.'"

But one of the Pharisees appeared to be hostile and continued to question him. "Why are you baptizing if you are not the Messiah, not Elijah and not the prophet?"

"I baptize with water," he answered. "But there stands among you, unknown to you, the one who is coming after me. And I am not fit to undo his sandal straps. He is more powerful than I. He will baptize you with the spirit of God and with fire. His winnowing fan is in his hand to clear his threshing floor and to gather the wheat into his barn. But the chaff he will burn in fire that will never go out."

Elisa and I were deeply moved by what we heard. This man admonished the rich to share with the poor and those in positions of influence to be fair and just. He spoke with power and with authority.

In our training we learned not to be swayed by oratory but to discuss what we hear and reach our own conclusions. But here was a man saying that the Messiah, the promised of God, has come — that he is presently among the people of Israel. This was something for which we were totally unprepared.

Luke, this man sounded so convincing that scores of people — the entire crowd save the Pharisees and Sadducees — followed him into the river, confessed their sins and asked to be baptized.

So engrossed were we in watching the scene in the river that Elisa and I had not noticed a man sit beside us. He was dressed like a native of the area. I nodded a greeting and he responded. I introduced Elisa and myself. He said, "My name is Zachea. I am a shepherd here."

"Who is that man who is preaching?" I asked.

The man smiled, steadied himself with his crook, and answered. "His name is John, but around here we call him John the Baptizer. One day he appeared preaching repentance and baptism.

"They say that his father was a priest called Zachariah of Ain-Karim near Jerusalem, who belonged to the Abijah section of the priesthood. His mother, Elisabeth by name, was a descendant of Aaron.

"They say that he was a quiet child as he grew up. As his spirit matured, he went to live in the wilderness, surviving on nothing but locusts and wild honey."

I interrupted and said, "That diet and activity accounts for his slight build." Elisa put her hand over mine as a signal for me to quit talking and to listen. Then the man continued.

"He comes here daily to preach repentance and to baptize in the Jordan. Then he disappears again. A few men have started to follow him and are called his disciples."

"Do you mean that this occurs every day?"

"Yes, he speaks here daily. He preaches on the same topic over and over again. And large crowds come to this place with every new day."

Elisa looked at the sun. It was about the ninth hour and it was a long ride back. We hated to leave because John was still baptizing in the Jordan. She whispered, "John talked about sharing. Let us give our leftover food to the shepherd. He may not have eaten all day." Zachea was very grateful for truly he had not had anything to eat since early morning.

We bid him farewell and went to our horses. As we placed our bags on their backs they seemed eager to start moving again. I watered them, then we mounted and rode quietly for a while, each in deep thought.

Finally I spoke. "What do you think of what we just saw and heard?"

And Elisa replied, "He surely knows the writings of the prophets, and he has no fear of speaking out against those in authority who are not following the Law."

"His preaching is so simple — to repent when we disobey the laws of God. But I cannot understand why he requires baptism."

Elisa thought for a moment. "Perhaps, as the Essenes believe, it is a sign of washing away sin. As I watched the people being baptized, I noticed that they came out of the water singing praises to God. They did seem changed in some way."

"Would you want to be baptized?"

"I don't know. But let us return tomorrow and listen to John again."

I nodded approval. "That is what I had wanted to do."

After a short time, Elisa spoke again. "I recall that in Malachi it says, 'Look, I am going to send my messenger to prepare a way before me. And the Lord you are seeking will suddenly enter his temple.'[2] Do you suppose that this man we just heard is a messenger, that he speaks the truth and that the coming of the Messiah is upon us?"

"That would be thrilling if the Messiah would come in our lifetime," I said, not voicing my doubts.

By sunset we were back at the inn. The servants took the horses and we went to our rooms to wash off the dust of the road.

At dinner, we spoke to Matthias about what we had witnessed. "Yes," he said, "that wild man has been preaching for several weeks. I have never heard him, but it is very good for business at the inn. Many people come from a distance to hear him and stay with us."

Elisa said, "We would like to go again tomorrow if we may borrow the horses again. Would you like to go with us?" Matthias replied, "I cannot leave the inn for that long, but I will arrange for the horses and some food again."

"About the sixth hour allows adequate time for us to get there to hear him. We will rest in the morning," I replied.

On the way back to our room, we stopped to see the sick servant. He had been able to retain food all day, and the bowel humors had just passed once today and had good firmness. It was obvious that he would recover.

Then Elisa and I sat in the garden in the cool breeze to talk. We reviewed what we had heard John say about honesty in work and confession of sins.

"It seems to me," Elisa said, "that John is saying we must confess our sins and resolve to lead a better life. He suggests that baptism is a sign of inward repentance. However, the baptism of the Messiah will be an act of God that brings salvation."

"Yes, that seems to say it all."

"But the predictions about the Messiah are difficult to understand. How will he baptize with the spirit of God and fire?" I had no answer.

We sat for a long time and then quietly walked to our room. As we entered she asked a question. "Will you follow the crowds tomorrow and receive the baptism of John?"

"I don't know," I answered truthfully. "He sounded so convinced that the Messiah is here. And further he said that baptism is for the remission of sins. And we both know that confession of one's sins is good. What about you?"

"This may be a way of introduction to the Messiah of God. I will follow you." Then Elisa added, "Joseph, the Lord has allowed this to happen to us for some reason. Perhaps in time we will understand."

Luke, she's right. There must be a reason we were witnesses today as John baptized on the banks of the Jordan.

Joseph

[1]   Isaiah 40:3-5

[2]   Malachi 3:1

Letter 13

Elisa and I had several dreams last night, dear Luke, and all were concerned with cleansing, running water and a man shouting. It is unusual that both of us have dreams the same night about the same thing. Throughout our morning meal, we discussed the teachings of John the Baptizer. If you have two tunics, he said, give one to someone who has none.

"Does he mean," Elisa asked, "that we should eat less and give the rest to the poor? Or does he mean that we should not waste anything? Eat enough, but not to excess. Share with others." She thought this over. "Perhaps he means that we should live simply and give to those in need."

"With our training," I pointed out, "we could soon earn enough to own a large house, have many servants, drive fine chariots and have many tunics."

"Joseph, do you really want to do that?" she cried. "It is completely foreign to my upbringing. Your parents and mine have always lived very simply."

"You mean," I said, "now that you may be able to afford a large home, dress in fine silks and have servants, you will not want to do that?" Elisa's reply was immediate. "Don't bring me any lavish clothes. I will not wear them. Let's give the money to the poor."

Luke, that is the philosophy by which we plan to live. We will not have a fine house like Dividimus. We will have a simple home, simple food and simple ways. Our lives will be devoted to the care of the sick, rich or poor, free or slave.

As we prepared to leave for the day, we went to the servants' quarters to check on our patient. As we arrived, he met us at the door and looked quite a bit better. He was very appreciative.

The horses were ready and off we went. We rode with joy in our hearts. Elisa was singing and I tried to join in, but as you know, Luke, singing is not one of my talents.

Soon we were at the same spot where we had stopped yesterday. We dismounted, led the horses to the Jordan to drink and then tied them in a grassy spot to feed. We picked up our medical bags and the meal prepared for us and walked up the same rock to look down on the river.

The breeze was gently blowing Elisa's hair, the leaves were rustling and everything was so peaceful. Elisa spread out the noon meal, and we ate an adequate amount but made sure that enough was left for Zachea, our shepherd friend.

Then we lay back, Elisa to rest and I to watch the clouds glide by in the heavens. Luke, I wondered about so many things. What is there above the clouds? What makes the stars and moon light at night?

We were awakened by people gathering on the riverbank below us. Elisa said, "Let us go and meet some of them." We placed our bags and the remainder of the food under a tree and carefully made our way down the riverbank.

There were shepherds, merchants, camel drivers, leather workers, gardeners, men and women, all local people. We could hear them talk among themselves.

"Did you hear him yesterday?"

"Have you been baptized by John?"

"Did you hear him take on the Pharisees and Sadducees?"

Soon John appeared out of the woods and everyone gathered to hear him. He was almost four cubits tall. He walked into the water until it was about knee deep and started to preach. "Repent and be baptized," he exhorted again and again. We stood and listened with the crowd. His words were so piercing, so convincing.

As he started to baptize, we were moved to step forward together into the cold water. As we approached, John said, "Repent. Confess your sins." Elisa spoke to John a few moments, then he placed his hand on her forehead and she sank briefly below the surface of the water. As she emerged he turned to me. I hurriedly thought of the times that I had disobeyed the Lord and the laws of the Scriptures, blurted them out to John, and he baptized me.

As we stepped back to the riverbank, our hair and clothing still dripping, Elisa said, "Look at that man." She pointed to a figure about ten paces away, approaching John. He was tall as well, four cubits or more, and clothed like us, as if he too came from Galilee. He was dusty, as if he had walked a long way. We could not see his face clearly, but there was a dignity about his bearing that was unusual.

As the man's turn came, John suddenly stopped preaching. "No. No!" he cried out.

"You should not be baptized by me. It is I who need baptism from you.

And yet, you come to me!"

"Leave it like this for the time being," the man replied. His voice was clear, deep and melodious. "It is fitting that we should, in this way, do all that righteousness demands."

John stood a moment, shook his head, then baptized the man. The Galilean stood in the water as in a trance. He appeared to be deep in prayer. Mind you, Luke, we were just a few paces away from him during this time.

Suddenly a bright light came from the sky, as if the heavens opened up. Then a white dove appeared and settled on the Galilean's head. Luke, it shone brighter than the sun, but it did not hurt the eyes to look at it. Then we heard a voice, seemingly from the skies above:

"You are my son, the Beloved. My favor rests on you."

Then the dove disappeared, the light faded and all was quiet.

The man thanked John and strode with dignity out of the Jordan and into the woods.

We could see that John was taken aback with what had just happened, as were we all. As his gaze followed the man, he spoke.

"Look. There is the Lamb of God who takes away the sin of the world.

"This is the one of whom I spoke when I said, 'A man is coming after me who ranks before me because he existed before me.' I did not know him myself, and yet it was to reveal him to Israel that I came baptizing with water.

"I saw the spirit coming down on him from heaven in the form of the dove and resting on him. It fulfills that which he who sent me to baptize with water had said to me, 'The man on whom you see the spirit come down and rest is the one who is going to baptize with the Spirit!'

"Yes, I have seen and I am the witness that he is the chosen one of God."

There was silence among the hundreds in the water and on the riverbank. Our eyes were drawn to the spot in the woods where last we had seen the man from Galilee. He did not return.

John came out of the water and his disciples followed. He had finished his preaching and baptizing for that day.

Elisa and I, who had been holding each other's hands during this extraordinary experience, climbed out of the river and up to our rock to dry off.

Elisa spoke first. "Did you see the man in deep prayer after he was baptized? And did you see the dove fly down and hover over him?" I nodded. "Did you hear a loud voice say, 'You are my son, the Beloved'?" Once again I nodded. "It is true then. I was afraid that I had imagined it."

"What does it all mean?" I wondered aloud. "Was that the voice of God?"

The more we thought about what we had witnessed, the more questions we had. If this is the Messiah, why should he look like an ordinary man? Why would he appear here? And why now?

The shepherd Zachea then appeared, as he had the day before. He had just arrived, having taken time to find a sheep that was lost. We told him eagerly about the Galilean and he listened attentively but, like us, he was confused about what he heard.

By this time it was past the ninth hour. We gave Zachea the remainder of the food, mounted our horses and rode back to Jericho, our minds in a whirl about the events.

After the evening meal, we sat in the garden and talked until the moon was high.

Joseph

Letter 14

At the morning meal at the inn, Elisa and I heard that John had left the area and gone to Ephraim, but no one spoke of the man from Galilee. Luke, we told our fellow travelers at the table what we had witnessed. Some of them were eager to hear more, but others had more interest in the goods they were trading and the high taxes of the Romans.

We left the table and went out to the garden, deciding that there would be no journey today or the last few days of our stay. The servant has fully recovered and we have no responsibilities for the several days before we leave for Capernaum. It is wonderful to be able to sleep late, have leisurely meals, take walks in the garden and, in the evening, hold hands under the stars while we talk of our future.

We have spoken of the hard work ahead of us, and the family we hope to have. "Enjoy these times," Elisa remarked one day as dusk fell. "They are very rare in the life of a physician."

But often the conversation returned to our experience at the river Jordan and the mysterious man from Galilee.

I went to visit the man who runs the caravan station and learned that a number of pilgrims from Galilee are expected back soon from a pilgrimage to the Temple. We could attach ourselves to their group for the five-day trip to Capernaum. I bought supplies for the trip and arranged for a donkey so that Elisa would be able to ride part of the way.

Matthias has a final dinner at the inn planned for us and he has already asked us to return to visit. As Elisa has said, "God only knows. This stay in Jericho may have changed our lives."

I will write again after we arrive and become settled in our new practice in Capernaum.

Joseph

Capernaum

Letter 15

We have arrived back in Capernaum, Luke, and I have much to tell you.

Our journey north from Jericho took us across the Jordan and up along the east bank of the river, passing fields of wheat, groves of olive trees and large vineyards. We saw many small huts, which serve as the homes of tillers of the soil. Many were made of stone, but a large number were made of mud with only a few wooden crossbeams to hold the roof because wood is expensive. In these homes, a family sleeps in the rear of a room in an elevation over the winter oven. The thatched roof is made of palm leaves and branches. I explained to Elisa that I was born and spent my childhood in a home like this.

It was wonderful to see the country after our stay in Jerusalem. And it was an inspiration to travel with the pilgrims. They were all so joyful that they had been able to see and visit the Temple.

Elisa and I talked frequently about our experience with John the Baptizer at the River Jordan. We mentioned it occasionally to our fellow travelers but they had no interest.

After several such encounters, Elisa said, "Perhaps we should not push the teachings of John at this time. If the Lord wants John's message to be heard, He will provide a time and place." I nodded and we spoke of our experiences only to each other for the rest of the journey.

The commander of the caravan was so glad to have us that he did not charge us for passage or for use of the donkey. He even helped us set up a daily clinic as, during our journey, several of our fellow travelers and caravan workers sustained severe injuries. We had to amputate a couple of fingers, we used a lot of Erasmus' healing balm for bruises and abrasions, and we treated a few sprains. We had one fatality: A man suddenly clutched his chest in the region of his sternum, struggled for breath and collapsed. We went to him almost immediately, but he gasped a few times and then stopped breathing. His pupils were dilated and we could not feel a pulse.

This is what Dividimus taught us was acute indigestion. Abraham believes that such an instance is not connected with the stomach but rather with the heart as, during similar attacks, he heard the heart skip beats and then stop altogether.

The caravan leader was a little unhappy about the delay, but we did feel we had to bury the man. He had no possessions or identification. He had paid his way with Greek money. Now he is buried in an unmarked grave near the Jordan, four day's journey north of Jericho.

Elisa walked much of the way. However, on long travel days, as the afternoon progressed, I insisted that she ride the donkey. Fortunately, the caravan leader took rather long rest stops at the noon hour.

Finally, we climbed the last hill and there was the valley and the Sea of Galilee below us. What a stirring sight!

By the ninth hour, we were in Capernaum and soon we were at my father's station. He welcomed us with a hearty smile. He was clearly pleased to see us, but too restrained to show his emotions. I unpacked the donkey and helped unload some of the other animals as I always used to do. It was good to see Joshua again. My father's caravan business has increased so much that he has hired two new helpers.

Finally, Elisa and I bid farewell to our new friends among the pilgrims and thanked the caravan commander for his kindness. He was so grateful for our services that he gave us a precious inlaid serving tray. In fact, he invited us to come with him whenever we wish to travel to Jerusalem.

We had not seen our parents in two years, so we had a great reunion. We went to the home of Erasmus and Sarah first. They both looked tired, particularly Erasmus. We plan to carry some of his burdens now and to allow him more rest. We caught up with the news about Elisa's sister, Rebekah, and brother, Samuel, and their families.

Our parents had become friends while Elisa and I were gone, which made our hearts glad, and Sarah decided that they should join us for the evening meal. Sarah began to busy herself with the task of cooking and would not let Elisa help.

Erasmus had work at the clinic, so we went to see my mother, Mary, and deliver the invitation from Sarah. She was tearful with joy that we were home safely. She had news to tell us of my sister, her husband and their two children. Reu has bought land closer to Capernaum and they are able to visit more often.

Soon my father joined us. He had finished with the major work with the caravan and left the rest to one of his helpers. It was good to talk to him about his business. You know, Luke, I worked with him in the supply business from the time I was twelve years old and I was interested in the changes he had made in the last two years.

Soon the four of us set out to the home of Elisa's parents, my mother carrying a date cake for dessert. Sarah and Erasmus were ready for us with a bountiful repast. It was a delicious meal with a lot of laughter. My father's hearty laugh echoed throughout the house.

After the meal, all of the parents spoke at once. "Come with us. We have something to show you." Elisa and I followed them out of the house, down the street on the west side of the town and up a hill. Soon I knew that we were on the property of one of the Pharisees, named Hupham. I had delivered goods to that location many times from the caravan station. I recognized the overseer's house, made of stone with a fine slate roof, beside a grove of fruit trees. There were mulberries, pears, plums and date palms. I remembered the delicious fruits that I would pick up off the ground as I passed through making deliveries to the vast storehouse. I wondered why one of Hupham's servants did not stop us from trespassing.

"What are we doing here?" I asked.

My father, Joseph, pointed to the overseer's house and said, "This is your new home." As we gasped, Erasmus pointed to the huge storehouse. "And that is where we will treat our patients."

We were overwhelmed and could not speak. Elisa and I hugged each other and all four of the parents in gratitude. As my father and mother and Erasmus and Sarah crowded around us, the story unfolded.

Hupham had larger storehouses elsewhere and needed to get rid of this one, along with some of the land. My father had heard of his desire, and since the Pharisee was indebted to him for a sizable sum, he approached him for the small piece of land and the buildings. Hupham was willing to dispose of it. Then my father and mother went to Erasmus and Sarah, and a deal was made. My father would acquire the four-room house, fruit orchard and the grove of trees across the road while Erasmus would acquire the storehouse for a place for all of us to practice the healing art. I just stood there with my arms around Elisa and could only say, "Thank you. Thank you."

Finally my mother said, "Don't you want to see your new home?" We walked up the three steps to the portico and were overwhelmed. This was so much larger than the room where we had lived in Jerusalem for two years. My mother walked on and said, "There is more. Come see."

We entered a large room that could serve as a dining room. It was about 14 by 14 cubits in size with two doors on the north side and a large one on the east side. The first door on the north side was the entrance to the cooking area, which was about 8 by 10 cubits, with a small room for storage. We returned to the large room and went through the other door that entered a large room about 10 by 10 cubits, where we would sleep. Then we moved back to the dining room and to the large door on the east side. This opened into a spare room that ran the length of the house, measuring about 14 by 24 cubits.

Luke, you cannot imagine the tears of joy and the embraces that followed. Elisa and I had planned to start the new period of our lives together in a one-room home. This was more than we had ever dreamed about. My mother and Sarah had furnished us a place to sleep and some vessels for cooking, but the rest we must obtain ourselves when we can pay for them.

I glanced at my father and he nodded. He knew that I understood he had made this purchase with his savings. I recalled the lesson that he had taught me from childhood: "Never purchase anything unless you have the total amount of money on hand to pay for it. Then you can look anyone in the eye and say, 'I owe no man any money. I owe only God.'"

"The orchard is the place where I will spend my spare time," he said. "I would love to clean it up, clear out the weeds and make it look nice." He looked at me. "You can help me if you have time." And then he added, "There are some dead cherry trees and walnut trees that we can saw up and make furniture for your home."

We will have much to do. I knew that we needed the furniture and could not afford to buy it. Luke, I had not had my fingers digging in the ground or working in wood for almost six years.

Erasmus then explained, "You know that I have always treated the ill at my home, but now they will come here. We will all work here." He looked at Sarah and motioned. "It is dark and we must go home. We start to work in the morning. Elisa and Joseph, come in one hour after sunrise so I can show you around. Let's go, Sarah."

As the four started to leave, we thanked them all again. I said a prayer thanking God for such wonderful parents.

When they were gone, I asked Elisa, "Does this fit the plan that we made at Jericho?"

She was quick to reply. "Simple, adequate room to grow, and for a guest. This is just right."

"But Joseph," Elisa said with a start, "we forgot to tell them about John and the man from Galilee!"

"Perhaps it is better," I said, "because that will take time. It may be better to do it some Sabbath after the meal."

By this time there was a knock at the door and one of my father's helpers brought in the rest of our belongings.

As we unpacked the few things that we had brought, Elisa stopped and remarked, "We have so much. The Lord has been so good to us."

And so, Luke, that is the way it will be for us as we start our new life in Capernaum.

Joseph

Letter 16

Dear Luke, we were up at dawn to enjoy our new home. I had been on the grounds many times but had only seen this house from the outside. Hupham built it well of stone, and the mortar is of excellent quality. The windows are small and high, and the floors are made of small stones covered with mortar. Large wood beams support the roof, which is built on a slant so that the water can drain off. The usual roofs here are of tightly woven grass but this one is of slate. There are doors on every side of the house, and a large portico along three sides of the house.

"Hupham really built a sturdy house for his overseer," I remarked to Elisa. "Thankfully he did," she replied. She went inside to fix some herb tea. I followed and found some bread that Sarah had left us, and we sat down for our first simple meal in our new home.

The house faces south on a hill just southwest of Capernaum. The fruit orchard behind the house blocks the view of town. But we had no time to linger and off we went, carrying our physician's gowns and bags of instruments and herbs to the place where we would practice with Erasmus.

We walked out of the house through the south door and passed by the well. It was deep, and I recalled that I drew up many a drink of cold water when I came here on deliveries. My father had said he thought this was the deepest well in this area.

Then we came to the storehouse. I remembered this very well, too, having unloaded the supplies from the station there. It was also built sturdy enough to withstand storms.

As we approached we could see Erasmus riding up on his horse. "You're up early," he shouted as he dismounted and tied his horse. "We wanted to be here early so that we could see it all," Elisa replied. I helped him carry in his bags. Erasmus opened the door and said, "Well, come and look it over."

The building was large, about 20 by 60 cubits. We entered an open area that was about half the size of the building, where Hupham's servants had stored their grain in sacks. It had several windows for good ventilation. Erasmus explained that this is the room where the patients will wait. Often an entire family comes in carrying the patient on a pallet.

The room was filled with new benches made of walnut. Erasmus said, "Your father and Joshua made these out of the trees in the grove." I examined the delicate work and said, "I must thank them."

Then he led us through into the area where Hupham had storage bins. There were six stalls, three on each side, each about 5 cubits wide and 8 cubits long, with a corridor 4 cubits wide in the center. These were the places where we were to examine our patients. There was one compartment for each of us, one for surgery, one for herbs and one for storage. Imagine, Luke, we each have a separate room in which to see our patients, not like the entirely open places that we had in Athens and Jerusalem, and the type that most physicians use.

Then Erasmus took us to the room where he will do most of his surgery. He had already fitted the room with instruments for incising boils and suturing wounds, saws for performing amputations, and many other instruments.

Behind that room is where the herbs and potions are being stored, which Sarah has been mixing under his direction while Elisa and I were in Jerusalem. As Elisa walked in and looked at all of the labeled bottles of herbs arranged neatly along the shelves, her eyes sparkled. She unpacked the plants she had so carefully nurtured from the time they were given to her by the members of the Essene community, stepped back a few paces and smiled.

Attached to the storehouse was a small building with two stalls for horses or donkeys.

Erasmus said, "Now, let us plan our work day." So we sat down and he described how he had been working the past few years.

"I start after dawn and ride my horse to visit the patients who are too sick to come to see me. This takes me three to six hours. Then I spend the rest of the day here." He slapped his thigh and continued. "Ach! That keeps me out of mischief!" Then he turned to Elisa and said, "I have not been fishing since you left for Jerusalem. I surely would like to go. "

So, Luke, we decided the following schedule: I will call on his patients in their homes in the mornings. Elisa will work at the clinic in the morning, rest after the midday meal, and then return. I will work in the clinic after I return from the sick calls. Erasmus plans to work four mornings and three afternoons a week.

Finally, Erasmus described the patients I am to see and where they live, and he showed me the herbs and potions he carries in heavy saddlebags. "Use my horse until you can afford to buy one yourself." I loaded the bags and mounted and off I went.

Riding away I could hear him laughing and talking to Elisa. "Oh! Now, I will catch all of the fish in Lake Galilee!"

Luke, it feels strange to enter houses where I had been many times in years back as a delivery boy and now I come as a physician. Some of the families were a little reluctant to accept me, and several times I overheard the remark, "This is Joseph's boy. What can the son of a caravan outfitter know about the healing art?" But since Erasmus had sent me, they let me come in and treat the patient. I took a history of the patient and did a complete examination, then discussed the treatment with the family. They seemed impressed with the thoroughness of my work, but I know that it will take time for them to accept me.

The morning passed and at noon I returned and told Erasmus about the cases I had seen. His detailed questions made me realize, again, that his depth of knowledge is as vast as that of Abraham. Then he mounted his horse and said, "Now I'm going fishing."

I went to our home where Elisa had fixed a light meal. We talked about the patients we had seen and the work that needed to be done. Then she went to rest and I went to the clinic to see the first of the afternoon's patients.

Our first day in practice was exhausting but a great pleasure. I implore the blessings of God upon you, Luke.

Joseph

Letter 17

Greetings, dear friend. It has been several weeks since our return to Capernaum, and our working arrangement with Erasmus is going well. We have already treated many types of illnesses and injuries.

Luke, you must see the drug room in our clinic. Elisa has filled the shelves with containers of drugs, all neatly labeled. It is easy to go into the room and obtain the necessary ingredients for a prescription for a patient and prepare it rapidly and accurately. She even has a scale on which we can weigh the herbs before we mix them. And her herb garden is progressing well, especially the sprouts that she brought from the Essene community.

So you see, dear friend, we are well situated here. The three of us are the only trained physicians in Capernaum. The people Elisa and I grew up with have come to accept us as physicians.

We work hard but I also make time to work with my father in the fruit orchard behind our house while Elisa tends her herb garden. My hands have not been accustomed to such work and I have developed a few blisters. I also spend time making furniture for our house. It is crudely done, I'm afraid, but it will do.

In the cool of the evening we try to take walks to the Lake of Galilee, and often we see Erasmus sitting on the bank fishing with a long pole.

One thing Elisa and I hate to do is to put a price on our work. We feel that God has been so good to us that we should do it without charge, but that is not very practical. We have adopted the policy of Erasmus and also Abraham to accept anything, trade or otherwise, as payment for our work. Erasmus leaves a basket at the door for coins, but he accepts chickens, vegetables, whatever the patient can give. Some patients pay well, others a little and some who do not have any coins do not pay. We treat them all the same.

Elisa and I have been able to buy some dishes for the kitchen. We do not purchase anything until we have the money to pay for it. We have managed to purchase a donkey. It is big and strong enough to carry my medical bags and me on my rounds to the sick. It must be an odd sight to watch him plodding along with me on his back as we go from home to home.

On the Sabbath, there is no work at the clinic. I make only those visits that are necessary to treat the critically ill.

A few days after we started practice here, one of the Pharisees chastised me severely for working on the Sabbath. Last week while Elisa and I were at Sabbath services, a messenger came from this same Pharisee, who had fallen down the steps of his home while on the way to the synagogue. Of course, I went and did not say a word about his previous criticism. I needed help so I sent for Elisa. We set his broken femur and fixed it in its proper place. As we left his room and entered the gathering hall of his home, his friends, all prominent Pharisees, surrounded us. We were very courteous in our report to them. It was obvious to them that we had worked hard. They did not say anything about it being the Sabbath, and neither did we.

We have been so occupied in our new life that we often are too busy or tired to talk. Only rarely do we speak of our restful days in Jericho or of our experiences on the Jordan with John the Baptizer. This lack of time to talk together bothers us, and we hope that we will be better able to adjust our work so that we have more free time for ourselves.

My dear Luke, I bid you farewell, and may the God of Abraham, Isaac and Jacob bless and keep you.

Joseph

Letter 18

Luke, Elisa and I are concerned that the Lord has not blessed us with a child yet. Of course, the leaving of descendants is one of the purposes of our race, and infertility is quite a curse for a woman. We discussed this with Erasmus and he just gave his usual laugh and said, "When the Lord wants you to have a child, He will arrange it."

Of course, we were taught that infertility is the fault of the wife, but Erasmus has a much different opinion. He feels that from one-fourth to one-third of the cases are due to the male seed. He told us of women who had been unable to bear a child to their first husbands, but after they were widowed and remarried they bore several children. Perhaps someday we will know more about this condition.

Elisa and I now arrange our work so that we eat our meals together and take a walk to the lake or in our orchard every evening. During our walks, we often discuss the teachings of John and what we witnessed at the Jordan River. We cannot get off our minds the man from Galilee and the voice that hailed him from above. We finally discussed the events in Bethany with our parents at a meal on the Sabbath. They seemed surprised that we were both so taken with John and the man from Galilee.

Erasmus said, "There have been many prophets in the history of Israel, and many more false prophets. Usually the true prophets have been killed or driven away because they said things the people did not want to hear. This man John seems to be doing that. He had better be careful. People do not want to be told that that they are sinners. As for the man from Galilee, there have been many claims to be the Messiah ..."

"But the voice was from nowhere and everywhere," I interrupted.

"Are you sure that you were not dreaming? Or had too much wine?" Erasmus remarked with a laugh.

Mary said, "We will see in time. My father, your grandfather, told me that there are many false prophets. Just be cautious."

Then Joseph, my father, who speaks his mind less often, added, "If it makes you better people by having had the experience, be thankful for it."

As Elisa and I walked home I said, "Perhaps we did not explain everything well enough."

"Let the Lord guide us" was her answer.

And so He will.

Joseph

Letter 19

Dear Luke, I have tried to describe Elisa to you in previous letters. But today I found a description of her in the writings of what we call the Proverbs. These were written years and years ago by an unknown scribe or scribes. This passage describes Elisa in better words than I am able to do:

A perfect wife — who can find her?
She is far beyond the price of pearls.
Her husband's heart has confidence in her,
from her he will derive no little profit.
Advantage and not hurt she brings him
all the days of her life.
She is always busy with wool and with flax,
she does her work with eager hands.
She is like a merchant vessel
bringing her food from far away.
She gets up while it is still dark
giving her household their food,
giving orders to her serving girls.
She sets her mind on a field, then she buys it.
With what her hands have earned she plants a vineyard.
She puts her back into her work
and shows how strong her arms can be.
She finds her labour well worth while.
Her lamp does not go out at night.
She sets her hands to the distaff,
her fingers grasp the spindle.
She holds out her hand to the poor,
she opens her arms to the needy.
Snow may come, she has no fears for her household,
with all her servants warmly clothed.

She makes her own quilts,
she is dressed in fine linen and purple.
Her husband is respected at the city gates,
taking his seat among the elders of the land.
She weaves linen sheets and sells them,
she supplies the merchant with sashes.
She is clothed in strength and dignity,
she can laugh at the days to come.
When she opens her mouth, she does so wisely.
On her tongue is kindly instruction.
She keeps good watch on the conduct of her household,
no bread of idleness for her.
Her sons stand up and proclaim her blessed,
her husband, too, sings her praises:
"Many women have done admirable things,
but you surpass them all!"
Charm is deceitful, and beauty empty.
The woman who is wise is the one to praise.
Give her a share in what her hands have worked for,
and let her works tell her praises at the city gates.[1]

We do not have servants in the household nor does Elisa spend her time weaving linen sheets. She works as a physician. But this is Elisa.

And, of course, we have no sons yet, but by the grace of God we will have them someday.

May God so guide you that you meet her.

Joseph

---

[1] Proverbs 31:10-31

Letter 20

Luke, Elisa and I were gone from Capernaum for most of the last six years and now have little in common with friends of our childhood. Both of us started to work at a young age helping our fathers and did not have much idle time. And as you remember, in Athens you and I had neither the money nor the desire to pass time drinking or with women. We spent most of our time studying.

In my courtship and marriage to Elisa I have found her to be my best friend, who helps me become a better person in so many ways.

We both enjoy meeting people with different experiences. We have begun to develop close ties with a few special people our age and older. We share interests in the Scriptures, in the writings of other cultures, and news of events in the land of Israel and in lands far away. We read and discuss the Torah, the Prophets and the Writings. We often meet on the day after the Sabbath in each other's homes and talk late into the evening. The women are expected to have an opinion and speak on equal terms with the men.

We have not yet shared our experiences with John at Bethany on the Jordan, wishing to get better acquainted first.

Among these new friends are John, a former officer with the Temple Guard in Jerusalem, and Esther, his wife, the daughter of a landowner. John has completed his service and now manages several properties. Then there are Samson and his wife, Hannah, and David and his wife, Rachel. Samson and David are teachers in the synagogue school. Hannah and Rachel are always helping the poor. The last couple is Abriam and Judith. He is a land procurement agent and she likes to care for the ill. Judith was a great help to Erasmus while Elisa and I were in Jerusalem for training.

We are all members of what could be called the working class, with professions or businesses.

The priestly class is the highest of all in Israel. Then there are the very rich and the landowners. These are few in number but seem to control almost everything. Then follow the merchants and the tax collectors. The working class comes after that and then the more learned, the teachers and scribes among them. Next are the artisans, the small shopkeepers in town and craftsmen of all types. Then there are the shepherds, who have a very difficult, isolated life, and the tillers of the soil, who barely make a living on small plots of land. Finally, there is the class of servants, the poor and beggars. We do well with all people in our practice and we receive, when paid, according to their means.

Luke, I know that you must feel dismay as you read about our friends and our evening discussions. "You men are meeting and discussing items with women! No! No!" I know your feelings on this matter, and mine were not so different when I was younger. But when I met Elisa and recognized her great wisdom and intelligence, I realized that God indeed does make us all equal. It is how we treat each other that makes the difference. The men in our group respect the women and their ideas.

Yes, Luke, we men have much to learn from women.

Joseph

Letter 21

Peace be with you, dear friend.

My father's caravan station is a leading source of news in Capernaum because visitors come from distant lands.

Today my father sent over a messenger with news of John the Baptizer. He has publicly denounced Herod Antipas, the tetrarch or governor of Galilee and Perea. In John's preachings throughout Galilee, he has condemned Herod's marriage to Herodias, wife of his brother, Herod Philip. This marriage has caused great scandal because it violates the Law. John's repeated condemnations are an insult to Herod, but it is Herodias who is most angered.

This evening, all of our friends gathered at our home. They had heard the news, but none of them knew much about John. It was then that Elisa and I told them of the events we had witnessed at the Jordan with John and the man he called the Chosen One of God.

Several months have passed since these events occurred, and I can no longer recall clearly the features of the Galilean, but I can still hear the words from above spoken over him that day. "You are my son, the Beloved. My favor rests on you."

As we finished, everyone sat quietly. Finally David, one of the teachers, spoke. "I have heard of John and his preaching of repentance and his baptizing in the River Jordan in Judea. He has had a group of followers, but I had not heard that he had come to Galilee."

"I can see," said Samson, "why Herod arrested him. He wanted no more attention to this scandalous marriage to his brother's wife."

"This man from Galilee," Esther said. "He made a deep impression upon the both of you, didn't he?" And we answered in unison, "Yes!"

"Have you seen him again?" she asked.

"Would you recognize him?" asked Hannah.

And Samson, her husband, wondered aloud, "What about this voice that you heard? Where did it come from? What did it sound like? Could you be mistaken?"

Luke, we answered all questions as clearly and as honestly as we could. Finally John the husband of Esther spoke, echoing the thoughts of Erasmus. "Prophets have been raised by God for centuries. We have had Isaiah, Jeremiah, Hosea and many others. They all accuse the people of their sinfulness and they all have been either driven away or killed. Very few of our people followed their teachings, but we do have their words in the Scriptures. If John is a prophet, and he sounds like one, he may receive the same fate." And the talk continued well into the night.

Luke, I wish you were here to take part in our discussions.

Joseph

Letter 22

Luke, our circle of friends has grown to about twenty, and we continue to learn from each other. All attend the synagogue regularly and are eager to deepen their understanding of spiritual matters. We meet the day after the Sabbath to discuss the readings and the preaching we heard the previous day, and to share our own readings of the Scriptures.

Remember, Luke, parchment is rare and expensive, so few of us have even pieces of the Writings. But they can all be found in the synagogue, where the faithful come to read the Scriptures and to commit to memory the words of the Prophets.

Tonight the group gathered in our clinic. The room where our patients wait is large enough to hold more than one hundred people. Esther and John brought date cake and wine. "Joseph," teased Abriam, "don't you wish these were all paying customers?"

Among the new couples are Eliab and Naomi, who both sing beautifully, and Daniel, a lawyer, and his wife, Leah.

We also have some widows in the group. Thalia, whose husband Aaron died of a liver ailment, is a little older than the others but very active. Miriam, the widow of Joachim, thirsts for knowledge and expresses herself beautifully.

Ruth, the widow of James, is a cheerful person who suffers from joint pains. Erasmus, Elisa and I have tried all types of mixtures of herbs to cure her but to no avail. Damp weather seems to make the pain more intense.

And finally there is Ana, the quiet one. Ana, the widow of Eleazar, is always carrying a piece of parchment on which she writes things that she wishes to remember. I wish that we could afford to pay her to keep records of our patients' illnesses. It would be a great help in our work.

Tonight Elisa suggested we offer the clinic as a regular meeting place. The benches that my father and Joshua made proved very comfortable for our long session tonight, and our offer was gratefully accepted.

As the evening ended, several of our friends stayed to help clean the clinic, and when we left the waiting room was ready for the morning's patients.

Joseph

Letter 23

Our practice is growing, Luke. Word is spreading that Elisa and I have taken special training under Abraham of Jerusalem and we are getting patients from the surrounding villages and towns. I am no longer called "Joseph's boy," but am treated like a learned physician. But today a new healer came to town.

I know you, too, are accustomed to the wandering healers who arrive, set up a booth and sell a tonic, usually made of cheap wine and a few herbs, which they claim will cure every sort of disease. These charlatans come, stay a few days, then move on, leaving the patients still ill but now with empty pockets. However, this new healer seems different.

Elisa encountered him first. She came upon a crowd of people gathered around a man they said was healing people of afflictions for which we have no cure. A deaf person could now hear, and a lame man was on his feet and walking.

She entered the crowd and saw a man in his early thirties. His clothes were clean and neat but plain, unlike the fancy clothes that so many wandering healers wear. She watched as he went from person to person, speaking to them, touching them, looking deeply into their eyes. He did not examine them in any way nor did he give them any tonic. She did not witness any cures, but the people he touched seemed somehow changed. She hurried to the clinic to share word of this new healer in town.

"Abraham taught us to be on the lookout for new methods of treatment," she said. "This man seems to have something that we do not have. Come with me. Let us learn more."

I know that Elisa is not easily fooled, so I decided to join her. We finished the work with our patients and went to find the new healer.

By the time we arrived the crowd had settled at the man's feet. He was sitting and speaking to those gathered, like the wise men do in the Temple. He was not speaking of healing but of performing good deeds, caring for those who are poor or in need.

He had a kind expression and a pleasant smile. His hair was neatly groomed, parted in the middle and braided in the back of his head in the Galilean manner. And yet he was a little taller than most Galileans. His muscles were pronounced, as if he had done heavy work. With the scars on his hands I would place him as a carpenter by trade.

Luke, I cannot find the words in Greek to explain, but just looking at him, listening to him, gave me a feeling of confidence and trust.

Whenever someone came close to the man and begged to be healed, he would talk to them quietly but intently. He did not ask questions as we do in trying to learn the history of an illness. He did touch them on the arm or shoulder. Then he would say something astonishing. "Your sins are forgiven. Go and sin no more."

Luke, his words clearly had an effect on each of the petitioners. The distress lifted from their eyes and a peaceful look came over their faces. They kissed his hand and began to praise God for sending this healer.

Elisa whispered to me, "I do not know this man, yet I feel I have seen him before."

"As do I. But I cannot recall where we would have met."

The crowd grew larger as word spread of the cures. But this stranger, this healer in plain clothes, somehow slipped away. Those who had gathered gradually left, still talking of what they had seen. We went to examine some of those he had touched.

"Look, there is the man with the withered leg," Elisa said. "My father treated him with the paralytic disease when we were both children. Now he walks normally with both legs."

"There is the woman who has been crippled in her back all of her life," I added. "She is walking upright and straight."

As we examined others, we found every case was the same. There was simply no explanation for these cures within our knowledge of medicine.

On our way back to the clinic, Elisa spoke. "Joseph, did you notice that he did not ask for any money? This man is not like any of the wandering healers we have known before."

"Yes," I replied, more than a little annoyed that this man seemed to cure with no effort. "I do not understand how he works these cures. It defies all that has been taught about the healing art since Hippocrates. But you are right, Elisa. We must be open to new methods of treatment. We must try to learn from this man."

After we closed the clinic for the day, we ate a hurried meal and set out again to find the healer. Unlike others, he did not seem to have a booth, or a camel or horse to carry wares and potions from town to town. We inquired but no one had seen him since he'd slipped away. Near dusk we found ourselves near the lake. We sat down for a moment to reflect on what we had seen and heard. In the distance the bluffs began to fade into shadow. The sun began to set and we started home, following a path through the trees.

We had just entered the depth of the woods near our home when I suddenly noticed a kneeling figure ahead of me. I stopped, recognizing the healer. Elisa was right behind me. "Oh," she uttered. That was just enough to disturb him. He arose and walked over to us.

"Peace be with you," he said.

We both nodded and then I spoke. "I am Joseph and this is my wife, Elisa. We are physicians here in Capernaum."

The man nodded and I continued. "We watched you this afternoon and we are eager to learn your way of healing. Could you come to our clinic tomorrow afternoon and then eat with us?" I stopped short. I had blurted out an invitation to a meal without asking Elisa.

But she stepped up and said, "Please come." He looked at her. "I will be glad to visit your clinic and then to break bread with you. But please remember I am accustomed to simple food. I will be at your clinic about the eleventh hour."

Elisa and I looked at each other and we were both pleased. As we turned back, the man was gone, he had disappeared into the trees. And Luke, we didn't even ask his name!

"Elisa, I should have asked you before I invited him to eat at our home but you see, I again spoke before I thought." She grasped my hand and smiled. "Joseph, he seems so nice. I will not mind doing the cooking. And he said 'simple food.' That is what he will get."

As we crossed the road from the wooded area to the orchard near our home we noticed a fragrance sweetening the air. The summer flowers are just starting to bloom. My parents, Joseph and Mary, were just leaving after tending the orchard and garden. It pleases them as in the days when they worked the soil, but it is not as strenuous. They really enjoy the quiet time working together.

Elisa was eager to tell them of the new healer. They listened intently and Joseph said, "You know what I always said about having competition. It makes you do better in your work. It keeps you challenged."

Luke, I remember that he spoke those words to me many times when I was working with him. "Do better work than your competition." And he not only talked about it, he practiced it. I watched him do extra little things for the travelers and caravan drivers. He always had some cold water from our deep well, which was welcomed, and he cared for the animals as if they were his.

We nodded and bid them farewell as they left. As we entered our house, Elisa said, "Somehow, Joseph, I do not feel that this new healer is competition."

I thought a while and replied. "Obviously, he can do things that we cannot do, but I feel just as you do about him. He seems more like a friend."

Luke, soon we may have new methods of healing to tell you about.

Joseph

Letter 24

Elisa left work early today to prepare a simple yet special meal for our guest. She went to Simon's dock to find fish. Luke, we are fortunate to have fresh fish at two markets here in Capernaum. Fish were not easily available in Jerusalem.

One of the fish markets is run by Simon and Andrew, brothers from Bethsaida. Zebedee and his two sons, James and John, operate the other. All of their boats set out at night and bring in a catch for early morning sale. We know these men well because we treat them for the cuts and other injuries that they receive in their work. They are strong men, well-muscled from long hours at the oars and nets.

I finished with the patients after the tenth hour and was cleaning up when suddenly the healer appeared at the door. With a broad smile he said, "Shalom. I am Jesus." "Shalom!" I replied.

I hoped to impress this man, so I showed him the entire clinic — the waiting room, the treatment rooms, the surgery and the barn. He went over all of our equipment and asked a lot of questions. After that we sat down to drink a little wine. I said that I was very impressed with the healing that he had performed the day before and I told him I was eager to learn his technique. He smiled and stroked his beard.

"Joseph," he said, "you have much to learn. It will all be revealed to you in good time."

I nodded but did not understand. I pressed on. "Elisa and I are eager to learn all that we can so that we can help our patients. May we observe you do your healing? Where did you train? I apprenticed with Dividimus in Athens, and Elisa trained under Abraham in Jerusalem. After we married we both spent two years of advanced training under Abraham in Jerusalem."

He replied, "Joseph, you will learn so much more than you can imagine. But be patient. It will come in time." Luke, you know that patience is not one of my attributes. But the way he answered ended further discussion.

Then the healer noticed the benches in the outer room. "Fine carpentry," he remarked as he checked for the smoothness of the finish and the grain of the wood. I answered, "My father and Joshua, his employee at the caravan station, made them. Joshua and I made most of the furniture in our home." And then I boldly asked, "You have worked with wood too?"

"Joseph, you are an observant physician. Yes, I have worked as a carpenter since childhood."

"That explains the calluses and cuts on your hands. I can see that those are not the hands of a physician." I closed the door and we walked the short distance to our home. Jesus remarked, "It is beautiful here, Joseph. You are blessed."

As we entered the house, he walked to the kitchen to find Elisa. "May I help you?" he asked, and started to stir the soup she had put on the fire. Soon all three of us were busy with preparations for the meal.

As we sat down to eat, I gave the traditional Jewish blessing. Jesus added, "And may we help those who do not have enough to eat." Elisa smiled in approval of the added prayer.

We had a wonderful visit over dinner, which lasted two hours. Jesus complimented Elisa several times on her cooking. She blushed and quickly changed the subject as cooking is not her strongest asset.

During the course of our time together, Jesus questioned us in detail about our education, why we went into medicine, how we met, how we are able to practice together. We laughed and joked as if we had known each other for years.

But whenever I started to ask Jesus about his training and his healing technique, he evaded the questions. In fact, he revealed very little, except that he was from the town of Nazareth and that he had attended the synagogue school there. His mother's name also is Mary, and his father, Joseph, died several years ago.

Then Elisa said, "Jesus, I am sure that I have seen you somewhere in the past."

"That is possible. I lived in Nazareth all of my life. Perhaps you visited there with your parents."

"No," she said, "I have never been to Nazareth."

"Perhaps we met at the Passover in Jerusalem. I have been there every year."

"Perhaps," Elisa said, "but I know that I have seen you in recent years. Your voice sounds familiar."

Jesus arose abruptly. "It is late and I must leave." He put his hands on each of our heads and said, "May the Lord bless you both in your work. Thank you for your hospitality."

As he left Elisa and I both called out, "Please, come back." "I will," he said, and disappeared into the dark.

We held hands and gazed after him for what seemed to be a long time. As we prepared to retire, Elisa spoke first. "Jesus found out all about us but we learned very little about him. He never mentioned an apprenticeship or any training as a practitioner of the healing art. Where did he learn his technique?"

I recounted what Jesus told me, including his admonishment to be patient when I had asked him earlier that afternoon to share his healing knowledge.

"Did you notice his piercing eyes?" Elisa said. "When he spoke he looked right into my eyes, as if he could see my thoughts."

"Jesus is certainly a mystery," I said. "There is something dignified, almost majestic about him. He is imposing yet not overbearing. He cures without the use of medicine but he is not a charlatan. The people whom he cured had real afflictions that we could neither treat nor cure."

Elisa was quick to reply. "A trickster he is not. He asks for no money like the usual traveling healer. He does not have a horse and a fancy cart like they all have. This is hard to understand.

"But I do not remember when we have laughed so much in one short evening," added Elisa.

Luke, we have met a new healer and yet we cannot comprehend him or the art of his medicine. But as we learn more about his methods, I will share the secrets with you.

Joseph

Letter 25

Dear Luke, tonight during the midnight watch Elisa awakened me. "Joseph," she said. "I know where we have seen that man, Jesus." I stretched and tried to wake up as she continued. "You remember in Jericho when we were baptized by John?" "Yes," I replied, still yawning.

"Remember when we stepped back and a man came forward to be baptized? John suddenly stopped baptizing and protested. 'No! No! You should not be baptized by me. It is I who should be baptized by you.' We heard the man say, 'Leave it like this for the time being. It is fitting that we should all do that righteousness demands.' Then John baptized him.

"And a bright light appeared, and a dove, and we heard a voice from above say, 'You are my son, the Beloved.'"

Elisa took a deep breath and her eyes gleamed in the moonlight. Luke, she is beautiful.

"It was he, the man from Galilee, the healer named Jesus!"

I was awake by now, listening intently. She was exact in every detail of her recollection. This was the man whom John had called "the Lamb of God who takes away the sin of the world."

"This man is specially blessed by God," Elisa concluded.

"But why, and why is he here now?" I asked.

She replied, "Only God knows," and, satisfied for the moment, she turned over and fell asleep. But I could not go to sleep. My mind was full of questions.

How could a man be the son of the one true God? All of the questions that had been suppressed in my mind these past few months, when I had been too busy to consider them, now came up. How can a man forgive sins? How can he cure the incurable? It is all beyond my understanding. I scarcely closed my eyes the remainder of the night.

Elisa was bright and fresh in the morning but I was not. I told her of the questions that came to my mind during the long sleepless night.

"I am going to ask Jesus these questions if I ever see him again."

"Wait," said Elisa, "there may be more to this than appears. Let us observe his actions."

"Yes, I will observe him. I still want to learn his technique of cure."

"Remember he told you that all will be revealed in time."

"But I do not like to wait!" I exclaimed.

"I knew that before we were married, Joseph. But try. If he is a deceiver — and I do not believe that he is — he will follow the usual course. Remember what Abraham said many times: 'A deceiver will reveal his true character if you just wait.' I am sure that the time will come when it will be appropriate to discuss all of this with him."

And so, Luke, we have a deepening mystery.

God be with you.

Joseph

Letter 26

Luke, Jesus has remained among us at Capernaum, along the Sea of Galilee. Our friends and patients come in and tell us stories of what they have heard and seen.

Miriam came in breathless one morning last week. "Elisa, I just heard that man Jesus speak, and he has a depth of knowledge of the Scriptures that surpasses that of the most learned rabbi. He can quote from the prophets with complete accuracy. And he speaks with such power, such force.

"Yet he has such a kindly look on his face all of the time, especially when he speaks of feeding the poor and taking care of those who have no family. He says that redemption is possible through the actions we take to help those in need."

Later Ruth came into the clinic and told how comforted she felt when she heard him say, "Your sins are forgiven."

Another day Samson and Hannah brought another story of a cure. David and Rachel came in with another story, and then Abriam and Judith arrived to tell of the teachings that they had heard throughout the day, which remind them of writings of the prophets.

You can imagine that most of the talk this evening at our meeting was about the new healer and his teachings. Everyone had a different experience and a different point of view. Some were skeptical. Who is this man and can he be trusted? Could this be a prophet for our times?

Finally David, who favors the Socratic method of teaching and learning, spoke. "These questions are pertinent but we have no answers as of yet. While Jesus is here in Capernaum, let us all observe his actions and listen to his teachings, and continue to debate what it all means. We may learn something from him, whoever he is."

But Luke, I am not so concerned with what he teaches. I am more anxious to learn how he cures people.

Joseph

Letter 27

It has been several weeks, Luke, since the mysterious healer and preacher named Jesus came to Capernaum. Today we learned that he has left to preach and work in villages to the south. We hear that he will someday return to Capernaum.

Luke, Elisa and I are still trying to learn more about him. Last month Elisa had an idea. "Joseph, your mother, Mary, and your sister, Acida, have traced many family ancestries. They know the background of everyone in Capernaum. Perhaps they could learn about the ancestry of Jesus."

We asked them to research his background, and they accepted this unusual challenge.

Today as we were sitting in the garden late in the afternoon, my mother came over with a parchment in her hand and handed it to us. "Elisa and Joseph," she said, "we have the complete ancestry of this man Jesus. He is of the House of David."

This is what we read:

> *Jesus, the son of Joseph, son of Heli, son of Matthat,*
> *son of Levi, son of Melchi, son of Jannai, son of Joseph,*
> *son of Mattathias, son of Amos, son of Nahum, son of*
> *Esli, son of Naggai, son of Maath, son of Mattathias,*
> *son of Semein, son of Josech, son of Joda, son of*
> *Joanan, son of Rhesa, son of Zerubbabel, son of*
> *Shealtiel, son of Neri, son of Melchi, son of Addi, son*
> *of Cosam, son of Elmadam, son of Er, son of Joshua,*
> *son of Eliezer, son of Jorim, son of Matthat, son of Levi,*
> *son of Symeon, son of Judah, son of Joseph, son of*
> *Jonam, son of Eliakim, son of Melea, son of Menna,*
> *son of Mattatha, son of Nathan, son of David, son of*
> *Jesse, son of Obed, son of Boaz, son of Sala, son of*
> *Nahshon, son of Amminadab, son of Admin, son of*
> *Arni, son of Hezron, son of Perez, son of Judah, son of*
> *Jacob, son of Isaac, son of Abraham.*

Elisa spoke first. "Mother Mary, you and Acida have traced him back to

Abraham. Amazing!" We thanked her, walked her to the garden gate and then went into the house to study the lineage in detail.

Luke, I realize that all the importance we place on ancestry must be confusing to you. However, in our tradition we want to trace our roots back to Abraham, who is the father of our race.

Elisa read the document slowly and paused at each name. "Some of his ancestors are saints, some are not saintly," she said, "and many of these names are unknown to me. The prophets mention a few of them. But he is the son of David and through him a descendant of our father Abraham."

"So we know about Jesus' ancestry," I said. "But where does he get his ability to cure the sick? His method is not through herbs or potions."

Elisa was quiet a moment, then she looked at me. "Joseph, didn't he tell you that all of this would be revealed in time? Should we not just wait and see what develops?"

I must admit she is right. Waiting is what we will have to do now.

Who is this strange healer named Jesus?

Joseph

Nazareth

Letter 28

Dear Luke, I am writing this letter from Nazareth after a very hard journey and very tense few days of work. Here's how it all started.

One late afternoon, two days after the Sabbath, a man arrived at our clinic riding a trim and spirited horse and leading two others. They had been traveling rapidly a long time and the horses were covered with sweat. Everyone on the streets stood around and admired them.

The man, clearly a messenger, entered the clinic and handed me a note addressed to the physicians Elisa and Joseph of Capernaum.

This is what it said:

> *Come at once to Nazareth to treat my ill brother.*
> *Abraham of Jerusalem informed me that if I ever need*
> *medical help, I should contact you. My brother is*
> *desperately ill. No one here can help him. The horses*
> *are at your disposal. Please come quickly.*
>
> *Jeremiah*

I recognized the name as belonging to a leading Pharisee of Nazareth, a town in lower Galilee.

Luke, this was a new request — to leave Capernaum to treat a patient. Elisa was as surprised as I was. We discussed the problem with Erasmus. It clearly was an emergency and the servant was not to leave without one or both of us. I finally said to Elisa, "We both cannot go. One of us must stay here. I know that you wish to go, Elisa, but the trip will be strenuous. No one knows what is waiting in Nazareth. You and Erasmus can take care of our patients while I am gone." She agreed reluctantly.

Since it was late and the horses had come a long way, we decided to let them rest and start early in the morning. We had the servant stay in our spare room.

Elisa helped me pack medicines and surgical instruments in separate bags. Needless to say, we had a restless night. Elisa and I had not spent a day apart since we had married.

We rose before dawn and had breakfast. Elisa packed some food for the journey. The servant brought the other two horses and I loaded one with my medical bags. As I kissed Elisa goodbye she whispered, "Nazareth was the home of Jesus. See if you can learn more about him." I replied, "I will try," as I mounted the spirited horse. I did not look forward to a hard day of horseback riding. I was used to a slow donkey.

Nevertheless, the servant was an excellent horseman and he led the way at a gallop. We would stop every few miles to feed, water and rest the horses.

By the ninth hour we reached the top of a knoll, and there below us, surrounded on three sides by hills, was Nazareth. Finally we arrived at the home of Jeremiah. The grounds were spacious. The gatekeeper had sent a messenger ahead, so the Pharisee was outside waiting for us.

I dismounted awkwardly and would probably have fallen had the servant not been there to steady me. Every muscle, bone and joint in my body hurt. The Pharisee introduced himself. "I am Jeremiah and am grateful that you came."

I informed him that Elisa had stayed in Capernaum to take care of our patients. "You must be tired, you have ridden a long way," he said. "Perhaps you should rest first and we should eat, and then you may see my brother, Neri."

"I know this must be an emergency because you summoned me," I replied, feeling my reserves of strength returning. "I would prefer to see your brother now."

I could see the relief on his face. I know that he wanted to show me hospitality, particularly after the long journey, but I felt that he was very anxious about his brother. I did ask the servant to carry my bags. We went through several rooms to the back of the house, and there I could see several servants around a bed. Jeremiah asked them to step aside so I could examine the patient.

Jeremiah told me that his twenty-year-old brother had fallen from a horse three days before. He was able to get up and walk home but complained of a severe headache. During the evening Neri had become unusually drowsy and by morning was unconscious. Jeremiah had called several physicians in Nazareth but no one could help. He knew that he needed Abraham as a physician but also knew that his brother could not last the many days it would take Abraham to arrive from Jerusalem. Then Jeremiah remembered that Abraham had recommended us as physicians and sent for us. As I leaned over to examine the patient, I saw that there was crusted blood on the left side of his head. His breathing was shallow and slow. His heart was beating slowly. My heart grew heavy.

Luke, I know you have already diagnosed this patient as having a hemorrhage in his head pressing on his brain. I stepped back, motioned to Jeremiah to follow me to an adjoining room and explained what was wrong. I told him that without treatment his brother would surely die within a matter of hours, and that the only thing we could possibly do was drill a hole in the skull and relieve the pressure by letting out the blood, hoping that the bleeding would stop.

Luke, you know how rare it is that we are able to locate the area of bleeding, stop it and drain it.

I told Jeremiah that the chances for success were slim but that I had brought all the necessary instruments. I would operate if he would give permission. "Do anything you can," he replied anxiously. I nodded and stopped for a moment and prayed to the Lord for guidance. Jeremiah appreciated that.

By this time it was well past sunset. I asked the servants to boil some water and I put my surgical instruments, dusty from the long journey, in the water. I have learned that if instruments are boiled they are cleaner and the wounds they make seem to heal better. I also washed my hands in soap and hot water and put on a clean outer garment.

Then I directed the servants to bring in a sturdy table and place Neri upon it. By this time he was so deeply comatose we did not need to administer an opiate.

I had the servant cut off his hair and beard and shave his scalp and face. There was a noticeable bulge, and I could feel the fracture in the skull.[1] I cleaned the wound with water and soap. Then I incised the skin and fresh blood seeped out. I tried to stop the bleeding with the cloth but it continued until I applied greater pressure. Finally it stopped.

Next, I took my trephine instrument and started to drill a hole into the skull. I could feel that the area in which I was drilling was fractured, but I continued to drill until I had penetrated the skull bone completely. At that time, Luke, the blood that oozed out was dark, almost black. By the grace of God I had selected the right place to drill a hole.

A good amount of blood drained out. I kept pressing until there was no more dark blood. By this time, the incision that I had made showed some clotting and the area of the incision was quite dry. I debated whether I should leave a piece of cloth or cord there to help the wound drain but decided not to do so. Patients sometimes develop yellow pus when we leave a drain in the wound. This time I chose just to close the wound, which was dry and did not bleed. I was very pleased.

Luke, by this time it was close to midnight. I had attendants carry the patient back to his bed while I washed my hands. The servants cleaned up behind me. I told them to wash the instruments in freshly boiled water and set them out to dry. It was only then that I began to feel my exhaustion. But I could not stop then.

I sat down beside Neri and could see that he was breathing better, about three times as rapidly as he had been previously, and he seemed to be taking deep breaths. His heart rate was a little faster. He still was not moving. He was obviously very dry. He had not taken any food or fluids in three days.

Jeremiah had remained in the room the entire time. I could hear him murmuring some of the Psalms. I explained what I had done, and we both said a prayer of thanksgiving. It was the third watch of the night.

Jeremiah had some food brought in to me and I ate well. It was the first time I had eaten since the meal Elisa had prepared for the journey.

I sat with the patient the rest of the night, and by dawn I could tell that he was breathing much better and was stable. He certainly was not getting worse.

Jeremiah, by this time, was relieved enough to admit he was tired and was going to bed. He had a special room prepared for me. I told him that I could not leave my patient. He had a mat brought in for me so that I could sleep in the room with Neri. I instructed the servants how to care for him and to awaken me every three hours. And sleep I did.

At the third hour Neri seemed to be stable, and there was no bleeding or bulging of the wound, so I went back to sleep. In three hours, when they awakened me, I could see that his breathing was practically normal and he seemed to be very comfortable. I went back to sleep again, and at the ninth hour he was continuing to improve. I had not talked to Jeremiah all this day. I thought that he was probably still sleeping.

By the twelfth hour the patient appeared much improved. In fact, I could almost see some swallowing movement. I asked the attendants to try to give him some fluid. He was unable to swallow, but we took some cloth and dipped it in water, and he was able to suck on this. This seemed to relieve him very much. I was pleased.

About this time, Jeremiah came in and I reported to him all of the progress that had been made during the day. He and I said a prayer of thanksgiving together. By this time it was the end of the evening watch again and time for the midnight watch to start.

I slept on a mat on the floor by the patient and asked the servants to awaken me midway through the night. At this time, I was very pleased. Neri had taken some fluids and was not as dehydrated. It is amazing how much water you can get sucking on a moist cloth.

At sunrise the next day, the servants again awakened me. I was glad to see a little motion in Neri's arms and legs. He seemed to be opening his eyes and looking around. I was happy that there was no bulging in the area of his wound.

By the time that Jeremiah came, I was able to report his brother's progress. We put a little liquid into the patient's mouth and he was able to swallow it. This was very encouraging. I ordered water and wine to be given to him as he could tolerate it.

Jeremiah asked me to join him at breakfast. We again gave thanks to God for the patient's progress so far. The servants brought a sumptuous meal — pastries, goat's milk, figs, pomegranates, honey, grapes, cheese, fish and eggs. It was the largest breakfast I had ever eaten.

On my return, I could see that the patient could swallow and that the dryness of his skin and on his tongue was disappearing. But I was concerned that he had had no action from his bowel or his bladder since I had come. I had hoped that we could get these flowing again. I knew that it would take time and I waited.

This stage dragged on very slowly, but as it progressed I noticed that the patient started groaning a little from pain. I did not feel the pain was sufficient for an opiate yet. I just continued with the fluid, prescribed some milk for him and a little clear soup. Neri took this very well.

When we called his name, he seemed to respond. As the sun set on this day, he recognized Jeremiah and began to speak a few words. He did not remember his accident. You know, Luke, this also happens with an injury of the head. The injured person does not have any memory of what had happened at that time. By night I was very relieved that he felt better. I was eager to get a good night's sleep.

Jeremiah asked me to sleep in one of his many guestrooms, which was adjacent to Neri's room. Then he showed me where I could bathe. Luke, that clean warm water really felt good. The servants brought me nightclothes — silk garments. I had never worn silk before. It felt cool and soft, and I remembered Elisa's wish to live a simple life, that she wouldn't wear silk garments even if we could afford them.

Luke, by the grace of God, and our training in Athens, this patient will survive.

Joseph

---

[1] A blow on the side of the skull may cause small blood vessels to rupture and slowly bleed into an area between the linings of the brain. The patient loses consciousness after one or two days. The accumulation of blood causes pressure on the brain and eventually is fatal. Recovery is possible if a hole is drilled into the skull, the blood drained and the bleeding stopped.

Letter 29

I had a good night's sleep, Luke, even in unfamiliar surroundings and silk garments. The sun was up when I arose and rushed next door to the patient's room. Neri seemed considerably improved even from the night before. He was talking, knew who he was and where he was and was able to take solid food. His bowel and his bladder had started to flow. I leaned over and listened to his chest and heard his heart beating regularly. There was no bulging of the wound on his scalp and no discharge of yellow pus, which meant there was no infection in the wound.

I told Jeremiah I should watch my patient about two more days, and he seemed pleased that I would stay that long. It was now the day before the Sabbath. I explained that I could leave the day after the Sabbath if all continued to go well. My host, being a Pharisee, was pleased that I did not plan to travel on the Sabbath, since the Law prohibits it.[1]

As we were leaving, Neri tried to sit up and I ordered him to stay quiet in bed. I was afraid it would strain him too much and start the bleeding again. He wasn't very happy with my instructions, but I did allow him to raise his head a little on a pillow. I was very firm in telling the attendants that he must stay still. Perhaps I was too firm with him, but we were trained to keep such patients quiet for several weeks.

Jeremiah and I said our morning prayers and then ate breakfast. As we finished he invited me to see his estate. There were grapevines and fruit trees of all types in his kitchen garden, which furnished all of the fresh food that was needed for his home and his guests. Jeremiah took me to his vineyards out in the country and also to his grain fields. We also saw some of the cattle that he has been raising

On my return, about the sixth hour, I had another visit with my patient. After the noon meal Jeremiah took me on a stroll through Nazareth. He told me about the owners of every home that we passed, especially the grand homes of his fellow Pharisees. We walked through the market place, as bustling as that of Capernaum though somewhat larger.

Then we arrived at the synagogue and entered. It was much like ours in Capernaum, but after we said some prayers of thanksgiving, Jeremiah showed me around and explained everything as if I had never been in one. I guess he thought that physicians did not attend the synagogue.

As one enters the main chamber one always faces Jerusalem. There is a platform beyond the middle and a pulpit, called the Chair of Moses, from which members of the congregation read when called upon. Then he showed the most important part, where the scrolls of the Law are stored. He gestured to the front row of seats, facing the congregation, where he and the rulers of the synagogue and other distinguished Pharisees sit.

The main objective of Sabbath worship is to teach the congregation. The rabbis read a section of the Law, then something from the Prophets, then discuss what they read.

Jeremiah introduced me to the people in the synagogue, most of them rabbis. We finished our tour of the synagogue and started back about the ninth hour.

I was pleased to see that Neri was doing well. He even joked with me. Then I strolled onto the portico of the house to enjoy the afternoon breeze. Jeremiah asked me to sit and have a glass of wine with him. At that time I asked the question I'd had on my mind since arriving in Nazareth. "Did you ever know a carpenter by the name of Jesus?"

Jeremiah, about to take a sip, stopped and put his wineglass down on the table. "Yes," he replied, clearly startled. "Why do you want to know?"

"He has been in Capernaum lately. Tell me about him," I replied.

"Tell you about him?" he cried. He seemed very angry. "That fellow, that blasphemer, has been the talk of this town for months. This carpenter's son claims to be the Messiah! Only my concern for my brother put him out of mind for the last few days."

Jeremiah took another sip of wine and his voice fell to its normal level.

"I knew his father, Joseph the carpenter, very well. He was a very good man. He taught his son the art of carpentry, and the two of them made some of the fine furniture in this home. They made the table and the chairs in this room. Joseph died several years ago and Jesus continued to work in the shop and support his mother, Mary, but he never married." As he took another sip of wine, I recalled the social pressure to marry I had felt since boyhood.

"Last year," Jeremiah continued, "Jesus left his mother in the care of his brethren and disappeared. We heard nothing more about him until several months ago, when we learned that Jesus was preaching in the synagogues of upper Galilee. Then he returned to Nazareth to visit his mother and relatives. And on the Sabbath he came to our synagogue."

Jeremiah took a deep breath and looked directly into my eyes. "Someone handed him the scroll of the prophet Isaiah. I watched him unroll it. He looked carefully, found his place and read from the scroll:

The spirit of the Lord has been given to me
for the Lord has anointed me.
He has sent me to bring the good news to the poor,
to bind up hearts that are broken,
to proclaim a year of favor from the Lord,
a day of vengeance for our God,
to comfort all those who mourn.[2]

"He then rolled up the scroll and gave it back to the assistant and sat down. The eyes of everyone in the synagogue were fixed on him. Here was a man of little education, a carpenter by trade, standing up and reading in the synagogue!

"Joseph, what Jesus said next angered me.

"'This text is being fulfilled today even as you listen.'

"All the Pharisees began to object. Here was a man claiming to be anointed by God! Someone challenged him, saying, 'This is Joseph's son surely.'

"But Jesus was resolute. 'No doubt you will quote me the saying, "Physician, heal thyself," and tell me, "We have heard all that happened in Capernaum. Do the same here in your own countryside."

"'I tell you solemnly, no prophet is ever accepted in his own country.'

"And then, Joseph, he went on to suggest that Gentiles may be worthy of salvation!

"He said, 'There were many widows in Israel, I can assure you, in Elijah's day. But heaven remained shut for three years and six months, and a great famine raged throughout the land, but Elijah was not sent to any one of these. He was sent to a widow of Zarephath in Sidon.'"[3]

Luke, the Scriptures tell the story how Elijah, a prophet of God, was sent to a town in Sidon to a widow who used her last food to feed him. After that, her jar of meal and jug of oil were never empty. Her son died and Elijah stretched himself on the child and called, "Oh Lord my God, let the life breath return to the body of this child," and it did. Elijah returned him to his mother.

Jeremiah continued. "'And in the Prophet Elisha's town,' Jesus said, 'there were many lepers, but none of these was cured, except the Syrian, Naaman.'"[4]

"Then there was an uproar," Jeremiah said. "Everyone in the synagogue sprang to their feet and started pushing and shouting.

"This man claimed to speak on the authority of the Lord himself! Here in the town where he lived, this carpenter's son claimed to be the chosen of God, the Messiah!

"Several among us grabbed him and hustled him out of the synagogue and out of the town. We took him to the brim of the hill on which Nazareth is built, intending to carry out the Law and throw him over the cliff. As we approached the brim, suddenly Jesus slipped through the crowd and escaped. We could not find him. And he was gone, yes, just gone." Jeremiah paused abruptly and looked at me.

Luke, I was completely shocked at what I had heard, and Jeremiah seemed to sense it.

"Jeremiah," I said, "I have met Jesus. Elisa and I have watched him and heard him speak when he came to Capernaum and ..."

A servant came and interrupted. "Master," he said, "we need you now." And Jeremiah excused himself and left. Luke, I sat there totally appalled at what my host had told me. Then I carefully organized what I wanted to tell him when he returned.

Soon there was a commotion in front of the house. I walked along the portico and saw several chariots driving up and richly robed people coming into the house.

As I retreated, planning to see Neri and then go to my room, Jeremiah appeared and said, "Sorry that I was called away, we must finish our conversation later. Now I want you to come and meet some of my friends." He took me by the arm and led me to the entrance of his house. "I am so overjoyed that my brother is recovering that I am giving a banquet in your honor."

I saw that many people had gathered. They were merchants of the city, Pharisees and scribes from the synagogue, and others. Luke, I was uncomfortable with this honor, because I knew that it was by the grace of God that Neri got better.

But I reclined at Jeremiah's right and the banquet was delicious. There were several courses with fresh plates each time. Jeremiah must have had thirty servants attending us. We had snail, cooked lamb, quail and fish. There were all types of vegetables and then came the dessert. Luke, imagine plates and plates of fine pastries, figs, honey, pomegranates, oranges, cheeses, nuts and wine-soaked dates. And the finest wine was served throughout.

I reluctantly accepted the praises that he piled upon me, as there was nothing that I could do to alter the situation without insult. When I did get up to talk, I said that we should thank God that the patient got well. But his friends insisted that I come to Nazareth to practice, and each vied with the other in making lavish offers to me to come. It became annoying.

Finally I excused myself to check my patient. Neri was doing well. I uncovered the wound and there was no bulge and no drainage. I covered it with a fresh dressing. Then I listened to his chest and to his heart. There were no bubbles in his chest and the heart was beating slowly and regularly. I returned to the banquet as the guests were leaving, and I bid them farewell with Jeremiah.

After all of the guests left, I thanked Jeremiah for the honor and started to ask again about Jesus. "Joseph, it is late," he said. "Let us continue our discussion in the morning before we go to the synagogue." I could not do anything but agree.

I checked the patient again, gave the night instructions to the servants and retired.

Joseph

[1]   Exodus 20:8

      Exodus 35:1-2

      Deuteronomy 5:12

[2]   Isaiah 61:1-2

[3]   1 Kings 17:7-24

[4]   2 Kings 5

Letter 30

I did not sleep much that night, Luke. I was planning what I would say to Jeremiah about Jesus. I determined to tell him of all the good that Jesus has done, the cures I have seen him perform and about some of his teachings, which echo the prophets of old.

I went first to check on my patient. Jeremiah came in and we had the morning prayers with Neri. At breakfast I again thanked my host for the banquet in my honor and then he said, "We have some time before we go to the synagogue. Tell me about your experience with Jesus."

Jeremiah listened intently, and when I was finished he said, "Perhaps he is a magician or a trickster of some sort."

"Tricksters and magicians perform for profit," I replied. "He accepts no money for anyone or anything that he does. Erasmus, my father-in-law, has been a physician for forty years and has treated many of the people Jesus has healed. Elisa and I have seen some of them, Jeremiah, and I tell you they were not fakers. These people had physical deformities and incurable illnesses and are now well."

"But his claim to be the Chosen One of God!" exclaimed Jeremiah. "He said that the Lord sent him — you know the verse in Isaiah."

"Yes," I replied. "But Jeremiah, Hosea, Jonah, Isaiah and all of the prophets were sent by the Lord."

"That I admit, but this man is a carpenter, he has done work for me. He cannot be a prophet. He is or was just a good carpenter."

"The Lord has picked men from unusual areas and occupations to be His prophets …"

Jeremiah interrupted. "But he used a verse from Scriptures that describes the Messiah of God, whom we are expecting, and he claimed to be the One. Jesus claimed to be the Messiah of the Lord. That is blasphemy!

"Joseph, I know my Scriptures. You stick to your medicine."

I could see that I was irritating my host and I did not want to go any further.

"Joseph," he continued more calmly, "I respect you very much. I have seen your work and know that it is excellent, but I cannot understand your feeling about the carpenter of Nazareth. He is nothing but a fraud." And he excused himself to prepare for the synagogue.

I understand why Jeremiah refuses to believe that Jesus is the Messiah we have been promised, but if we have no faith that God's promises will be fulfilled, then how are we to ever trust enough to accept the truth when it is before us?

At the service I met many of the people who had been at the banquet the night before. They were just as lavishly dressed. Jeremiah went to sit in the front row with the others, while I took a seat toward the back. The service was inspiring, but I could see that many of the Pharisees were more interested in showing off their clothes than listening.

After the service we had our midday meal, which was prepared yesterday. This household really does nothing on the Sabbath. Neither Jeremiah nor I mentioned Jesus again.

I checked Neri and he was progressing well. There was no sign of yellow discharge from the wound. If it has not appeared by this time, it will not come. There was good healing of the wound, but a depression in the skull where I had made the trephine hole. I instructed the servant to keep it covered with a clean cloth and keep him in bed four more weeks. Then he could sit up in a chair for two weeks and then gradually walk. Neri did not like my instructions at all, but that is what we were taught in Athens. I left some of Erasmus' ointment to use if yellow pus ever comes. It was near nightfall and the start of a new day would come soon.

I retired early to start the return journey by dawn. It would be another long horseback ride and my muscles ached in anticipation.

But by the next nightfall I would see my dear Elisa. What a pleasant thought on which to sleep.

Joseph

Capernaum

Letter 31

Dear Luke, this morning I rose early, dressed and went to see Neri. He had already eaten and was sitting up, but I could see that it didn't hurt him so I did not say anything. He was quite cheerful and there was no bulge in his temporal area. I dressed it again. I told Neri he could wear a head covering until his hair grew out. I gave everybody final instructions and left the room. Jeremiah and I said morning prayers and then had a full breakfast. He seemed very thoughtful and considerate as I packed all of my equipment in one bag. I had used up all of the bandages and most of the medications I had brought.

Jeremiah handed me a small pocket sack, and I could see that there were many gold pieces in it. I said, "Jeremiah, I cannot accept this. This is altogether too much for my time."

"Joseph, you spent several days here. You saved my brother's life. I owe this to you. Don't insult me by not taking it." I knew that I had to accept his generosity. I thanked him very much. However, I did not want to carry the gold coins in my knapsack, so I hid the sack in an empty medicine bottle among my surgical instruments.

Then Jeremiah led me down to his corral. "Joseph, I have some of the finest Arabian horses in Nazareth, in fact, in all of Judea and all of Galilee. Any one of these horses can be yours. I have picked out one of the best for you." And he had his attendants bring the sleek, highly spirited horse that I had ridden from Capernaum. "Certainly, Joseph, a man in your position should ride a horse like this." He handed me the reins. "I want you to take him."

I thought for a moment, then handed the reins back to Jeremiah. "I know it is hard for you to understand, Jeremiah. I appreciate the gift of a horse very much because I need one. My donkey is slow and sometimes stubborn. But if you don't mind, I would like to select a less majestic horse from your corral and take that. Many of our patients are very poor and do not have any luxuries, so Elisa and I try to get by with as little as we can."

"Joseph, I do not understand, but I respect your opinion. Take any horse that you want." And he pointed to the corral. I went through his herd of horses, checking each one. I picked a good horse, one that was young and very strong, one that could carry my instruments and me. I noted that he had a good set of teeth and no sign of injury.

"Jeremiah, I will accept this horse."

"Have it as you will. Now will you accept a saddle?"

"Yes, but not your best."

He selected an older saddle and had a groomsman prepare the horse for the journey. I led the horse to the front of the house, thanked him most graciously, loaded my sack of instruments and medicine behind the saddle and mounted.

In a low tone, Jeremiah said his final words. "Joseph, I didn't sleep much last night, thinking about what you told me about Jesus. If you hear more about him, please let me know."

"Jeremiah, I will. Please keep me informed about the progress of your brother. If anything serious happens, please send for me right away." We bid each other "Shalom" and I left.

All of the way back, I thought about the anger and hatred Jesus had stirred in his hometown.

The distance passed rapidly but not quickly enough for me. I was so eager to see my Elisa and tell her all about my experiences. Finally I came in sight of Capernaum.

As I tied the horse to the post in front of the clinic, a crowd gathered around admiring him. I walked inside and there was Elisa in the hall. We embraced intensely, so very pleased to see each other, and I said I had much to tell her. She stepped outside with me as I unpacked the medical gear and took the horse to a stall in back of the clinic. There was adequate room for him with the donkey, which had been out in the pasture in the orchard while I had been gone.

Elisa knows horseflesh and admired him. "Where did you steal the horse?" she said.

"It is a long story. Let me tell you when we finish with our patients."

Later, as Elisa and I walked home hand in hand, I began to relate the entire story of the trip to Nazareth.

Elisa was interested in the operation, the way the patient progressed and his recovery, but most of all she wanted to know about Jesus' appearance in the synagogue and the shameful way that the people had treated him. She recited the passage in Isaiah that he had read. "Certainly, he could be a prophet, but this passage seems to describe the Messiah. Are you sure that he used it?"

"Yes, which is why it raised the ire of Jeremiah and of everyone in the synagogue."

"Joseph," Elisa said, "we need to discuss this further. But first let me ride the horse. Then I will feed you."

Luke, Elisa mounted the house and rode off with her hair flying. The horse sensed that she was an excellent horsewoman and responded to her. When she returned, she said, "I will have to do this more often."

Later, after one of her nourishing meals, we walked to the home of her parents. There would be no meeting tonight at our clinic. Erasmus had just come back from fishing and Sarah was busy giving the fish away so that she would not have to clean them. We told them briefly all that had happened. Erasmus was especially interested in the surgery. We didn't dwell too much on the episode involving Jesus since it would take some time to explain everything.

After that we went to see my parents, Mary and Joseph. My father was particularly interested in the horse. He said he had hated to see me riding around on that old donkey.

And so, dear Luke, I end this accounting of a remarkable week. I shall leave these letters for the next caravan to Antioch.

May the Lord God watch over you.

Joseph

Letter 32

Dear Luke, Elisa and I awakened at dawn, said our morning prayers and broke our evening's fast. Then we walked to the clinic, I put my bag and blanket on my horse and off I went to call on our patients. It was quite early but there were a number of people on the street. They were all surprised to see me riding a horse.

I finished my rounds in about half the time and was able to get back to the clinic earlier than usual. It was good to see my patients again, although Erasmus and Elisa had done a wonderful job with them. You know, Luke, many of the patients prefer to see Elisa rather than me. She seems to be gentler with them. And she is so attentive, as if there is nothing else on her mind but care of the patient. They appreciate this and flock to her.

Upon seeing Erasmus I told him the full story of what had occurred at the synagogue with Jesus. He listened intently, asking many questions. Erasmus is very well-versed in his faith but open to new ideas and interpretations. He seemed intrigued but said he was late for his fishing and we would talk all about it later.

This evening, Elisa and I walked along the lake and talked about Jesus, who has been teaching in the towns and villages around Capernaum.

Luke, when I returned from Nazareth I found your letter responding to my first reports about Jesus and his cures. I could almost hear your voice in the words you wrote. "What is the matter with you, Joseph? Is the water in Capernaum bad? Have you had too much of your mother's wine? I'll have to come to Capernaum to straighten you out." Do come to Capernaum, Luke. Then we can learn together the truth about this man Jesus.

Elisa and I then talked about the sack of gold pieces I had so carefully packed in the empty medicine bottle. We decided to replace all of the bandages that I had used in Nazareth, and obtain a few more surgical instruments and suture material. The rest we will use for drugs, herbs and potions that we give to the poor. We know that they need medicine and cannot buy it. Now we will have plenty.

Then Elisa said, "Joseph, my father and I have been talking about the clinic and we both feel that we need more help. It is too much for the three of us. We need someone to welcome the patients and help us with them like my sister does for my brother in Cana. We need someone to keep the place clean."

"Can we afford it?"

"Yes, with the increased numbers of patients that we are getting."

Luke, I knew that she had figured out all of the finances. But there was more. "Judith was a great help to my father when we were in Jerusalem in training. She loves to work with the sick. I think we should ask her to work with us again."

"Of course," I agreed, seeing the need once she had pointed it out.

Luke, it is great to sleep in my own home again with Elisa, even though we have coarse nightwear and a firm bed. The fancy sleepwear and soft bed that I used as a guest of Jeremiah did not suit me as well as what we have at home.

May the Lord High God watch over you and all of us.

Joseph

Letter 33

Luke, Jesus is now teaching in the synagogues in Galilee. News came to my father's station that he is drawing a crowd of followers.

Today, the day after the Sabbath, our friends gathered to hear about my journey to Nazareth. Now, as our meetings begin, we sing the Psalms rather than read them. Eliab and Naomi have such good voices that others sing quietly so we can hear them. Then I told our friends all that I had learned about Jesus.

Luke, when I finished telling the story of Jesus being hauled out of town to be thrown over a cliff, all were dismayed. "I cannot believe they did that to such a good man," the widow Miriam said.

I tried to explain. "They considered him a blasphemer, claiming to be the anointed one, the Messiah. Jesus finished reading the passage from Isaiah and told them, 'Today in your sight, this is being fulfilled.' But they knew he was only one of them, a carpenter of Nazareth."

"And when they objected," said Samson, who is often our leader in these discussions, "Jesus delivered what they must have considered an insult, saying that a prophet is not accepted in his own country."

David had been quiet until then. "Jesus also told them that God had sent prophets to people of many lands — Elijah to a Sidonian and Elisha to a Syrian," he said. "In this he implies that God loves all of mankind and not just us, his Chosen People. That must be the statement that most angered them.

"Let us listen again to those words of Isaiah," David directed.

Quiet Ana, whose memory of the Scriptures we all envy, quoted the exact passage.

> *The spirit of the Lord has been given to me*
> *for the Lord has anointed me.*
> *He has sent me to bring the good news*
> *to the poor,*
> *to bind up hearts that are broken,*
> *to proclaim a year of favor from the Lord,*
> *a day of vengeance for our God,*
> *to comfort all those who mourn.*

John the husband of Esther said, "This man may indeed be a prophet, but to be the Messiah, that is different. What do we know about the Messiah?"

His wife, another student of the Scriptures, answered quickly. "Jeremiah says he shall be of the House of David. 'I will raise a virtuous branch for David, who will reign as true king and be wise, practicing honesty and integrity in the land. In his days Judah will be saved and Israel dwell in confidence.'"[1]

"Isaiah speaks of the day of salvation," said Rachel. "'The wolf lives with the lamb, the panther lies down with the kid, calf and lion cub feed together with a little boy to lead them. The cow and the bear make friends, their young lie down together. The lion eats straw like the ox. The infant plays over the cobra's hole. Into the viper's lair the young child puts his hand.'"[2]

"Wouldn't it be a marvelous place," Thalia, the eldest among us, drawled in her deep voice, "if all that would happen?"

Then Eliab spoke up. "It is also written in Isaiah that the Lord comes with vengeance and with retribution[3] — that is, with justice and power."

Elisa objected. "Jesus does not use physical power. He uses only words, but we have all heard him confuse the scribes and the Pharisees with his knowledge and wisdom. And he does seem to be guarding people like a shepherd. He has several followers already."

Tonight, Luke, everyone had an opinion and a favorite quote of the Scriptures to share. Hannah spoke next.

"Isaiah goes on to say that the eyes of the blind will be opened, the ears of the deaf unsealed, the lame will leap like a deer and the tongues of the dumb sing for joy.[4] Jesus has done this!" she continued. "He has opened eyes of the blind, unsealed ears of the deaf. The words of the prophet are coming to pass!"

Naomi broke in eagerly. "Malachi says that a messenger will be sent to prepare the way.[5] Do not we have John the Baptizer announcing that the son of God has appeared?"

Well, Luke, the discussion went on like this for some time, with each of us offering what we knew or believed about the Messiah.

"He will be from Bethlehem of Judea," said Ana, who quoted a passage from Micah. "'But you, Bethlehem-Ephrathah, the least of the clans of Judah, out of you will be born for me the one who is to rule over Israel. His origin goes back to the distant past, to the days of old.'[6]

"On the other hand," she said, "the Holy Writings of Hosea say he will be called out of Egypt."[7]

"Isaiah says that a virgin shall be with child and shall bear a son and shall name him Immanuel,"[8] said Abriam. "According to Isaiah, then, this child must be born of a virgin."

"That is impossible," I blurted out. But Elisa put her hand on mine and said, "Joseph, anything is possible with the Lord."

Then I spoke of the study my mother and sister had made of the ancestry of Jesus, confirming he was of the House of David. And several asked to see our copy of his lineage.

I continued. "My mother also told me a story she recalled about what happened in Bethlehem about the time Jesus was born. Her father heard the story from a traveler. As I recall, some astrologers came to see Herod the Great, and soon after that he ordered the massacre of all the boys two years old and under in Bethlehem and nearby. About thirty little boys were killed, and no one knew why. There was a rumor that he was trying to kill the future king of Israel. But nothing more was said about it.

"Mother said Herod was very cruel. In fact, the Romans would say it was safer to be his enemy than to be his son."

Others said they had heard about this tragedy as well.

Elisa had been silent much of the time, carefully weighing every word. Finally she spoke up, bringing the discussion to a conclusion.

"In truth we know very little about the background of Jesus. If he is the Messiah," she said, "he will reveal himself when he is ready to do it."

After all had left and Elisa and I were alone again, she spoke quietly but with determination. "Joseph, I believe that this man Jesus has been sent somehow very specially from God. Do you?"

"I do not know what to believe."

"Well, Joseph, let us see what happens. Suppose we observe everything that he says and does. I will try to confirm that he is the Messiah promised by God — and you should try to prove he is not."

"You mean that you want me to play the part of the devil?"

"Not exactly, but you can try to find a natural explanation for the cures."

"That suits me. But let us not disclose our findings until we are certain of the truth."

It was very late when we reached home.

Joseph

1 Jeremiah 23:5-6

2 Isaiah 11:6-8

3 Isaiah 35:4

4 Isaiah 35:5-6

5 Malachi 3:1

6 Micah 5:1-2

7 Hosea 11:1

8 Isaiah 7:14

Letter 34

Luke, Jesus has returned to Capernaum, and I have borne witness to a cure for which I have no explanation. It happened this morning at the synagogue.

Our service is rather structured. We begin with a reading from the first five books of the Scriptures, also called the Pentateuch. This is followed by readings from some of the prophets. Then someone, usually a noted scholar or a Pharisee, gets up to discuss the readings.

Today, as often happens, the service was delayed in starting until all of the Pharisees came and filled up the front seats. Shortly after we finally took our places, Jesus walked into the assembly. He greeted the men gathered, then turned to me and smiled. "Joseph, how is Elisa?"

"She is well and with the women."

"Good," Jesus continued. "Tell her that I would like to come to your home again soon for her special fish dinner." I was pleased and knew Elisa would be also.

All of a sudden we heard a commotion in the rear. A man in rags had followed Jesus to the synagogue and now was charging into the assembly. Erasmus and I recognized him as Isaac, a man who has seizures. We have treated him many times for injuries caused when he fell during his seizures.

Isaac was agitated and ran toward Jesus, shouting in a voice that was low-pitched but deafening. "Ha! What do you want with us, Jesus of Nazareth? Have you come to destroy us?" He pointed an accusing finger at Jesus.

"I know who you are — The Holy One of God!"

All eyes were on Isaac and on Jesus, whose face grew grim.

Then Jesus spoke sharply. "Be quiet! Come out of him!"

Suddenly a spell seized Isaac. He uttered a cry, fell to the floor, started to shake all over and foam at the mouth. Erasmus and I rushed to him and I attempted to get a cloth between his teeth to prevent him from biting his tongue. Then, abruptly, his muscles stopped twitching and Isaac rose to his feet. He smiled, bowed and thanked Jesus and took a seat beside him.

You know, Luke, these patients usually go into a very deep sleep after one of their spells. But this man was alert and active.

Erasmus was astounded. The entire congregation of the synagogue was

---

in an uproar. We could hear the cries of disbelief. "Did you see that man? He gives orders to unclean spirits and they come out!"

Jesus remained calm while the leader of the synagogue called for order and the Sabbath service began. Some time later, as the service ended, I looked toward Jesus, and he was gone. Isaac had also slipped out and disappeared into the crowd.

My parents were joining us that day for Sabbath meal at the home of Erasmus and Sarah, so I rushed to relate what had happened this morning to Elisa and our mothers.

Luke, my father is a man of few words but he, too, was moved to speak.

"The voice that we heard almost accusing Jesus, saying, 'You are the Holy One of God' — it did not sound at all like the voice of Isaac."

Erasmus responded. "Ach! Ach! What do you mean, that the voice we heard was of a demon? That Isaac was possessed, and the devil left him at the sight of Jesus?"

We continued to debate what we had seen and heard. Finally Erasmus concluded the discussion with his remarks. "Well, if Jesus is what he says he is, we will soon know. If not, his cult will pass like that of the many others who have preceded him."

As Elisa and I walked home, I began to doubt what I had witnessed. "Is Isaac really cured? I will not believe it until weeks pass without any more attacks."

"Joseph," said Elisa, "could you look beyond what you have seen?

"Do you not recall how Jesus said in Nazareth that a prophet is not accepted by his own people? It seems that today in the synagogue the demons, the unclean spirits, recognized Jesus as being from God."

And Luke, she may be right. But it is difficult to believe what my own eyes have seen.

Joseph

Letter 35

It is evening of the same Sabbath as my last letter. Elisa and I went for a walk along the lakeshore. We had gone but a short distance when we saw a crowd following Jesus and we joined them. Suddenly he turned up the lane to the house of Simon the fisherman. Luke, I have made calls to this house each day for the past week. Simon's mother-in-law was ill with what Erasmus calls the "right-sided fever." We have seen many of these cases here, more than we wish to see because they are almost always fatal.

You know that those affected with this condition develop a little nausea and vomiting, then a slight fever and tenderness in the middle of the abdomen. The next day the tenderness is very definite in the right lower abdomen. Then vomiting becomes worse and the right side becomes hard and very tender. When one presses on this area and lets go rapidly, the patient screams with pain. Soon the entire abdomen is hard and swollen. The abdomen gives off a hollow sound when we tap on it. The patients have a high fever, their bowels become locked, they sweat profusely and their skin and tongue become very dry. All of this continues until they die a miserable death.[1]

Abraham in Jerusalem told us of a rare case when the swelling lessened, the fever gradually came down and the bowel humors were excreted as normal. The patient began to take nourishment and improved in a period of weeks.

Luke, we have never cured any of these patients. We use abdominal poultices but still we cannot make the bowels move. There is no way that we can get them to retain fluids because they vomit whatever they take. The bowels seem to be paralyzed.

Simon, a widower with grown children, called me to the house about two weeks ago to see his mother-in-law. He is usually quite gruff, but that day he was anxious. I recognized the disease and told him of the outlook. I brought Elisa and Erasmus into consultation and they agreed with me. We have been treating her for a week. She is now in the final stages with a distended abdomen, dry skin and very high fever. She exudes the odor of death. I had seen her this morning and felt that she would not live much longer. Now, Jesus was going there.

I spoke to Elisa. "She may have died since I saw her this morning. Perhaps he is going to pay his respects."

Jesus knocked on the door. He nodded to us as Simon, looking exhausted and forlorn, opened the door and motioned us to follow. That horrible odor of sickness came out of the room. The patient was breathing very rapidly, her abdomen was distended to the size of a late pregnancy, and there was a look of terminal agony on her face. I told Jesus about her illness and he leaned over the bed where she lay.

After a moment he spoke, rebuking the fever. "Be gone!" he said, and there was an immediate reaction. Her skin became moist, the look of agony on her face disappeared, and the abdomen returned to its normal size. She opened her eyes and smiled. Then, to our amazement, she arose and welcomed us to Simon's house. She went into the other room and returned with a tray of date cakes and cups of the juice of pomegranates and served them to us. But Jesus had slipped away.

The word got out to the crowd that Jesus had cured Simon's mother-in-law of the "right-sided fever." There was much rejoicing and praising God.

Believe me, Luke, this did happen! I have Elisa and Simon as my witnesses. A woman who was in the terminal stages of the right-sided fever was cured instantly.

I insisted on examining the patient thoroughly. But Elisa and I found nothing wrong. She was again the same woman we had known for years, jovial, alert and very active.

"Unbelievable," said Simon. "This is a miracle. I have heard that a strange man is in town doing some unusual cures, but I have never spoken to him. Why did he come to my household?"

I then told him of the cure of the demoniac in the synagogue, as fishermen rarely attend services and Simon was not there this morning. He and his brother Andrew are the most seasoned fishermen of Capernaum, but they have little formal education and have no patience with the righteousness of Pharisees.

Elisa was quiet and thoughtful as we walked home, but I said, "Anyone who has a fever for days and days requires weeks to regain strength. Simon's mother-in-law recovered right away."

"Yes, and your explanation?" she asked.

"I have none."

"I have one," she said. "I believe that we have seen Jesus show power over both the natural and the supernatural today. Only God can do that."

Luke, is it possible his power does come from God?

Joseph

---

[1] Appendicitis or inflammation of the appendix, with rupture and spread of the infection over the entire abdomen.

Letter 36

Dear Luke, last night, as Elisa slept peacefully, I arose during the third night watch and walked out into the orchard. In the moonlight I saw a figure at the edge of the woods. It was Jesus, again kneeling in prayer. Luke, in the synagogue it is our custom to stand and pray. As I stepped closer he turned and asked, "Joseph, what are you doing up at this early hour?"

"I could not sleep," I said, and then all my words came in a rush.

"I cannot understand how you perform these cures. There is no explanation among all the teachings of the medical profession. And frankly, I am a little upset that you do not share your knowledge. We are taught — we even take an oath as physicians — to teach others what we have learned."

Jesus walked up to me and put his hand on my shoulder. His gaze was piercing even in the moonlight.

"Joseph, you and Elisa and Erasmus have spent years in your training and are doing wonderful work. The cures I perform cannot be done by human means. These are all the work of the Lord God. And they are not why I am here. I have a teaching mission that I am pursuing."

I dismissed that remark and pressed my case. "Who are you? Elisa believes you may be the Messiah."

He sighed. "Joseph, all of this will be revealed when the time comes."

He turned to leave, but I felt the need to know him better. Luke, this is a man of flesh, and how he does what he does must have an explanation. "Won't you join us for the morning meal?" I asked.

"Thank you, yes," he said, and we walked through the pre-dawn haze to the house. Elisa was just arising and saying her morning prayers. We joined her and then shared a full meal. Jesus ate heartily and with good cheer.

Before he took his leave, Jesus told us he would be leaving Capernaum again today but he would return. He explained, "I must proclaim the good news of the kingdom of God to the other towns, too, because that is what I was sent to do. I must preach in the other synagogues of Galilee and Judea." This, he said, was the mission of which he had spoken earlier.

As Jesus walked across the road and into the wooded area, I described to Elisa what had happened before dawn. We carefully considered all his remarks in light of the cures we have witnessed. "What Jesus has done is not in the power of man alone," Elisa concluded. Then a thought came to her.

"Joseph," she said, "could he be both man and God?"

"Oh! There you go again," I said. "Just be careful with such remarks before any Pharisee. They will drive us away," and we both laughed.

"If Jesus is God," she said, "he seems to be one of joy and cheer. He is not the vengeful God of the Scriptures."

"The Scriptures!" I said. "They are so hard to read. They are full of murders, deceit and wars. I get annoyed when I hear many of the stories read in the synagogue."

"Jesus sees another teaching in them," Elisa said. "He talks about the love of God and of neighbor.

"While he travels to other towns preaching, let us see if we can get a new light on the message of God through our own studies."

And so, Luke, we are on a search of new meaning in the Scriptures.

Joseph

Letter 37

Luke, I understand your misgivings about the cures I have witnessed. But in the last few weeks I have examined both Simon's mother-in-law and Isaac, the man with the seizures. Both are in good health with no sign of their afflictions. I cannot explain it. Elisa says it is by the power of the Lord.

Today Elisa and I arose early and went for a walk along the lake. The mist still lingered over the water and we could hear the sound of oars and the voices of the fisherman as they were coming in from their night's work. They sounded tired and dejected, and we knew fresh fish would be scarce at the market today.

A short distance ahead we saw a group of people gathered. As we approached, Elisa whispered, "It is Jesus teaching. He is back in Capernaum. Let us hurry. Maybe we can hear him."

But as we approached, Jesus left the group and walked toward the two boats on the bank. They were empty and two fishermen were washing their nets. I recognized Simon and his brother Andrew.

They are strong men, browned by the sun and used to long hours hauling nets. Simon is of larger build, with a dark, unruly beard, and considered something of a leader. People come to him with their problems. Andrew is lighter in coloring than his brother, more thoughtful and milder in manner.

Jesus stepped into Simon's boat, sat down and resumed his teachings to the crowd who had followed. We watched and listened. This time there were no mysterious cures. His message was about the obligation to care for the poor, for children who are orphaned and for widows with no means of support.

When he had finished speaking, he climbed out of the boat and turned to Simon, who had continued to clean his nets during all of the time that Jesus had been teaching.

"Put out into the deep water," Jesus instructed, "and play out your nets." Simon objected. "Master, we worked hard all night long and caught nothing."

But Jesus held his gaze and Simon reconsidered. "If you say so, I will play out the nets."

By that time Andrew had approached and had heard the conversation. I could tell that both were reluctant to go out again. But they climbed into the

---

boat, pulled at the oars with long strokes and were in deep water shortly. Jesus stood on the shore and watched. So did everyone else, including the two of us.

Simon and Andrew threw out their nets, and immediately they were filled with so many large fish that the nets began to tear. They signaled to their companions in the other boat to help them. James and John, the sons of Zebedee, set out and in less than an hour the two boats were filled to the sinking point.

As his boat neared land, Simon was standing at the bow. As soon as he could, he jumped into the water and waded ashore. He came to Jesus, who was sitting by this time, fell to his knees and said, "Leave me, Lord, for I am a sinful man."

Andrew, James and John secured the two boats and approached Jesus themselves. We could see that they were completely overcome by the catch they had made.

Jesus looked at each of the four and smiled. "Do not be afraid. From now on it is men whom you will catch." And he arose and started to walk away.

To my astonishment, these men did as he asked. They left their fish, their nets, their boats, and followed Jesus out of Capernaum.

It was late and I knew we had patients waiting. But I shared my dismay with Elisa as we headed to the clinic.

"Elisa, Jesus made two boatloads of fishermen look foolish. This man who has been a carpenter in Nazareth, where there is no water, knew where there were fish."

"Joseph," she said, "Simon must have known there were no fish to be caught. He knew that daytime is not the time to catch fish. It took great trust in Jesus for him to set out from shore. What power Jesus had over him!"

"I cannot believe that four successful fishermen would abandon their way of life and follow a man who is preaching and teaching. He told Simon, Andrew, James and John that they would now become fishers of men. It is insane."

"Perhaps they see something beyond success in this life."

"Surely these men will return to their docks in the morning. What are they going to do, catch men on a hook? Is this how they will put food on the table?

"What are their families to think? How will they survive?"

"Jesus has shown there is another way," she replied. "Perhaps he will teach them to catch the attention of men by the words they speak, like he does."

But her words did not calm me this time, Luke. I was too upset. I can only pray that the Lord will give me a greater understanding.

Joseph

Letter 38

Luke, this morning I decided to go by the wharf before beginning my morning rounds. I tied my horse and went first to Simon's boat. Some men were cleaning their nets, others were selling the day's catch. I looked for Simon and Andrew but could not find them. Finally, I asked one of their hired fishermen. He said, "Simon and Andrew left with that man Jesus yesterday. We are trying to carry on the business."

I thanked him and went to the next boat. There were old Zebedee and two hired men. I raised my voice, as Zebedee has trouble hearing. "Where are your sons?"

"Hup!" he groaned. "They followed that Nazarene and are gone. I don't know where they are. They had better come back. I cannot stand this heavy work."

These four men have given up their occupations. It does not make any more sense today than it did yesterday. As I left I said, "Don't worry, Zebedee. They will be back." And off I rode.

There was much talk at the clinic that afternoon about what had happened. My mother came with word of where Jesus and his new followers had gone. A caravan had just arrived with the news. They were in a nearby village. As had happened here in Capernaum, crowds of people were following Jesus, listening to him speak and awaiting cures.

I shook my head again. "I must ask Simon why he did this. I cannot understand."

"Joseph," Elisa replied, "when the Lord wants you to understand he will arrange for it to happen."

And so I am learning patience, Luke, not because I want to learn it, but because there is no other choice.

Joseph

Letter 39

Luke, today I made my weekly visit to the leper colony about an hour's ride from Capernaum. But it was not to be the usual visit.

As you know, leprosy is a most dreaded disease, and lepers are ostracized in our society. They must leave home and live away from other people. They usually band together and live in a group outside a town or city. If they do walk among us, they must go bareheaded and wear special clothes. Whenever anyone approaches, they must call out in a loud voice, "Unclean! Unclean!" or "Leper! Leper!"

If anyone should be cured, he must follow the detailed set of instructions in the Book of Leviticus.[1] He must make three burnt offerings and be certified clean by a priest. Only then can he return to normal life.

The prophet Elisha told Naaman, the commander of the Syrian army who had leprosy, to wash seven times in the Jordan River, and he was healed.[2] This was attributed to God. But, Luke, I have not seen anyone healed by medication. I believe the ones who are considered healed had some other condition that looks like leprosy.

But even lepers need medical care. Years ago Erasmus decided that, as a dedicated physician, he must accept them as patients. Since they could not come to see him, he went to their camp once a week. Now I have the job. Needless to say, I do not cherish it, but I still do it. I make certain that it is the last call in the morning so that I may go home and change clothes and wash completely afterwards. The clothing that I wear during each visit is boiled later in hot water.

This colony of lepers is located in a grove of trees near a neighboring town. Luke, I see patients here with the early stages of the disease — with sores or white patches on the skin that are devoid of feeling. They do not feel any pain with an injury. Then there are those with nodules on the skin of the hands and face. They look grotesque. Finally, there are those in the late stages when the fingers and toes shorten from injury or infection. The odor from the pus and dead tissue is horrible.

Today I used all of the bandages and Erasmus' balm that I had with me.

As I was riding home through the town, I saw a seated group of people in the distance. I recognized Jesus among them, with the four fishermen of Capernaum, and dismounted, planning to speak to them. Then we heard the call "Leper! Leper! Leper!" A man from the colony was approaching.

Most people rose to their feet and scattered, but Jesus sat still, and so did Simon, Andrew, James and John.

The leper's disease was far advanced. He had massive nodules on the cheeks, making his face look like that of a lion. He had two stubby fingers on his right hand. The odor from the sores was almost intolerable.

Seeing Jesus, he went up to him, knelt, leaned forward so that his face touched the ground, and implored him. "Sir," he said. "If you care to do so you can cure me."

Jesus stretched out his hand, touched him and said with a smile, "Of course I care to! Be cured."

Luke, I know that you will not believe it, but I saw it in the midday sun. The leper's white spots cleared, his face lost its grotesque appearance, the skin became smooth, and the shortened fingers became normal.

The man looked at his hands, felt his face and let out a scream of joy. He knelt again before Jesus and thanked him, praising God.

Jesus put his hand on his head and softly said, "Do not tell anyone, but go and show yourself to the priest and make an offering for your healing as Moses prescribed it, as evidence for them." Then the man left to do as had been prescribed in the writings in Leviticus.

I stood there in amazement a few paces from Jesus. "Joseph," he said, "what brings you here?" I explained that I was returning from my weekly visit to the leper colony.

Jesus smiled and said, "The Lord bless the three of you for your charitable works. How is Elisa?"

"Just fine. She is treating patients while I ride around the countryside enjoying myself," I said, and we all laughed.

"Tell her we will be back in Capernaum in a few days and we will be over for her fish dinner." He got up and they left. I mounted and rode home in a gallop. It was late. I bathed and changed my clothes and went to the clinic where I told Elisa the entire story.

Joseph

1   Leviticus 14:1-32

2   2 Kings 5:8-14

Letter 40

Dear Luke, Jesus and the fishermen have returned to Capernaum. John, the younger of Zebedee's sons and slighter of build, came in this morning to say that the five of them would join us for the evening meal. Elisa left early to get some fish at the wharf and busied herself with lentils, beans, cucumbers, lettuce, melons and blackberries. She also had some fig cakes that her mother had sent over.

Jesus blessed the food before we ate and offered thanks to God for the meal. We talked and laughed and ate for a long time. Luke, this man Jesus is really a very joyful man. He tells stories that bring hearty laughter from everyone, but the stories never ridicule anyone or anything. It seems he respects everything that has been created by God.

Jesus took his leave early. "Thank you, Elisa, for the wonderful meal and we thank both of you for your hospitality. It is time for me to find a spot in your woods here and spend the night in prayer." But Elisa hastened to extend her hospitality even more.

"Jesus, whenever you are in Capernaum, feel free to use the large room in our clinic to teach if the weather is bad outside." He graciously accepted.

Simon, Andrew, James and John remained behind. It seemed they were all expecting my questions. I first asked where they had been.

"Joseph," Simon began, his voice booming as if he were still at sea, "since we left Capernaum, we have traveled from village to village and watched Jesus heal and listened to him teach. His reputation continues to grow. Large crowds gather to hear him and to have their sicknesses cured. When the day is done, he leaves us to be alone and pray. Now we, too, have developed a habit of prayer." The others nodded approval.

"What did you do all of that time? Why did you leave everything and follow Jesus? Why do the crowds follow him when he heals only a few?" Luke, my questions tumbled out and everyone laughed. Then came the responses, one man at a time, with Simon again taking the lead.

"Joseph, we listened to Jesus explain the Scriptures. He showed us how to look deeper, beyond the tales of wars and deceit, and see that the Scriptures are a story of God's love. He gives his people everything, but they rebel repeatedly and bring suffering onto themselves. Yet God always forgives them and even follows the Jewish people to Egypt and to Babylon to bring them back."

Then Andrew, who had spent more time studying the Scriptures than his brother, took over. "We learned so much about God and His love for us. Jesus went through all. of Genesis, Exodus, Leviticus, Numbers and Deuteronomy, Joshua, Judges, Samuel, Kings and Chronicles. He showed us the constant love of God for his creation, the repeated revolt of mankind and the unfathomable forgiveness of God.

"Periodically, God raised such prophets as Isaiah, Jeremiah, Baruch, Ezekiel, Joel, Amos and others, all trying to call our ancestors back from their sinfulness. But the prophets were all persecuted.

"The story of Jonah, he said, was written to show the persistence of God to bring the sinners back. Jonah's resentment when people were not punished is an example for each one of us. We learned that we often resent in this way.

"And the story of Job shows the need for steadfastness of faith even in terrible suffering."

"He spent much time teaching us about the Psalms — all one hundred and fifty of them," said James, a tall and vigorous young man. "About one-third are laments or complaints to God, but that only proves the close relationship of God to His people, and their closeness to Him." And Luke, I remembered how reciting the Psalms had comforted me in Athens when I first learned of Elisa's illness.

"The Lord created the entire world — the earth, stars and moon — for man and woman to enjoy it and bask in His love," James continued. "But they and their children disobeyed throughout the years and brought punishment upon themselves. Still, God always calls them back, forgives them and gives His love, only to be rejected again and again."

Luke, these fishermen seem to have acquired insight into the sacred writings that would take men of learning years to acquire.

"The message in the Scriptures," said young John, "is that He and He alone made the earth out of nothing but love."

James resumed the story of creation. "In time there were many offspring, and soon wickedness was rampant. This disobedience of the Lord required a total cleansing, and water covered the earth. Only the family of Noah, who had found favor with the Lord, was saved. After the waters receded, God told Noah to 'be fruitful and multiply.'[1]

"From them came many descendants. Some again chose to be greater than the Lord and built the Tower of Babel, bringing total confusion upon themselves and dispersion.

"Man has brought all this chaos and pain upon himself," Andrew concluded. "Punishment is the consequence of sin, just as hunger is a consequence of not eating, but God, in his mercy and love, forgives us."

"But you left your families, your way of life, all of you! Why? How could you leave the work that you have spent years developing?"

"What we have received is of far greater value," Simon said. "There is no comparison."

"What do you live on and where do you stay?"

"Whatever and wherever something is offered to us, or out in the open, enjoying the beauty of God's creation."

"And why do those people just follow and listen to him?"

"They are hungry for the knowledge of God," Andrew responded, "and He gives it in such lovely ways."

"We have learned that God is love," said John.

"With all the killing in the Scriptures?" I asked.

"That is man's rebellion against God," John replied. "It is not His will that it happen, but He gives men and women free will, and sometimes they rebel and use it in selfish ways."

"To answer your question about leaving everything," Simon interjected, "we have found a new way of life that is far more meaningful to us. Andrew and I have disposed of our boats to our workers."

"John and I feel the same," said James. "Our father has hired two men to take our places."

Luke, the energy and zeal of Zebedee's sons seem to be a good match for Simon's leadership and Andrew's wisdom.

Simon then rose to his feet. "It is late and we must leave. Thank you, Elisa and Joseph, for your hospitality and also for your many questions. Joseph, do not try to figure out how Jesus performs his cures. Just listen to his messages."

The others nodded approval and thanked Elisa, taking their leave. We stood in the doorway and watched them disappear on the road between the two groves of trees.

Elisa squeezed my hand, looked me in the eye and said, "Isn't it wonderful how these men have changed? Jesus must be a powerful teacher. They are entirely different in their outlook on life. They have learned to love the Lord God with their entire being. When someone does that, all of the teachings of the Scriptures, the Ten Commandments and the Law must fall into place.

"Perhaps, if we tried, we could somehow approach what they have."

So Luke, with Jesus and the fishermen as our example, we are renewing our zeal to learn more about God.

Do not worry. I will not abandon my medical teaching. Elisa says that everything good comes from God and in treating the sick we are doing God's work.

Joseph

[1]   Genesis 9:1

Letter 41

In your last letter, Luke, you warned against inviting strangers in our home, as I did the new healer. You also warned us to be careful about the food we eat and the water we drink.

The sharing of meals is a tradition of our faith. You remember when we were in Athens that I always wanted to eat with several of our fellow apprentices. It is ingrained in us. When Elisa and I were children we saw our parents invite friends and strangers into the home to share the meals. So now it is our custom to invite others to share our simple meals at our home.

We eat many fish. The Sea of Galilee is a short distance away. We are fortunate that we can get fresh fish almost every day. So many other places in our country have to be content with dried and salted fish because seafood cannot be carried far and remain fresh.

Bread and wine are essential for Jewish meals. There are many vineyards near here and wine is plentiful. Bread is a staple food most women prepare in the home, but there is a good bakery in Capernaum. The baker is young and has a growing family. In many other regions of Galilee, wine is preferred with meals because the water often makes people sick if they drink it. However, we have good water here in Capernaum if one is able to dig a well, but Erasmus taught us it must be in a high section of land where there is no drainage.

Luke, I must tell you a story about Erasmus and the well of Capernaum that illustrates his practical approach to medicine.

Many years ago, before Erasmus returned to Capernaum after training, most of the people here drew their water from a central well. A few months after he returned, the leading citizens decided to dig another well. This would be in another section of the city, at a lower level, and would not cost so much to dig.

The water was plentiful, but Erasmus soon had an epidemic of intestinal flux on his hands. The patients had frequent flows of a soft bowel humor, a high fever and were nauseated for several days. The old folks and the young children did not fare well and some of them died. They would dry out from the tremendous loss of fluid as the bowel humors flowed so much. Erasmus mixed some water with the juice from apples and salt, and tried it on a patient with loose bowels. He also gave him some mandragora. These

---

patients did not die. We still prescribe this mixture for patients we see with the bowel flux.

In the meantime, Erasmus began to try to determine what was causing so many to suffer from the bowel flux. People said it was the devil but Erasmus felt differently. He noticed that not everyone in a family would get ill. By careful questioning and keen observation, he learned that those people who drank only wine and not water did not get sick. He kept close records of the cases and questioned everyone who drank the water from the new well, everyone who drank from the old well, and those who drank only wine. Luke, only the people who drank water from the new well became ill. He wondered whether something was draining into the new well, which was lower than a large part of Capernaum. As you know, the bowel contents of man and beast are deposited all over the streets, and water from the roads drains into low areas during rains.

Erasmus appeared before the council of elders who were managing the town and presented his findings. There was no way he could convince them there was a problem with the new well. He noticed that they all lived on the elevated section and each had deep wells of their own. He also learned that the well was on the land of one of the elders and that he was receiving a great profit from it. The owner of the land said to Erasmus, "I will prove to you that you are wrong. My household and I will drink that water for a week." Erasmus was horrified. He shouted, "No, please. You will all get sick and some of you may die." There was a commotion in the council chambers as he continued.

"Please, close the well for four weeks and let us keep a record of the new cases. If I am correct, there will be no new cases and you will not be endangering the lives of members of your household." The other members finally persuaded the elder on whose land the well was located to agree. The well was closed, and many of the townspeople were unhappy because they had to walk farther for their water.

In one month, Erasmus came to the council chambers and reported that there were no new cases. This time, fortunately, the council respected his wisdom. They closed the well and selected an area of higher ground to dig another well, and no more cases of bowel flux occurred.

Luke, the reluctant elder who owned the land on which the shallow well was located turned out to be very appreciative and became a lifelong supporter of Erasmus.

Joseph

Letter 42

Greetings in the name of the God of Abraham, Moses and David.

Tonight, as we were gathering with our friends the day after the Sabbath, the sky darkened with an approaching storm. We had just begun our meeting when the door opened and there was Jesus.

"Elisa, I decided to accept your invitation to teach in your clinic, but I see that I am interrupting." Everyone got up and said, "Come in," as I explained to him why we were gathered. The room was soon filled with people. Jesus is well-known in Capernaum now, and throngs of people gather whenever he appears.

In addition to his usual followers, often dressed in worn and plain garments, this crowd contained Pharisees and doctors of the Law from almost every village in Galilee, and even from Jerusalem in Judea. They had come to hear and question Jesus.

As he was speaking, the sick and the paralyzed were brought up to him and he touched them. Sores were healed and crippled limbs restored to normal function. Shortly, the storm ceased and the sky cleared. As word spread of the healings, more people gathered outside the clinic trying to get in. I was standing inside the door when I heard a noise outside. I was told that some men had appeared carrying a paralyzed man on a pallet. They wanted to bring him in and lay him before Jesus, but it was not possible to clear a way. We were foot-to-foot, shoulder-to-shoulder. I thought they had decided to wait until Jesus left, because it became quiet.

Suddenly there was a clatter on the roof of the clinic. Someone was removing the slate tiles from my good roof! There was nothing I could do about it, I could hardly breathe, let alone move. Soon a large hole was made in the roof and the pallet bearing the paralyzed man was lowered into the middle of the gathering, right in front of where Jesus was standing. Somehow, room was made.

Jesus gave the man that look I have seen many times now, just before he heals. It seems that he sees the faith in the eyes of the person to be cured. He said, "My friend, your sins are forgiven."

The room had fallen silent, even the scribes and Pharisees. But I could almost hear the unspoken questions. Is this blasphemy? Who is this man? Who can forgive sins but God alone?

Jesus sensed the disbelief. "What are these thoughts that you have in your heart?

"Which of these is easier to say, 'Your sins are forgiven you,' or to say, 'Get up and walk'?

"But to prove to you that the Son of Man has authority on earth to forgive sins," he said to the paralyzed man, "I order you to get up, pick up your pallet and go home." And immediately, the man rose, picked up his pallet and started to walk out, praising God. And way was made in the crowded room for him to leave.

Jesus thanked Elisa for the use of the clinic and left, trailed by his four companions.

"Praise God," cried some in the crowd. "We have seen many things today."

But the faces of the scribes and Pharisees were unreadable, as if they did not want to believe what they had just seen. When I finally got outside I could see men repairing the roof, putting the slate tiles back in place. They were singing praises to God, and working beside them, singing louder than anyone, was the man Jesus had just healed.

Finally we were left with the group that had first gathered. "Joseph," asked Samson, "do you know this man? Have you examined him?"

"Erasmus has been treating him since he was a child, when he developed the paralytic disease and both of his legs became useless. His muscles were all withered."

"Can you explain this?" he asked.

"No, I cannot. I have treated this helpless man many times and now he is doing the work of roof repair."

"Jesus read the minds of the Pharisees and scribes," noted Ruth. "He was aware of their thoughts and answered them clearly."

"And in full view of the authorities from Jerusalem," Elisa added, "Jesus said, 'Your sins are forgiven you.' What's more, he called himself 'The Son of Man.'"

"His use of the title 'Son of Man' follows from the Book of Daniel," offered the learned Samson, "where the 'Son of Man' receives dominion and kingship.[1]

"But outright forgiveness of sins! That is different. Only God can do that."

Samson's wife, Hannah, thought for a moment. "If only God can forgive sin," she began, her voice growing stronger as she voiced her conclusion, "and he forgives sins … he must be God!"

"Inconceivable!" said one. "Absurd!" cried another.

But I looked at my Elisa and remembered her own deduction: "What Jesus has done is not in the power of man alone."

May the Lord God of Israel be with you and all of your friends and patients, Luke, and may he guide us here in Capernaum in our quest for the truth.

Joseph

---

[1]   Daniel 7:13

Letter 43

Luke, the cure of the paralytic at our clinic has stirred up talk throughout the area. As I made my rounds this morning, people stopped me on the road and asked me about it. Many of the patients I visited asked to be taken to Jesus to get cured. Patients who come in from outlying towns have even heard about Jesus and wanted to know more about his cures. Then there are simply the curious who come just to see the repaired roof. This afternoon, when I returned to the clinic, it became crowded again as people lingered to hear about the cures from those who had witnessed them. I passed Elisa in the hall, and she winked at me and whispered, "Perhaps some of them will listen to him now and heed his teachings."

Later in the afternoon Ana came by to tell us, to our great surprise, that Jesus has a new follower, a tax collector named Levi.

As you know, Luke, many tax collectors are dishonest and exact far more than the government requires in taxes. They must turn over to Rome a specified amount, but whatever they collect above that amount is theirs. Although they may become very rich, they are barred from the Temple and deemed of the same social class as prostitutes.

Ana said that as Jesus walked by the customhouse earlier today, he noticed Levi sitting there collecting the taxes. Jesus stopped, looked at him and said, "Follow me." Levi left his post at that moment and followed Jesus. Of course, the coins that he left on the table disappeared very rapidly.

Luke, I could not believe her story. I left the clinic and hurried to the place where the tax collectors set up their booths. Sure enough, Levi's booth was empty.

So Jesus now has five men following him much of the time — Simon, his brother Andrew, James and John the sons of Zebedee, and Levi.

Of course, no one misses Levi, and soon others will take his place. But we do miss the four fishermen.

Joseph

Letter 44

Greetings in the name of the Lord God of Israel.

Luke, you have asked if we had written Abraham regarding the cures of Jesus and what his response was. Yes, we have heard from him. He had heard reports of the new healer and was glad to hear our direct observations. Abraham is cautious. He often instructed us, "Do not be the first to adopt a new treatment. But also, do not be the last." He taught us to study everything that is new very thoroughly, and use it if we become convinced that it is effective and safe for the patient. He cautioned us to look carefully for any signs of fraud and deception. However, he was very interested in Jesus. In fact, he wants us to record whatever he teaches about the Scriptures and write of it to him. So, I am writing to you and Elisa is writing to Abraham all about the works of Jesus.

Today a runner came to our clinic with an invitation from Levi the tax collector to a banquet tonight in honor of Jesus. Levi is the new follower of Jesus who has decided to leave his profession and most of his possessions behind. Elisa and I are known to be friends of Jesus and therefore were invited to the banquet. "You know," I told Elisa, "Levi is considered a sinner." She replied, "But Jesus will be there. We are going."

It was after sunset this evening when we arrived. Levi lives in a rather modest house compared to the homes of others of his profession. The dining room was full of tax collectors, most of whom we know as patients. Many were lavishly dressed and we felt out of place in our plain garments. But when Jesus and the four fishermen arrived, they wore clothing similar to ours.

The banquet table was low, about one and one-half cubits high, and arranged in a deep curve, with Levi and Jesus, the honored guest, reclining on the end. We reclined on several cushions and were attended to by servants. Levi will be giving all of this up to be a follower of Jesus. He will carry no personal possessions, but walk with Jesus and eat and sleep where he can, even in the open. And he is overjoyed.

As we left the house of Levi, we noticed that scribes, Pharisees and others had gathered beyond the gate. One Pharisee stopped Simon and asked, "Why do you eat and drink with tax collectors and sinners?"

Jesus overheard the comment, turned and replied. "It is not those who are well who need a doctor, but the sick. I have not come to call the virtuous but the sinners to repentance."

Then a leading Pharisee named Hezekiah came up to Jesus and taunted him. "John's disciples are always fasting and saying prayers and the disciples of the Pharisees too, but yours go on eating and drinking."

Jesus seemed to be expecting this remark. "Surely," he said, "you can not make the bridegroom's attendants fast while the bridegroom is with them? But the time will come when the bridegroom will be taken away from them. That will be the time when they will fast." The Pharisees and scribes looked at each other and none seemed to have an answer.

Now Luke, fasting is a form of prayer. The Pharisees fast two days a week in addition to the times that Jews normally fast. And John the Baptizer encourages fasting among his followers. They fast more than the Pharisees because they are preparing for the coming of the Messiah.

Jesus cast his eyes on his challengers and continued. "No one tears a piece from a new cloak to put it on an old cloak. If he does, not only will he have torn the new cloak, but the piece taken from the new one will not match the old."

He paused but no one spoke a word, so he continued. "And nobody puts new wine into old skins. If he does, the new wine will burst the skin and then run out, and the skin will be lost. No, new wine must be put into fresh skins. Nobody who has been drinking old wine wants new. The old is good, he says."

Confused and frustrated, the Pharisees and scribes had no answer to this but turned on their heels and walked away into the darkness.

As we started home Elisa spoke first. "Jesus has shown that an unclean public sinner like a tax collector can reform and respond to the preaching as completely as anyone. Levi has given himself totally to Jesus. It shows that all people, whether good or bad, can come to God, reform and be accepted and loved."

We walked a short way before I shared what was on my mind. "I am concerned with the riddles, these parables of Jesus. What did he mean that the bridegroom will not be present all of the time?"

"Perhaps that he himself will not always be with his followers. It seems obvious that Jesus is the bridegroom in the parable."

"What about the new and old cloths and the wine skins?"

"Perhaps he is giving new meaning to some of the old teachings, a deeper meaning. And he may mean that some of the people will still prefer to worship the old way instead of adapting to the new." After a few moments of silence, Elisa continued.

"We know that John's disciples fast in anticipation of the coming of the Messiah. Do you suppose that the reason that Jesus does not have his disciples fast is because the Messiah is here — that Jesus is the Messiah?"

"But why would he not want to tell everyone?"

"God in his infinite wisdom will inform us at the proper time."

So, Luke, we have a new experience every day to share with you and with Abraham.

Joseph

Letter 45

Dear Luke, this Sabbath morning began as many of the others have since we returned home from Jerusalem. I left early to visit sick patients and Elisa arranged to meet me after morning services at the home of my parents, where we would eat the Sabbath meal. The women each prepare something the previous day so they do not have to cook on the Sabbath.

Today I had to visit a patient with dropsy.[1] Luke, I have purged him and sweated him but to no avail. He has swelling of the feet and legs, and his abdomen is now distended with fluid. He has to sit up in a chair to breathe. Usually when I listen to his chest, I hear bubbling and wheezing sounds. Today when I pounded with my fingers on the lower part of his chest I heard a flat sound, which indicates fluid. He needed some immediate relief of this distress so he could breathe.

I made a small stab wound in his chest with a scalpel and inserted a hollow reed, and out came clear yellow fluid. His breathing became much easier after about two logs[2] of clear yellowish fluid drained from the incision. I sewed up the small wound with the hope that it would stop leaking and not get infected. Perhaps tomorrow I will try the other lung or even the abdomen.

As I was on my way home, I passed a cornfield owned by Hezekiah. He was walking with some of his fellow Pharisees about the field. I stopped, dismounted and greeted them. But he started to chastise me.

"Joseph, you know that you should do no work on the Sabbath."

"A physician is allowed to do whatever is necessary to save a life."

Just then there was a disturbance in the field ahead of us. Out walked Jesus and his followers. We could see that the disciples were picking the grains, rubbing them in their hands and eating them. Luke, our law allows anyone who walks through a neighbor's field to eat what he needs at that time, but not to carry any away.

But this infuriated Hezekiah. He shouted, "Why are you doing something that is forbidden on the Sabbath day?"

Jesus just smiled as he approached us. "So you have not read what David did when he and his followers were hungry — how he went into the House of God, took the loaves of offering and ate them and gave them to his followers, loaves which only the priests were allowed to eat?"[3]

Now Luke, you, as a Gentile, may not know the rules of the Jewish Law.

The loaves of offering are reserved for the priests to eat, and no one else is allowed to eat them, or even enter the area where they are kept. However, in the Scriptures there is a story told of David, who when he and his men were hiding from Saul and they were hungry, went to the local shrine to ask for some food. Nothing was available but the special bread allowed only for the priests, but the priest allowed the men to have the bread because the human need was greater than the Law.

Now all of this is well-known to the Jews because it is often read in the synagogue.

Jesus again had answered the charge of a Pharisee with a question to which there was no reply.

Then he said, "The Son of Man is master of the Sabbath."

This was a remark Hezekiah and his friends could neither stomach nor answer, so they turned and left.

Jesus turned to me and smiled. "Good morning, Joseph. I see that you are about your work treating the ill."

"Yes," I replied. "But my results are dismal compared with yours."

I described the case of dropsy I had just seen. Jesus listened as his disciples continued to eat the grain. Then he said, "We have great need for physicians like you and Elisa and Erasmus. You relieve suffering and give comfort to the afflicted. You are doing the work of the Lord.

"Come," he said, "we must hurry to reach the synagogue in time."

I joined the group, leading my horse. As we passed the clinic I turned the horse loose in the pasture, changed my outer garment and caught up with the group on foot. Entering the synagogue, Jesus greeted each person warmly. None of the Pharisees nodded or greeted Jesus or any of us.

Jesus did not teach this Sabbath. As soon as the service was over he and his followers disappeared in the crowd.

Over the Sabbath meal there was much to discuss. Erasmus still was very concerned about Simon's mother-in-law. He wanted to know if she had had any recurrence of the fever. Elisa said, "I saw her at the synagogue today and she was as healthy and jovial as when we saw her after her recovery."

"That beats all understanding!" exclaimed Erasmus.

We reviewed the cure of the paralytic several days ago, the call of Levi, the banquet at Levi's house — and Jesus' remark that the well do not need a doctor. "He surely is right there," Erasmus added.

I recounted the experience of this morning in the grain field, and Jesus' remark that the Son of Man is master of the Sabbath. This astounded everyone except Elisa. Erasmus said, "That to me means he claims a very close connection with the divine."

"But how could it be? A mere carpenter?" Sarah asked. She rarely says much but thinks deeply. "Does that mean that he is greater than our ancestor Moses?"

"God made the Sabbath and only he can change it," my mother added. "Could he be the long-awaited Messiah?"

"And," I asked, "one of the tribe of David, born in Bethlehem of a virgin, out of Galilee and who lived in Egypt?"

"There is one thing we do know," my mother said. "We know he is of the tribe of David."

At that time a messenger came to the door to notify my father that a caravan was coming over the hill to Capernaum. So the two of us took our leave to work the rest of this Sabbath afternoon and evening.

Joseph

[1] Heart failure usually secondary to massive increase of the heart size from long-standing high blood pressure, from an infection or from blood clots in the arteries of the heart. This makes the heart muscle weak and unable to pump the blood throughout the body. The back pressure causes fluid to accumulate in the lungs, which makes a bubbling sound. Later, fluid accumulates between the chest wall and the lungs, around the heart and within the abdomen, enlarging the liver, and massive swelling occurs in the feet and legs.

[2] A log is a Hebrew measurement. It is about one-third of a quart.

[3] 1 Samuel 21:2-7

Letter 46

Another week has passed, Luke, and another Sabbath has arrived. I appreciate your letter and your disbelief about the cure of the leper. I accept the fact that spontaneous cures have been reported. But have qualified practitioners of medicine reported them? It may happen. I have not seen any such reports yet. Neither has Elisa nor Erasmus. But, Luke, these healings by Jesus are different. They are cures of all types of diseases. None of our advanced medical knowledge can explain, for instance, the case that happened today in the synagogue.

Our patient Eleazar had a withered right arm and hand from birth. Erasmus attended him. Luke, you remember that we saw several of these types of deformities in Athens under Dividimus.

Today I was seated in the synagogue with Erasmus and my father when I saw Eleazar slip into the back, hiding his malformed arm behind a pillar. I asked him to sit with us. We know he is embarrassed to be seen in public but, with urging by Erasmus and my father, he joined us.

As we became settled, Jesus and his followers came in quietly. The leader of the synagogue handed Jesus the scroll, and he got up and unrolled it to Exodus. He began to read the portion telling how God delivered the Ten Commandments to Moses.[1] Then he paused and drew all eyes to him.

"Remember," Jesus continued, "to keep holy the Sabbath day. Six days you may labor and do all your work, but the seventh day is the Sabbath of the Lord, your God. No work may be done then by you or your son or daughter or your male or female slaves, or your beast, or by the alien who lives with you."

Then he took his eyes off the scroll and looked over the assembled congregation. Some of the Pharisees were whispering to each other, nodding their heads and looking at the three of us. Erasmus, my father and I do necessary work on the Sabbath. I was a little embarrassed. Jesus' eyes moved to where we were seated and settled on Eleazar.

All of the scribes and Pharisees were watching Jesus to see if he would cure him on the Sabbath, hoping to find something to use against him. Jesus seemed to know their thoughts. He spoke to Eleazar.

"Stand up! Come out into the middle." Visibly embarrassed, Eleazar rose and moved forward.

Then Jesus looked around and said to the assembled congregation, "I put it to you. Is it against the Law to do good on the Sabbath or to do evil, to save a life or to destroy it?"

No one answered. He fixed his gaze on one Pharisee after another and then turned to Eleazar.

"Stretch out your hand," he said. Eleazar obeyed. There, before all our eyes, the deformed hand of the man we all knew straightened and became normal.

I looked at Erasmus, sitting beside me, and the expression on his face was beyond description. He whispered to me, "It is truly miraculous."

We looked to see what Jesus would do next but he had slipped quietly out the side door. "Where did he go?" Erasmus asked.

"Some secluded spot where he will spend the rest of the day and night in prayer," I answered. I looked to find Eleazar, but someone told me that he had left hoping to find Jesus.

Our path homeward took us past a group of Pharisees who were arguing heatedly. They were furious at the actions of Jesus and were discussing the best way of dealing with him. When we had passed them and were beyond hearing distance, Erasmus said, "You had better tell your friend Jesus that he should be careful around here or they will arrest him."

"We have warned him repeatedly but he doesn't seem to care. He says whatever he feels needs to be said and then leaves unharmed."

"Those rascals will get him some way some day."

During the Sabbath meal Elisa, as has become her way, searched for a deeper meaning to what we had witnessed. "Could the withered hand represent the withered soul of a sinner? Could he mean that God could restore even a withered soul to normal?"

Luke, Jesus refers to himself as the Son of Man. He speaks of his Father in heaven. He spends much time secluded in prayer. And he works miracles.

He may be the Messiah but I am not ready yet to admit it.

Joseph

[1]   Exodus 20:2-17

Letter 47

Jesus has been in Capernaum for several days now, Luke. He teaches at the synagogue in the mornings, in the shade of the trees on the lake in the afternoon, and in the woods at night. Simon, Andrew, James, John and Levi — who now is called Matthew — are always with him, but he has many other followers. They sit at his feet as he talks, as we often did with Dividimus, and are eager to learn everything that they can from him. This method of learning also occurs with the teachers of the Law in the Temple in Jerusalem, such as Gamaliel the Elder, with whom students often spend four years.

Today, as we finished with the patients in the clinic in the late afternoon, I stepped outside and noticed that the sky was very dark and the air felt heavy. I hurried inside to close the shutters against the rain. I had just finished when the door burst open and Jesus walked in, followed by a large group.

"Elisa and Joseph, may we stay here throughout the storm?"

By that time all of the followers had come in, filling the large room. As we closed the door, the storm broke in fury with thunder, lightning and a driving rain.

Jesus started to teach as soon as the storm quieted enough that we could hear him. This time he centered on the Wisdom literature in the Scriptures. He spoke of the practical advice that it gives to help us get along with one another. It is a summation of human experience. Proverbs, he said, offers insight on relationships, and the contrast between the righteous and the wicked. The whole Wisdom tradition speaks of the value of good friends and a good wife, the virtues of honesty, generosity and justice, the value of hard work and the problems that develop as the result of foolish and careless behavior.

The entire assembly listened so attentively that we did not even realize until he finished that the storm was over and the sun was shining. Jesus rose, thanked us and took his leave. "I wish to go to the mount and pray alone."

On the walk home I admitted to Elisa, "Just listening to Jesus makes me want to go to the Scriptures and read them more carefully. He gives new meaning to them. This is what you have been telling me all of the time."

She nodded. "Joseph," she said, "did you notice that Jesus showed a determined attitude as he left? He really wanted to be alone. He usually goes to a secluded place to pray, but this time he specifically said 'the mount.' When Moses went to the mount, the Lord spoke to him and gave him the Ten Commandments.

"Jesus must be planning a great decision," she concluded, "and wanted to commune with God during the night alone."

Luke, we will wait to see what Jesus will do next.

Joseph

Letter 48

Dear Luke, this evening Simon came over to sit with us in the garden. It has been more than a week since we have seen him or Jesus. He told us what happened after Jesus left our clinic the night of the last storm.

"Jesus spent the entire night alone on the mount in prayer. At daybreak the following morning I brought about twenty of his followers to the wooded area where Jesus was praying. As the sun started to rise Jesus called for us to come to him. He stood up, greeted and welcomed us. Then he spoke. 'I need all of you to help me do the work of my father who sent me to you. I will have special work for each of you in the future. Right now I will select the first twelve whom I want to be with me all of the time. Therefore, I will call these apostles.' Everyone grew quiet as Jesus continued.

"'They are Simon and his brother Andrew, James and John, Philip, Bartholomew, Matthew, Thomas, James the son of Alphaeus, Simon the zealot, Jude the son of James, and Judas Iscariot.'

"As he called us each by name, he nodded in our direction. We were all pleased, even though we did not know exactly what we were to do. We looked at him and his head was bowed low."

"And then what?" I asked.

"Jesus turned and walked away. The twelve of us gathered into a group and set out into the woods to follow. We found him kneeling in prayer, so we joined him. After some time, Jesus rose and said, 'We will be together a long time and you must become accustomed to the fact that I spend a lot of time communing with my Father.'

"We have been together since that time. Jesus spends his time teaching us as well as the other followers." Then Simon looked at the setting sun. "I must leave and meet with him and the others."

I wanted to ask, "Why twelve?" but Simon was out of the garden. Elisa and I watched him disappear in the woods. Finally I spoke.

"Jesus selected twelve ordinary men for this special mission. And look, none of them are learned. You and I and Erasmus have treated several of these men at one time or another. We know their backgrounds. Why them?

"Simon and Andrew originated in Bethsaida and are fishermen on our lake. James and John are likewise fishermen. Philip is also from Bethsaida, and so is his friend Bartholomew. Matthew is the name Jesus has given to Levi, the former tax collector. Thomas is called the Twin. Simon practiced law. James the son of Alphaeus and Jude the son of James, they say, are kinsmen of Jesus. They are all Galileans except Judas Iscariot, from the village of Kerioth in Judea. Why them?"

Elisa, in deep thought, opened her eyes wide. "We have had prophets throughout the history of Israel, through whom God sent messages to our ancestors. We had Moses, Samuel, Isaiah, Jeremiah, Ezekiel, Jonah, Hosea, Job, Malachi and David. All of these had messages from God for reform of the Israelites. None of these were learned men. God did not go to the Temple to find educated men who would be His prophets. God selects ordinary people to show that great things can be done by Him through them."

"But here are twelve who have left everything behind. Levi left a position of wealth to wander through the countryside from village to village and listen to Jesus teach. It does not make any sense!"

"Joseph, you are so practical. They must feel there is more to life than what they had, and they want to learn to be like Jesus and teach his way of life to others."

"With no home, sleeping in the open?"

"But Jesus talks of the kingdom of God. And do you not realize that in appointing twelve he wants to restore Israel?"

"You mean start the Twelve Tribes again?"

"No, just to restore the symbol of the Twelve Tribes with a leader, a new type of Israel and a new Jerusalem."

All that I could say was "Let us wait and see."

So, Luke, I send another letter in great confusion.

Joseph

Letter 49

Today Elisa and I finished with our patients early and went for a walk along the shore of Lake Galilee. We saw a crowd gathering and heard that Jesus had returned. He has been teaching in the villages, Luke, and the twelve chosen ones have been with him. Elisa and I joined the followers, walking past the fish market and the boat docks. The flies were thick. The docks are not kept as clean now since the four fishermen left to be with Jesus. We saw Erasmus sitting on the bank. We told him that we were following the crowd to hear Jesus, and he decided to leave his fishing and come with us.

We were soon out in the country where a pleasant wind was blowing off the sea. People were already gathered on a plain near the lake, at the foot of the hill we call the mount. By their clothing and their accent, we recognized people from Judea, from Jerusalem, from the coastal region of Tyre and Sidon and elsewhere. Some were on crutches, others were labored in their breathing. They had come to hear Jesus and to be cured of their diseases.

Elisa remarked, "I wonder how many of these sick people came to us in Jerusalem and we could not cure them. I know some of our incurables from Capernaum are here."

Suddenly there was a great shout as Jesus and his twelve apostles came down the hill. They stopped at the level area where the people had gathered. The ill and the maimed began to approach Jesus, and he laid his hands upon them. He spoke softly to each.

Elisa whispered, "Joseph, all of these people who are sick must really believe that they will be healed. Jesus knows who believes and who does not believe."

There were several local Pharisees and scribes in the crowd, and I judged them to be among the nonbelievers.

Finally everyone settled down to hear Jesus teach. We were fortunate to be close to where he was sitting. I could see Ana, Miriam and Thalia among the listeners. Jesus rose, fixed his eyes on his followers and spoke.

"Happy are you who are poor, for yours is the kingdom of God.

"Happy are you who are hungry now, you shall be satisfied.

"Happy are you who weep now, you shall laugh.

"Happy are you when people hate you, drive you out, abuse you, denounce your name as criminal, on account of the Son of Man.

"Rejoice when that day comes and dance for joy, for then your reward will be great in heaven. This was the way their ancestors treated the prophets."

Jesus paused, and his tone became reproachful.

"But alas, for you who are rich, you are having your consolation now. Also, for you who have your fill now, you shall go hungry. Alas, for you who laugh now, you shall mourn and weep. Alas, for you when the world speaks well of you, this is the way their ancestors treated the false prophets."

The Pharisees and the scribes shook their heads in disgust.

"But I say to you who are listening," and here Jesus paused again, "love your enemies. Do good to those who hate you. Bless those who curse you. Pray for those who treat you badly.

"To the man who slaps you on one cheek, present the other one too. To the man who takes your coat from you, do not refuse your tunic.

"Give to everyone who asks you, and do not ask for your property back from the man who robs you.

"Treat others as you would like them to treat you."

Luke, so much of this is different from what we have been taught in the synagogue. The Scriptures say, "An eye for an eye, a tooth for a tooth."[1]

But Jesus had an answer for the confusion I had not yet voiced.

"If you love those who love you, what thanks can you expect? Even sinners love those who love them. And if you do good to those who do good to you, what thanks can you expect? For even sinners do that much. And if you lend to those from whom you hope to receive, what thanks can you expect? Even sinners lend to sinners to get back the same amount.

"Instead, love your enemies and do good and lend without any hope of return.

"You will have a great reward and you will be sons of the Most High, for He himself is kind to the ungrateful and the wicked."

I again glanced at the Pharisees, who appeared to be very uncomfortable. It seemed that they were looking for a way to leave, but could not because of the immense crowd. And Jesus continued.

"Be compassionate, as your Father is compassionate.

"Do not judge and you will not be judged yourselves.

"Do not condemn and you will not be condemned yourselves.

"Grant pardon and you will be pardoned.

"Give, and there will be gifts for you. A full measure, pressed down, shaken together and running over, will be poured into your lap, because the amount you measure out is the amount you will be given back."

Luke, all of this is a new teaching. Jesus is preaching a very different way of life. Erasmus took in every word and nodded approval. Elisa smiled and looked at Jesus as he began to seem more demanding.

"The disciple is not superior to his teacher. The fully trained disciple will always be like his teacher.

"Why do you observe the splinter in your brother's eye and never notice the plank in your own? How can you say to your brother, 'Brother, let me take out the splinter that is in your eye,' when you cannot see the plank in your own? Hypocrite, take the plank out of your own eye, and then you will see clearly enough to take out the splinter that is in your brother's eye.'

"There is no sound tree that produces rotten fruit, nor again a rotten tree that produces good fruit. For every tree can be told by its own fruit. People do not pick figs from thorns, nor grapes from brambles. A good man draws what is good from the store of goodness in his heart. A bad man draws what is bad from the store of badness. For a man's words flow out of what fills his heart."

Jesus stopped again, but no one moved. He looked at the disciples and asked rather sharply, "Why do you call me 'Lord, Lord' and not do what I say?"

He gazed over the crowd on the shores of Lake Galilee. From our position we could see boats on the lake. There was a haze over the water so the distant shore was not clearly visible. All was quiet, the sun was sinking behind the hill and the shadow of Jesus seemed to extend over the vast crowd as he ended his sermon with a parable.

"Everyone who comes to me and listens to my words and acts on them, I will show you what he is like. He is like a man who, when he built his house, dug deep and laid the foundation on rock. When the river was in flood, it bore down on that house but could not shake it, it was so well-built.

"But the man who listens and does nothing is like the man who built his house on soil with no foundations. As soon as the river bore down on it, it collapsed and what a ruin that house became!"

Then Jesus stopped, turned and walked back up the mount, followed by

---

his disciples. Soon the Pharisees got up and pushed their way through the crowd. I could see the irritation on their faces as they passed us.

Soon everyone was leaving. Elisa, Erasmus and I walked back with Daniel and Leah, other friends we had found in the crowd, discussing what we had heard. Daniel, who practices law, was struck by how Jesus continues to confound those who wish to trap him. "His precepts are simple but revolutionary," he remarked. Leah said her heart was full and she had much to share with their young daughters when they returned home.

Erasmus stopped to pick up the fishing gear he had left in the water. As he pulled up the line he had a good-sized fish. "Ach! Look what I caught!' he exclaimed, and he carried it home.

After we arrived home Elisa and I talked a long time about the way of life Jesus preached. "Joseph," she said, "this is how we have been trying to live ever since that day on the Jordan when we were baptized by John. Jesus spelled it out today in clear terms. These are the ideals. Perhaps if we try hard, we can achieve most of them at least some of the time, and a few all of the time."

We were so exhausted that we ate very little and prepared to retire early. There was so much to consider in the teachings of Jesus, it was as if we had been through a long examination in our training.

And now Luke, I share them with you. May the Lord God of Israel guide us all in knowing His Way.

Joseph

---

[1] Leviticus 24:20

Letter 50

Luke, the sermon we heard from Jesus, on the plain by Lake Galilee, has been the talk of all our patients for the past three days. While we are working at the clinic Erasmus often stops between patients and starts to discuss one of the teachings with whoever is available. He told me that he spent an entire afternoon discussing what he heard Jesus say with one of his fishing partners on the lake, and they did not even put their hooks into the water. And the Sabbath meal at my parents' house yesterday lasted four hours because we talked and talked.

Tonight, for our weekly meeting, the clinic was as full in the evening as it had been all day. Our friends were discussing the teachings as they came into the door. When the place was filled I called for an opening prayer for guidance, and we sang one of the Psalms. I had Ana recite Jesus' exact words as best she remembered. Luke, she did a magnificent job.

Daniel made the first comments. "Leah and I listened to him speak to the multitudes on the plain yesterday, and our home has not been the same since. Every sentence he spoke provoked thought. And I don't believe he was speaking just to Pharisees, he was speaking to each one of us. Are we helping the poor, hungry, or those who weep? Do we really bless those who curse us?"

"Alas for the rich," said the widow Miriam. "Those who hoard their wealth and do not share with those in need are cutting themselves off from God. Jesus said, 'Give to everyone who asks you, and do not ask for your property back from the man who robs you.'"

John, who had served with the Temple Guard, shook his head and said Jesus had set an impossible standard for behavior. "To love and serve one's friends is normal. But to love one's enemies is not what anyone does."

"But would not it be wonderful if everyone did just that?" Miriam responded. "No more wars. No more killings. No stealing. No hatred."

John shook his head, but his wife, Esther, touched him on the arm and her deep voice carried across the room. "Not to judge or condemn, John, would stop a lot of hatred, as would to forgive without counting the cost."

Luke, the debate went back and forth, and the gathering broke up into groups of two and three to argue a particular point. It was a very noisy place. I finally realized that it was very late and I rapped on the table for quiet.

Elisa had been silent until now, but she arose to be heard, and her quiet voice suddenly carried great authority. "Could it be that Jesus had another entirely different meaning with all of his statements on the plain? Could he have used the word hunger to mean a great yearning for the word of God? Could he have meant that, if we hunger for God's word, if we are poor in spirit and if we seek the word, we will find the kingdom of God?

"To be poor means total dependence. Could he mean that we must be totally dependent upon God? Could he have meant that those who weep wish to know the Word of God, and they will receive it and be joyful?

"Could he have meant that those who are persecuted for their beliefs will be rewarded in heaven? And those who receive glory now will go the way of the false prophets — to oblivion?

"I do not know which one of us has any enemies. But supposing someone came to Capernaum who chose to persecute this group, what would we do? Would we love him or would we hate him?

"Jesus says that we should be compassionate as our Heavenly Father is compassionate. How many of us can say we do that? Which one of us is the hypocrite in the blind man's story? How many of us have our spiritual foundations built on rock?" Then she sat down.

She said it, Luke, she said it all. My Elisa, whose mind can penetrate the depths of a question, has come to the heart of the message of Jesus.

After a thoughtful silence David the teacher took up her unspoken challenge. "Taking that a little further, do we give of ourselves to those who need us in full measure and running over? And are we free from fault in our faith before we try to teach someone else? The bad tree and the bad men each signify those who have a fault or are guilty of a wrong, and they will try to justify it and teach that it is the right thing to do."

"The house built on soil with no foundation," said Samson, "was swept away by the river. We must be totally solid and knowledgeable about our faith or we will be swept away with the distractions of life."

Everyone was now thinking on a deeper level, and that must be what Jesus means for us to do.

A short time later Elisa signaled an end to the night's discussion. "Come, it is time for the refreshments that Hannah and Rachel brought." We feasted on fig cakes and mulberries with the juice of pomegranates, and, one by one, said our goodbyes.

Luke, I am beginning to see Jesus through Elisa's eyes. I pray to the Lord to help my unbelief.

Joseph

Letter 51

Grace and peace from the Lord God. The town of Capernaum is still alive with talk about Jesus. People on the street and at the market are discussing what they have heard him say or seen him do. This morning as I was returning from my rounds, I saw Jesus once again and a crowd of the curious gathering around him. I dismounted and walked toward the group, leading my horse. At the same time, some of the Jewish elders approached him. I tied the horse to a tree and followed, hoping they were not there to challenge Jesus. To my surprise the leading elder, named Ira, greeted Jesus very warmly.

"Jesus," he said, "we come to ask a favor of you. The centurion in charge of the Roman troops in Capernaum has a favorite servant who is near death. The soldier has heard about you and sent us to ask you to come and heal his servant." Before Jesus could answer, another of the group pleaded, "He deserves this of you because he is friendly towards our people. In fact, he is the one who took charge of building the synagogue."

Jesus turned to follow the elders, and the rest of us followed them. We had gone only a short distance when we saw the centurion's house and several people approaching us. One hailed Jesus. "Sir, we are friends of the centurion, and he has sent us to give you this message: 'Do not put yourself to trouble, because I am not worthy to have you under my roof, and for the same reason I do not presume to come to you myself. But give the word and my servant will be cured. For I am under authority myself and have soldiers under me, and I say to one man "Go" and he goes, to another "Come here" and he comes, to my servant "Do this" and he does it.'"

A look of respect crossed the face of Jesus. He turned to the crowd, saying, "I tell you, not even in Israel have I found faith like this."

The messengers took their leave and returned to the centurion's house. Jesus and the crowd remained behind. A short time later messengers poured out of the centurion's house shouting, "The servant is cured! The servant is cured!" We all turned to Jesus, but he was gone.

I returned to my horse, rode to the clinic and told Elisa all that had occurred. The rest of the day, as we dressed wounds, examined patients and prescribed treatment, I marveled at what had happened. Jesus had cured a pagan without touching him, without even seeing him.

In the evening, I expressed my thoughts to Elisa. "Joseph," she said, "your mind stays on the practical. Much of this is in the spiritual realm. It appears that Jesus has a message and a ministry to others, in addition to the Jewish race. The centurion and his servant are both Gentiles.

"Could it be that Jesus came to unite Jew and Gentile, and to start a whole new form of worship which would embrace us all?"

"The centurion showed humility and faith in Jesus' ability," I noted. "And he had second thoughts about inviting Jesus to his home because he knew that a Jew entering the home of a Gentile would be ritually unfit to worship. He showed that he was concerned about Jesus.

"But the part that astounded me," I continued, "was that the elders of the Jews were asking Jesus for help. Many of these are the ones who have been very critical of his actions in the past."

"Yes, but do you not see that the centurion himself, being a man of authority, seemed to recognize that Jesus has a special relationship with God?"

And so, dear Luke, the influence of Jesus on the people of Capernaum grows ever stronger, especially upon me.

Joseph

Letter 52

Dear Luke, Elisa and I have been very involved with our patients while Jesus and his disciples have been out teaching and healing in the surrounding villages. Today, as we were ending our work, in walked James, the older of the sons of Zebedee, to tell us that they have returned to Capernaum.

I welcomed him. "James, come in and tell us about your experiences with Jesus."

"I can only stay a short time," he replied. James is somewhat impatient, but that stems from his passionate nature.

Elisa brought some water from the well and James, still on his feet, began his story. "After Jesus cured the servant of the centurion, he went off into the woods to pray for the night. The next morning we found him still in prayer. He finally noticed that we were present and informed us that we would now spend some time going from village to village teaching. We all left with him. News of his travels spread rapidly and crowds would develop around Jesus wherever we went. The twelve of us stayed very close to him all of this time in order to learn as much as we could of his teachings.

"About a week later Jesus and the rest of us, and a great crowd of followers, were approaching a town called Nain. As we neared the gate of the town we met a procession carrying a dead man to his burial. Jesus stopped and asked who had died. He was told that a widow had lost her only son. Jesus asked to see her, so he was taken through the crowd of townspeople.

"He touched her shoulder and she looked up at him. 'Do not cry,' Jesus told her. Then he went up and put his hand on the open coffin. The bearers stood still. Jesus looked at the dead man and said, 'Young man, I tell you, get up.'"

James stopped and looked me straight in the eye. "Joseph, I saw that dead man sit up and begin to speak.

"Then Jesus took the man's hand and placed it in his mother's hand, and they embraced.

"Everyone was filled with awe and we turned to praise Jesus, but he had left. However, word of this deed quickly spread across the countryside.

"I have seen many miracles performed by Jesus," James concluded, "but I am staggered at each new one that I witness."

Luke, curing illness and expelling demons is one thing, but raising the dead, that is another. "James, are you sure that he was dead?"

"Joseph," he thundered, offended at my disbelief. "This man was on his way to be buried! Many of the townspeople had been with his mother since he had died. His body had the odor of death. I was there!"

"I hear you, James, but it is hard for me as a physician to believe that a dead body can be returned to life. What's more, touching a dead body is ritually unclean according to the writings in Leviticus,[1] and the only reason we do it is because we are physicians."

Then Elisa spoke. "Elijah raised the son of the widow of Zarephath of Sidon[2] and Elisha raised the son of the woman of Shunem.[3] Both of these men were prophets of God and it was through Him that they raised the dead."

James nodded, but he was not familiar with the passages and still in awe of what he had seen. And he was eager to be gone, so he quickly took his leave.

Luke, the powers of Jesus are more and more of a mystery. Elisa may be correct. This man of miracles may be the long-awaited Messiah.

Joseph

[1] Leviticus 21:1-2

[2] 1 Kings 17: 17-24

[3] 2 Kings 4:18-37

Letter 53

From your last letter, Luke, I see that you have been going to the synagogue in Antioch and reading the Scriptures under the tutorship of Rabbi David. True to the Luke I knew in Athens, you question everything that you cannot understand. Now, to answer your question, "Who is the God of Israel and why is He different from the Greek gods?"

I know that other religions worship several or even hundreds of gods, but our God is the creator of everything. He was here before anything else existed. We know that everything that happens is caused by something that precedes it. God is the one who started it all.

In medicine we are accustomed to factual information and abandon the writing if it is not. The Scriptures were not written to be read as a work of science like the writings of Hippocrates. These stories were passed from father to son for centuries, then finally they were written down.

We are taught that each story of the Scriptures is to be read verse by verse, meditating on each to discover the underlying meaning, which is usually of profound importance. In the mind of our ancestors, the facts of a story were not as important as the message it was supposed to tell.

We believe that each author was inspired by God to write what he did. That is why we consider the Scriptures the Word of God.

Now, Luke, you will find a collection of historical facts, legends and myths in the various stories. That does not distract from the authenticity of what they teach.

I see that your first question has to deal with the two stories of the creation of man as found in Genesis.[1] The message in these is that God created the universe, the earth, the sky and stars and everything in it. The story of the fall is related to show that man disobeyed the one rule that he was given by God and therefore was punished.

The story of Cain and Abel [2] shows how jealousy leads to sinfulness and murder. Yes, many of the people became corrupt. The story of the flood tells of God's love and His desire to save the just, and He did.

And then we have Abraham accepting God as the one and only God and worshipping only Him, and that is how our race started. However, you also asked, "Why would God choose the Hebrew race to be his people?"

Well, the first thing to remember is that He picked a very insignificant people. Certainly He knew that there were many more prominent and plentiful peoples. Luke, we do not know how many others God asked. Perhaps He had asked many other nations and they were not willing to give up the worship of their many gods for just one.

We pray that the Lord God will guide you as you continue your study of the Word of the One True God.

Joseph

1   Genesis 1:5-25
    Genesis 2:5-27
2   Genesis 4:1-16

Letter 54

Greetings in the name of all that is holy.

Today, after we'd had a demanding day of work, Jesus asked to meet with his followers at our clinic. More people with afflictions arrived at our doors, among them people who could not see or could not hear and people who could not walk. They came not to see us but to be cured by Jesus.

Then two messengers arrived and walked up to Jesus. "We are disciples of John the Baptizer," they said.

Luke, you remember that Elisa and I heard John preaching and baptizing on the River Jordan when we were on our way home from our two years in Jerusalem. It was then we first saw Jesus, though we did not know him.

"We heard the news of the miracles that you are doing," the messengers explained, "and John selected the two of us to come to you and ask, 'Are you the one who is to come or are we to wait for someone else?'"

Jesus did not immediately answer but continued to cure many people of their afflictions. Finally he stopped and turned to the messengers. "Go back and tell John what you have seen and heard. The blind see again, the lame walk, lepers are cleansed and the deaf hear. And the dead are raised to life. The good news is preached to the poor, and happy is the man who does not lose faith in me."

Having received their answer, they thanked Jesus and prepared to leave. Since it was late, I asked the messengers to stay overnight and allow us to give them some provisions for their journey. "I know the road along the river and in the dark it is full of hazards. There are holes in the road and often rocks block the path and, on rare occasions, there are robbers who leave their victims penniless and badly beaten."

But they feared not. As they left they said, "God will provide," and walked off into the night without food or water.

I went back inside and Jesus was speaking about John. He said, "What did you go to the wilderness to see? A reed swaying in the breeze? No. Then what did you go out to see? A man dressed in fine clothes? Oh no! Those who go in fine clothes and live luxuriously are to be found at court. Then what did you go out to see? A prophet? Yes, I tell you, and much more than a prophet. He is the one of whom Scriptures say, 'Look, I am going to send my messenger to prepare a way before me.'[1]

"I tell you, of all the children born of women, there is no one greater than John. Yet the least in the kingdom of God is greater than he. All the people who heard him, and the tax collectors too, acknowledged God's plan by accepting baptism from John, but by refusing baptism from him, the Pharisees and the lawyers had thwarted what God had in mind for them." Jesus took a drink of the water that Elisa had provided, then resumed.

"What description, then, can I find for the men of this generation? What are they like? They are like children shouting to one another while they sit in the market place. 'We played the pipes for you and you wouldn't dance. We sang dirges and you wouldn't cry.'

"John the Baptizer comes, not eating bread, not drinking wine, and you say, 'He is possessed.' The Son of Man comes, eating and drinking, and you say, 'Look, a glutton and drunkard, a friend of tax collectors and sinners.' Yet Wisdom has proved right by all her children."

Luke, it was obvious that Jesus was addressing those in the crowd who were opposed to his teachings. When he talks to believers, his face is kind, his voice is soft, and he has a smile. But when he talks to critics, his face becomes stern, his voice sharp, and his general stance determined and forbidding. We could recognize the spies of Pharisees in the crowd because they hung their heads and said nothing.

Then jubilation arose from those people recently cured, and it became a celebration. Jesus was pleased with the merriment and took part in the singing. And then suddenly he was gone.

When the evening ended, Elisa and I left for home, recalling our own experience of John and our baptism by him and how, after hearing him, we developed the philosophy by which we lead our lives.

Thoughtfully Elisa said, "Jesus had a very sharp criticism for the Pharisees in his story of the children playing in the market. They could not please their friends. If they played a joyful tune they would not be joyful, and if they played a sad tune they would not be sad.

"Now the Pharisees do not follow John's teachings, which are strict, nor do they want to follow Jesus' teachings for us to love one another. In other words, nothing pleases them."

We walked quietly for a short distance and Elisa spoke again. "You remember when we heard John preach on the bank of the Jordan? He seemed to predict a judgmental Messiah, not one who is kind and forgives everyone, and not one who eats with tax collectors and does not condemn anyone. This is not the type of Messiah that John seemed to expect. That is why he sent his disciples to ask Jesus the question, 'Are you he of whom it is written?'"

"Do you think he will believe when he hears the reports of his disciples?" I asked.

"He will see the truth in Jesus!" was Elisa's reply as we entered our home.

Luke, we will hear again of John the Baptizer. Of this I feel sure.

Joseph

[1] Malachi 3:1

Letter 55

Peace and grace be unto you, dear Luke. Today we had the pleasure of attending a banquet at the home of Simon, one of the Pharisees of Capernaum we had recognized at the sermon on the mount. Elisa, Erasmus and I have been his physicians. Erasmus prefers not to attend social functions and did not join us.

As we arrived, there was the usual greeting with a kiss from the host, and a servant washed our feet. In this city the streets are cleaned often but the ritual is still kept. This is the most menial of jobs but is done for every guest as they come into the house. After the feet are washed, the servant anoints the head of each guest with fragrant oil.

Elisa was the only woman at the banquet, but we did not find that unusual. As a physician she has often been invited to places where it is customary for only men to be guests.

All of the Pharisees and most of the guests were in richly colored robes and were standing in small groups of three and four discussing their estates and their successes. Elisa and I have no estate. Our successes are the patients we treat, but we do not talk about them.

As we were standing to one side we saw Jesus walk in. Elisa looked at me and whispered, "Do you suppose Simon has arranged this evening to entrap Jesus with more of his questions?" I nodded and felt anxious. "Don't worry," Elisa said. "Jesus cannot be trapped."

I noticed that our host appeared to be busy with his other guests and had not greeted Jesus with the accustomed kiss, nor had the servant knelt before Jesus to wash his feet. I did not know if this was an intended slight.

Jesus came over to speak to us, as everyone else was engrossed in conversation. We exchanged greetings, and as I was about to ask about The Twelve, the servant called everyone to the banquet.

Jesus, Elisa and I settled near one end of the table, not at the place of honor. When we were all in our places and the host was about to start the prayers before meals, there was a commotion at the door and we all turned to see what was happening.

A woman was pushing the servants away and forcing her way inside. Elisa and I recognized her as Sherah, one of the local prostitutes. We have treated her often. She comes in late in the day, as no one will sit beside her in the waiting area. She has never been caught in the act of her trade or she would have been stoned. We wondered what she could want here at this great banquet.

Luke, both of us knew from confidences she had shared with us that several of the guests reclining at the table were her clients. I am sure they were worried that she would embarrass them. But then, who would believe the words of a prostitute?

She wore a rather old robe, soiled and tattered. Her hair was long and uncombed. The servants could not stop Sherah as she barged into the banquet room. We saw that she was carrying an alabaster jar, and holding it very tightly. She set off toward the section of the table where the host and his guests sat. I could see the host was provoked. But she continued past Simon, stopped suddenly and knelt at the feet of Jesus. She began to weep. Her tears fell on his feet, and she wiped them off with her hair. Then she started to kiss his feet. The rest of us were too startled to move. Even the servant stood still. Then the woman took the alabaster jar, filled with ointment, and turned it over to anoint the feet of Jesus.

By this time Simon had recovered and said, almost under his breath, "If this man were a prophet, he would know who this woman is who is touching him, and what a bad name she has."

Jesus turned to his host and said, "Simon, I have something to say to you."

"Speak, Master" was the reply.

Elisa and I were surprised that he called Jesus "Master."

Jesus pulled in his outstretched legs, sat upon them and looked at Simon. "There was once a creditor who had two men in his debt. One owed him five hundred denarii and the other fifty. They were unable to pay, so he pardoned them both. Which of them would love him more?"

Simon answered, "The one who was pardoned more, I suppose."

Jesus nodded in approval. "You are right."

Then he turned to the woman. "Simon," he said. "You see this woman? I came into your house and you poured no water over my feet, but she has poured out her tears over my feet and wiped them away with her hair. You gave me no kiss, but she has been covering my feet with kisses ever since she came in. You did not anoint my head with oil, but she has anointed my feet with ointment. For this reason I tell you that her sins, her many sins, must have been forgiven her, or she would not have shown such great love.

"It is the man who is forgiven little who shows little love." Jesus said this clearly and loudly so that everyone could hear.

Then Jesus bestowed on Sherah a look of compassion, a look Elisa and I have seen many times. We knew what would come next. "Your sins are forgiven," he said to her.

We could hear some of the guests murmuring to each other. "Who is this man that he forgives sins?"

Jesus continued, addressing the woman. "Your faith has saved you. Go in peace." Sherah leaned over, kissed the feet of Jesus again, picked up her alabaster jar, bowed very courteously to the host, stepped back, bowed to all the guests and walked out.

As she passed the servants who were guarding the door she said, "I am sorry to have forced my way in. Thank you."

There was a great hush over the entire banquet table. The only one who seemed in a mood to celebrate was Jesus. He bantered with his neighbors at the table. He complimented every servant who served him and offered jests and pleasantries. Jesus got all of the attention from the servants. Obviously, he was the only one who had ever paid them such respect.

When the meal was over, everyone but Jesus thanked the host and left. Elisa and I heard him thank Simon the Pharisee most graciously, then the servants and the cook. Then he went on his way into the darkness.

As we walked home discussing what had happened, Elisa said with a laugh, "Poor Simon. So many of his guests seemed uncomfortable when Sherah walked into the banquet hall."

"And you know why," I replied. "Jesus was so gracious the entire time. Can you imagine a Pharisee thanking the cook and the servants?

"And did you notice that Jesus got the most attention?" I added.

"Joseph, you know that is not the reason he did it."

"I know," I admitted, rather ashamed. "But forgiving the sin-ridden Sherah!"

"He must have seen the basic goodness in her," Elisa finished as we came to our home. "It will be interesting to see what she will become now. Will she cease to follow the life of sin?"

Luke, forgiveness for sins, yes, great sins, is one of the teachings of Jesus. This time he forgave Sherah's sins without accusing her of anything. Did he know that she would be cured of her desire to sin?

I have seen him look into the eyes of people as if he could read their hearts. He must know the inner thoughts of each person he cures because he does not cure everyone.

He must know, then, dear Luke, that my love and respect for him grows, but my mind is still full of doubts.

Joseph

Letter 56

Dear Luke, Jesus has a company of disciples now, not just The Twelve.

Being with him has become a way of life for these followers. They all try to follow his example of total goodness. Jesus seems to "live in them," especially in The Twelve, who are always with him and listen to all of his teachings.

But, Luke, let me now tell you about the women in his company of followers. Jesus has cured many of them of afflictions, including evil spirits.

There is Mary of Magdala, from whom seven demons were cast out. I do not understand how this happened, but there are so many things Jesus does that I cannot understand. Magdala is a town half a day's walk from Capernaum. Mary is a woman of means whose husband died a few years after they married. She gives generously to the poor and has been contributing to the living expenses of Jesus and the apostles. She often accompanies them as they teach in the villages of Galilee. She has a kind smile but her face is drawn, as if life has not always been easy for her.

Then there is Joanna, the wife of Chuza, a steward for Herod Antipas at his palace in Tiberias.

The Herods, you may recall, rule Judea under the Romans even though they are not of David's lineage and are not pure members of the race. Herod the Great, who ruled when I was a child, was half-Jewish but was religiously indifferent. He observed the Jewish feasts but also those of various cults.

He was made king of Judea, including the regions of Idumea, Samaria, Galilee, Perea and Bashan. He built the great Temple of Jerusalem, the Greek Theatre, the Hippodrome, many palaces and gardens, the Fortress of Antonia in Jerusalem and the city of Caesarea Philippi on the sea. But he was a vicious man. It is he who killed all the male infants in Bethlehem more than thirty years ago. He also had his wife killed, as well as three sons and a brother who was the high priest. However, he was a shrewd politician and extended the boundaries of Judea almost to the size it had been at its glory under Solomon.

Now one of his sons, Herod Antipas, is the tetrarch of Galilee serving under the Roman governor of Judea, Pontius Pilate.

Chuza and Joanna are both followers of Jesus — Chuza in secret — but Joanna has been public with her beliefs and follows Jesus along with others in the company.

Then we have Susanna, another widow. Susanna walks with a little limp as she had the crippling disease of children as a girl. She and several other women give Judas Iscariot money to buy food for the company, which they then prepare. Without them, the company would not survive.

Luke, it seems that the women who follow Jesus are even more determined than the men are. They do not waver in their belief. Like Elisa, they remain pillars of the faith in spite of trouble.

Now, in Jesus' company these women are not treated as servants. They are present at all of his teaching sessions. They take part in questioning Jesus and in other discussions that follow. The men in the company of Jesus have learned to treat these women with respect, as he does.

In Jewish society the woman is still considered inferior to the man. All of the prayers refer to men alone. And the woman is to serve the man first before she is allowed to eat. A widow often has great problems because only a man is allowed to conduct business.

But all the men in my family have a deep respect for their wives. Since my father grew up as an orphan with four brothers and four sisters from three to sixteen years of age, the siblings learned that they must depend on each other. After he married, my mother would help with the fieldwork and my father would help in the house, so they always sat down to eat together.

It was this training that made it easy for me to treat Elisa as my partner. I do not let her serve me first and then eat later. We do everything together.

This is also the way that the husbands among our set of friends treat their wives.

Now that I have grown accustomed to questioning the ways of the world, I have to wonder. Did God will that men should rule, or did man will it?

Joseph

Letter 57

Dear Luke, it seems that Jesus is emphasizing his teaching ministry. He now spends more time teaching his disciples and teaching the crowds than he does healing. However, he speaks in parables, a powerful and effective method of instruction that has its roots in the Scriptures and in the rabbinical literature.

One example is in the writings of Samuel.[1] David took Uriah's wife, Bathsheba, and lay with her, then had her husband killed in battle so that he could keep her. Nathan the prophet told him a story about a rich man who had many lambs, but when a guest came he took the only lamb of a poor man and slaughtered it, and he and his guest feasted upon it. David became angry and said, "The man deserves death." And Nathan replied, "The man is you."

But as someone trained in science, I sometimes find parables hard to follow. Jesus often seems as if he is speaking in riddles. Elisa seems to understand his stories better than I do and often needs to explain their meanings to me.

Tonight, Jesus came into the clinic for a meeting with his disciples and other followers. We were all sitting in the large room and he was sitting on a table in front of everyone. After discussing the writings of David and the Psalms that he wrote, Jesus told this parable.

"A sower went out to sow his seed. As he sowed, some fell on the edge of the path and was trampled on, and the birds of the air ate it up. Some seed fell on rock, and when it came up it withered away, having no moisture. Some seed fell among thorns and the thorns grew with it and choked it. And some seed fell into rich soil and grew and produced its crop a hundredfold." Then he stopped for just a moment.

"Listen, anyone who has ears to hear!" he cried out, rising to his feet.

Some murmuring among small groups broke the silence of the crowd. Even the disciples of Jesus seemed confused, and Thomas asked him, "What does that mean?"

"The mysteries of the kingdom of God are revealed to you," Jesus said, looking at him, then catching the eyes of each of us round the room. "For the rest there are only parables, so that they may see but not perceive, listen but not understand."

We remained quiet, wanting to hear more of an explanation. Jesus grew impatient.

"This, then, is what the parable means:

"The seed is the word of God. Those on the edge of the path are people who have heard it, and then the devil comes and carries away the word from their hearts in case they should believe and be saved. Those on the rock are people who, when they first hear it, welcome the word with joy. But these have no root. They believe for a while, and in time of trial they give up.

"As for the part that fell into thorns, these are people who have heard, but, as they go on their way, they are choked by the worries and riches and pleasure of life and do not reach maturity.

"As for the part in the rich soil, these are people with a noble and generous heart who have heard the word and take it to themselves and yield a harvest through their perseverance."

All was quiet. But Jesus was not finished.

"No one lights a lamp to cover it with a bowl or to put it under a bed. No, he puts it on a lamp stand so that people may see the light when they come in. For nothing is hidden but it will be made clear, nothing secret but it will be known and brought to light.

"So take care how you hear, for anyone who has will be given more, or anyone who has not, even what he thinks he has will be taken away."

After this he stopped but this time he did not explain. The crowd broke up into small groups to discuss these teachings and Jesus left quietly.

Soon only our circle of friends was left and David led the discussion. "The parable of the sower can be applied to each one of us in this room as we hear the word of God from the Scriptures. Are we like the seed on the rock and do not let it take root? Or are we like the thorns and the seedlings smothered by the distractions and pleasures of life? Or does the seed find rich soil in us?

"This is about reading and hearing the Word of God, understanding it, making it a part of us and living it day by day."

"I like the parable of the lamp," said Abriam. "By the light, he must mean the Word of God, the wisdom we are learning and the love for others. Are we spreading this Word like a light on a post or are we hiding it within ourselves?

"And that last statement is very powerful — 'For anyone who has will be given more.' If one lives in the Word of God and spreads the Word, more will be received.

"Further, if we think that we know everything and do not try to learn more, if we do not spread the Word, we may lose it all!

"Of course, because of the hardness of their hearts, some who hear will not listen or understand. What a challenge Jesus has given to us!"

There was silence as every one of us considered our personal beliefs and our own actions in light of those beliefs. But I was still puzzled, certain there was more to the meaning of Jesus' last words. As Elisa and I walked home I remarked, "Jesus could not have been speaking about material possessions, because he is always telling us to give to those who don't have anything. He must mean something else." We walked on in silence.

As we neared home she stopped and spoke. "Joseph, I believe that he meant spiritual goods. If we develop spiritually, we continue to gain more and more in spiritual values. If we do not have any and do not try to get any, we lose everything.

"The lamp is a clear message to everyone who believes in the Word of God. It means that we should tell the world about God and not just keep it to ourselves."

Luke, working through the meaning of these parables is a rewarding experience, especially with my dear Elisa.

Joseph

---

[1]   2 Samuel 11:1-27, 12:1-15

Letter 58

Praise be to the Lord God of Israel.

Jesus has been teaching in the surrounding towns and villages the past week, and this time three of our group were among his followers. John, Esther and Miriam accompanied him. They returned today as we were closing the clinic for the day. They were tired and thirsty so we offered them some cold water from the well. We asked them to stay but they were eager to return to their own homes. "Tell us just one thing that happened," Elisa pleaded.

Esther exclaimed, "We met his mother!" Elisa's eyes sparkled. "What did she look like? What was she wearing?"

Miriam answered first, her voice rising and falling dramatically as she drew a picture with her words. "She wore a blue robe which covered her from her neck to her ankles. And her face! Her face bore an expression of such kindness, and she always had a pleasant smile. But," and she paused, "Elisa, I could sense that she was worried about her son. She appeared to be afraid that he will be hurt by someone who does not understand him."

John interrupted. "Don't you want to know how we happened to meet her? We had followed Jesus during his teaching sojourn to the town of Nain, which is near Nazareth. One afternoon he was preaching, and the lessons were much like those we had heard on the plain by the lake several weeks ago. The crowd was again very receptive.

"Suddenly someone pushed through the crowd toward Jesus, and I was prepared to stop him since I did not know whether he was planning to hurt him or not. But he called out, 'Jesus, your mother and brothers are standing outside and want to see you.'

"Jesus stopped abruptly and answered. 'My mother and brothers are those who hear the word of God and put it into practice.'"

Now Luke, I must explain to you that in our language we often refer to our cousins or distant relatives as our brothers and sisters, or just brethren.

"Then he excused himself," John continued, "followed the man outside and there found relatives from Nazareth. He embraced his mother, his aunts and cousins. As we had followed him, he then turned to introduce all of them to us. They were all glad to see him. We withdrew and let them have a private visit. Soon they were laughing and joking, and Jesus seemed to be enjoying himself."

"Were his brethren as tall as Jesus?" I asked.

"No, they are short like many in Galilee," John replied. Then he got up and suggested that it was time for them to leave.

As Elisa and I walked home, I finally voiced the question on my mind. "Why would he deny his family in front of a crowd after they had walked so far to see him?"

"Joseph," she replied, "he did not deny his brethren. He spent much time with them. But he wanted to impress upon everyone the value of a spiritual relationship.

"Don't you see? His family includes everyone who hears the Word of God and puts it into practice."

I could see she was right, Luke. As usual I was thinking in practical terms while Jesus was speaking in the spiritual realm.

Joseph

Letter 59

Now that you are studying the Hebrew Scriptures, dear Luke, you seem to be more interested in what I write you about Jesus, especially his new teachings. Yes, some of them seem radically different in our culture.

Today, the day after the Sabbath, our friends gathered to hear from John, Esther and Miriam about the week they had spent with Jesus. The first questions most of the women asked were about Mary the mother of Jesus. They wanted to know about her robes, her hair, the appearance of her hands and the type of sandals that she wore. But the men were growing impatient. Finally David broke in. "This is all well and good but I would like to hear what Jesus taught you during this time."

"He taught so much," Miriam said, "but his main topic was the importance of women in the history of the Tribe of Abraham."

"He taught about women all week?" someone asked.

"Yes, about how God had inspired women to fulfill His plans," replied Esther. "He used a sinful woman, a harlot named Rahab, to hide Joshua's spies,[1] then Ruth, the childless young widow of Moab, who accompanied her mother-in-law on her return to Judah and there found a new husband, later becoming the great-grandmother of King David."[2]

"And then there was Esther," Miriam said, "the Jewish wife of Ahasuerus, the king of Persia, who appealed to her husband to save the Jews from extinction at the hands of the evil Haman."[3]

Luke, the women went on and on and we men just listened and learned.

"I want you to know," Miriam ended with a flourish, "that it was a very joyful experience. Jesus seemed to keep the entire company cheerful and happy. As we walked we sang various songs, usually from the Psalms. I can see why the apostles just enjoy being with this great teacher."

"It really was an enjoyable and instructive week. But remember," John added, "Jesus can be very firm when the occasion demands. He does not stand for any foolishness or jokes that ridicule anyone."

The night was cool and the moon bright as Elisa and I left the clinic for home. Elisa remarked, "Wouldn't it be nice if everyone in every culture respected women as much as Jesus and the men in our group do?"

Luke, Jesus seems to be leading the men among his followers to a new perspective on the gifts that women offer.

This respect for women is among his most radical teachings.

Joseph

1   Joshua 2:1-24

2   Ruth 4:5-17

3   Esther 8

Letter 60

Dear Luke, we had an exhausting day at the clinic. We sutured wounds, fixed broken arms and treated more than a dozen with various illnesses. After such a day Elisa was too tired to prepare a meal. "Let us just eat some bread and cheese and go to bed," I said, and we set off for home.

As we came near, we heard voices and laughter from behind the house. Elisa recognized the voices and started to walk fast. Elisa said, "It is Jesus and The Twelve and I have no food in the house."

Jesus and his followers had been away from Capernaum for several weeks.

Jesus saw us approach and a wide grin appeared on his face. "Elisa," he said, "we thought that we would feed you tonight."

And Luke, feed us they did. They had brought fish, bread and lentils. They prepared everything over a fire in the grassy area between our home and the fruit orchard. They had laid a large cloth on the ground and the food was ready.

Jesus said, "Joseph, all we need is some of the delicious wine that your mother makes." And I brought out several wineskins full. All of this contributed to a joyful evening and delicious meal. Jesus kept everyone laughing. He and The Twelve did not let us do anything and even cleaned up after the meal. Then we gathered around the fire and sang songs. Jude has a fine bass voice. Young John sings tenor very well. So does James the son of Alphaeus. Smaller and more slender than John's brother, he is being called James the Lesser.

Some time later it became quiet and Jesus started to teach. He warned us not to spoil the pure faith of a child with the doubts of a man.

"Obstacles are sure to come, but alas for the one who provides them! It would be better for him to be thrown into the sea with a millstone put round his neck than he should lead astray a single one of these little ones. Watch yourselves!"

Jesus then looked at all of us in the group, one at a time, and said, "If your brother does something wrong, reprove him, and if he is sorry, forgive him." Several among us nodded at that.

"And if he wrongs you seven times a day, and seven times comes back and says, 'I am sorry,' you must forgive him." Now, that was a lot harder to take. Several of the disciples had some difficulty with it and marveled that Jesus could be so forgiving.

Andrew spoke for all the others. "Increase our faith," he pleaded.

Jesus admonished them. "Were your faith the size of a mustard seed you could say to this mulberry tree, 'Be uprooted and planted in the sea,' and it would obey you."

With that, Jesus got up, thanked us for the use of our land, and we thanked all of them for dinner. And The Twelve left with him.

Joseph

Letter 61

Greetings to my friend and fellow physician.

Erasmus, Elisa and I have a number of fishermen among our patients. Fishing is a major industry along the Sea of Galilee. These men are very strong because they spend so much time rowing boats and throwing nets. But in recent weeks several have come in complaining of pain in the lower part of their backs after long hours on the water. As you know, Luke, we are always inquisitive about the cause of ailments. We discussed this development and determined to identify the cause. I discussed the idea with Aaron, who had purchased the fishing boat from Simon, and suggested that I go out with him and his crew as an oarsman and observe. He agreed, but warned me that I might get sick if a squall came up. I did not tell him that I had spent many days on a boat going to and from Athens.

The next afternoon Aaron sent a message that they were going to cross the lake and they could use my help.

I returned with the messenger to the boat dock and, to my surprise, found Jesus and The Twelve there prepared for a journey. Aaron asked Simon to take the helm and explained why I was on board. The sea was calm, there was no wind, the sky was clear. It was clear that if we wanted to get anywhere we would have to row. As I sat down to take the oar, I noticed that the plank seat and the brace for the feet were not as comfortable as the ones I had used going to Athens. Everyone on the boat watched me as I picked up the oar.

"Mighty big scalpel you have there, Joseph," Jesus remarked with a smile. As we shoved off I started to row with a steady methodical rhythm. Everyone who had been watching me was very surprised. Simon called out, "Joseph, where did you learn how to row a skiff?"

I answered in between strokes, "How else do you think I got to Athens to study medicine? That was a much larger boat and I rowed for days." Everyone laughed.

As the time passed, even Jesus took a turn at the oars. I could see that he used the smooth motions of an experienced oarsman too. I wonder where he had learned the technique.

My shoulder and arm muscles grew tired as I responded to the steady count of the helmsman. But I noted further that the lower part of my back had started to hurt. I felt a strain with every stroke. But I continued to row until it was my turn to be relieved.

Then I went to Aaron and informed him I felt the cause of the back pain was that the seat was too low. He replied, "I lowered those planks because the short oarsmen could not reach the studs where they brace their feet." I realized that the fishermen who came in complaining of backaches were tall. We had no complainers who were of short stature.

"Could you give me two blocks of wood," I asked, "in order that I might sit higher during my next turn?" Aaron agreed, and soon found small blocks of wood that could fit. When my next turn to row came I tried the now-elevated seat and I did not feel the back strain.

I asked Jesus if his back had hurt and he said that it does whenever he rows this skiff. I asked him to try sitting higher, and when he did he also was able to row without a strain.

Soon, a brisk wind came up and with it our spirits. Simon ordered that the sail be raised and everyone should pull in the oars. It was as if he'd never been away. He relished being in command again, barking out orders, watching the wind and the sails, even letting the boat heel a little to make it go faster. Luke, we had a glorious time just skimming over the water by the power of the wind alone. I wished that Elisa could be with me. I resolved that someday we would have the opportunity to experience this together.

The sailing was so smooth that Jesus lay down and fell asleep. Simon spoke to me. "Jesus must be tired. He spent all night in prayer again. Do you think he gets enough sleep?" I shook my head. "I doubt if he does, but he does always seem fresh and alert. Some people require less sleep than…"

Before I could finish, the wind suddenly shifted and the boat began to list dangerously. Simon ordered the sail down, and the experienced boatmen began to strap down everything that was loose. Simon was shouting orders, but thunder and the roar of the wind drowned out the commands. Soon everything was secure and we were all holding onto something solid.

Then the rain came with the wind, driving it almost horizontally. I had been in squalls before on the Aegean Sea but this was worse. The boat rocked from side to side and up and down. The bow would rise on a swell and almost point straight up and then suddenly slap back down as a great wave broke over the boat. We were soon soaked and the boat began to take on water. We held on with one hand and scooped water out with the other, using hands, buckets or anything handy.

Luke, I must admit I was frightened. I felt little hope this small vessel with eighteen men in it would hold out in such a storm.

Throughout all this, Jesus was still asleep.

But even Simon was shaken by now, and he motioned to the disciples nearest Jesus to awaken him. "Master, Master, we are going down," they cried. The water now filled half the boat.

Jesus sat up, saw that he was soaked from head to foot, and looked around at the rest of us. Then he steadied himself on the bow, stood up and rebuked the wind and the rough seas.

The thunder ceased that instant and the sea became still. We looked about in wonder.

Then Jesus admonished us. "Where is your faith?" He settled back on his cushion and went to sleep.

The other crewmen shook their heads as they dipped water out of the boat. "Who can this be who gives orders to winds and waters and they obey?"

Then we took to the oars again. I sat on my extra two pieces of wood and had no further backache. Rowing is hard work. I hoped that there would be a little breeze, but I did not want to ask Jesus for that favor. I was too thankful to be alive.

Soon we docked. Simon awakened Jesus and we all thanked him for saving our lives. He smiled, stretched his arms and legs, and said, "Thank you for the rest. That is just what I needed."

We had landed in Genesareth, across the Sea of Galilee from Capernaum. A large herd of pigs was calmly grazing on the side of the mountain near the shore. We all stepped on land. Just then a naked man came screaming toward the boat.

I had heard there was a man possessed by devils in this area. He wears no clothes and does not live in a house but lives among the tombs. The authorities of the area have tried to secure him with chains and fetter, but he always breaks out of the fastenings and runs into the wilds as if driven by the devil. It must take tremendous strength to break the chains.

Luke, here he was coming towards us, shouting and screaming, his long hair full of sticks and grass. His face and skin are scarred from bruises that he has received in demonic attacks. His feet are large and the soles very thick. It was obvious that he had not bathed for years.

As he caught sight of Jesus, he gave a shout and fell at his feet and cried out at the top of his voice, "What do you want of me, Jesus, Son of the Most High God? I implore you, do not torture me."

Now, Luke, I do not know much about demonic possession, but how could this man know of Jesus unless some supernatural powers told him? No one knew that we were coming to this area, yet this wild man seemed to recognize him.

"What is your name?" Jesus asked.

"Legion," the man replied. And we could hear many different voices coming from the man pleading with Jesus not to order them into the abyss.

Then another most unusual thing happened. The voices began to plead with Jesus to send them into the pigs. Jesus nodded and suddenly the voices stopped and the man ceased to shout. He became still. He pulled up some large leaves to cover his nakedness and sat at the feet of Jesus. But the pigs suddenly started to charge forward at unnatural speed. They ran as if they were being pulled by something. They ran off the cliff into the lake and drowned.

The swine herders watched from the field in wonder. Then they ran and told the story to the people in the countryside and the town. In the meantime, the man who had been possessed walked into the Sea of Galilee to wash himself. A few of us from the boat gave him some of our garments in order to cover his nakedness.

Luke, Dividimus taught us that science is the cause and explanation of everything, that everything we know must be felt, heard, smelled, seen or tasted. However, in our work with Abraham, Elisa and I were shown there are some things we cannot explain with our present state of knowledge. None of what I had just witnessed can be explained by science.

Jesus moved to sit in the shade of a tree and play with children who had come to see the boat. He was laughing and telling them stories, and each one wanted to sit on his lap.

It had not rained on this side of the lake. Simon and Andrew took out some of the fish that had washed into the boat with the storm. John collected some sticks and made a fire, and we all gathered around.

There was a cool wind off shore and the sun was low in the sky. The former wild man ate five fish. I am sure that he had not eaten for a long time.

Then a number of townspeople appeared, alerted by the herders who had left in a panic. They charged into our circle to see for themselves the man they had put in chains. He was sitting calmly at the feet of Jesus and eating, fully clothed and in possession of his senses.

The mothers of the children had also arrived. I could see that they were alarmed and afraid for their children. As other townspeople arrived, the story of the demons was told and retold, and soon it seemed that the entire population of Genesareth was in a state of panic, as if they were afraid the demons would return. They implored us, "Leave, please leave."

But Jesus only smiled at them. As we started toward the boat, he took the time to say goodbye to each child by name.

The man no longer possessed asked to be allowed to leave with Jesus, but was sent away. "Go back home," Jesus said, "and report all that God has done for you."

As we shoved off, the townspeople, still upset, threw rocks at the boat. It angered me and I picked one up to throw back. But Jesus held my arm. "Joseph, they do not understand, forgive them." He went to the bow of the boat to enjoy the breeze while he hummed a tune. He seemed very happy.

Now we had the steady breeze that I had wished for earlier. It did not take long to return to Capernaum. We watched the sun set behind the western hills as we clambered ashore. I thanked Aaron and told him that a couple of blocks of wood on the plank would save their taller oarsmen from a backache. I turned to thank Jesus, but he was gone.

Joseph

Letter 62

Luke, you have asked me about the people Jesus has healed. Are the cures permanent? Yes, Elisa and I have been watching these patients closely.

We see the mother-in-law of Simon almost daily because she often helps some of the infirm walk to the clinic. She is completely well. Elisa has examined her several times and she has absolutely no lingering effects of "right-sided fever." The leper that Jesus cured now has a leather shop in Capernaum and there is no sign of the dreaded disease. The paralytic has learned the trade of a carpenter and I see him working on houses throughout Capernaum. You asked about the man with the withered hand. He, of all people, has obtained a job as a fisherman with Aaron, the man who bought Simon's boat. He was on the stormy cruise with us several days ago. I have also heard from reliable sources that the centurion's servant and the widow's son are well and working. The cures seem to be complete and permanent. But I understand your disbelief and suggest that the only way you can truly realize the power of this man Jesus is to come and observe him yourself.

But today I have more to tell you about Jesus, and both stories are astonishing.

He has returned from visits to the small towns around the Sea of Galilee. Elisa and I joined the followers who gathered to welcome him back, and he embraced a good number of us.

Suddenly, a man pushed through the crowd. I recognized him as Jairus, an official of the synagogue. I had just returned from a visit to his home to see his twelve-year-old daughter. She had a simple sore throat about two weeks ago, the kind that leaves most children in two to three days. But hers did not. I saw her at home about one week later with very inflamed joints, red and hot. She had a high fever, her heart was beating rapidly and she was beginning to get short of breath.[1] In fact, she wheezed and had rattles in her chest when she breathed like some of our old folks with dropsy.

Luke, I called Elisa and Erasmus in consultation. The only diagnosis that we could come up with was an inflammatory rheumatism that affects the heart.

I could thump my finger on her chest and by the change of the sound tell the outline of the heart. It grew larger every day. In fact, this morning it was half the size of her little chest. I could hear the bubbles in her lungs and also wheezing when she breathed. She coughed constantly. We placed more pillows under her head so that she could breathe.

"Jairus," I said, "I know of no physician who has any medicine that would help her." Of course they were shocked, but I continued. "My friend Jesus has performed cures that I never expected. I know how all of you at the synagogue feel about him, but he is your only help that I know." Luke, I too was depressed, and we all three cried together, as the girl continued to cough and wheeze. This was not a very good morning, Luke.

As soon as I recognized Jairus in the crowd, we made our way to his side and together we approached Jesus. Jairus fell down on his knees and pleaded. "Please, Master," he said. "Please come to my home and cure my daughter. There is nothing that the physicians can do. Ask Joseph here. He just left my home and suggested that you could help. Please come. She is my only daughter and is dying." Jesus looked at me and I nodded to confirm everything that he said. Jesus lifted Jairus up from his knees and started to make his way through the crowd following him.

However, I noticed another one of our patients forcing her way toward Jesus. She is a woman who has had a blood flow for twelve years.[2] She had even seen Abraham of Jerusalem and he was unable to cure her condition. She came to Elisa recently and after reviewing all of the things that had been done for her, Elisa told her that everything had been tried and there was nothing that could be done. But she added that Jesus has cured many of those we have found incurable.

I watched the woman as she reached Jesus, knelt down behind him and touched the fringe of his garment. I could see relief on her face. I found out later that the hemorrhage stopped at that instant. Jesus halted and asked, "Who touched me?" But no one around seemed to know. Simon and his companions said, "Master, it is the crowds around you, pushing." But Jesus persisted. "Somebody touched me. I felt that power had gone out from me."

Seeing herself discovered, the woman came forward trembling and fell at his feet. She explained in front of all the people why she had touched him and that she knew she had been cured at that very moment.

"My daughter," he said, "your faith has restored you to health. Go in peace."

Luke, this woman had so much faith in Jesus that she dared to touch his cloak. As you know, in our culture women are made to feel dirty, unwanted and unclean when they have a bloody flow. It is considered such a curse.

It is easy to recognize a woman who has an issue of blood when she

---

Capernaum

comes to the clinic. She always finds a place to wait away from someone else. In our religious tradition, cleanliness is holiness, and touching human blood makes us unclean.

Can you imagine how a woman must feel? For half of her life she bleeds for a few days at monthly intervals. During this time she is to be shunned. After childbirth she must go through the ritual of cleansing at a prescribed time in order to be accepted back into the community.

Elisa and I have talked this over and we feel that the laws of cleanliness are basically good, but the monthly flow of blood and some bleeding after childbirth are part of the normal body function of a woman and should not be considered unclean.

I could see that Jairus was fidgeting at this delay and anxious to get started again. But just then, someone arrived from his household. He had a stricken look on his face. "Sir, your daughter has died. Do not trouble the Master any further."

Jesus overheard this and turned to Jairus. "Do not be afraid," he said. "Only have faith and she will be safe."

The synagogue official nodded through his tears. Elisa and I held him by the arms as we walked. The crowd had heard the words of Jesus and began to talk amongst themselves. "What's the use of going?" "Why is Jesus going to see a dead girl?" But no one was willing to break away.

As we reached the house of Jairus we saw that it was full of friends of the family. All were mourning. We walked in and spoke to the child's mother, who was weeping profusely.

"Where is the girl?" Jesus asked.

Friends pointed upstairs to the room. Jesus went upstairs and Jairus, his wife, Simon, John, James, Elisa and I followed. A servant opened the door and the room was filled with mourners. Jesus politely but firmly asked them all to leave, and they did so reluctantly. He turned to the parents and said, "Stop crying. She is not dead, but asleep."

Luke, by this time I had, as is my custom, checked the girl. Her pupils were dilated and fixed. She was not breathing and there was no pulse in the hand that I was holding. She was dead.

Jairus and his wife could not believe the words of Jesus. The people at the door started to laugh because they knew that the girl was dead. But Jesus just walked up to the girl, took her other hand and called to her.

"Child, get up."

And Luke, while I was holding her hand, her pulse returned, a pink color came over her skin and she started to breathe.

She opened her eyes, sat up and rose from her bed. Jesus led her to her parents and said, "I believe this young lady is hungry. Give her something to eat."

Luke, there were no more swollen joints, no cough, shortness of breath or wheezing. She was a girl in good health who only a few seconds before had been dead. I examined her. The heart was normal in size and there were no bubbles in her chest.

Jesus ordered Jairus and his wife not to tell anyone what had happened. He also looked meaningfully at the five of us — Simon, James, John, Elisa and me. We all nodded. Then Jesus stepped out of the room into the crowd, who were still in mourning. Then the parents walked out with the girl. Everyone was astounded. I looked for Jesus but he was gone.

One of our patients came to Elisa and started to ask what had happened, and then the mother asked the maidservant to bring the girl something to eat. Everyone was astounded. Just then the girl became aware of the crowd of people in the house. She asked her mother, "Are we having a party?" And her mother answered, "Yes, to celebrate your recovery from a serious illness."

Luke, Elisa and I today were privileged to witness two cures. It is difficult to believe what we know to be the truth.

May God in all of his infinite knowledge watch over you, Luke, and direct all of us in our search for divine guidance.

Joseph

[1] Rheumatic fever starts as a sore throat and makes the joints hurt. It also affects the heart by damaging the valves and occasionally causes an inflammation of the heart. This may cause it to dilate and may lead to accumulation of fluid and blood in the lungs, which is called congestive heart failure. This condition usually leads to death. Antibiotics have practically eliminated this disease.

[2] Menorrhagia or excessive and prolonged menstruation.

Letter 63

Luke, Jesus and his followers have spent the last week teaching in the surrounding villages. They came back about the sixth hour today. We received a message that Jesus would like to meet at our clinic with his followers this evening.

His teaching was the book of Ecclesiastes, and how it shows that life is not always predictable, that one has to trust God without the consolation of understanding His purpose or meaning. This book urges us to be faithful even when we are frustrated, depressed or just tired. And then he quoted the last words of the book, "Fear God and keep his commandments since this is the whole duty of man. For God will call all hidden deeds, good or bad, to judgment."[1]

As Jesus finished he looked around the room and summoned The Twelve to come forward. He called each by name: Simon. Andrew. James the Greater. John. Philip. Bartholomew. Matthew. Thomas. James the Lesser. Simon. Jude. And Judas Iscariot.

"I now give you power and authority over devils and to cure diseases," he said. "I send you out to proclaim the kingdom of God and to heal."

He paused a moment. "Take nothing for the journey, neither staff, nor haversack, nor bread nor money, and let none of you take a spare tunic.

"Whatever house you enter, stay there, and when you leave, let it be from there. As for those who do not welcome you, when you leave their town," he said, calling to mind what every Jew does when leaving Gentile territory, "shake the dust from your feet as a sign to them."

All was quiet in the room. The twelve men before us were rather surprised at the commission that had been given them. They are to set out in the morning and go from village to village proclaiming the good news of the kingdom of God and healing people everywhere.

Then Jesus rose, thanked Elisa for the hospitality and departed, with the apostles following one by one. The rest of the followers were quiet for only a few moments. "Jesus commissioned these men to do his work," someone said. "He must have great confidence in them to grant them these powers." But it was already late and people gradually departed.

As we walked home, I kept to myself my first reaction on watching Jesus confer power on The Twelve. I had begun to follow Jesus in order to learn his technique of healing, and today he gave to twelve other men — none of whom has any medical training — authority over the devil and the ability to cure illnesses.

I did voice my second, less selfish, reaction. "I am happy for The Twelve. They have been training for this by listening to teachings of Jesus all of these weeks.

"But he wants them to travel without any provisions and depend upon the charity of the people for their very existence," I said. "What if they are rejected?"

Elisa took my hand to reassure me. "Jesus tells them not to react with violence. The disciples are just to leave the town. If the people refuse to believe the truth that is given to them, it is their own fault.

"And his instruction not to take any provisions must mean the apostles are to live on the gifts of others. They must not concentrate upon their individual needs. Their mission is to spread the Word of God, and they cannot make a profit from their efforts. They must depend upon food and shelter from the people to whom they speak."

After we entered the house she added, "Jesus told us that we would learn more in time, and so we are doing."

Joseph

1   Ecclesiastes 12:13-14

Letter 64

Grace and peace be yours from the Lord God of Israel.

Today Joanna, wife of Chuza, a steward of Herod, came to the clinic at about the tenth hour. Like other followers of Jesus, she spends time sitting at his feet, listening and learning. She stays with us or with Esther when Jesus is in Capernaum. After that she returns to be with her husband in Herod's palace.

Joanna arrived looking exhausted, as if she had been running a great distance. Her hair was wet and matted and her clothing soaked with sweat and discolored from the dust of the road.

Elisa and Judith gave her water and fanned her. Judith asked, "Joanna, why have you run so hard?" Finally Joanna caught her breath and was able to speak.

"Herod has arrested John," she said, "and has had him put into prison!"

"Why? Why would he do that?" Judith exclaimed.

"Well," Joanna answered, "it's Herodias, his wife. Herod married her while she was his brother Herod Philip's wife, and this is against the Law of God. John has never stopped preaching about the sinfulness of their marriage. Herodias is furious that Herod has not had John silenced. I heard her screaming at Herod, calling him all kinds of names, until finally he ordered John arrested and put in prison.

"But this, I am afraid, is not enough for Herodias. She wants to have him killed. Herod has him in prison, where he is safe for now. He knows that John is a good and holy man and has given him protection. John is in prison and there is no way that we can get him out." She finished and drank some more water.

Elisa and Judith took her into a quiet room to let her rest. I sent a messenger to summon other friends of Joanna. Judith and Abriam decided to accompany her back to Herod's palace to help her comfort John. Samson would go to notify Jesus. We all prayed that John would be released unharmed.

One week later Judith and Abriam returned. They had been to see John daily. He was well cared for and was able to preach to the guards. They said that often when he was preaching, they thought they saw a figure listening attentively but staying in the shadows. Once, they stationed themselves closer to the shadows and were able to recognize the figure. It was Herod himself. He listened intently and often appeared to nod in approval. But as he left, he seemed perplexed. Still, he kept coming back to listen.

Joanna had told them that Herodias continued to be angry over John, but Herod would not give in to her. She taunted Herod. "You are afraid of a barefoot man who has no sword or knife. And you call yourself the king of Galilee! A soft king you are. An ant could push you over." Joanna reported that Herodias stormed through the castle but Herod held out. And John's disciples were keeping watch at the prison.

Luke, I wonder who will win this dispute, Herod or his vicious wife. And the sad part of it is that the life of John is the pawn in this great domestic battle. Jesus called John a messenger preparing the way. "Of all the children born of women, there is no one greater than John," he said.

John is right. Herodias is wrong. And Herod knows it. He just does not have the will to stand up to his wife.

May the Lord God of Israel protect John.

Joseph

Letter 65

Two weeks have passed, Luke, since Jesus sent The Twelve out to teach and heal. Jesus has dropped into the clinic twice and stayed a few minutes, but spent the rest of the time in the woods in prayer.

Late yesterday the apostles returned to town, two by two. They came to our home to ask where they might find Jesus. Luke, believe me, they were all changed men. The wonder of their experiences was on their faces.

Simon expressed it best. "We did just what Jesus told us. We carried no staff, no haversack, or bread or money, but people took us in their homes and fed us well. We were able to cure the ill and proclaim the kingdom of God. People listened to us. Andrew and I visited one town where every person came out to see and hear us. First we healed the sick, but then we repeated all of the teachings of Jesus."

"It was the same with John and with me," said James the son of Zebedee. "The words we needed just came to us when we talked about the kingdom of God."

"Philip and I healed a woman who was crippled," said Bartholomew. "We were amazed at the hunger these people have for the word of God. We also sang the Psalms with everyone."

"Thomas and I felt inspired all of the time," said Matthew. "In fact, we felt that to sleep was wasting time."

"James and I," said Jude, "did all of this in the name of God, and the sick were healed as we touched them."

Finally, Simon the zealot spoke. "For the first time, Judas Iscariot, our treasurer, did not have to part with money. We were well fed as we preached and cured."

So it went, Luke. The Twelve had a spirited reunion.

Elisa and I fixed them some food. As they were eating, Jesus arrived and the greetings were loud and joyful. Everyone talked at once and Jesus was pleased.

Finally Jesus also sat down to eat. When he finished, he said to the apostles, "Come with me to my place in the woods to thank my Father for such a successful mission. In the morning we will leave for Judea." They all thanked us and left.

As Elisa and I stood at the door and watched them depart, we held hands in silence.

"What a blessing God has given us," Elisa said, "to be able to experience this. And He has blessed us in many other ways. We have each other and our parents are here and well. But above all He has given us the opportunity to have this relationship with Jesus."

She stopped and then added, as if she could see what lies ahead for us, "To whom much is given, much is expected!"

Joseph

Letter 66

Luke, the past two weeks have been the most trying time since Elisa and I became physicians. We have had an epidemic of what we call "inflammation of the lung."[1] The patients suddenly develop a chill and become hot all over. They complain of a pain in the chest, which is worse when they take a deep breath. They develop a cough and produce pink sputum. At least one in three patients dies. We have noticed that infants and older folks die more often than patients who are better fed, younger and healthier.

We have had an occasional case here previously but this has changed.

A few weeks ago Elisa saw her first case this season, gave him the medications we have been using and sent him home. I went out to see him everyday. His fever became higher. At first he had a dry cough but later he started to cough up a bloody material. He died within a week. The condition seemed to spread through Capernaum and soon we had many cases.

We have tried all types of medication and applied hot poultices and mustard plasters on the chest. We do everything, but they continue along the same course. The patients continue with a hot skin, perspire tremendously, cough constantly and lose weight. We have found that we must get liquids into these patients and that we must keep the fever down. Sponging them off with cool water seems to be the best way.

In those patients who do recover, the fever drops suddenly, the sputum changes from being bloody to one of a darkened character and the patient starts to eat. We have noticed that this recovery is sudden. Everything seems to happen at once. Luke, this crisis often occurs on alternate days, either the fifth day, the seventh day, the ninth day or the eleventh day. I often have gone to the home in the morning and after examining the patient have told the family the patient may die soon. But the temperature would drop during that night and there would be marked improvement. I could not explain this with our treatment. Some people would get well, others not.

Elisa, Erasmus and I discuss our cases every day. Elisa once said, "Do you suppose there is something in the air that causes this, something that gets into the tissue of the patient and produces the condition? If we could just see what that something is."

We have found that bloodletting is not the best treatment for this condition. In fact, every time that we tried to let blood from a patient, he died very quickly. Erasmus had been trained in bloodletting but in learning of these findings, he was quick to adopt our method.

There is another thing we have noticed, Luke. The patients, of course, lose a great deal of weight. Typically we can see their ribs and a depression between each of the ribs, and most of them complain of pain when they breathe. However, occasionally there is a bulging between the ribs.

One day, I had some of the people attending a patient hold him while I incised the skin in this area and inserted a hollow tube in the chest. Yellow pus gushed out.[2] I went back the next day and the patient was better, and again I drained the chest. I continued to do it until the patient got well.

Luke, it has been a difficult time. We try to get adequate rest ourselves as those who are tired seem more susceptible to the illness. Sabbath services and our meetings at the clinic have been suspended. We do hope the epidemic will end soon.

Jesus has been away teaching somewhere in Judea. He had sent the apostles out to teach and cure and we have not heard from any of them. We are eager to have him back and we hope that he will help us and cure this condition. But his cures have been specifically in a few people. I will beg him to help us as soon as I can.

Please pray for the people of Capernaum, Luke.

Joseph

[1] Lobar pneumonia, the infection of one or more sections of the lung caused by the Diplococcus pneumoniae. Antibiotics developed in the 1930s have resulted in cures for most of the patients.

[2] Pus develops between the lung and the chest wall.

Letter 67

Luke, we almost lost Jesus to the epidemic.

He and The Twelve returned to Capernaum nearly four weeks ago, and a few nights later Simon came to our door. "Elisa and Joseph, please come," he said. "Jesus is very sick."

We hurried to their campsite, which was just outside of town. We were horrified when we saw Jesus. He was mumbling, breathing rapidly, coughing and producing tremendous amounts of frothy, bloody sputum. His heart was beating rapidly, his skin was hot and dry and his tongue was parched. He was covered with a robe and yet he was shivering. We each examined him and heard a dull sound at the base of the right lung when we thumped the chest. We looked at each other and knew that Jesus had inflammation of the lungs and it was an advanced case.

Luke, my first thought was that if he cured others, why doesn't he cure himself? But I didn't voice the thought. I said, "Jesus, you are sick. You need to stay inside. You cannot stay outdoors."

Elisa added, "You have inflammation of the lungs. We have had an epidemic of it here and almost one-third of the patients die. If you stay out here in the woods, I know you will die. We have to take you in and take care of you." He was too weak to resist. By this time he was so spent and shivering that he couldn't walk.

We improvised a litter out of a couple of robes. Simon, James, John and I carried him into town. We took him to the home of Esther and John. I knew they had a large home that was mostly empty. It was late at night when we knocked at the door. "Esther," Elisa said, "Jesus is desperately ill. We found him out in the woods. I know that he will die if he is left there. Will you keep him in your home?" Graciously, Esther and John welcomed us in. They aroused a servant, and we put Jesus to bed in a spare room.

We went back to our clinic and gathered all of the medications that we could find, including something to purge him. Esther, her servant and I spent the night trying to cool Jesus' skin by washing him with tepid water. I gave him what medications we have and sent Elisa home so that she could care for other patients in the morning. Jesus had a very difficult night, and it seemed that he was getting sicker by the hour.

In the morning I went back home, told Elisa what was going on and lay down to rest. I made my calls on other patients in the afternoon. Elisa went in the afternoon to see Jesus, whose illness was progressing like that of so many of the other patients. His skin was hot and he continued to cough up bloody sputum.

By this time, we had alerted many of the followers of Jesus. They organized themselves to take turns at his side, each to care for him for four hours at a time. Among them were Ana, Miriam, Ruth, Judith and Abriam, Eliab and Naomi, Rachel and David. Others were ill themselves or tending family members. The disciples also took their turn attending Jesus. Fortunately, none of them became ill.

I would go to Jesus in the morning, Elisa would go in the afternoon and we would both go in the evening. Occasionally Erasmus would come and examine him. We always appreciated the advice he gave us.

Jesus' condition worsened. We continued to give him fluids so that he didn't dry up as so many others did. However, he was just too sick to eat. The cough continued and the fourth day passed. We waited through the fifth day, but there was no crisis. Many times I thought of the cures Jesus had performed.

We continued through the seventh day, praying for the crisis that might signal his recovery. Jesus, who had been able to speak a little at first, had fallen unconscious by now. He had a high fever and was delirious.

On the morning of the ninth day, I told Elisa, "Let's hope that this day he will have his crisis and recover." But when I arrived I could see that he was still desperately sick. There was no bulging of the muscles of the chest. The sounds I had heard in the chest were unchanged.

When Elisa returned to the clinic in the afternoon, I asked her anxiously if there had been any change. "No," she said wearily. And that night when we checked him, there was still no change. I could see that the caregivers were also getting worn out. We were very anxious about this special patient of ours. The tenth day passed and the morning of the eleventh day came. Again no improvement. I was sore at heart for I did not think Jesus could last much longer. His breathing was still rapid, he was still coughing up frothy sputum and his skin was still hot. He was constantly being sponged in an effort to cool him off. We could not get enough fluid into him. There was no change in the sounds of his lungs. We all prayed to God that this special man would recover.

I came back and told Elisa, "This is the eleventh day and I don't think he will make it." She left for the home of Esther and John prepared to spend the afternoon. But she came back late that afternoon rejoicing. "Jesus had his crisis! He is going to get well!"

While she was there, the temperature of his skin dropped, his heart rate slowed and the character of the sputum that he coughed up changed. He opened his eyes and he spoke clearly. We thanked God that he was recovering and rejoiced with all of his followers.

When we returned that evening, Jesus was sitting up and talking clearly. There was no bulging in his chest, a good sign. The dullness and loud breath sounds were still there, but he was able to take food for the first time since he had fallen ill. I instructed all the caregivers to feed him so he could gradually regain his strength. Jesus had been in bed for so long that he needed support even to sit up.

I sat down and explained everything that had happened to him during the last eleven days. He had only fleeting memories of people coming and going and of feeling parched. He thanked everyone for taking such good care of him and reacted like most patients do — he was impatient to get well.

"I will be able to go about my duties soon," he said.

"Jesus, you are too weak and it is going to take you several weeks to regain all your strength."

"Joseph, I am young. I can do it. I must be about my father's business."

But it didn't take him long to realize that I was right. He had not the strength to feed himself, much less to stand and walk.

"Jesus," I said, "you have cured many people and why you didn't cure yourself, I do not know. You have been desperately ill and it is going to take you a long time to get your strength back. You are going to have to do what we tell you."

"Joseph," he replied, "I know that you are right and I will try to be a good patient." And, Luke, he has been. He thanks everybody for everything. He doesn't want to be much of a bother and tries to do as much as he can for himself.

Of course, the disciples and his caregivers praised God that Jesus had recovered. During the entire illness, there had been constant prayers rising to God. Judith and Abriam had organized a prayer vigil, and others spent many hours individually in prayer.

After about a week, Jesus was able to walk by himself. It may be a month before he is really able to resume his activity, but he is recovering more quickly than I had expected. He had lost much weight, but he seems to be regaining this by the extra food brought in by many of his followers. And Esther and John are noted for the generosity with which they feed their guests. Jesus is already planning to set off with The Twelve for Bethsaida and Chorazin.

Erasmus, Elisa and I are exhausted. This epidemic is more than six weeks long and we have been going day and night. I still insist that Elisa get her afternoon rest and I pray that she does not fall ill with consumption again. It is almost a miracle that none of us who took care of Jesus have come down with the inflammation of the lungs.

Luke, I have learned one thing through this trying time. Jesus may have a very close relationship to God, he may cure people and bring the dead to life, but he is human and subject to the same illnesses as the rest of us.

Joseph

Letter 68

Thank the Lord God of Israel. The epidemic is over.

Luke, I insisted that Elisa rest for several days after Jesus recovered. This has been very tiring for her. But there is other unsettling news to share.

Joanna, the wife of Herod's steward Chuza, rushed into the clinic today. She was disheveled and breathless. "Herod has beheaded John!" she exclaimed. "Herod beheaded John!"

Hannah and Samson were at the clinic, having just told us Jesus was away in prayer. In our shock, it took some time for the five of us to calm her down and listen, but here is how the story unfolded.

For his birthday, Herod held a banquet for the nobles of his court, his army officers and the leading citizens of Galilee. Chuza and Joanna were in attendance. There was much food and wine. Many of the guests had heard that Herodias was preparing a surprise for Herod. Suddenly, there was a blare of trumpets, a ruffle of drums, and out from behind the curtains came the daughter of Herodias in a dance of many veils.

"I hate to say this," Joanna said, "but Salome put on a very good dance. When she had finished, applause thundered from the guests. Herod, of course, was delighted that his guests were so pleased. As the girl took her last bow before him, he called out to her. 'Ask me anything you like and I will give it to you. On my oath, I will give you anything you ask, even to half my kingdom.'

"The girl turned to her mother, who was seated near me. 'What should I ask for?' she whispered. 'The head of John the Baptist' was the reply. I was shocked when I heard this and ran toward the girl to stop her, but she darted up to Herod and made her request boldly.

"'I want you to give me the head of John the Baptist, here and now, on a dish.'

"Herod was stunned. His face turned pale. He looked around as if for help but no one moved. Herodias had by now resumed her seat beside him. As he looked into her stony face, she nodded in satisfaction.

"Herod seemed frantic. He looked over the gathering, and all his guests, who shortly before had been loud and boisterous, fell silent. The nobles, the officers — all were looking at him. No one moved.

"Sweat began to run down Herod's cheeks and his face grew red with anger. He waved his robes as if he were hot, but did not move.

"Herodias whispered to him fiercely, 'You gave an oath. You must do it. You cannot break your word in front of all these guests. Or are you the mouse that I said you were?'

"Finally the king motioned to one of his bodyguards. 'Go at once and bring me the head of John on a plate.' The hall was still silent. The face of Herodias now beamed in victory. The girl waited.

"Finally the guard reappeared. He had the head of John on a dish. Herod gave it to Salome, who turned and gave it to her mother.

"Friends," Joanna continued, "I wanted to scream 'Murderer! Murderess!' to Herod and Herodias, but my husband restrained me. And he was right. It would have done no good. But the banquet was over. The guests, their faces grim, rushed out without thanking Herod for the meal, as if to distance themselves from what he had done.

"Herod stood up and moved to the curtains. With a sagging head and mottled face, he left the banquet chamber. I burst out in tears and so did others who had heard John speak. We were saddened beyond belief.

"We went to the prison. Some of John's apostles were already there. They had wrapped up his body, and we left together to place it in a tomb."

The five of us sat in silence when she had finished. Hannah and Samson, burdened with the news, left to seek Simon or one of the other apostles. Joanna will stay with us for a few days until she can recover some of her composure. The shock of witnessing all of that had a great effect on her.

Luke, we have lost a great man of God.

Joseph

Letter 69

Luke, the news of the beheading of John shocked the friends and followers of Jesus. He has been out of the city teaching. It would have been good to have him here to comfort us and explain how this could be God's will.

Joanna stayed with us about a week. Elisa spent hours listening to her and counseling her. Judith and Abriam accompanied her when she felt ready to return to her home and husband, Chuza.

After their return they gave us more news about Herod. Word had come to Herod at court about Jesus and all of the cures that he had performed, and this confounded him. Some people were saying that John had risen from the dead, while others said that Elijah had reappeared, and still others told him that one of the ancient prophets had come back to life.

"John I beheaded," Herod said. "So who is this I hear such reports about?" He told his court that he wanted to meet this man Jesus. But Chuza kept his silence.

We were all disturbed about this threat to Jesus. Ruth asked, "Do you think that Jesus knows of the beheading of John and of his own danger?"

"The news of John's beheading will spread all over Galilee shortly," Elisa replied. "He will hear of it wherever he is teaching. We must pray that Herod does not imprison Jesus."

And so dear Luke, Jesus may be in peril, as Erasmus once predicted.

We pray that he may escape the fate of John and many of the earlier prophets.

Joseph

Letter 70

Luke, our workload is increasing rapidly as word spreads of Elisa's talents. She gets the complete confidence of the patient and thereby gets a very detailed history of the illness. She learns about other problems occurring in the patient's life that might affect the illness. Then she does a thorough examination and often finds conditions of which the patient is unaware. She learned her superb diagnostic technique from Abraham and from Erasmus.

Her father has cut back on his hours at the clinic as he more often feels a pain in the chest that makes him weak. There is enough work for another physician, and there is a new member of the profession in town, but he cannot help us. He has chest pains more severe than those of Erasmus.[1]

Jonathan and his wife Elisabeth moved to Capernaum several months ago and we met them one evening walking by the lake. Jonathan trained at the school in Carthage. He is a very good surgeon, particularly with broken bones. But after three severe episodes of pain in the chest, he was advised to quit his profession and so they decided to move away.

During each episode, Elisabeth said, he developed severe pain in the center of the chest and down the left arm.[2] He sweated profusely, became ashen in color and passed out. He stayed in bed for a few days and then gradually got up and returned to work. But after the third attack he was not able to walk without pain coming on in the chest.

We have invited Jonathan to see our clinic and he was impressed. We also invited him and Elisabeth to our meetings the day after the Sabbath.

Jesus and the apostles have been teaching in the towns and villages around Capernaum for the last several weeks. There has been no further word of Herod.

This afternoon, as we were finishing early, Philip, one of The Twelve, walked into the clinic with a bloodstained arm. He is a man of Bethsaida near Capernaum, the home also of Simon, Andrew and Bartholomew, a friend of Philip who has also become an apostle of Jesus.

We could tell by his expression that Philip was in pain. Judith rushed to him and took him into the room set aside for surgery. We found a long gash on his right upper forearm. He had fallen on a rock this morning and Jesus had told him to come and have Elisa take care of it. And she did, while I finished up with the other patients. First she gave him a glass full of strong wine to help deaden the pain. Then she washed the wound with water from our well.

We are grateful to our fathers for having the foresight to purchase property with its own well for us. Erasmus taught us that if a wound is washed over and over again with water before it is sutured, it heals much better. There is less pus. Because of that we need a lot of fresh, clean water. It would be a problem to carry it from the common well.

Elisa then poured strong wine and oil into Philip's wound and started to stitch it, leaving a wine-soaked string so the pus would drain out and the wound heal from the bottom. After she placed the drain she wrapped it with bandages of white cloth and put him to rest on a pallet that we have for just this purpose. By this time I was finished with the other patients and we had cleaned up the clinic. Philip slept off the wine and sat up. We all had a drink of cold water, and I asked him what Jesus and The Twelve had done during the past few weeks.

"Well, there is much to tell," he said. "The day we left here, we prayed most of the night, slept a little, and at dawn we started for Bethsaida. Jesus wanted to be alone with us. Well, it was wonderful for two days. We prayed, Jesus taught, we learned much. We laughed and had great fellowship, just Jesus and the twelve of us."

Philip took another sip of water and continued. "By the third day the crowds had found Jesus, and our quiet time was over. Jesus welcomed them, talked about the kingdom of God and cured those in need of healing. And the people listened, eager to hear his message of love, forgiveness and reconciliation."

Then I asked, "Philip, tell me what Jesus said when he got word about Herod beheading John."

"That was a tragedy, and we learned of it a few days after it happened. Jesus became pale, held back the tears and went off to a wooded area and knelt and prayed. He stayed there for a long time. And we also knelt and prayed.

"Finally, Jesus got up and so did we. He said, 'Prophets are always hated and often killed because they tell the truth. Herod and Herodias are living in sin and they know it. They silenced John but they have not silenced us.

"'Remember that prophets are persecuted because they speak the truth and remind the people of their sins against God. And that is what may happen to us.'"

Philip then looked at his wrapped arm and asked Elisa, "May I go now to meet him near the lake?" Elisa replied with a twinkle in her eye, "Only if you take your physicians with you."

We closed the clinic, stopped at home to change tunics, and the three of us headed to the lake. There we found Erasmus fishing and told him where we were going. He eagerly joined us. He was not obeying our orders about walking slowly. He walked ahead of us. But apparently he did not have any pain in his chest.

The breeze off the lake was cooling. We passed the synagogue, the house of Simon, and many fishing boats. People were coming from every house and joining the crowd. Word had spread that Jesus was going to teach on the plain near the lake.

As we walked we noticed there were no fishermen on the lake and no one working in the fields near the lake. It appeared that all had left their work and were joining the multitude gathering to hear Jesus. We made our way through the crowd and soon could see Jesus coming down a slope. A throng of people surrounded him as he made his way toward us, smiling broadly.

He greeted us and spoke to Philip. "I told you that Elisa would take good care of you." Then he turned to Erasmus. "You are missing some good fishing."

"Ach, that can wait," Erasmus said with a laugh.

Jesus looked over the noisy crowd, which now numbered about five thousand. He strode forward to a small mound and motioned for the men, women and children to be seated and be quiet. Then he started a long discussion which was more detailed than the one he had given to the people on the plain a few weeks ago.

"Happy are the lowly. They shall have the earth as a heritage.

"Happy are they who mourn, for they shall be comforted ..."

And then, Luke, he described the life God wants all his children to have. There would be justice, freedom, mercy, purity of heart, peace for everyone. Further, he talked about the boundless love of God for everyone everywhere. That means that God loves you as much as he loves me, Luke.

All who listened were enthralled. Once Jesus stopped speaking, the ill and the lame came up one by one to be healed. Luke, it was a wondrous sight to behold.

It was then late in the afternoon. The sun had slipped down behind the mountains, and a chalky gray settled over the distant shore of the lake. Soon it would be evening.

Philip stepped up to Jesus and said, "Send the people away, and they can go to the villages and farms round about to find lodging and food, for we are in a lonely place here."

"Give them something to eat yourselves," Jesus said. We were only a short distance away, Luke, and could hear this exchange clearly.

"But Master," he said, "we have no more than five loaves and two fish, unless we are to go ourselves and buy food for all these people."

Then Jesus said to The Twelve, "Have the people gather in parties of about fifty." They did so and made us all sit down. Then he took the five loaves and the two fish, raised his eyes to heaven, and said a blessing over them. He then broke them and handed the pieces to his disciples to distribute among the crowd.

And each of us, Luke, ate our fill! It did not seem possible. And when the scraps remaining were collected, they filled twelve baskets. This set the crowd astir.

We looked for Jesus to explain what had happened, but he was gone. Said Simon, "He has gone to a secluded place to pray the rest of the night."

It was getting dark and it was a long way back to town. The thousands drifted off, each to their own homes. We passed by the lake to pick up Erasmus' fishing pole and bait. Then we sat down on the shore and discussed the events of the day. Elisa was already looking for a deeper meaning to the miracle we had witnessed.

"God fed our ancestors with manna in the desert," she said. "Could this be a sign that God is planning to give us some unending nourishment in the future?"

"You mean, like constant learning?" asked Erasmus. "Yes, that is one way," replied Elisa. "But perhaps there is another. Some way that we cannot even imagine now. Perhaps something to nourish our bodies while his teachings nourish our hearts."

Deep in thought, her eyes opened wider. "Jesus talks about the special mission from the Father. Is he talking about the father of all Israel, the Lord God?

"We have had prophets throughout the history of Israel, through whom God sent messages to our ancestors. Is Jesus another prophet sent from God in our midst? Or is he more than a prophet — His Son?"

Once again Elisa had come up with questions that I could not answer. It was now my turn to say, "Let us wait and see."

Erasmus got up and said, "It is time for sleep. Thank you for taking me with you." And we all went home.

So Luke, I end another letter with a heart filled with wonder.

May God, in His wisdom, bless and guide you.

Joseph

[1] Angina pectoris—pain in the anterior chest on exertion in a patient with coronary heart disease, which causes narrowing of the interior of the blood vessels supplying the heart muscle. When the heart is subjected to increased demand by exertion, the muscles do not get enough blood and cause pain. Resting or medication usually relieves it.

[2] Myocardial infarction (heart attack) is a complete obstruction of an artery supplying the heart. This causes destruction of the section of the heart supplied by the obstructed blood vessel. A scar results if it is a small vessel. If it is a large vessel the heart stops.

Letter 71

Peace, grace and mercy be unto you. The days are long now and the sun does not set until late. On our evening walk last night, Elisa and I came to a wooded area near the lake where Jesus often comes with his disciples to pray. There we found The Twelve sitting in a circle with Jesus in the center. He was on his knees, his head raised to the heavens. The only motion I could detect was of his lips. Some time passed with Jesus in prayer.

Suddenly he arose and looked around. He saw Elisa and me standing quietly behind the apostles, but he did not seem to care whether or not we were listening. He put this question to The Twelve.

"Who do the crowds say that I am?" He looked to each one for a response.

"John the Baptist."

"Elijah."

"You are one of the ancient prophets come back to life."

I was about to speak myself — I am not really sure what I would have said — but Elisa took my arm and whispered, "Joseph, he did not ask you." That annoyed me, but she was right.

"But you," Jesus said to them insistently. "Who do you say I am?"

"The Christ of God," said Simon, using the Greek form of the title Messiah.

Jesus nodded in approval. "Simon, son of Jonah, you are a happy man! Because it is not flesh and blood that revealed this to you but my Father in heaven." Then he spoke more solemnly to the First Apostle.

"So I say to you: You are Peter and on this rock I will build my Church. And the gate of the underworld can never hold out against it.

"I will give you the keys of the kingdom of heaven," he added.

"Whatever you bind on earth shall be considered bound in heaven. Whatever you loose on earth shall be considered loosed in heaven."

Simon, now named Peter or the Rock, straightened his shoulders and stood with a certain dignity, as if he accepted this great responsibility. It seemed to be a conferring of power from Jesus to Simon Peter, to carry on his mission.

"Now I give you strict orders," Jesus said, "not to tell anyone about this."

He looked at the disciples one by one, then at Elisa and me. We all nodded in acquiescence.

At that he withdrew deeper into the woods to pray. Elisa and I left, as did The Twelve.

As we walked home, Elisa spoke. "Joseph, that is the second time that he has said that he is the Messiah, and again he told us not to tell anyone. This time he involved The Twelve in the secret."

Luke, Jesus must want to keep this revelation among his very close followers, but I do not see how this news can be silenced. It seems that everyone in Galilee and even in Judea is talking about him.

But to make this claim in public would rouse the chief priests and elders. They might consider the claim a blasphemy and prescribe the death sentence.

Luke, Elisa and I are worried about Jesus. This man of peace represents a threat to civil and religious authorities.

Joseph

Letter 72

Dear Luke, we assembled at the clinic after sunset today to make sense of the teachings and doings of Jesus, the man whom we know and yet we do not know. Who is he? What is he?

Elisabeth and Jonathan joined us for the first time and everyone welcomed them. All were there but Thalia, who was ill with wheezing.[1] We all prayed for her recovery. I had seen her at her home this morning. Erasmus, Elisa and I have treated her condition but are not getting anywhere with her breathing problem. Yes, Luke, I wonder why Jesus does not cure her.

David and Rachel had been at the lakeshore this week listening to Jesus teach. "After one long session," David told us, "Jesus stopped and everyone became quiet. Then he made a grave pronouncement that even now bewilders me. This is what he said:

"'The Son of Man must undergo many sufferings. He is destined to be rejected by the elders and chief priests and scribes and put to death, and to be raised up on the third day.'"

We gasped. "What does this mean?" I asked David. But he only shook his head and sat down. Rachel resumed the story.

"Jesus then spoke to all of us assembled there. 'If anyone wants to be a follower of mine, let him renounce himself and take up his cross every day and follow me. For anyone who wants to save his life will lose it, but anyone who loses his life for my sake, that man will save it.

"'What gain, then, is it for a man to have won the whole world and to have lost his very self?

"'For if anyone is ashamed of me and of my words, of him the Son of Man will be ashamed when he comes in his glory and in the glory of the Father and his holy angels.'

"Then he added, 'I tell you truly, there are some standing here who will not taste death before they see the kingdom of God.' And then Jesus disappeared into the crowd and was gone."

Now, Luke, Jesus refers to himself as the "Son of Man," and in our tradition that title specifies someone sent from God who would be a leader. And now Jesus seemed to be prophesying his own death.

"But he would have to be in Jerusalem," David said, "where the elders, chief priests and scribes, those with power in the Temple, would reject his teachings. I can see that, because he teaches love and forgiveness.

"Rejection, yes, I can understand that." David then shook his head. "But to be put to death for teaching love, this is another matter.

"But we must remember that the prophets taught this and many of them were killed. Could it be that Jesus will meet the same fate? I pray that he will not."

Then Jonathan, the newest member of the group, spoke up. "I believe that early in the Wisdom literature[2] this phenomenon is described. A virtuous man, who claimed to have knowledge of God and called himself the Son of God, reproached those in power because of their breach of the law. They planned to treat him cruelly and torture him and test his endurance and condemn him to a shameful death. They further state that if this virtuous man is God's Son, God will rescue him. That seems to me to describe just what we have here."

"Well, it seems that all of this has been written long, long ago," Daniel said. There was silence for a while and then we heard Leah, his wife, say with assurance, "If Jesus says it will happen, it will happen.

"But to rise again from the dead on the third day," she added, "that is difficult to understand, to believe, or to even conceive that it could happen. And I don't want to see him suffer. He has done nothing but good." And we all agreed.

"We know that Jesus is very close to God," Rachel said, "or he could not do the things that he does."

"These pronouncements of Jesus worry me," said Miriam. "What does he mean by losing life and then gaining it? Can we come back to life here?"

And so went our discussion, the time passing rapidly.

Later, as we were walking home, Elisa said, "It is hard to understand how anyone who does nothing but good has to suffer and be put to death. I can see where he has often disagreed with the elders and the other authorities when they are obviously wrong, and it does anger them. But I cannot understand why they would put him to death for that."

"Jealousy," I replied. "They may be afraid that he will take their power from them, their position."

Elisa fell silent for a few moments. Then she turned to me and said, "Joseph, should we give up our lives here and our work and follow him?"

"No," I was quick to answer. "I am sure that his twelve disciples must give total devotion, but the rest of us are needed to live as God wills us within our own community. We must not let our worldly goods and duties so completely envelop us that we forget about God and fellow members of the community. The goal of this life is to possess eternal life with God in the future, and that must be foremost in our lives."

I am not sure that answer satisfied her, Luke.

"If Jesus is the Messiah," I continued, "he obviously is not the glorious political and military leader that the prophets foretold. Nor is he the vindictive Messiah that John spoke of on the Jordan. He says that he will suffer and be put to death. And he implies that his followers must be ready to suffer and to die too."

"Perhaps he also means that to lose one's life is to give up trying to control our destiny and leave it all to God!" Elisa replied.

May the Lord of Abraham, Moses and David guide us all in this search for knowledge and wisdom.

Joseph

---

[1] Asthma or spasm of the bronchi (breathing tubes) due to an allergy or infection, causing a wheezing sound when breathing.

[2] Wisdom 2:13-20

Letter 73

Grace and peace from the Lord God.

This evening Elisa and I went to hear Jesus teach near the lake. There was already a large crowd gathered in wait. As Jesus and The Twelve were seen coming down from the mountain, everyone surged towards him.

Suddenly a man from Capernaum cried out, "Master, I implore you to look at my son, my only child," and he pointed to his boy.

Elisa and I both recognized the eight-year-old as a patient who has had seizures since he fell and hit his head on a rock at the age of two.

"A spirit takes hold of him," the man said, "and my boy is thrown into convulsions and foams at the mouth. The demon is slow to leave him, and when it does, it leaves him worn out."

Then the man pointed to The Twelve and said, "I begged your disciples to cast out the demon but they would not."

Jesus also looked at the disciples. "Such a faithless and perverse generation! How much longer must I be with you and put up with you?"

Just then the lad darted toward Jesus but uttered a cry and was thrown to the ground in a convulsion. Elisa and I rushed up to try to prevent any injury. I held the boy's head to keep it from hitting the ground, and Elisa tried to get a cloth between his teeth so that he would not chew on his tongue.

From where he stood, Jesus rebuked the unclean spirit — and the boy quit shaking. The foaming cleared and dried up. His rigid body relaxed and he scrambled to his feet without help. Jesus took him by the hand and led him to his father, who cried "How great is the Lord God!" as they walked away.

I helped Elisa up from the ground and we wiped the dust off our clothing. Later, as we set off for home, I asked the question that had been bothering me. "If Jesus gave The Twelve the power to cast out devils, why could they not do it in this case?"

Elisa was quick with her answer. "Their ministry of healing and teaching depends upon him," she said. "They cannot do it by their own power."

"And where does Jesus derive his power?"

Capernaum

"From his Father," she said, "the great Lord Almighty."

Luke, Elisa astonishes me when she speaks with such conviction. I still have questions and doubts.

Perhaps Jesus is the Messiah. But he is a man. He has eaten at our table, laughed and prayed with us. And we have nursed him to health when he almost died.

How can he be the Son of God?

Joseph

Letter 74

Greetings to Luke of Antioch.

The physician Jonathan, who was forced to retire because of chest pain, has become a great help in our practice. He visited at the clinic several times and offered to be of assistance when Erasmus is out. I like this because he relieves Elisa of some of the surgery. Whenever he notices that his pain is coming back, he sits and rests a few minutes until it disappears.

Jonathan is an intelligent physician and we like to discuss our patients' illnesses with him. He has good insight. He had years of experience working as a surgeon to the Roman legions in the battlefields.

Knowing that Jonathan is available allows me to spend more time on home visits. I learn a lot about my patients when I see them in their own environment. And I enjoy the challenge of making the diagnosis myself. I have no one in the next room to consult. I must rely only on what I hear, feel, see and smell.

This morning I came in early from my rounds and found another injured disciple. This time it was James the son of Alphaeus — the smaller James, as he is known. He had injured his left wrist in a fall. He had a deep cut that bled profusely but finally had stopped. Elisa examined it and found that there were no bones broken and no tendons cut, but sutures and a splint were needed.

"You know, James," she said as she was working, "everyone in Capernaum is full of admiration for all that Jesus has done." As she pulled the stitches tight, James gritted his teeth but nodded his head in understanding.

"Joseph and I have had a special problem understanding and explaining the prophecy he uttered that he must suffer and die."

"Elisa," James answered, "we cannot explain that either. Just yesterday, the Master, as we have become to call him, said to the twelve of us, 'For your part you must have these words constantly in your mind: The Son of Man is going to be handed over to the power of men.'

"We could not understand what he meant, and we were afraid to ask. Even Peter, who often is the one to speak first, did not ask."

Elisa had the wrist wrapped by that time, but James was in no hurry to leave. He seemed to want to talk. He looked at his bandaged wrist and spoke softly.

"Last night we were sitting around the campfire and feeling rather self-important. Jesus was in prayer deep in the woods nearby. We started arguing which one of us was the greatest, and Jude and I boasted of our kinship to Jesus.

"Suddenly the Master appeared and we all fell silent, ashamed of ourselves. Elisa, he must have known what was in our minds because I know that he did not hear our words.

"He walked to the side, where a group of followers was assembled, took a small boy and sat him by his side. Then he directed his gaze to us.

"'Anyone who welcomes this little child in my name welcomes me,' he said, 'and anyone who welcomes me welcomes him who sent me. For the least among you all, that is the one who is great!'"

You know, Luke, in your culture and mine, children are of little consequence, and no one bothers to listen to them, comfort their fears or be nice to them. Speaking this respectfully of children is another unusual thing about Jesus.

James continued. "It was John who spoke next. 'Master,' he said, 'we saw a man casting out devils in your name, and because he is not with us we tried to stop him.'

"Jesus looked disturbed and was firm in his answer. 'You must not stop him,' he said. 'Anyone who is not against you is for you.'

"That surprised us," James continued, "but it made good sense, as all the statements of Jesus do, except when he speaks in parables." He rose to leave and Elisa told him to come back in two days to have his wound checked.

As you can see, Luke, we keep hearing about Jesus constantly and find that his words challenge our way of life.

Tonight we met at the clinic to discuss his latest teachings. Samson and Hannah had taken a week to follow Jesus as he and his disciples went from village to village in Galilee, and they had returned with a story to tell.

"One day as we were all walking along," Samson said, "we met a man on the road who had a sack full of his belongings and seemed to be prepared for a journey. As we approached, he spoke to the Master. 'Jesus,' he said, 'I will follow you wherever you go.' We thought that was a rather determined statement.

"Jesus stopped and so did all of us. 'Foxes have holes,' he said, 'and the birds of the air have their nests, but the Son of Man has nowhere to lay his head,' and he continued on his way.

"The man joined the group, but I don't know how long he will stay."

Hannah then picked up the story. "Later we encountered another man along the way, and to this man Jesus said, 'Follow me.' The man seemed willing to go but he said, 'Let me go and bury my father first.'

"That seemed reasonable to me, but Jesus answered, 'Let the dead bury the dead. Your duty is to go and spread the kingdom of God.'

"And that is not all," Hannah continued. "Another man spoke up and said, 'I will follow you, sir, but just let me go and say goodbye to my people at home.' Now, that seemed reasonable too, at least it did to me, but Jesus was quick to respond. 'Once the hand is laid on the plow,' he said, 'no one who looks back is fit for the kingdom of God.'"

After she finished, each of us was deep in thought about the meaning of these words.

Finally Abriam spoke up. "That seems such a major commitment, to leave home and family to follow Jesus."

Ruth added, "But that is what The Twelve have done. It takes very dedicated people to fully do his work as disciples. But surely the rest of us can be followers of his way."

Elisa agreed. "We must not let our attachments rule us but consider them as belonging to God and use them as He would want us to use them."

We talked for some time about how we could follow these difficult teachings in our present lives, with our families, our work and our other responsibilities.

Luke, we are all beginning to think of ourselves as followers of Jesus and his teachings. The way of living he has shown us will not be easy, but surely it is in accordance with God's will.

Joseph

Letter 75

Luke, the ministry of Jesus grows ever stronger. This afternoon after we finished our work at the clinic, Elisa and I walked to the lakeshore to hear Jesus teach. Erasmus was pleased to be with us. He is always eager to explore new thoughts and teachings. His own depth of knowledge ranges widely, including the different customs and building styles of the Greeks and Romans, the Babylonians and the Egyptians. Of course, he is very familiar with the Scriptures and can quote them extensively when needed. He likes to continually increase his knowledge and is very interested in the teaching of Jesus.

We arrived at a spot where about two hundred people had gathered. The hills were far in the distance with the Sea of Galilee just beyond us. The water was a still deep blue, and just a few boats could be seen. There was a slight breeze drifting in from the sea.

We settled comfortably on the grass with the others and were prepared to hear Jesus teach. But Jesus had something else in mind. He made his way through the seated groups of three or four people and tapped certain men on the shoulder as he passed, calling them by name. He smiled as he passed us but did not pause. Then he stopped, faced the crowd and spoke.

"All of you whom I tapped on the shoulder, please come forward."

We looked around and slowly everyone whom Jesus had selected rose and joined him. There were seventy-two men, young and old. A few were finely dressed but most were in plain clothing like ours.

"Earlier I chose my twelve disciples," Jesus explained, "and now I appoint you. Go out in pairs to the towns and places where I plan to visit.

"The harvest is rich," he said, "but the laborers are few, so ask the Lord of the harvest to send laborers to his harvest.

"Start off now, but remember, I am sending you out like lambs among wolves. Carry no purse, no haversack and no sandals. Salute no one on the road. Whatever house you go into, let your first words be, 'Peace to this house!' And if a man of peace lives there, your peace will go and rest on him. If not it will come back to you. Stay in the same house, taking what food and drink they have to offer, for the laborer deserves his wages. Do not move from house to house. Whenever you go into a town where they make you welcome, eat what is set before you. Cure those in it who are sick, and say, 'The kingdom of God is very near to you.'

"But whenever you enter a town and they do not make you welcome, go out into its streets and say, 'We wipe off the very dust of your town that clings to our feet, and leave it with you. Yet be sure of this: The kingdom of God is very near.' I tell you, on that day it will not go as hard with Sodom as with that town."

Luke, the Scriptures tell us the cities of Sodom and Gomorrah were destroyed for their wickedness by a rain of fire and sulfur from the heavens. Lot, the nephew of Abraham, had been living in Sodom with his family when two messengers from God came to visit him. The men of Sodom attempted to assault them. The messengers made Lot and his family leave and told them not to look back. But Lot's wife looked back as the city was destroyed, and she was turned into a pillar of salt.[1]

Then Jesus seemed to suggest that the people of the towns of Galilee, where he has spent more than a year preaching and working miracles, carry a greater burden in knowing the truth than those who have not heard his words.

"Alas for you, Chorazin! Alas for you, Bethsaida! For if the miracles done in you had been done in Tyre and Sidon, they would have repented long ago, sitting in sackcloth and ashes. And still, it will not go as hard with Tyre and Sidon at the judgment as with you. And as for you, Capernaum, did you want to be exalted high as heaven? You shall be thrown down to hell."

Then he assured those selected of their authority. "Anyone who listens to you listens to me. Anyone who rejects you rejects me, and those who reject me reject the one who sent me."

Elisa and I listened intently and were pleased that Jesus was commissioning more to go out and do his work. Then he withdrew to pray with The Twelve and the seventy-two.

Erasmus seemed amazed at what he had just seen and heard. As we started to walk home, he spoke. "Jesus is telling us very frankly that we had better listen and believe. The towns of Galilee must do what he tells us or be destroyed. That reminds me of what prophets said in the past. Isaiah, Ezekial and Jeremiah all warned that the ancient cities of Tyre and Sidon must repent. The people of those cities rejoiced when Jerusalem fell to Babylon and the Temple was destroyed, only to see their cities suffer the same fate."

But my questions had to do with the commissioning of new apostles. "Why did he select seventy-two?" I asked.

"According to the teaching of the rabbis, there are seventy-two nations in the world. That makes one for each nation," Elisa replied. "Jesus wants his teaching spread to every nation in the world, not only to Israel!"

"Why should they go two by two?"

"Could it be that they are to witness for each other? You know that there must be two witnesses in the Israeli courts."

"Why are they not to greet anyone?"

"Jesus may not have wanted these seventy-two to engage in useless chatter, as so many travelers do when they meet each other on a lonely road, but to feel a great urgency in spreading the message."

We were now at Erasmus' home and as he left he said, "Wait until I tell Sarah." We knew that Erasmus would tell her all that he had witnessed.

As we walked home, I must have been quieter than usual for Elisa asked, "Joseph, what is bothering you?"

I was startled. "Oh, nothing. Nothing at all."

"Now, Joseph, I have been married to you more than three years and I know when something is on your mind. You have a particular expression when you are worried." And, Luke, she was right.

"All right. I am disappointed that Jesus gave those seventy-two men the ability to cure all diseases and did not give it to us."

"I thought of that, too," she replied. "But let us look at it this way. 'If he had made it too easy for us to cure our patients, we would not continue to investigate the causes of the diseases. It would be too easy.

"And, also, all of our patients are accustomed to giving us something in return for our treatment — a chicken, some fish, or a few coins if they can. Jesus never takes anything for his cures. The graces that he gives must be given freely and without recompense.

"And remember he always forgives sins. That, Joseph, is beyond us too." And that finally satisfied me, at least for this evening.

May the Lord God who created all things guide us all closer to Him.

Joseph

---

[1]   Genesis 19:1-26

Letter 76

Dear Luke, you have asked a question I expected when you got into the Book of Numbers.[1] "Joseph, how does looking at a bronze serpent raised on a pole cure snake bites?" There is nothing about looking upon a bronze serpent that cures snakebites. However, there is a message to the story, which concerns the rebellion of the Israelites against God. He had brought them safely out of the land of slavery and was feeding them in the desert. But some chose to rebel and they were punished with an infestation of snakes. The people asked Moses to intervene for them and save them from death by snakebite. God forgave them in the form of a cure but asked those who followed his instructions to look at the image of a snake. They had to have faith in God to do what seemed useless. Rebellion and punishment were followed by repentance and forgiveness.

Elisa wonders if there is a still deeper meaning to this story. She says sometime in the future, perhaps, we will all gaze up at someone who is raised high on a pole in forgiveness for our sins. I cannot understand exactly what she means but she often is right in her predictions.

Jesus, the twelve apostles and the seventy-two whom he just appointed have been preaching in towns and villages in Galilee. Sometimes we go days without news about them. When we do hear of them it is a familiar story. The people are eager to listen to his teachings and occasionally experience a cure.

Today Joel, one of the many children of Capernaum who enjoy sitting and playing at the feet of Jesus, dashed into our clinic. "Jesus is back!" he cried. "He is on his way into town, and many of his disciples are with him. He says he is on his way here!" Elisa and I worked quickly so that we could finish and sweep the room before they arrived.

In the early evening our friends and other followers of Jesus gathered at the clinic. Among the group were most of the seventy-two, who came rejoicing. The room was nearly full when Jesus appeared at the door with The Twelve. He smiled broadly as he looked around, then everyone rose and cheered as he walked in. He greeted most of us by name and some of us with banter. "Joseph!" he said as he approached. "So how many did you cure today?"

His apostles were together at one side, eager to share their tales.

"Lord," they said, "even the devils submit to us when we use your name."

They recounted what had happened as they spread the word of the Lord in the towns they visited two by two, as he had commanded. Each pair had a different story, but all had successes in the name of the Lord. Jesus smiled as he listened.

When all were through and the chatter had stilled, Jesus spoke. His joy showed in his face. "I watched Satan fall like lightning from heaven," he said.

"Yes, I have given you power to tread underfoot serpents and scorpions and the whole strength of the enemy. Nothing shall ever hurt you. Yet do not rejoice that the spirits submit to you. Rejoice rather that your names are written in heaven." He raised his head and his hands in prayer.

"I bless you, Father, Lord of heaven and of earth, for hiding these things from the learned and the clever and revealing them to mere children. Yes, Father, for that is what it pleased you to do. Everything has been entrusted to me by my Father, and no one knows who the Son is except the Father, and who the Father is except the Son, and those to whom the Son chooses to reveal him."

Then, Luke, he turned to his disciples. "Happy the eyes that see what you see, for I tell you that many prophets and kings wanted to see what you see, and never saw it, to hear what you hear, and never heard it."

Suddenly, a man in the rear of the room rose to speak. I recognized him as a shrewd lawyer and a devout Jew.

"Master," he said. "What must I do to inherit eternal life?" Everyone fell silent.

"What is written in the Law?" Jesus asked him in return.

The lawyer replied, "You must love the Lord your God with all your heart, all your soul, all your strength and all your mind, and you must love your neighbor as yourself." You have read these passages, Luke.

Jesus smiled. "You have answered right. Do this and life is yours." He turned to address the disciples again.

But the lawyer seemed anxious to justify his presence. "And who is my neighbor?" he called out. But Jesus was not to be tricked. He began to tell a parable.

"A man was once on his way from Jerusalem to Jericho and fell into the hands of brigands. They took all that he had, beat him and then made off, leaving him half dead. Now a priest happened to be traveling down the same road, but when he saw the man, he passed by on the other side. In the same way, a Levite who came to the place saw him and passed by on the other side. But a Samaritan traveler who came upon him was moved with compassion. He bandaged his wounds, pouring oil and wine on them. He then lifted him onto his own mount, carried him to the inn and looked after him. Next day, he took out two denarii and handed them to the innkeeper. 'Look after him,' he said, 'and on my way back I will make good any extra expenses you have.'"

Jesus looked directly into the eyes of the lawyer. "Which of these three do you think proved himself a neighbor to the man who fell into the brigands' hands?"

Now, Luke, the lawyer knew the priest could not take time to touch the traveler, who was presumably dead.[2] He would have been defiled and could not take his assigned place of worship at the Temple without going through purification. And the Levite, as assistant to a priest, would also be defiled. The lawyer also knew that many Israelites despise Samaritans, who married Gentiles. Their offer to help was spurned when the Temple in Jerusalem was being built, so they built their own.[3]

But the answer was clear. "The one who took pity on him," the man replied.

"Go and do the same yourself," Jesus said quietly.

With these words, the evening of preaching ended and Jesus, his apostles and the seventy-two made their way to the door and left. The lawyer watched them go, standing his ground, and then left, shaking his head.

Luke, Jesus used the example of a Samaritan, a people so many Jews despise, to illustrate an act of charity. This tells me that all are the same in the eyes of God and that we should help everyone regardless of race. That must have been a revolting thought to the pious lawyer.

Remember, Luke, the talks we used to have about the poor and the helpless? We as practitioners of the healing art have been taught to treat the person and the illness, whether the patient is a Jew or a Gentile, Samaritan or Assyrian.

Still, in our society sickness is considered a punishment for sin. This belief Elisa, Erasmus and I cannot accept.

Now Jesus asks everyone to do what they can to care for the ill, the injured, the victims of robbers or whoever the unfortunate may be.

As we walked home Elisa asked me, "Are you still jealous of the seventy-two?"

"No. I am not. I am beginning to see that the Lord God may have other plans for us in our own profession."

Elisa stopped and exclaimed, "Joseph, I thank God that you have finally realized that point."

Luke, I do not know where following the words of Jesus will lead us, but may the God of Israel guide us all.

Joseph

[1]   Numbers 21:4-9

[2]   Leviticus 21:11

[3]   Ezra 4:1-5

Letter 77

Luke, it is good of you to ask how Elisa is holding up under the heavy load of work. I thank the Lord she is healthy and seems to have a lot of energy. Of course, we insist that she get adequate rest. Erasmus and I listen to her chest regularly and hear no abnormal sounds. She has no cough and maintains her weight well. We report to Abraham.

For the past several weeks Jesus and his apostles have been teaching throughout Galilee and Judea, even in Jerusalem. We were overjoyed today when we learned he has returned to Capernaum. He has secluded himself in the woods to pray, but we hope we shall soon see him. However, Simon, the apostle who left the practice of law to follow Jesus, made his way to our clinic today. Luke, I must share the story he told us.

"We were on our way to Jerusalem," he said, "and were planning to spend the night in the village of Bethany in the home of Mary and Martha and their brother Lazarus. Jesus has known them since he was a child. He and his parents would stay with them at Bethany when they would go to Jerusalem for the Passover. Bethany is less than an hour's walk from the Temple. They are a very prominent family in the area, but none of the three has married.

"As we approached the house, Martha welcomed us and made us all comfortable. She called and introduced us to her sister Mary, who came and sat at the feet of Jesus. Martha, meanwhile, was busy doing the necessary work of a hostess preparing and serving the meal, but Mary continued to sit and listen to Jesus. We all became uncomfortable watching Martha work alone. Finally she stopped in front of Jesus and said, 'Lord, do you not care that my sister is leaving me to do the serving all by myself? Please tell her to help me.'

"We were surprised with the answer Jesus gave her. 'Martha, Martha, you worry and fret about many things and yet few are needed, indeed only one. It is Mary who has chosen the better part. It is not to be taken from her.'

"Martha was stunned. We all were."

Luke, I was a bit appalled myself, as I have been raised to be responsible and work hard. Martha must have been deeply embarrassed.

"Then Jesus broke out with that disarming smile of his. 'I meant to shock,' he said, 'and I see that I did.' Martha regained her composure. We relaxed and listened intently as he continued.

"'Here we have two women,' he said. 'Martha and Mary are both doing good works. But in the final decision, to devote everything to the knowledge and the worship of God is the better.

"'Now, I will quit teaching, and Mary, go and help Martha.' And she did."

Elisa had been smiling as if she understood the story. "There are men and women now who spend their entire time in prayer. Then there are those who are so overwhelmed with the cares of the world that they do not spend any time in prayer. Most of us seek a balance between a contemplative and active life.

"But I often wonder how it would be to spend an entire lifetime in prayer. It would seem to be as close to God as one could get. Some of the mystics have gone to the desert to live alone and just meditate on God."

She stopped and looked at me as she continued. "But we have chosen to serve God and also man."

Simon nodded. "Jesus approves of that too although the love of God is primary. All other things are secondary to it. Our goal is to please God." And he was on his way.

Joseph

Letter 78

Luke, today Elisa and I learned a new way to pray.

I had finished my morning rounds early and was able to help Elisa in the clinic, enabling us to finish about the tenth hour. We had a light meal and went in search of Jesus and the apostles. There's a place in the woods where they gather and where Jesus spends much of the night and morning in prayer, sitting, kneeling, sometimes lying on the ground. I don't think he gets enough sleep.

As we arrived, we found The Twelve waiting for him. We had just seated ourselves at the edge of their group when Jesus emerged from the woods.

"Master," said young John, "you spend hours communing with our Lord God. What is it you say to him?"

Andrew added, "Lord, teach us to pray, just as John taught his disciples."

"Hmmm, yes," Jesus said. "Say this when you pray:

Father, may your name be held holy,

Your kingdom come.

Give us each day our daily bread,

And forgive us our sins,

For we ourselves forgive each one who is in debt to us,

And do not put us to the test.

The disciples repeated the prayer over and over. Elisa and I did too until we remembered it. And later we went over every line together until we realized how powerful this simple prayer is.

The starting word "Father" is very personal. Jesus used the word "Abba," which is a very loving term for father.

Luke, in these few phrases, Jesus seemed to include every type of prayer we learn at the synagogue. First there are prayers of praise to our God and prayers of thanks for all He has given us. There are prayers of contrition, in which we express sorrow for our sins and ask God's forgiveness. And finally there is the most common form, prayers of petition, to ask God for something.

This prayer calls to mind our ancestors. We know that the Lord gave Moses and his people manna in the desert to feed them.[1] Today we also experience hunger, but of a more spiritual nature.

Further, with this prayer we ask not just to be forgiven but we pledge that we will in turn forgive others — a pledge that will be difficult to uphold.

And finally, we petition the Lord not to test our faith.

As we were still committing these lines to memory, Jesus gave us more reason to pray and to persevere in prayer.

"Suppose," he said, "one of you has a friend and goes to him in the middle of the night to say, 'My friend, lend me three loaves, because a friend of mine on his travels has just arrived at my house and I have nothing to offer him.' And the man answers from inside the house, 'Do not bother me. The door is bolted now, and my children and I are in bed. I cannot get up to give it to you.' I tell you, if the man does not get up and give it to him for friendship's sake, persistence will be enough to make him get up and give his friend all he wants.

"So I say to you: Ask, and it will be given to you.

"Search and you will find.

"Knock and the door will be opened for you.

"For the one who asks always receives. The one who searches finds. The one who knocks will always have the door opened to him.

"What father among you would hand his son a stone when he asked for bread? Or hand him a snake instead of a fish? Or hand him a scorpion if he asked for an egg?

"If you then, who are evil, know how to give your children what is good, how much more will the heavenly Father bless those who ask Him."

Then he withdrew into the deeper area of the woods to resume prayer. Elisa and I bid the disciples farewell and went home. We repeated the prayer Jesus taught us over and over again until we knew it well enough to teach our friends.

"Jesus is setting us another example," Elisa said. "He comes closer to God through prayer. He must hear God speaking to him. This is what we have to imitate."

She stopped and then added, "Jesus seems to pray the deepest when he is alone, but he seems to also speak to God at most any time. We can do the same. We can pray, we can speak to God at any time."

That is as far as we got before we reached our home. There was a patient waiting on the doorstep who had cut his hand. We took him to the clinic and by the time we got the wound cleansed, treated and covered with bandages, it was late. We returned home to eat a little and retire.

Joseph

---

1   Exodus 16:1-36

Letter 79

Greetings in the name of the God of Abraham, Moses and David.

Elisa and I see many faces of our friend Jesus. He is a healer, a lover of children, a humble man who takes his place among sinners, and a smiling companion. But today we saw a different side of Jesus — a fierce fighter for the oppressed.

We had finished our work early and walked out to the place where Jesus was to teach today. It was a short distance from our house. As we were gathering, Jesus came out of the woods with his disciples. A man pushed his way through the crowd and stood in front of Jesus.

It was obvious that he could not speak since he made gestures and signs with his hands and pointed to his mouth, but no sound came out. Someone nearby told me this man had been unable to speak from birth. We saw Jesus touch the man's throat, look heavenward, offer a prayer — and the man began to speak clearly, in a Galilean dialect. I have never seen this happen before.

Jesus did not linger but made his way quietly through the crowd.

As he passed near us, we overheard two people arguing where Jesus derives his power. "It is through Beelzebub, the prince of devils, that he casts out devils," said one. The other decided to test Jesus. "Master, give us a sign from heaven."

Jesus looked at the man and at those around him, his eyes seeming to read their thoughts. He turned and walked a few feet up to a little elevation and turned around to speak.

"Every kingdom divided against itself is heading for ruin," Jesus said, "and a household divided against itself collapses. So too with Satan, if he is divided against himself, how can his kingdom stand, since you assert that it is through Beelzebub that I cast out devils.

"Now, if it is through Beelzebub that I cast out devils, through whom do your own experts cast them out? Let them be your judges then." He stopped and looked around. No one answered. Clearly Jesus was claiming power from a higher source, someone with authority over demons.

"But if it is through the finger of God that I cast out devils, then know that the kingdom of God has overtaken you."

There must have been about one hundred gathered before him. No one moved. All eyes were staring up at him.

"So long as a strong man fully armed guards his own palace," Jesus continued, "his goods are undisturbed, but when someone stronger than he attacks and defeats him, the stronger man takes away all that he relied on and shares out his spoil."

As he looked at some of his questioners, he said, "He who is not with me is against me, and he who does not gather with me scatters."

This seems to be a challenge, Luke. If one who has heard the word of God from Jesus does not follow him and support him, it is just as if he is against him.

Jesus continued. "When an unclean spirit goes out of a man, it wanders through waterless country looking for a place to rest, and not finding one it says, 'I will go back to the home I came from.' But on arrival, finding it swept and tidied, it then goes off and brings seven other spirits more wicked than itself, and they go in and set up house there, so that the man ends up by being worse than he was before."

Then he stopped. Before anyone else in the crowd could react, a woman raised her voice and proclaimed, "Happy the womb that bore you and the breasts you sucked."

Now, Luke that is an expression reserved for one who is extraordinary. It would have been said in the Greek culture to Alexander the Great, to Socrates or Hippocrates.

Jesus called back to the woman, "Still happier those who hear the word of God and keep it."

By this time the crowd was growing larger and larger. It seemed that everyone from the village and the surrounding countryside was there. Many of them implored him to work a miracle, give a sign of his divine power. But Jesus reprimanded them. "This is a wicked generation. It is asking for a sign. The only sign it will be given is the sign of Jonah.

"For just as Jonah became a sign to the Ninevites,[1] so will the Son of Man be to this generation. On Judgment Day the Queen of the South[2] will rise with the men of this generation and condemn them because she came from the ends of the earth to hear the Wisdom of Solomon, and there is something greater than Solomon here."

Luke, the Queen of Sheba did bring all her entourage to hear the wisdom of King Solomon. And Jonah, a very reluctant prophet, preached to the large city of Nineveh that they should repent for their sins or face destruction.

"On Judgment Day," Jesus continued, "the men of Nineveh will stand up with this generation and condemn it because when Jonah preached they repented, and there is something greater than Jonah here."

As I looked around I saw all eyes focused on Jesus. After a moment he again spoke.

"No one lights a lamp and puts it in some hidden place or under a tub, but on a lamp stand so that people may see the light when they come in.

"The lamp of your body is your eye. When your eye is sound, your whole body is filled with light, but when it is diseased your body too will be all darkness. See to it then that the light inside you is not darkness. If, therefore, your whole body is filled with light, and no trace of darkness, it will be light entirely, as when the lamp shines on you with its rays."

Luke, all of these parables are rich with meaning. Darkness is the absence of God's word. But if we listen to Jesus and follow his teachings, Jesus says, the word of God will light us from within.

Jesus had just finished speaking when Ezra, a Pharisee and patient of ours, pushed his way through the crowd and addressed him. "Sir," he said, "Will you and your company dine with us tonight?" Jesus seemed surprised and said, "There are about twenty of us." The Pharisee replied, "I can accommodate them all." As Ezra passed near us we greeted him. He looked up rather startled, returned the greeting and said abruptly, "I want both of you to come too." And we nodded in acceptance. As the family's physicians we felt we could not decline.

Gradually, the crowd dispersed. Jesus withdrew deeper into the woods to meditate, and his listeners divided into groups of three or four to discuss what they had just heard. Elisa and I went home to get ready for the dinner.

We walked the distance to the rather grand home of the Pharisee. We were ushered in, went through the usual ablutions and took our assigned places. We knew most of the people there because they were our patients.

When Jesus came to the door he walked right into the banquet hall. Elisa and I looked at each other. He had passed up the ritual washing before meals. Jesus never passes this up.

The host had also seen Jesus enter and had noticed that he had not washed. He walked up to Jesus and looked at his hands and feet, in a way that attracted the attention of every one in the room. Jesus stood up and spoke loudly and clearly. "Oh, you Pharisees! You clean the outside of cup and plate, while inside yourselves you are filled with extortion and wickedness. Fools! Did not he who made the outside make the inside too?

"Instead, give alms from what you have and then indeed everything will be clean for you."

And that was not enough. "But alas for you Pharisees! You who pay your tithe of mint and rue and all sorts of garden herbs and overlook justice and the love of God! These you should have practiced without leaving others undone.

"Alas for you Pharisees who like taking the seats of honor in the synagogues and being greeted obsequiously in the market squares."

Elisa and I looked at each other. We had never heard Jesus speak like this. His face was grim and his eyes flashed like they had fire in them.

"Alas for you," he continued, "because you are like the unmarked tombs that men walk on without knowing it!"

And he looked at all of the guests, who were shocked that a guest would speak like that to his host. And so were we. Then we noticed a man come forward. We recognized him as one of the unscrupulous lawyers of Capernaum.

"Master," he said righteously, "when you speak like this you insult us." He received nods of approval from the others.

Jesus looked directly at him. "Alas for you lawyers also," he replied, "because you load on men burdens that are unendurable, burdens that you yourselves do not move a finger to lift."

To our surprise, no one responded right away to these harsh words. "Never have I seen a lawyer at a loss for words!" Elisa whispered.

Jesus continued. "Alas for you who build the tombs of the prophets, the men your ancestors killed! In this way, you both witness what your ancestors did and approve it. They did the killing, you do the building.

"And that is why the wisdom of God said, 'I will send them prophets and apostles. Some they will slaughter and persecute, so that this generation will have to answer for prophet's blood that has been shed since the foundation of the world, from the blood of Abel[3] to the blood of Zechariah,[4] who was murdered between the altar and the sanctuary. Yes, I tell you, this generation will have to answer for it all.'"

Luke, you may remember from your reading of the Scriptures that Abel was slain by his brother Cain in a fit of jealousy. And Zechariah was a prophet who had tried to call Israel back from their sins and was killed in the Temple about eight hundred years ago.

Jesus continued. "Alas for you lawyers who have taken away the key of knowledge! You have not gained access yourselves, and have prevented others going in who wanted to."

Then Jesus got up, thanked Ezra and left, followed by The Twelve. Luke, Elisa and I were torn between leaving, out of loyalty to Jesus, and staying, out of respect for our host.

The problem was settled for us in a moment when we heard a scream of pain from the rear of the banquet hall. A servant came rushing to the host to tell him that one of the other servants had fallen and was badly hurt. Elisa and I rose immediately and went to the injured servant. He had tripped over a break in the stone of the floor that needed repair. Both bones of the right forearm were fractured. The servant was in great pain, so I asked for the strongest wine that the host had. One servant said, as he looked at the host, "May I get your special stock?" Ezra objected. "No, not that!" But I interrupted. "We need the best. Get it!" The host was furious. Elisa tore up the costly table linens for wrappings and found some wood for splints. By this time I had enough wine in the servant to serve as a mild anesthetic. I had two servants hold the man at the shoulder while I pulled at the wrist, and after prolonged tension the bones snapped into place. Elisa applied the splint with skill. Then we gave his fellow servants instructions to give to his family on how to care of him and when to bring him to the clinic.

By the time we were finished, the banquet was well under way. Ezra had insisted the meal proceed as planned. However, the servants were so thankful to us that they served us in the kitchen. Luke, we felt more at home there. We were both exhausted and also hungry. They served us delicious meats, several types of breads that we had never tasted before and sauces and vegetables. Then we had fruit for dessert, which the Pharisee had brought from afar. They gave us the remainder of the host's special wine. It was really choice wine. We thanked them, checked our patient and finally returned to the banquet room, informing the host of the instructions that had been given for the care of the injured man. We thanked him for the invitation, excused ourselves and left.

We had heard Ezra blame the servant for falling on the broken floor and delaying the banquet. We knew that he felt no responsibility for the servant's injury. We knew also that the servant had a wife and several children, so we knew without discussion that we would not charge for this service. Elisa found out where the servant lived, so she could bring food to the children until he could work again.

As we were leaving, we could hear the scribes and Pharisees mounting

---

a furious attack on Jesus. "How dare he say such things about us?" "What business is it of his how we treat others?"

They were organizing a plan to try to force answers from him on innumerable questions. "We must be on the alert to hear what he says," we heard. "We must set traps to catch him in something he might say."

As we got out into the quiet of the darkness, we sighed in relief. Both of us had felt uncomfortable in Ezra's house and among his guests. We walked a while and I said, "Jesus spoke truly about the Pharisees. We have seen how they treat those under them."

Elisa replied, "Jesus is the first one ever who said what needed to be said at the place where it should be heard. Never has anyone had the nerve to do this. Now all the authorities — the Pharisees and scribes, the priests and Levites — will be against him. Do you think that he realizes that?"

"Yes," I replied. "He knew exactly what to say and when to say it. Still, I doubt if any one of those guests who heard him tonight will change."

"Today we have seen a different Jesus," Elisa said. "He fought for the rights of those to whom society gives no rights. And he has left the best lawyers in town speechless with his remarks."

By this time we were at our home, tired yet invigorated by what we had seen Jesus do tonight.

May God bless you, Luke.

Joseph

[1] Jonah 3:1-10

[2] 1 Kings 10:1-13

[3] Genesis 4:1-14

[4] 2 Chronicles 24:20-22

Letter 80

Dear Luke, Rachel and David have just returned from a week with the followers of Jesus as he preached in the villages of Galilee. We gathered at the clinic tonight for a special meeting to hear what they had seen and learned.

"Just to be in his company made it the most memorable week of our lives," David said. "The very first day, as we came to a village, people gathered very quickly around us. There were many, many people in the crowd, so many that we were treading on one another. Rachel and I had to struggle to stay on our feet and stay close to Jesus.

"Jesus spoke that day first to his disciples. 'Be on your guard,' he said, 'against the yeast of the Pharisees — that is, their hypocrisy. Everything that is now covered will be uncovered, and everything now hidden will be made clear. For this reason, whatever you have said in the dark will be heard in the daylight, and what you have whispered in hidden places will be proclaimed on the housetops.'

"Then he turned to the multitude that had gathered to hear him and said, 'To you, my friends, I say, Do not be afraid of those who kill the body and after that can do no more. I will tell you whom to fear. Fear him who, after he has killed, has the power to cast into hell. Yes, I tell you, fear him.

"'Can you not buy five sparrows for two pennies? And yet not one is forgotten in God's sight. Why, every hair on your head has been counted. There is no need to be afraid. You are worth more than hundreds of sparrows.'"

"Ana, are you taking this down?" I said. Ana only nodded, too busy taking notes to reply.

"Some of the crowd grew restless," David told us. "Many were eager to see Jesus work a cure of some sort. But most were there to learn from him, just as we were. There is a great desire for knowledge out there among the people.

"Jesus looked over the crowd, which was still gathering, and addressed his disciples. 'I tell you, if anyone declares himself for me in the presence of men, the Son of Man will declare himself for him in the presence of God's angels. But the man who disowns me in the presence of men will be disowned in the presence of God's angels.'

"'Everyone who says a word against the Son of Man will be forgiven, but he who blasphemes against the Spirit of the Lord will not be forgiven.'

"'When they take you before synagogues and magistrates and authorities, do not worry about how to defend yourselves or what to say, because when the time comes, the Spirit will teach you what you must say.'"

"My dear friends," David continued, "just the question of this Spirit he speaks of could be debated an entire evening…"

But someone interrupted David. "Go on! Let us hear more about what Jesus said." So he continued.

"Another day, a rather well-dressed man came up to Jesus and said, 'Master, tell my brother to give me a share of our inheritance.'

"'My friend,' Jesus replied, 'who appointed me your judge or an arbitrator of your claims?'

"Jesus must have known that the man was trying to trap him," David said. "I know this because of what he said next: 'Watch, and be on your guard against avarice of any kind, for a man's life is not made secure by what he owns, even when he has more than he needs.'

"Jesus gathered his thoughts for a few moments. Then he began a parable, speaking in that clear, distinct voice that carries so well over the crowd.

"'There was once a rich man who, having had a good harvest from his land, thought to himself, "What am I to do? I have not enough room to store my crops."

"'Then he said, "This is what I will do. I will pull down my barns and build bigger ones, and store all my grain and my goods in them, and I will say to my soul: My soul, you have plenty of good things laid by for many years to come. Take things easy, eat, drink, and have a good time."

"'But God said to him, "Fool! This very night the demand will be made for your soul, and this hoard of yours, whose will it be then?"

"'So it is,' Jesus said, 'when a man stores up treasure for himself in place of making himself rich in the sight of God.' And everyone was quiet.

"Jesus then turned to his disciples. 'That is why I am telling you not to worry about your life and what you are to eat, nor about your body and how you are to clothe it. For life means more than food and the body more than clothing.

"'Think of the ravens. They do not sow or reap, they have no storehouses and no barns, yet God feeds them. And how much more are you worth than the birds! Can any of you, for all his worrying, add a single cubit to his span of life? If the smallest things, therefore, are outside your control, why worry about the rest?

"'Think of the flowers. They never have to spin or weave, yet I assure you, not even Solomon in all his regalia was robed like one of these. Now if that is how God clothes the grass in the field, which is there today and thrown into the furnace tomorrow, how much more will he look after you, you men of little faith!

"'But you, you must not set your hearts on things to eat and things to drink, nor must you worry. It is the pagans of this world who set their hearts on all these things. Your Father well knows you need them. No, set your hearts on His kingdom, and these other things will be given you as well.

"'There is no need to be afraid, little flock, for it has pleased your Father to give you the kingdom.'

"And then he continued to address the disciples. 'Sell your possessions and give alms. Get yourselves purses that do not wear out, treasure that will not fail you in heaven where no thief can reach it and no moth destroy it. For where your treasure is, there will your heart be also.'

"Do you see, my friends?" David said, interrupting his story. "The treasure that Jesus is talking about must be in heaven, not here. And this directive to sell all your possessions, what a powerful command that is!

"Some of the disciples, I noticed, seemed upset by these words. But I looked at The Twelve and I realized that they had already given up everything to follow Jesus.

"Just look at Peter and Andrew, James and John. They all left a good livelihood as fishermen to follow Jesus. And Levi — he went from being rich to having no possessions."

David stopped and motioned to Rachel to finish the story. "Jesus had even more to say," she said.

"'See that you are dressed for action,' he told us, 'and have your lamps lit. Be like men waiting for their master to return from the wedding feast, ready to open the door as soon as he comes and knocks. Happy those servants whom the master finds awake when he comes. I tell you solemnly, he will put on an apron, sit them down at table and wait on them. It may be in the second watch he comes, or in the third, but happy those servants if he finds them ready. You may be quite sure of this, that if the householder had known at what hour the burglar would come, he would not have let anyone break through the wall of his house. You too must stand ready, because the Son of Man is coming at an hour you do not expect.'

"Then Peter spoke up and asked, 'Lord, do you mean the parable for us or for everyone?'

"Jesus looked at him and replied. 'What sort of steward, then, is faithful and wise enough for the master to place him over his household to give them their allowance of food at the proper time? Happy that servant if his master's arrival finds him at this employment. I tell you truly, he will place him over everything he owns.

"'But as for the servant who says to himself, "My master is taking his time coming," and sets about beating the men servants and the maids, and eating and drinking and getting drunk, his master will come on a day he does not expect and at an hour he does not know. The master will cut him off and send him to the same fate as the unfaithful.

"'The servant who knows what his master wants but has not even started to carry out those wishes will receive very many strokes of the lash. The one who did not know but deserves to be beaten for what he has done will receive fewer strokes.

"'When a man has had a great deal given him, a great deal will be demanded of him. When a man has had a great deal given him on trust, even more is expected of him.'

"Here again is another profound statement," David said. "It seems that we are obliged to spread our love and knowledge of God and not keep it to ourselves.

"But his next words still confuse me. The tone of his voice became even more forceful as he proclaimed the following: 'I have come to bring fire to the earth, and how I wish it were blazing already. There is a baptism I must still receive, and how great is my distress till it is over!'"

David shook his head. "That is something that I cannot understand."

It fell to Rachel to pick up the story. "Jesus returned to this message again on the last day. It was a rather disturbing afternoon. At one point Jesus said, 'Do you suppose that I am here to bring peace on earth? No, I tell you, but rather division. For from now on a household of five will be divided — three against two and two against three, the father divided against the son, son against father, mother against daughter, daughter against mother, mother-in-law against daughter-in-law, daughter-in-law against mother-in-law.'

"Such a thought really upset me," Rachel said.

"Then Jesus spoke rather harshly again. 'When you see a cloud looming up in the west you say at once that rain is coming, and so it does. And when the wind is from the south you say it will be hot, and it is. Hypocrites! You know how to interpret the face of the earth and the sky. How is it you do not know how to interpret these times?

"'Why not judge for yourselves what is right? For example, when you go to court with your opponent, try to settle with him on the way, or he may drag you before the judge and the judge hand you over to the bailiff and the bailiff have you thrown into prison. I tell you, you will not get out till you have paid the very last penny.'"

"And just then," David interjected, "a number of people pushed their way through the crowd to Jesus. They had just arrived, and their leader told Jesus about the Galileans whom Pilate had murdered, mingling their blood with that of their sacrifice.

"You may remember that some years ago a group of Galileans came to Jerusalem on a pilgrimage and Pilate's soldiers thought that they were starting a riot and killed them. Herod and Pilate have not spoken to each other since that time.

"Jesus looked at them and said, 'Do you suppose these Galileans who suffered like that were greater sinners than any other Galileans? They were not, I tell you. No. But unless you repent you will all perish as they did. Or those eighteen on whom the tower at Siloam fell and killed them? Do you suppose that they were guiltier than all the other people living in Jerusalem? They were not, I tell you. No, but unless you repent you will all perish as they did.'"

Finally, dear Luke, Rachel recounted the last words of Jesus to this group of followers, a parable to leave them something more to think about.

"'A man had a fig tree planted in his vineyard, and he came looking for fruit on it but found none. He said to the man who looked after the vineyard, "Look here, for three years now I have been coming to look for fruit on this fig tree and finding none, cut it down. Why should it be taking up the ground?" "Sir," the man replied, "leave it one more year and give me time to dig round it and manure it. It may bear fruit next year. If not, then you can cut it down," he said.'"

"But what does that mean?" Ruth had found her voice before the rest of us. "Perhaps," said Samson, "Jesus means that with loving care the tree will produce. That we will get good out of our friends and those who are not our friends, if we treat them with kindness."

We broke up into small groups about this time and started talking about what we had heard from David and Rachel, and the discussion continued until the hour was late.

Joseph

Letter 81

Greetings in the name of the Lord God, the God of Abraham, Moses and David. May His blessings be upon you on this Sabbath day!

It was good to hear from you and to know that you are deeply involved in reading the Scriptures. Rabbi David must make a fine teacher.

Today Jesus was teaching in the synagogue when there was a great stir at the door. I looked and saw an older woman, stooped and bent, walking into the room reserved for men. I recognized her as a patient Erasmus had first treated many years ago. She had the crippling disease of the spine that some women get.[1]

You remember, Luke, we saw a lot of this in Athens in women who lived long enough to have stopped their monthly flow. Their skin gets dry and wrinkled, the muscles seem to gradually disappear, and they get a forward curve in the chest. They shorten in height, walk with their heads down and fall forward if they do not balance themselves on a stick. They lose a lot of weight and it appears that their spark of life is slowly burning down.

This woman hobbled in with the walking stick she has had to use for eighteen years. To see Jesus across the room, she had to strain her neck muscles to lift her head high enough. When Jesus saw her, he stopped his teaching. "Come near, woman," he said.

I could see that she was both embarrassed and pleased — pleased because the teacher had spoken to her, embarrassed that she was unable to make her way forward very rapidly and also because she was in a place in the synagogue where she did not belong.

Jesus waited patiently as she shuffled up to him and strained to look directly at him, then he laid his hands on her.

"Woman," he said, "you are rid of your infirmity."

Luke, there in front of all of us, this pitiable old woman suddenly stood upright, her sunken face filled in, the wrinkles disappeared, and she looked pink and healthy! She dropped her stick, knelt down and kissed Jesus' feet. She turned to leave the synagogue, proclaiming "Praise God! Praise the Lord God!"

I looked at the presiding synagogue official and I could see his face get red. Jesus had healed on the Sabbath! He had his assistant ring the bell for order, then got up and addressed the people. "There are six days when

---

work is to be done. Come and be healed on one of those days and not on the Sabbath."

The smile left the face of Jesus.

"Hypocrites!" he cried out. "Is there one of you who does not untie his ox or his donkey from the manger on the Sabbath and take it out for watering? And this woman, a daughter of Abraham whom Satan has held bound all these eighteen years — was it not right to untie her bonds on the Sabbath day?"

The official bristled at this insult. He and other opponents of Jesus began to argue with each other. Most of the men assembled for worship, however, were excited at the wonder that Jesus had worked and eager to hear what else he had to say. Jesus obliged, resuming his teaching.

"What is the kingdom of God like? What shall I compare it with? It is like a mustard seed, which a man took and threw into his garden. It grew and became a tree and the birds of the air sheltered in its branches.

"What shall I compare the kingdom of God with? It is like the yeast a woman took and mixed in with three measures of flour till it was leavened all through." I noticed that the officials of the synagogue were holding their hands over their ears so as not to hear the words of Jesus or the praises of the crowd. When I looked back at Jesus, I discovered he had left the synagogue.

Later, over the Sabbath meal, Erasmus recounted with joy what had happened at the synagogue a short time before. "Ach! Ach! I have treated that woman for years and she got progressively worse. I saw her suffer. And now she is well! We saw a miracle this morning. This man Jesus is more than a prophet!

"Did you see the officials of the synagogue object that the cure was made on the Sabbath? But that is not all. They are mad that this upstart Jesus has a great following and continues to defy them. They do not see through their own prejudices!"

My mother Mary spoke thoughtfully. "Jesus was teaching the value of every single person," she said, "even women who are well past their child-bearing years.

"Jesus likened the kingdom of God to yeast, that it spreads and soon all of the dough is leavened. That must mean that the kingdom of God will spread throughout the world."

"Even to Gentiles?" asked Sarah.

"So it seems" was her reply. Luke, the teachings of Jesus are debated like this in homes throughout Galilee.

Perhaps someday they will be debated in Antioch as well.

Joseph

---

[1] Osteoporosis (softening of the bone) due to loss of calcium is common in women after menopause. The vertebrae become compressed. The anterior portions collapse and cause a forward curvature of the spine.

Letter 82

Grace and peace be unto you, dear Luke. Today a messenger came to the clinic from Geru, one of the leading Pharisees. He asked me to come immediately to help two of his servants who had been injured. I told Elisa and Erasmus that I probably wouldn't be back until late, loaded up my horse with poles and canvas for litters and all of the medicines that I usually carry.

Erasmus had warned us about this particular Pharisee earlier. He was a hard taskmaster and would never take care of his servants or his hired help. Whenever Erasmus was called to treat an injury, Geru instructed him to collect payment from the patient, not from him. But he would also cut off all pay and sustenance to the servant at the time of the injury.

It was about an hour's ride to the place of the accident. Geru had been building a bigger storehouse for the abundant harvest he expected. It was the type of work that usually requires eight strong men, but he had insisted six men do the work of eight. The six were lifting a heavy beam and it had fallen and pinned two of his workers. They had finally lifted it off the men by the time that I arrived. I examined the men and found that one had a fracture of his forearm and the other a leg injury. There was no break in the skin of either so I again felt very blessed, as this meant that there would be no infection.

I first prepared a mixture of wine and extract from the sap of the poppy, gave it to both of the men, and waited for it to start working. One servant held the first man while I pulled on the hand. The bones snapped into place and I was able to set the forearm into its proper position. After this I set the arm in a splint, wrapped it and hung it in a sling from around his neck. I instructed him to watch his fingers, to make sure they didn't swell and discolor, and I asked him to come to see me at the clinic in about a week.

Then I went to the other man. He was quite numb from the medication by then, and I was able to examine his leg very well. Both bones were broken. The small bone snapped into place but we were unable to get the larger bone in alignment. A splint would help, but he would have a limp. I fashioned a stretcher and put the man on it.

After I finished I went to see Geru, who was cursing the rest of the workers for not being able to lift a heavy beam. I told him that I needed two men to carry the second injured man back to his home.

"Let him get home on his own," the Pharisee retorted. "I don't have men to spare to take him."

Luke, there was no reasoning with this man. I explained to him the danger of putting weight now on the injured limb, that the worker would be able to walk with a crutch in a few days, but Geru did not want to hear this. He told the foreman to use the lash on the remaining men, to force them to work harder. I was aghast at this.

Just then two men came up and saw the men struggling with the beam and the foreman brutally lashing their backs. It was Jesus and Peter. They immediately stepped over to offer their aid. With their help the workers raised three long wooden beams and put them in their proper places. Geru continued to berate his foreman to make the men work faster.

When the job was done, Jesus and Peter brushed the dust off their clothes. Geru did not thank them but ordered the foreman to put the workers to other tasks. Jesus and Peter walked over to see the injured men and me. I explained what happened. Jesus remarked, "Good work, Joseph," and they both continued on their way.

Geru rode away with a scowl on his face. The messenger who had summoned me helped me lift the injured man onto my horse, and I led the horse as gently as possible to the place where the patient was staying. I instructed him to stay off his leg, and from the limb of a tree I made a crutch for him to use.

By then it was sunset and time to return home. I told Elisa how Jesus and Peter had done the work of the injured men with no word of thanks from the Pharisee. She just bowed her head and said, "We must pray for Geru."

Luke, that is the last thing that I would have thought of doing. I wished that the Lord would send fire upon him. But Elisa's way is more in keeping with the prayer of forgiveness Jesus taught us to say.

Joseph

Letter 83

The two injured workmen are recovering quite well, Luke, but are still unable to work. Each of them has come to me and said, "I must pay you for helping me, but I am no longer employed and I have no money. I have children who are hungry." I told them, "Don't worry."

I went to see Geru and told him of their circumstances. He scowled and said, "If these two workers had been careful, they would not have been hurt. I am not responsible for their actions nor am I responsible for taking care of them."

I left because I knew that there was no further reasoning with him. Yet when I see this man taking the front seat in the synagogue, I can't help being annoyed.

Today is the Sabbath and I was at the synagogue with Jesus and the disciples when the Pharisees and the scribes came in. They were dressed in rich fabrics and showing off their broad and long phylacteries.

Luke, these are capsules worn by all males after the age of fourteen that contain quotes from the Torah and profession of their belief in God. They are worn during prayer time and are wrapped or strapped around the forehead or upper arm, near the mind and the heart.[1] The longer the tassels, the more closely these people think they are obeying the Law.[2]

Jesus had only scorn for them today.

He gestured to those in the front seats as he addressed the rest of us. "Look," he said. "The scribes and the Pharisees occupy the chair of Moses. You must therefore do what they tell you and listen to what they say. But do not be guided by what they do, since they do not practice what they preach."

"They tie heavy burdens and lay them on men's shoulders, but will they lift a finger to remove them? Not they!

"Everything they do is done to attract attention, like wearing broader phylacteries and longer tassels, like wanting to take the front seats in the synagogues and having people call them Rabbi."

Luke, I was pleased to hear Jesus rebuke this behavior in public even as he asks us to love and forgive those who injure us.

Elisa has been out to visit the families of the injured workers. She often goes out and visits the families of such patients and brings them food and clothing. She also leaves money with the food that she brings them. No one knows it. She just does it. Often she has someone else deliver the food.

Elisa and I realize that we will meet people like Geru often in our lives and it is only by God's grace that we are able to help their victims.

May the Lord God watch over you.

Joseph

[1] Exodus 13:9-16
Deuteronomy 11:18-19

[2] Numbers 15:37-39
Deuteronomy 22:12

Letter 84

Our days have been very busy, Luke. It will soon be spring, our second since our return to Capernaum, and in our free time Elisa and I help my father and mother in the garden they planted near the orchard. We also prune the fruit trees and grape vines and fertilize them with manure from our stable. We should have a productive garden and fruit orchard again this year. Last week we cleaned out the dead branches and scrub trees in the woods on the other end of the property. We left one heavily wooded area untouched, however. It is where Jesus often goes to meditate.

He and The Twelve have been teaching and preaching in Jerusalem much of the winter. Today we received word that they had returned to Capernaum, and this afternoon Jude, also called Thaddeus, came to the clinic. He was eager to tell us how Jesus had been received in Jerusalem and what the disciples had learned from Jesus.

His fame has grown as word of his miracles has spread from Galilee to Judea, Jude said. "Everywhere we went, people gathered to see and hear Jesus. One day someone said to him, 'Sir, will there be only a few saved?' But Jesus answered him indirectly, as he so often does. 'Try your best to enter by the narrow door, because, I tell you, many will try to enter and will not succeed.'

"And another day, Jesus said this, 'Once the master of the house has got up and locked the door, you may find yourself knocking at the door, saying, "Lord, open to us." But he will answer, "I do not know where you come from." Then you will find yourself saying, "We once ate and drank in your company. You taught in our streets," but he will reply, "I do not know where you come from. Away from me, all you wicked men!"

"'Then there will be wailing and gnashing of teeth, when you see Abraham and Isaac and Jacob and all the prophets in the kingdom of God, and yourselves turned outside. And men from east and west, from north and south, will come to take their places at the feast in the kingdom of God.

"'Yes, there are those now last who will be first, and those now first who will be last.'"

Jude stopped, took a long drink of cold water and went on. "We spent about a week at the Temple, where Jesus taught and prayed all of the days. We spent the nights in a cave in the Garden of Gethsemane. I must tell you, the view of the Temple in the morning sunlight from Gethsemane is indescribable. The golden dome glows like a ball of fire. You must see it from this spot sometime."

Elisa and I looked at each other as we both recalled the time that we saw this very sight during our years in Jerusalem.

Jude took his leave and Elisa and I finished cleaning up and went home. We ate our meal sitting on the bench in the flower garden that my parents had planted, enjoying a gentle breeze.

"Those were harsh words coming from Jesus," Elisa said, "that it is not easy to be saved."

"But he also says that people will come from all over into the kingdom of God. He must mean more than Jews."

"Of course," Elisa answered. "All are God's people. Jesus performed miracles for the centurion's child. God sent Elijah to a widow of Zarephath and Elisha to cure Naaman the Syrian of his leprosy. That shows that he loves everyone."

Then Elisa continued. "The narrow door could mean that it is not easy to be saved, there must be a determined relationship with God. Further, the chosen people are free to accept or reject these teachings. So are the Gentiles. They can all reject the Word of God, although I cannot understand who would do that."

She hesitated and then said softly, "God gave us free will. He would not want it any other way. We must accept Him willingly."

Then I attempted my own analysis. "It seems to me there is a deeper meaning of Jesus' statements that those who ate and drank with him may be locked out. Does he mean that those who do not believe in his teachings will be excluded? And then he says that people will come from all over. It seems to mean that Gentiles will be involved. Does he mean that some of the chosen people will choose not to believe and he will go to the others?"

Luke, Elisa looked at me with an expression of amazement on her face. "Joseph!" she exclaimed. "You are really getting the point of Jesus' teachings." We sat and talked in the evening shadows until it was late.

And so it is, my dear Luke. The God of Israel will save all people if they ask for it.

Joseph

Letter 85

Praise be to the Lord God.

Judith and Abriam have returned from a visit with Joanna and Chuza at Herod's palace. You may remember this couple was in Herod's court the night the head of John the Baptist was delivered on a tray. Their hearts as well as ours still ache from that event.

Now we learn that the rumors we hear about Herod are true. He wants to be rid of this troublesome preacher Jesus. "I wonder if Jesus knows this," Judith asked us.

"He has full knowledge of Herod's intentions," Elisa answered. "But he does not seem to fear anyone, even Herod."

This evening, Elisa and I joined others of Capernaum at the lakeside, sitting and listening to Jesus teach. We saw several Pharisees coming toward us. Now Luke, not all of the Pharisees are against Jesus. Some have listened and accepted his teachings. As these men approached, it was obvious that they were among those friendly to Jesus.

After the usual greetings they spoke words of warning. "You must go away," they said. "Leave this place, because Herod means to kill you." But Jesus did not seem dissuaded. His expression grew hard.

"You may go and give that fox this message: Learn that today and tomorrow I cast out devils and on the third day attain my end. But for today and tomorrow and the next day I must go on, since it would not be right for a prophet to die outside of Jerusalem."

Jesus stopped and looked at each of us, silencing our protests before we could voice them. Then he looked to the south in the direction of Jerusalem, his expression veiled.

"Jerusalem, Jerusalem, you that kill the prophets and stone those who are sent to you," Jesus said. "How often have I longed to gather your children, as a hen gathers her brood under her wings! And you refused!

"So be it! Your house will be left to you. Yes, I promise you, you shall not see me till the time comes when you can say, 'Blessings on him who comes in the name of the Lord!'"

Then we followed his gaze up to the sky, as if we could better discern the meaning of these statements. And as our eyes returned to where Jesus had stood, he was gone. The crowd dispersed in silence.

Elisa took off her sandals and put her feet in the cold water, then we sat on the shore and talked until the sun set.

Luke, Jesus spoke of Jerusalem as if it is evil. Yet we know that he loves Jerusalem as we do. It is the center of the Jewish faith. It is literally the home of God. He seems to say that great pain will afflict the city. He said that if Jerusalem does not listen to him it would be destroyed.

What worries us most is that Jesus seems to believe he will meet the same fate as so many of the prophets of old.

Joseph

Letter 86

Peace be with you, Luke. Today is the Sabbath. Elisa and I were invited to a banquet at the home of Menahem, the leading Pharisee and a patient of ours. Most of the other guests were lawyers, Pharisees and scribes.

Menahem greeted his guests on the portico and he seemed pleased that we came. His home is one of the largest and most ornate in Capernaum. I will not describe all of this to you. What a waste! Luke, suffice it to say that both Elisa and I felt uncomfortable. A servant washed our feet, anointed our heads with aromatic oil and ushered us into a large, magnificently furnished reception room. The other guests, most of them our patients, were cordial to us. Elisa and I mingled in the group and politely listened to their conversations about business.

Suddenly, we noticed that everyone was looking toward the entrance. Elisa whispered, "Jesus and The Twelve are entering the room." They, too, went through the usual greeting of the host and the washing of feet. Jesus was smiling and laughing.

All of the guests had heard of Jesus and many were eager to meet him. His fame as a teacher and a healer has spread. Only a few of the very rigid Pharisees did not join the group. I heard them saying to each other how unwise it was for the host to invite Jesus and his followers. Moments later we were surprised to see a merchant named Thrasas, one of our patients, come in with two servants assisting him.

Now, Luke, here is a man with dropsy whom we have been treating for a very long time. We have purged him and given him medication to make his bladder flow, but he continues to swell, bloat and to be short of breath. His legs and feet are twice normal in size, with the flesh of his feet bulging painfully over his sandal straps. His hands and face are puffy and his abdomen protrudes. You know what these patients look like.

We went to speak to him and he greeted us between gasps of breath. We arranged a comfortable chair for him to sit in. There he sat while his servants fanned him and continued to wipe perspiration off his face and arms. "I wanted to come to this banquet," he said, "but now I do not feel well." He became acutely short of breath and started to cough up pink froth. He looked like a terminal case of dropsy, and Elisa and I feared that he would expire there in Menahem's home.

Thrasas looked around the room and then in the direction of the crowd around Jesus. "Who is over there?" he asked, and I answered, "Jesus of Nazareth." At that Thrasas got up from his chair and started in the direction of Jesus. The two servants, Elisa and I struggled to keep him from falling. Guests and other servants stopped what they were doing and watched this strange procession.

As Thrasas neared Jesus, he stopped to catch his breath. "Jesus," he said, wheezing as he spoke, "you could cure me. I know you can. I believe you can cure me."

Jesus looked around and saw the lawyers and Pharisees watching. Addressing them he said, "Is it lawful to cure on the Sabbath or not?" There was no answer. Jesus then looked at Thrasas. He looked into his eyes as I have seen him do so many times, as if he knew that this was a man of deep faith. Then he said, "Your sins are forgiven. Be you healed. Go on your way."

Luke, Thrasas suddenly stopped his coughing and heavy breathing. And as we watched, the swelling left his face, hands and feet, and his abdomen went down so rapidly that he had to grab his garments or they would have fallen off.

He fell down on his knees before Jesus and thanked him, but Jesus raised him up and suggested that he go and thank God. Thrasas summoned his servants, nodded to us, thanked his host and left. The guests were aghast.

At that moment a servant, not knowing what had just happened, announced that the banquet was ready, and everyone moved toward the banquet hall.

Jesus stood to one side. He watched the guests crowding around the head of the table, trying to find their places there. Suddenly he spoke, his voice rising above the noise and commanding our attention.

"When you are invited by someone to a wedding party," he said, "do not sit at the place of honor. A more distinguished person than you may have been invited, and the person who invited you may come and say, 'Give up your place to this man.' And then, to your embarrassment, you would have to go and take the lowest place.

"No, when you are a guest, make your way to the lowest place so that when the host comes he may say, 'My friend, move up higher.' In that way, everyone with you at the table will see you honored."

By this time, the Pharisees who had taken their places at the head of the table had turned their backs to Jesus.

"For everyone who exalts himself," Jesus said, "will be humbled, and everyone who humbles himself will be exalted."

With that he stepped to the foot of the table where the apostles, Elisa and I were gathered.

Clearly other guests considered these words of Jesus inappropriate on such an occasion. But they reminded me of what Abraham told Elisa and me before we left Jerusalem: "Do not brag about your work. Just do your work with excellence and your patients will brag for you."

In a short time, Menahem walked into the room and strode to the head of the table. He checked to see that there were sufficient pillows on which the guests would recline while eating. He looked around at the guests and his eyes rested on Jesus. He walked over to Jesus and asked him to come up and sit at his right. He also asked several others to come up higher, and the Pharisees who had taken the high places now had to come and sit near us. The expressions on their faces showed that they were really annoyed. But now we as followers of Jesus saw an opportunity. We talked about the teaching of Jesus, the cure of the paralytic, the boy with epilepsy and all of the others. The Pharisees tried to ignore us, but we only spoke louder.

The servants started bringing in the delicious food and Luke, it was good, but in such large amounts we knew much of it would go to waste. Elisa and I both thought of the many poor people who would have nothing to eat tonight.

Between one of the courses, Jesus turned to his host and spoke in a voice that carried down the table. "When you give a dinner, do not ask your friends, brothers, relatives or rich neighbors, for fear that they may repay the courtesy by inviting you in return. No, when you have a party, invite the poor, the crippled, the lame and the blind. That they cannot pay you back means that you are fortunate, because repayment will be made to you when the virtuous rise again."

On overhearing this, one of the guests near the middle of the table exclaimed, "Happy the man who will be at the feast in the kingdom of God!"

Jesus turned to him and began a parable. "There was a man who gave a large banquet, and he invited a large number of people. When the time of the banquet came, he sent his servant to say to those who had been invited, 'Come along, everything is ready now.' But all alike started to make excuses. The first said, 'I have bought a piece of land and I must go and see it. Please accept my apologies.' Another said, 'I have bought five yoke of oxen and am on my way to try them out. Please accept my apologies.' Yet another said, 'I have just got married and so am unable to come.'"

By this time, everyone in the room was quiet. The guests and servants alike all were listening to Jesus.

"The servant returned and reported this to his master. The householder in a rage said to the servant, 'Go out quickly into the streets and alleys of this town and bring in the poor, the crippled, the blind and the lame.' 'Sir,' said the servant, 'your orders have been carried out and there is still room.'

"Then the master said to the servant, 'Go to the open roads and the hedge rows and force people to come in and make sure my house is full, because, I tell you, not one of those who have been invited shall have a taste of my banquet.'"

No one spoke for some time. Finally, the servants brought in the next course and conversations resumed, though somewhat subdued. The host and Jesus carried on a conversation through the rest of the banquet, but we could see that several of the guests were annoyed.

Soon it was over. We thanked our host as we left. I could hear him quietly thanking Jesus for the advice given. As we walked home, Elisa said thoughtfully, "You know, Joseph, we do not invite our friends to dinner or the poor and beggars."

I replied, "We don't have guests because you do not have time to cook and we cannot afford servants. Your work among the sick is more important. And in the clinic we do not distinguish between our friends and the homeless."

"Yes," she replied, "but we must be on the alert so that we do not become the ones about whom Jesus was talking."

May God bless you, Luke, as he has blessed me with dear Elisa.

Joseph

Letter 87

Praise be to the one true God of Israel. Word spreads quickly of any new teaching of Jesus, as great crowds follow wherever he goes. They marvel at the evidence among them of his many cures.

The merchant Thrasas is now carrying on his business with new energy. I have had him come into the clinic several times just to be checked. The harsh sounds of his heart are gone and he has the soft lub-dub lub-dub sounds of the normal heart. His lungs are clear, he has no cough, his abdomen is flat and he can walk several miles without shortness of breath.

Today, the day after the Sabbath, Ruth heard Jesus speak and brought the news tonight to our meeting.

"Jesus had a great crowd around him, and he told several parables that I believe relate to us as his followers. He seems to be saying that being disciples of the Lord's way cannot be taken lightly. Here is what he said:

"'If any man comes to me without hating his father, mother, wife, children, brothers, sisters, yes, and his own life, too, he cannot be my disciple. Anyone who does not carry his cross and come after me cannot be my disciple.

"'And indeed, which of you here, intending to build a tower, would not first sit down and work out the cost to see if he had enough to finish it. Otherwise, if he laid the foundation, and then found himself unable to finish the work, the onlookers would all start making fun of him, saying, "Here is a man who started to build and is unable to finish."

"'Or again, what king marching to war against another king would not first sit down and consider whether with ten thousand men he could stand up to the other who advanced against him with twenty thousand? If not, then while the other king was still a long way off, he would send an envoy to sue for peace.'

"Here he paused and seemed to look into our very souls," Ruth said.

"'In the same way,' he said, 'none of you can be my disciples unless he gives up all his possessions.'

"And then he concluded with this riddle: 'Salt is a useful thing. But if the salt itself loses its taste, how can it be seasoned again? It is good for neither soil nor the manure heap. People throw it out. Listen, anyone who has ears to hear!'"

We wondered aloud at Jesus' remarks. To hate our families, to hate even our own lives, isn't that rather harsh?

David, our student of language, felt Jesus was using extreme words to make his point. "Surely a disciple can still love his family but perhaps be detached from it. Then again, if family members stand in the way of accepting God and caring for our fellow man, then he must renounce them."

"Giving up all his possessions is not easy either," said Rachel, David's wife. "Perhaps, some time in our lives, we may achieve this for a short time. But it is an ideal, perhaps, for which we should strive."

"The reference to salt losing its taste is rather unusual," Samson said. "As I see it, disciples must keep doing good and praying or they will slide back.

"As followers of Jesus we must become leaders too. Jesus does not want us to be satisfied with learning about the kingdom of God, he wants us to live it."

And so it went. It was another long evening of discussion, just like you and I used to have in Athens when we studied together. There were just two of us then. Now there are twelve to twenty, and all want to talk. I wish you could join us.

Joseph

Letter 88

Luke, I assure you that Jesus uses no medicine or maneuvers in curing the ill. He heals by the help of the Lord God of Israel, and so do the ones to whom he has given the power. Even so, his teachings are more fascinating than the cures, even revolutionary.

Today he described the mercy of God. He told two parables that give great hope to those of us who have made mistakes or feel unworthy in the eyes of others.

I rose early this Sabbath morning to visit my patients so I could meet Elisa and our parents at the synagogue. As I walked in to sit with the men, Erasmus said, "Look there. Jesus just came in to teach. This should be interesting."

Soon we could hear murmurings among the Pharisees and scribes. "There is that man Jesus coming to teach here. Does he expect us to listen to him? Tax collectors and other sinners seek his company to hear what he has to say. He should know that a good Jew does not associate with the likes of them." And one man from the group of scribes pointed to Jesus and said in a loud voice, "This man welcomes sinners and eats with them!"

Jesus must have been expecting that remark. He looked at the man who spoke and then around the entire synagogue, which fell silent, waiting for his reaction. He did not disappoint them.

"What man among you with a hundred sheep, losing one, would not leave the ninety-nine in the wilderness and go after the missing one until he found it? And when he found it, would he not joyfully take it on his shoulders and then, when he got home, call together his friends and neighbors? 'Rejoice with me,' he would say. 'I have found my sheep that was lost.'

"In the same way, I tell you, there will be more rejoicing in heaven over one repentant sinner than over ninety-nine virtuous men who have no need of repentance."

He paused to let the meaning of these words become clear.

"Or again, what woman with ten drachmas would not, if she lost one, light a lamp and sweep out the house and search thoroughly till she found it? And then, when she had found it, call together her friends and neighbors? 'Rejoice with me,' she would say. 'I have found the drachma I lost.' In the same way, I tell you, there is rejoicing among the angels of God over one repentant sinner."

Then he slipped away to his favorite corner of the synagogue and in one moment was deeply absorbed in meditation with God. No one approached him.

At the Sabbath meal, the conversation centered on these parables. "Surely," Erasmus said, "one lost sheep out of one hundred would not be a disastrous loss, but Jesus says that is man's way of thinking, not God's."

Sarah said thoughtfully, "Mothers put aside money so their sons will be able to offer a dower in marriage. The loss of one drachma could delay a betrothal."

"I had not thought about that," I said.

And so it went through the meal and continued afterwards when we sat on the portico. Finally Elisa said. "God is beating at the door waiting for us just to open it so he could come into our hearts."

Elisa and I are so happy to share with our parents the wonders and wisdom of Jesus. My dear Luke, I share these also with you and pray that soon you will visit and meet Jesus yourself.

Joseph

Letter 89

Yes, Luke, I am keeping a close watch on these cures of Jesus. You and I know that sometimes a disease seems to be cured suddenly, with no apparent reason, but later recurs. These afflictions have not recurred.

We have seen the merchant Thrasas repeatedly and he has no further signs of the dropsy. It has now been several months since Jesus cured the boy with seizures and he has had no further spells. The man with the withered hand has learned the trade of a weaver and has the full use of both hands. The paralytic whose friends let him down through the roof of the clinic is now a carpenter and working daily. The centurion was transferred to another post and took his servant with him. I have heard reports that he was well. I also heard that the widow's son whom Jesus raised from the dead is supporting his mother and plans to marry. The woman with the hemorrhage has been in several times with minor ailments, but she has had no more issue of blood. Jairus' daughter is growing normally and now runs and plays with all of the other children. She has no more signs of the enlarged heart and fluid in the lungs. And Peter's mother-in-law is still well.

All of Capernaum now knows Jesus and has heard him teach. As I pass through town every morning I hear many discussions. Most of the people seem to favor his ideas, but a number of Pharisees are harsh in their criticism. I can hear them from a good distance away discounting his teachings. "Feed the poor? If they would work harder they would not be poor." "Care for widows and orphans? It is not our fault that they are in those conditions. Why should we worry about them?" And it goes on and on.

Jesus has been in town for several days, teaching in the synagogue or at our clinic. It is wonderful when he comes to our place. The room is always full when he teaches here.

Tonight as we gathered, Jesus came early and was visiting with the people, asking about their children and their work. Everyone wants him to come to eat at their home while he is here. He seems to enjoy these evenings, just as he does the dinners with us. As the room became crowded, Jesus stood up and told a parable that at first disturbed me and others among the listeners.

"A man had two sons," he began. "The younger said to his father, 'Father, let me have my share of the estate that would come to me.' So the father divided the property between them. A few days later, the younger got together everything he had and left for a distant country, where he squandered his money on a life of debauchery.

"When he had spent it all, that country experienced a severe famine, and now he began to feel the pinch, so he hired himself out to one of the local inhabitants, who put him to work on his farm feeding the pigs. And he would have willingly filled his belly with the husks the pigs were eating, but no one offered him anything. Then he came to his senses and said, 'How many of my father's paid servants have more food than they want, and here I am, dying of hunger!

"'I will leave this place and go to my father and say, "Father, I have sinned against heaven and against you. I no longer deserve to be called your son. Treat me as one of your paid servants." So he left the place and went back to his father.'"

From my place at the door I could see the whole room was intent on his story.

"While he was still a long way off," Jesus continued, "his father saw him and was moved with pity. He ran to his son, clasped him in his arms and kissed him tenderly. Then his son said, 'Father, I have sinned against heaven and against you. I no longer deserve to be called your son.'

"But the father said to his servants, 'Quick! Bring out the best robe and put it on him. Put a ring on his finger and sandals on his feet. Bring the calf we have been fattening and kill it. We are going to have a feast, a celebration, because this son of mine was dead and has come back to life. He was lost and is found.' And they began to celebrate.

"Now the elder son was out in the fields, but as he drew near the house, he could hear music and dancing. Calling one of the servants, he asked what it was all about. 'Your brother has come,' replied the servant, 'and your father has killed the calf we had fattened because he has got him back safe and sound.'

"He was angry then and refused to go in, and his father came out to plead with him. But he answered his father, 'Look, all these years I have slaved for you and never disobeyed your orders, yet you have never offered so much as a kid for me to celebrate with my friends. But for my brother, when he comes back after swallowing up your property, you kill the calf we had been fattening.'

"The father said, 'My son, you are with me always and all I have is yours. But it was only right we should celebrate and rejoice, because your brother here was dead and has come to life, he was lost and is found.'"

That, Luke, was Jesus' message for the evening, and he left, motioning his disciples to stay. We spent the rest of the evening arguing about this new teaching of Jesus. I had to agree with Eliab when he said, "If I were the elder son, I too would resent the favor shown to the younger son."

"The prodigal son must have said some harsh words to his father when he demanded his share," said Naomi. "He probably had no intention of ever returning."

"He left and cut all ties with the family," said Thalia, whose own sons were grown. "This is a blow to any Jewish family, a deeply hurtful blow. And for a Jew to care for pigs — that is the lowest form of degradation."

"He could not have expected much when he returned," said Daniel, our expert in the law. "The eldest son gets half of the family estate and the other son get one-third of what was left at the death of the father. The estate is not to be divided earlier without penalties."

"But when he came back," said Leah, "the father greeted him warmly and dressed him like one of the family, not as one of the servants, which is what the son had expected."

"This reminds me," David said, "of the story in Genesis of Esau's meeting with Jacob after years of separation. We all know that Jacob took advantage of his brother to get him to sell his birthright to him and then by deception stole his father Isaac's blessing from him. They had not seen each other for years. Jacob expected a vindictive Esau but instead he greeted him with love.[1] Here the father had every right to ostracize the younger son and not to employ him because he had brought disgrace to the family. But instead he was interested only in reconciliation. Jesus is telling us that God acts like that."

Miriam said, "Jesus is talking about the love of God toward the repentant sinner. He seems to be saying that God awaits his return so eagerly that He will even go out to meet him."

"Yes," said Elisa finally, drawing the conclusion for all of us. "God is our father and He lets us, His children, make our own decisions. If we choose wrong He lets us go, but all of the time He is eager for us to return. This parable seems to say that we are not to act and judge by the laws of the world but by the laws of God, who is totally forgiving and totally loving. If we acted like the world acts, we would be like the jealous son."

Luke, it is the jealous son I most identify with in this parable. But I now see it from the side of the other son.

It is deeply comforting for all sinners to know that God will forgive no matter how serious the sin.

Joseph

1   Genesis 33:1-7

Letter 90

Greetings in the name of the Lord. Jesus is doing more and more teaching, but it disturbs us as his friends and followers to see that a group of Pharisees has stepped up their efforts to discredit him. They try to trap him into saying something they can condemn as heresy or blasphemy. What they heard today was not blasphemy, but it was directed at their own greed and hypocrisy.

Eliab and Naomi were among the followers of Jesus today as he was teaching by the lake. They came to the clinic in the late afternoon with the story.

"There was a rich man," Jesus told his disciples, "and he had a steward who was denounced to him for being wasteful with his property. He called for the man and said, 'What is this I hear about you? Draw me up an account of your stewardship because you are not to be my steward any longer.' Then the steward said to himself, 'Now that my master is taking the stewardship from me, what am I to do? Dig? I am not strong enough. Go begging? I should be too ashamed. Ah, I know what I shall do to make sure that when I am dismissed from office there will be some to welcome me into their homes.' Then he called his master's debtors, one by one. To the first he said, 'How much do you owe my master?' 'One hundred measures of oil' was the reply. The steward said, 'Here. Take your bond, sit down and straightaway write fifty.' To another, he said, 'And you, sir, how much do you owe?' 'One hundred measures of wheat' was the reply. The steward said, 'Here, take your bond and write eighty.' The master praised the dishonest steward for his astuteness. For the children of this world are more astute in dealing with their own kind than are the children of light."

I started to object at this point, Luke, because it seemed as if Jesus was praising dishonesty, but Elisa silenced me with the touch of her hand.

Then Naomi took over the story. "'And so I tell you this,' Jesus said. 'Use money, tainted as it is, to win you friends, and thus make sure that when it fails you, they will welcome you into the tents of eternity. The man who can be trusted in little things can be trusted in great, the man who is dishonest in little things will be dishonest in great. If then you cannot be trusted with money, that tainted thing, who will trust you with genuine riches? And if you cannot be trusted with what is not yours, who will give you what is your very own?

"'No servant can be the slave of two masters. He will either hate the first and love the second, or treat the first with respect and the second with scorn. You cannot be the slave both of God and of money.'

"You see," said Naomi, "Jesus is saying that if money is used as a means to give glory to God or to help the poor, it is good, but if it becomes a means by itself, that is bad."

"You know how much some Pharisees love money," Eliab continued, "and Jesus knows it, too. Well, there were several in the group who were listening and when he finished, they just stood there and laughed. Jesus looked at them and I was close enough to see that he was angry. He looked at them one by one, and they suddenly stopped laughing.

"Then he said, 'You are the very ones who pass yourselves off as virtuous in people's sight, but God knows your hearts. For what is thought highly of by men is loathsome in the sight of God.'"

"And then," said Naomi, "Jesus further criticized those who live by the letter of the Law of Moses but violate its spirit.

"'Up to the time of John it was the Law and the Prophets,' he said. 'Since then, the kingdom of God has been preached, and by violence everyone is getting in.

"'It is easier for heaven and earth to disappear than for one little stroke to drop out of the Law.'

"Then he looked around at the many people listening, some of whom have cast aside their first wives and married another. 'Everyone who divorces his wife and marries another is guilty of adultery, and the man who marries a woman divorced by her husband commits adultery.'"

Jews follow the Law of Moses, Luke, but Jesus has added a few refinements and claims authority from God. While Moses said that divorce was permissible, Jesus very clearly says that remarriage is not.

"Jesus stopped then but continued to glare at each one of the Pharisees," Naomi said. "They had no answer and we watched them gradually slip away." As she finished she said, "It is late and our children are waiting for us. We must go."

Elisa and I closed the clinic and walked home in silence, each deep in thought. "Perhaps," Elisa said, "we should put as much enthusiasm into spreading the Word of God as the people of the world use in the spread of their worldly pursuits. Even though the steward was dishonest, he was energetic about it."

That made sense, dear Luke. We have become followers of Jesus but we are not very active in spreading the Word of God. That will change.

Joseph

Letter 91

Grace be with you, dear friend. This evening Elisa and I walked to the lakeshore and joined a group of followers sitting at the feet of Jesus. As we approached we heard Jesus begin a parable again addressing the peril of wealth.

"There was a rich man who used to dress in purple and fine linen and feast magnificently every day," he said. "And at his gate there lay a poor man named Lazarus, covered with sores, who longed to fill himself with the scraps that fell from the rich man's table. Dogs even came and licked his sores. Now the poor man died and was carried to the bosom of Abraham. The rich man also died and was buried.

"In his torment in Hades he looked up and saw Abraham a long way off with Lazarus in his bosom. So he cried out, 'Father Abraham, pity me and send Lazarus to dip his finger in water and cool my tongue, for I am in agony in these flames.'

"'My son,' Abraham replied, 'remember that in your life good things came your way, just as bad things came the way of Lazarus. Now he is being comforted here while you are in agony. But that is not all. Between us and you a great gulf has been fixed to stop anyone, if he wanted to, crossing from our side to yours, and to stop any crossing from your side to ours.'

"The rich man replied, 'Father, I beg you then to send Lazarus to my father's house, since I have five brothers, to give them warning so that they do not come to this place of torment too.' 'They have Moses and the prophets,' said Abraham, 'let them listen to them.' 'Ah, no, Father Abraham,' said the rich man. 'But if anyone comes from the dead, they will repent.' Then Abraham said to him, 'If they will not listen to Moses or the prophets, they will not be convinced even if someone should come from the dead.'"

Elisa turned to me and said, "Jesus is right. It has all been stated by Moses and the prophets. It is all in the writings that are read at the synagogue."

Then Jesus turned to his disciples and said, "Which of you, with a servant plowing or minding sheep, would say to him when he returned from the fields, 'Come and have your meal immediately'? Would he not be more likely to say, 'Get my supper laid. Make yourself tidy and wait on me while I eat and drink. You can eat and drink yourself afterward'? Must he be grateful to the servant for doing what he was told?

"So with you. When you have done all you have been told to do, say, 'We are merely servants. We have done no more than our duty.'"

"That's a reminder to be humble in service," I said as Jesus finished speaking and withdrew to pray. "Joseph, you seem to be getting into the deeper meaning of the stories of Jesus," Elisa said teasingly. The followers who had been listening to him gradually left, and Elisa and I returned home in the twilight.

May the Lord God bless you and keep you.

Joseph

Letter 92

Luke, greetings in the name of the God of Abraham, Moses and David.

As often as possible, Elisa and I walk to the lakeshore to hear Jesus teach. Every evening he goes there and teaches the crowds that gather. It is a naturally beautiful area with trees and grass.

Today we arrived just as the sun set and a breeze picked up from the lake. The crowd was large. We could pick out The Twelve and other disciples among the hundreds from all walks of life.

As we approached, Jesus was talking about the kingdom of God, but a Pharisee pushed up just then and rudely interrupted. "When is this kingdom of God coming?" he said derisively, then looking toward his friends to receive their plaudits.

Jesus stopped, looked firmly at the questioner and said, "The coming of the kingdom of God does not admit of observation, and there will be no way to say, 'Look here! Look there!' For you will know that the kingdom of God is among you."

There was no reply from the questioner. Jesus waited for more questions and then said to his disciples, "A time will come when you will long to see one of the days of the Son of Man and will not see it. They will say to you, 'Look there!' or 'Look here!' Make no move. Do not set out in pursuit for, as the lightning flashing from one part of heaven lights up the other, so will be the Son of Man when his day comes.

"But first he must suffer grievously and be rejected by this generation."

Luke, Jesus speaks as if the kingdom of God is near. But he also speaks of suffering, of rejection and the day that he is no longer among us. I know he continues to present a threat to Herod, and Elisa and I fear for his safety.

"As it was in Noah's day," he continued, "so will it be in the days of the Son of Man. People were eating and drinking, marrying wives and husbands, right up to the day Noah went into the ark, and the flood came and destroyed them all.[1] It will be the same as it was in Lot's day. People were eating and drinking, buying and selling, planting and building, but the day Lot left Sodom, God rained fire and brimstone from heavens and it destroyed them all.[2] It will be the same when the day comes for the Son of Man to be revealed.

"When the day comes, anyone on the housetop, with his possessions in the house, must not come down to collect them, nor must anyone in the

---

fields turn back either. Remember Lot's wife. Anyone who tries to preserve his life will lose it, and anyone who loses it will keep it safe. I tell you, on that night two will be in one bed, one will be taken and the other left. Two women will be grinding corn together. one will be taken and the other left."

Jesus had spoken commandingly, as he meant these words to be heard by all. But the Pharisees did not respond. No one did, as we were filled with foreboding. Finally, one of the disciples spoke — I do not know who but it was probably Peter — asking, "Where, Lord?" And Jesus answered, "Where the body is, there too will the vultures be." Then he left, and the Pharisees turned on each other in exasperation.

I started to go and listen to their heated argument, but Elisa put her hand on my shoulder. "Joseph, they will go on for hours and get nowhere. We have more important things to do than listen to them." And Luke, she was right, as usual.

It was dark as we set off for home. The roads are rough and irregular and the walk was not easy. Finally we reached the lane between the two groves of trees near our home. This road is smooth since my father takes pains to keep it so. As we passed by the woods on our right I remarked, "I wonder if Jesus has chosen this place again for his meditation."

We moved cautiously along a path that led to the deepest section of the woods, and there in a very secluded area was Jesus, kneeling in deep prayer. We watched for a moment and then left quietly.

As we came clear of the woods and on the road to our house and clinic, Elisa spoke in a whisper. "I wish that someday I could meditate so deeply with God. It seems that their souls are in communion." All I could do was agree.

Joseph

1   Genesis 6:5-22, 7:1-16

2   Genesis 19:23-26

Letter 93

Luke, the messages of Jesus continue to inspire Elisa and me. They have changed our lives and those of others here in Capernaum.

Today someone asked Jesus about the amount of time that he spent in prayer. In reply, Jesus told a parable about the need to never lose heart but to pray continually.

"There was a judge in a certain town who had neither fear of God nor respect for man. In the same town there was a widow who kept coming to him and saying, 'I want justice from you against my enemy!' For a long time he refused, but at last he said to himself, 'Maybe I have neither fear of God nor respect for man, but since she keeps pestering me I must give this widow her just rights or she will persist in coming and worry me to death.'

"You notice what the unjust judge has to say? Now, will not God see justice done to his chosen who cry to him day and night even when he delays to help them? I promise you, he will see justice done to them, and done speedily.

"But when the Son of Man comes, will he find any faith on earth?"

As the crowd grew today on the shores of the lake, I recognized three Pharisees who walked up but stood apart. I whispered to Elisa, "They always make a big show of giving their tithes so that everyone sees them. They pride themselves on following the Law to the letter."

Jesus looked directly at them and spoke calmly. "Two men went up to the Temple to pray, one a Pharisee, the other a tax collector. The Pharisee stood here and said this prayer to himself. 'I thank you, God, that I am not grasping, unjust, adulterous like the rest of mankind, and particularly that I am not like this tax collector here. I fast twice a week. I pay tithes on all I get.' The tax collector stood some distance away, not daring even to raise his eyes to heaven, but he beat his breast and said, 'God, be merciful to me, a sinner.' This man, I tell you, went home at rights with God. The other did not. For everyone who exalts shall be humbled while he who humbles himself shall be exalted."

The faces of the three men were expressionless, but I was close enough to notice their fists clench. When Jesus had finished, they slipped out of the crowd.

I asked Elisa, "Do you think his words had any effect?"

"Not on them," she replied. "But," she continued, "Jesus' parables do apply to all of us and we must all be careful not to show off our giving. The Pharisee did everything he was supposed to do and expected God to reward him for this. He had the sin of pride. Furthermore, he had contempt for the tax collector, which is also a sin."

Luke, this sin of pride is something I recognize in myself on occasion. But arrogance has never been a fault of Elisa. She leaves gifts of food and clothing at the homes of the poor unnoticed. She sets an example for me in my own weakness.

Joseph

Letter 94

Dear Luke, when fruit is ripening in our orchard and vineyard, we often hear voices and laughter. This is the domain of my parents, Joseph and Mary, and they spend many hours pruning the trees and fertilizing. But the trees produce so much fruit each year that they invite the people of Capernaum to come and pick all that they need.

It is a joyful time, Luke, as most of the people who come cannot afford to buy the fruit. They seem to appreciate it and always thank Joseph and Mary. The children all enjoy picking the apples and pears, figs, plums, mulberries and apricots. Even when there is no fruit on the trees the children enjoy playing in the shade of the trees.

Today, after our evening meal, the laughter from the orchard seemed particularly lively. Elisa and I went to the portico to see what was happening, and there we saw Jesus laughing and playing with a group of children. Parents were bringing their infants to Jesus just to have him touch them.

Just then Peter and the disciples arrived, and they started to turn the children away. But Jesus stopped them quickly.

"Let the little children come to me, and do not stop them," he said, "for it is to such as these that the kingdom of God belongs. I tell you solemnly, any one who does not welcome the kingdom of God like a little child will never enter it."

Jesus continued to play with the children and shortly most of the disciples joined in too. Finally it grew late and the parents gathered their children to take them home. Jesus left without notice, and soon the orchard was empty again.

As we sat on the portico enjoying the evening breeze, I said, "Elisa, some parents mistreat their children, but Jesus believes we should treasure them. He preaches against fathers who oppress their children, just as he preaches against the rich who oppress the poor and the lawyers who oppress the widowed.

"He believes every person should be treated fairly, and these are some of the teachings that anger those in power."

"Yes," she replied, "he teaches us there is no distinction of class or privilege in the kingdom of God, and that is one reason he is so beloved by the people.

"We must be very careful in our clinic," she said, "that we make no distinction between those who can pay and those who cannot."

"That is what Erasmus and Abraham have taught us to do and I believe we already do it. I have had complaints from rich Pharisees when they were made to wait their turn."

"Yes, so have I," Elisa remarked. "Even today the wife of a lawyer walked out because she would have to sit beside a poor woman. But she did come back and then had to sit between two poor widows who arrived earlier."

After some thought I ventured a question. "Should our attitude toward good be like that of a little child, trusting and innocent? Does that mean we cannot have doubts?"

Elisa was quick to respond. "To doubt is good provided we study and resolve our doubts. Haven't we discovered that the more we study the Scriptures and the words of Jesus, the deeper is our faith in God?"

And so it is, dear Luke.

Joseph

Letter 95

Luke, you write of aging patients with fractured hips. That is a condition Elisa, Erasmus and I have discussed often. The patients are unable to rise from their bed, and after some months they lose the strength to move at all. So many of these patients develop inflammation of the lungs and die. We have known some patients, however, who are able to rise from their bed earlier and regain their strength. There is little known about this kind of recovery as so many of our people die of other conditions before they develop the fragile bones of the aged.

Luke, it is our privilege as practitioners of the healing art to help those in need. Here in Capernaum our practice includes aged widows and many other patients who cannot pay. Elisa and I do not expect to be wealthy, but are grateful that we have the means to live comfortably.

Since we met Jesus and began to listen to his teachings, we have talked more about wealth and how it is meant to be used. You may remember our discussions about this in Athens. In our culture, riches are considered a sign of God's blessing and poverty a sign of God's displeasure. But Jesus teaches differently and he stirs people up with these teachings.

Many of his parables are about rich men who share their goods. The father of the prodigal son gave him one-third of his property and then a banquet, fine clothes and a ring after he had squandered his inheritance. We have come to understand that Jesus does not condemn riches but how a wealthy person may misuse the riches. They should be used to help others. He does not condemn tax collectors, but tells them they should not exact any more from their clients than is just, and should continue giving to the poor and to God.

We know that Jesus eats at the banquet table of the wealthy, but he does not hesitate to criticize them. And he always has the poor and the sinners with him.

Prophets all through the ages, Jesus points out, have taught that we should care for the poor and others in need. It is the Pharisees who have distorted the Scriptures to suit themselves.

This evening Elisa and I were listening to Jesus as he was teaching to a crowd on the steps in front of the synagogue. Elias, a member of the leading family of Capernaum, worked his way to Jesus and put this question to him.

"Good Master, what have I to do to inherit eternal life?"

Jesus said to him, "Why do you call me good? No one is good but God alone." Then he answered the question.

"You know the commandments. You must not commit adultery. You must not kill. You must not steal. You must not bring false witness. Honor your father and mother."

Elias replied, "I have kept all these from my earliest days till now."

"There is still one thing that you lack. Sell all that you own and distribute the money to the poor, and you will have treasure in heaven. Then come follow me."

But when Elias heard this he was filled with sadness, for he was very rich. Jesus looked at him and said, "How hard it is for those who have riches to make their way into the kingdom of God. Yes, it is easier for a camel to pass through the eye of a needle than for a rich man to enter the kingdom of God."

"In that case," said Elias, "who can be saved?"

"Things that are impossible for men," Jesus replied, "are possible for God."

Luke, what Jesus asked for is greater even than what he has asked of his disciples. I could see stirring among them and they motioned to Peter to speak to Jesus.

"What about us?" he said. "We left all that we had to follow you."

Jesus said to them, "I tell you solemnly, there is no one who has left home, wife, brothers, parents or children for the sake of the kingdom of God who will not be given repayment many times over in this present time and, in the world to come, eternal life." With that, Jesus stepped into the crowd and disappeared, leaving us all much to ponder over.

We pray for you daily, dear Luke. We know that God loves you as much as He loves us.

Joseph

Letter 96

From all the teachings of Jesus that I have written to you in my letters, dear Luke, you may have a picture of a stern teacher like some we knew in Athens. On the contrary Jesus smiles most of the time and enjoys making us laugh. He is a good friend as well as a teacher. He likes to reminisce in the evenings by the campfire or in a home as our friends and other followers gather around. We all talk about our childhood and the mischief that we got into as youths. And when we play games, Jesus enjoys winning like the rest of us.

I have never fully described him to you. Jesus is almost four cubits in height, taller than most men, and well-muscled for a man of more than thirty years. He has a beard and a broad forehead. His hair is parted in the center of his scalp and is plaited into a braid hanging from the back of his head. He keeps his garments neat and clean. Most of them were woven by his mother.

Of course you know that he worked most of his life as a carpenter. The calluses on his hands have diminished since he began teaching, although he does help whenever there is any physical work to do, like building a fire, carrying wood or building a temporary shelter. I have noticed that his bones are all straight. Either he never had a broken bone or if he did, it was set perfectly. He has all of his fingers, too. As you know, Luke, it is not unusual for carpenters to crush or cut off parts of their fingers in their work.

Jesus often talks of his experience as a carpenter. He discusses the fine points of a piece of furniture and how much time it took to make it. Often he finds some faults in the wood and in the workmanship and explains how they could have been avoided.

Jesus questions us and others to learn more about our professions. He asks about fishing, building houses with stone, shearing lambs, gardening, the care of trees. He asks Elisa and Erasmus about the herbs and ointments that we use.

Jesus is humble, gracious and cordial. His voice is moderately deep and carries far among the crowds. His eyes are kind and forgiving, but he can be very commanding and sarcastic when the occasion demands it. He has a penetrating gaze as if he is exploring your thoughts. No one ever tries to lie to him.

Aramaic is his primary language, but he is familiar with Hebrew and Greek.

The mind of Jesus is beyond my understanding. He has had no advanced education beyond synagogue school, yet he can outwit the smartest lawyers, scribes and priests. His knowledge of the Scriptures is unsurpassed, and he quotes accurately the teachings of the rabbis that he heard in discussions. He never seems to forget what he has learned.

Jesus is more than a friend to us. He acts as a concerned parent when we need it or like a loving, supporting brother. Everyone in our company of friends feels free to come to him at any time. He is adamant about keeping a promise.

Jesus is always prompt at meals, at prayers and at gatherings at our clinic. He is considerate of latecomers unless they are consistently late. Then he lets his disapproval be known and, as a rule, they are not tardy again.

It is clear from his countenance that Jesus has experienced sorrows and pain in his life as well as joy. So much of his concern is for the poor, and he helps us understand that they should be our concern as well.

Elisa and I share the joy of knowing this man and following his teaching. I have come to believe that Jesus is a prophet for our times, but I know his teachings represent a threat to Herod. I feel a need to protect him, but the dangers are not yet clear.

Joseph

Letter 97

Greetings in the name of all that is holy. It is early spring and the fruit trees are in full bloom. "It will soon be time for Passover," Elisa said one evening as we walked through the orchard. "I wonder if Jesus and The Twelve will go to Jerusalem. He has never missed a Passover there." "I hope not," I replied. "He has enemies among the Pharisees who would be there. I am afraid that Jesus would be in danger in Jerusalem this year."

Luke, it is the duty of every Jewish male to go to Jerusalem for the Passover if he possibly can. Pharisees and others with means begin their preparations several weeks in advance. Elisa and I did attend when we were in Jerusalem but have not been able to go since then.

Elisa looked up and said, "Really, Joseph, I would like to go to this Passover while my father and Jonathan can take care of our work."

Jonathan had told us he felt he could work longer hours. He does well if he paces himself and gets his rest. And Erasmus has said he would like to try making some of the house calls again. He enjoys visiting in the patients' homes. But I was worried that the journey and all of the activities of the Passover would be too much for Elisa.

She clearly had been thinking this over for some time. "I would like to have Abraham see how well I am doing," she said. "And on the way we could probably see Deborah, the physician of Ephraim. I have not seen her since we came back to Capernaum." Luke, by that time I knew that we were going, no matter how much I might object.

As we approached a field of wildflowers beyond the orchard we heard voices. There were Jesus and The Twelve. He looked up and saw us. "Elisa and Joseph, come join us, we are planning our Passover journey. It would be good to have you with us. We might need your medical help."

"We were just talking about going this year," Elisa said.

"Fine," Jesus replied. "We plan to leave in three days. We will stop at Magdala to pick up Mary, then we will go to Nazareth, where my mother will join us. I look forward to you meeting her. We will spend the Sabbath there." We bid farewell to Jesus and The Twelve and started for home to make our plans.

Now I was as eager to go as Elisa. Just to spend time in the company of Jesus and listen to his teaching would be worth the hardship of the trip. And perhaps I could be of help if the Pharisees did present a threat.

Stopping in Nazareth would prolong the trip, as it is west and a little south of the direct route to Jerusalem. "But having Jesus' mother with us will be worth the time," Elisa said.

As we arrived at Erasmus' home, we saw that he had just returned from the lake and had given all of the fish to the neighbors. We told him of the proposed journey and he said, "Great, I envy you. I wish that I could go. Of course I will take care of the patients. I need to spend more time in practice and less in fishing. The fishermen will be glad since I give all of my fish away. Maybe they will sell more! Hah!"

Sarah was not so keen about Elisa taking the trip. I assured her that we would take our donkey to carry supplies and Elisa could ride if she was tired.

Luke, the next two days were full of activity, cleaning and packing garments, medical instruments and Elisa's herbs and medicines. Elisa looked at the packs and said, "I don't think the donkey will like to be put to work. You know, he has been in the pasture since you got the horse." We obtained some supplies from my father's station. My mother was not happy to see us go. She cried as we bid her farewell.

As we prepared to retire for the night, I said, "Enjoy the night's sleep indoors. We will be sleeping under the stars a lot."

The Passover Journey

Letter 98

Praise be to the Lord, dear friend. We arose early and were fastening the last satchel on the donkey when Jesus and the disciples arrived with Joanna, Salome the mother of James and John, and Mary the mother of James the Lesser. We knew all of the women because they were our patients. Salome is short like Elisa's mother and reserved where her husband Zebedee is boisterous. Mary is stout, jolly and friendly.

Mary had a few things to add to our satchel. I remarked to Elisa, "Now there will be no place for you to ride." She replied, "I know that I will not need to ride."

The sun was rising over the hills as we set out for Jerusalem along the path that led along the Lake of Galilee. The fields were filled with flowers. Soon Jesus started to sing in his clear baritone voice. The others followed and time passed rapidly.

At the third hour Jesus stopped in the shade of some eucalyptus trees to rest. It was a welcome respite. My feet and legs were starting to ache and my shoulders hurt from the pack that I was carrying. As we gathered around, Jesus turned our attention to the wildflowers.

"Behold the lilies of the field. Even Solomon in all his glory was not clothed like one of them."

Elisa picked a flower and showed it to me. Really, Luke, I have seen spring flowers for years but this time I looked into the center of the blossom and marveled at what God had created. For the first time I saw the brilliant colors and the details of the structure.

We stopped at Magdala at the house of Mary. Jesus had asked her to accompany the group to Jerusalem, and she had the noon meal ready for us. After a refreshing rest we continued the journey.

Late in the afternoon Jesus found an area where we could make camp. I know that Elisa was tired because she lay down as soon as we made a place for her.

After a short rest the women fixed the evening meal. Jesus led the prayers and then we ate. It was an evening of laughter and fellowship, making me forget momentarily the aches and pains of the day.

I hope that I will get used to this walking.

Joseph

Letter 99

Dear Luke, I had a bad night. I am not used to sleeping on the ground. Elisa rubbed my muscles with Erasmus' balm and I finally was able to sleep. Everyone arose early but Jesus was already up and at prayer a short distance away. He joined us for our morning prayers and meal.

Jesus took a direct route to Nazareth but it was still a long walk. We stopped at midday for a meal and short rest. Jesus did not talk much today because he was determined to get to Nazareth before sunset. We will have a day of rest there so that he can visit with his relatives.

As the time passed my muscles seemed to hurt less, or perhaps I became accustomed to the pain. In the late afternoon I remarked to Elisa, "I would like to see Jeremiah and Neri again, but after the way Jesus was treated in the synagogue, I do not want to cause further trouble."

"From what you say, Jeremiah is a just and honest man."

"Yes."

"Then do not worry. He will recognize the good in Jesus." And on we went.

At about the ninth hour, we had just reached the crest of the hill above Nazareth. I recognized several of the places I had been when I came here. Jesus stopped and we were all glad to get some rest. Soon two men came up the hill riding spirited horses. They stopped and the older one asked if they could help. He and I recognized one another at the same time. It was Jeremiah. "Joseph, what are you doing here?" he said as he dismounted, and we embraced.

"We are on the way to Jerusalem for the Passover. Come, meet my wife, Elisa."

"And you must greet my brother," Jeremiah replied as the younger man dismounted. "Do you recognize him?" It was Neri, the man I had gone to Nazareth to treat. He was big and strong, with a full head of hair and a dark beard. I had not recognized him. We embraced.

I introduced Elisa then and Jeremiah said, "Elisa, you were the only one Joseph missed while he spent a week with us treating Neri. He did not do justice to you in his description."

Then I walked Jeremiah over to Jesus. "You remember that I also talked about Jesus and his teachings." I told him that Jesus had come to visit his mother and relatives who live in Nazareth.

Jesus stepped forward and Jeremiah greeted him. "Jesus, son of Joseph, we meet again. I have been hearing favorable reports of your works and teachings. I was among those who threw you out of the synagogue on your last visit there. Perhaps it is time to set aside my disbelief and listen to what you have to say." Luke, I was relieved. Jeremiah had not only spoken to Jesus but seemed eager to talk to him.

Then I introduced the rest of the company. Jeremiah and Neri welcomed them warmly. When the introductions were completed, Jeremiah asked, "Where are you staying?"

"Out under the stars," I replied.

"Not in Nazareth. You will all be guests at my home tonight."

"No, no. We do not wish to impose. There are too many of us." An invitation like that is not to be refused. But it is the custom here that if one person is invited, all of the people with him are invited too.

"Joseph, I insist! You all must come. Joseph, you know the way. Neri and I will ride ahead and make the arrangements. It should take you no more than an hour to get there." Jesus excused himself to visit with relatives and friends but agreed to bring his mother to dinner the following evening. And they both mounted and left. I could see hidden smiles on the tired faces of the women, the disciples and other followers. We would sleep inside and have warm food tonight and tomorrow.

Shortly we arrived at the home of Jeremiah. He was there to welcome us and had several servants take us to our rooms and had one care for the pack animals.

After washing away the dust of our travels, Elisa fell asleep. I went to visit with Jeremiah and told him of all the things I had seen Jesus do. The dinner was delicious and everyone had a wonderful time. It was cool in the gardens but almost everyone was tired and retired early. Elisa went to bed but Jeremiah and I had a long talk about the teachings of Jesus.

"Joseph, this sounds so much like the prophets of old. Is Jesus another prophet?"

"Prophets have been known to perform miracles. But he says that he is the Son of Man," I replied, convincing myself as I spoke to Jeremiah that Jesus must be something more than a prophet.

It was late and we retired.

Joseph

Letter 100

Dear Luke, we had a restful night, slept late, and had a bountiful breakfast. Elisa and I walked in the gardens. It was cool and there was a slight breeze. Jeremiah and his brother were overseeing the work in the fields.

At about the tenth hour we heard a commotion near the entrance of Jeremiah's estate. We went out to investigate and there was Jesus with about a hundred people gathered around him. Apparently it had become known that Jesus was in town, and friends, followers and the curious found and followed him. They came into the estate and Jesus sat under a tree and talked about the kingdom of God. He spoke of showing compassion and love to those in need, of visiting those in prison and, of course, God's mercy to those who have sinned. We have heard these themes before, but each time we found something special in the teachings. As I looked over the crowd I spied Jeremiah. He had just come in from the fields. He was listening very carefully to every word that Jesus spoke and nodded his approval.

After about an hour, Jesus slipped away and the gathering gradually dispersed. Jeremiah saw me and led his horse to me. "Joseph," he said, "I have never heard anyone with such a vast knowledge of the Scriptures. He quotes Isaiah, Jeremiah, Malachi and all of the prophets with such assurance. Where did you say that he studied?"

"In the synagogue here in Nazareth," I replied.

"So did I," he was quick to respond, "but I did not get the depth of knowledge that he has. He also calls us to show the same forgiveness to others as we ask of God. I can see why you and Elisa are attracted to his teachings.

"But when he was last among us, he claimed to be the Messiah, the Chosen One of God for whom we have waited for centuries. Our friends in Jerusalem tell us there are people there who believe he will overthrow the Romans and restore the kingdom of David to glory.

"This I cannot accept. Jesus of Nazareth may be a prophet, but he is not the Messiah."

That evening Jesus came for dinner with his mother and his relatives. They were working people but Jeremiah cordially welcomed them. The banquet hall was filled.

At last we met Mary the mother of Jesus. She and Elisa quickly became friends and were together most of the evening.

To my embarrassment, Jeremiah told his guests the story of my previous visit to his home and the successful surgery on his brother, who was also present. Then Jeremiah spent most of his time talking to Jesus, and I could see that he was very interested in everything that Jesus said.

After the banquet ended, Jesus and his relatives took their leave, and he said that we would resume our journey at dawn.

Luke, the difficult part of the journey lies ahead of us.

May the Lord God bless you and keep you in the palm of his hand.

Joseph

Letter 101

Luke, it has been a momentous day and one I shall never forget.

We rose early and Jeremiah had breakfast and provisions for several days' journey prepared for us. Jesus and Mary arrived and went directly to Jeremiah and thanked him for the hospitality, the banquet and the thoughtful discussion. Jeremiah showed warmth in his parting with Jesus and said, "I do hope that we meet again, perhaps during Passover in Jerusalem. I want to hear more of your thoughts about the Scriptures."

Then Jesus approached us. "Elisa, would you please care for my mother on this journey? I may be busy doing other things and I want her to be in your care." Elisa was elated. "Jesus, I will consider it a privilege," she said as she took Mary by the arm.

Everyone thanked Jeremiah again and as we left he shouted, "Neri and I will ride our horses to Jerusalem and be there for the Passover. We are staying with my close friend Joseph of Arimathea." I happened to glance at Jesus and his smile indicated that he was acquainted with this man. Off our little band went.

We set our course eastward toward the Jordan River. Villages line the banks and it would be easier to find water and supplies for our journey. It was pleasant walking along the well-traveled road, though I felt annoyed occasionally when a carriage passed, raising a lot of dust and forcing us to get out of the way into the grass or thicket.

Elisa walked with Mary in the company of women, and I set off at first with Peter. To our south I noticed a low mountain rising out of the plain and I asked Peter about it. He told me it was Mount Tabor, and I dropped back to tell Elisa.

"Mount Tabor!" she exclaimed. "When we were at the Essenes, they showed us a plant with a pleasant scent that grows on the top of Mount Tabor. Do you remember, Joseph? They recommended using it in salves and ointments to make them smell good." I did remember, and I resolved that someday I would climb the mountain and collect the herbs for Elisa.

Then she told me that she felt something remarkable would happen today. Mary had told her that Jesus spent the previous night in prayer, as he often does before a special mission or revelation. And Elisa was right, as we would learn later.

Just then Jesus changed course and turned toward the right, taking a rarely used path that headed to the mountain. Everyone was surprised. There was a little grumbling among the disciples, but Jesus' face seemed set.

Arriving at the base of the mountain at midday, we stopped in the shade of some sycamore trees and ate the bountiful food Jeremiah had given us. After the meal Jesus surprised us all by saying, "We will camp here tonight."

I looked at Elisa and said, "That should give me enough time to get to the top of Mount Tabor and collect the herbs." She objected but I had already removed an empty bag from the medical satchel. Soon I had disappeared into the trees that covered the path.

The path was rocky and steep, and soon I regretted my decision. I found a fallen branch about 3 cubits long and used it to help me keep my balance. Thorns began to tear my clothing and cut me, but finally I reached the top.

I quickly found several patches of the herb and filled the bag. But since I was at the top I decided to look around. Stepping around some tall shrubs, I came to a clearing where I could look east over fertile plains toward the Jordan. It seemed I could see the entire world from this height, and I thought of how God had appeared to Moses on a mountaintop.

Behind me I began to hear voices and then footsteps. It was Jesus, Peter, James and his brother John. Young John is quite a favorite among the company, and the women have begun to call him the Beloved Disciple.

Luke, Jesus sometimes calls James and John the Sons of Thunder, because they are so passionate in their beliefs. They want Jesus to rain fire on those who oppose him.

Through the bushes I could see the three disciples find rocks and fallen logs on which to sit and rest. They were clearly very tired. Jesus had apparently planned to come here all along and that's why we had made camp so early in the day.

Jesus, his look more determined than ever, then crossed to the center of a small clearing, knelt and began to pray. He was close enough that I could see his face through two branches.

I did not want to disturb Jesus in prayer, so I didn't call out to the other three. I settled down myself to wait. After a few moments, the disciples themselves quietly rose, then knelt to begin their own prayers up on the mountain, closer to God.

Luke, what happened next I still find hard to believe. But it has changed my life forever.

The face of Jesus began to radiate a soft light, like the moon on a clear night. His tunic and cloak, which had become a little soiled and torn, began to bleach out under the light until they were almost incandescent. The glow became sharper and brighter until it caught the attention of the kneeling disciples as well. I remembered the brilliant light that shone upon Jesus all those months ago when Elisa and I first saw him at Bethany on the Jordan.

Suddenly, Jesus was standing and talking with two men. One was dressed in skins and carried a walking stick. He was bearded and burned from the sun. He reminded me of John the Baptist, but his stature and facial characteristics were different. The other had a long beard and a shepherd's staff. Now all three were bathed in the brilliant light.

But who were these men and where did they come from?

Believe me, Luke, this was a sight that I cannot adequately describe and never will forget, the brilliance of the three men on this lonely mountaintop. If only Elisa could see it, I thought to myself. How will I ever describe it to her?

Or did she already see it? I wondered if any of the company waiting in the camp below could see the brilliance on the mountaintop.

I tried to hear what they were talking about. Jesus was talking of his passing, which was to happen in Jerusalem. That worried me, as Jesus has said that he would be killed in Jerusalem. I had hoped that somehow, by being with him, I could prevent that happening.

Then I heard Jesus address the men. He called the first one Elijah, the prophet of old, and the second one Moses!

Elijah, who was taken up to heaven in a flaming chariot,[1] and Moses, who had been denied the passage into the Promised Land before he died[2] — the two were here, on the mountaintop, with Jesus. This could only be done with the power of God, only by the hand of God, and I was witnessing it all.

And so were Peter, James and John, now sitting back on their heels in awe. They still had not caught sight of me.

Then Moses and Elijah began to bid Jesus farewell. I thought, no, it couldn't be over. I wished this moment to last forever. And so, it seems, did Peter. Scrambling to his feet, he called out to Jesus, "Master, it is wonderful for us to be here, so let us make three tents, one for you, one for Moses, and one for Elijah." But even as he spoke, a cloud came and covered Jesus, Moses and Elijah like a shadow. I could see that the apostles were afraid, as I was. Was Jesus leaving us now? All kinds of thoughts came to my mind.

The Passover Journey

There we were, Luke, up on the mountaintop with a cloud in front of us, in which had vanished Jesus, Moses and Elijah. Long moments passed as we waited and wondered what would happen next.

Suddenly, we heard a booming voice coming from the cloud.

"This is my Son, the Chosen One. Listen to him."

I wondered if the others could hear the voice down below the mountain.

Luke, it was the same voice Elisa and I had heard on the bank of the River Jordan as we watched John baptize Jesus.

Then the cloud disappeared, and there in the fading light of the afternoon sun was Jesus alone kneeling in prayer, just as he had been before. No Moses. No Elijah.

But Peter, James and John were all on their feet. Jesus rose and gave them the same look I had seen often when he did not wish to have anyone talk about his cures. It meant "Don't tell anyone what you have seen."

Then he turned around and looked through the bushes toward me. Luke, he had known I was there all the time! And now he was silently seeking the same promise from me.

Then the four of them left together.

Still stunned at what I had witnessed, I lay back and closed my eyes.

Was the voice from the cloud that of God? He spoke to Moses from a burning bush,[3] but he did appear as a cloud to protect the chosen people.[4] Yes, God did appear in a cloud to the Israelites in the past. Had I just witnessed His appearance again? But why me? Why would I be allowed to witness this?

I wasn't one of The Twelve, or even one of the seventy-two. But for some reason I had been allowed to hear the voice of God. And not once, but twice.

Did God do this just for me? For months and months I had followed Jesus, witnessing his cures, hearing his teachings, with only one aim in mind, to learn his technique of cures so that I could use it in the healing art. I had been blinded to the origin of his power. Elisa seemed to see this clearly and did not place so much emphasis on the cures. For weeks she has believed Jesus is the Messiah, the Chosen One, the Christ.

How dumb can I be? I have followed, heard and witnessed Jesus all this time and did not know him! My mind has been so slanted toward medicine that I have been blinded to anything else.

Luke, in the wake of that brilliant light on top of Mount Tabor, I saw clearly for the first time the entire life of Jesus and all that I had witnessed during our association with him.

Perhaps there is something higher than the calling to be a practitioner of the healing art! Perhaps medicine is not the epitome of knowledge.

Today on the mountain, dear Luke, I realized that we must spend our lives doing good and trying to get to a higher level of the knowledge of God. And here I have wasted months and months of closeness with Jesus, the Son of God and the Chosen One, following him for the wrong reason.

Then I realized, as Elisa had often said, that the miracles of Jesus are just a means to teach people who he is and attract them to listen to his words, to refrain from sin and to worship God.

I had been on the mountaintop alone for some time. I suddenly realized that Jesus, Peter, James and John must be back at the camp now, and Elisa must be worried about me. I hurried at first, slipping a couple of times and catching a bush to keep from falling. Then I decided to follow the path.

As I was about to come out of the thicket to the camp, Jesus appeared. He looked at my scratches and torn cloak and said, "It is best to stick to the path on this mountain."

"I was gathering herbs for Elisa to use in her medicines," I said, and showed him the fragrant sack.

"You may tell Elisa and my mother everything you saw on the mountain," he said. "But no one else."

"May I write of this to my friend Luke in Antioch?"

He nodded. "By the time he reads your letter, it will all be over." And he walked away before I could ask, "What will be over?"

At the camp I found Mary with Elisa, who had been worried about my delay. I gave her the herbs and we walked to the brook, where Elisa washed my wounds and put Erasmus' balm on them. I began to tell Elisa and Mary what I had seen and heard on Mount Tabor, and my thoughts as I lay back on the ground.

For Elisa it was a confirmation of her beliefs about Jesus. Mary was not surprised, but reserved about her feelings.

As I finished, Jesus came up to where we were sitting and joined us.

"Jesus," I said, "this is the second time I have heard the voice of God speak over you. You were the Galilean Elisa and I saw being baptized by John at the Jordan."

Jesus laughed and replied, "Joseph, I had wondered when you would finally tell me this." Elisa and I were surprised. "You knew that we were there?" she asked.

"Yes, I saw you in the water."

"Then you are the Chosen One of God, the Messiah!" she exclaimed.

"As you say. But Elisa, Joseph, the time is not right to reveal this to others. You will know when the time comes. Until then, perhaps you should know more about me." He turned to his mother. "You may tell them whatever they want to know. But first let us join the rest of our company for the evening meal."

Luke, there is more to tell you, but it must wait for another letter.

Joseph

[1]   2 Kings 2:11

[2]   Numbers 20:12

[3]   Exodus 3:2-6

[4]   Exodus 13:21-22

Letter 102

Luke, Elisa and I were eager to hear more about Jesus from his mother. After the meal was over Jesus motioned to Mary, to Elisa and me to follow him. He had picked out a place where we could not be heard by the rest of the company. We arranged comfortable places for Mary and Elisa to recline. Jesus then said, "Mother, tell them the story that you told me many years ago," and left to pray.

"It is a long story and I have not told it to anyone else except to my late husband, Joseph." Elisa pleaded, "Please tell us." Then Mary began.

"My parents were Jacob and Ann of Nazareth and I had a normal childhood. However, I did spend a lot of time reading the Scriptures and in prayer. As I approached womanhood, my father and the father of a young carpenter named Joseph, of the House of David, arranged for us to marry, and we went through the betrothal ceremony in the synagogue. Joseph would come and visit me on the Sabbath and we planned to be married soon. Then one Sabbath afternoon while I was at prayer, a bright light appeared in the room and startled me. There was a figure in the light, an angel who greeted me by name.

"'I am Gabriel,' the angel said, 'and I have been sent by God to deliver this message to you. Rejoice, so highly favored! The Lord is with you.'

"I was deeply disturbed by these words, and wondered what this greeting could mean. But the angel continued.

"'Mary, do not be afraid. You have won God's favor. Listen! You are to conceive and bear a son, and you must name him Jesus. He will be great and will be called the Son of The Most High. The Lord God will give him the throne of his ancestor David. He will rule over the House of Israel forever and his reign will have no end.'

"The angel stopped because he could see that I was disturbed. I asked, 'How can that be, since I am a virgin?'

"'The Spirit of the Lord will come over you,' Gabriel answered, 'and the power of The Most High will cover you with its shadow. And so the child will be holy and will be called Son of God. Know this too: Your kinswoman Elisabeth has, in her old age, herself conceived a son, and she whom people called barren is now in her sixth month, for nothing is impossible to God.'

"I answered, 'I am the handmaid of the Lord. Let what you have said be done to me.'

"And the angel left, the bright light disappeared, and there I was alone. The more I thought about what had happened, the more bewildered I became. But I knew it was not a dream. I had heard the voice, I had seen the light and the angel.

"Shortly after that my mother came to the door and said that Joseph had come to visit and was waiting for me.

"Elisa, I must have looked as confused as I felt, because she said to me, 'Are you all right, Mary?' I replied, 'I think so.'

"'Perhaps Joseph can cheer you up,' my mother replied. Joseph greeted me and also noticed that I seemed distracted. We went for a walk and sat on a bench in the garden. Joseph said, 'Mary, something is bothering you.' I burst out in tears. I don't know if they were in joy or fear. And then I told Joseph everything that had just happened to me. Well, he was as shocked as I was. And afterward I thought of all the questions that must have come into his mind. Here I was, his betrothed, and I was to have a child and it was not his! And I said that I was a virgin! How could this be? Why did it happen? What should he do? I should be stoned according to the Law. He could put me away. What would he do?

"For some time we just sat, holding hands. Finally Joseph said, 'Mary, you know that I love you and I am a man of honor. I do not want you to be exposed to the Law. Let me pray about this and I am sure that God will give me some answer,' and he left.

"Elisa, I did not tell my mother and father about what happened, but that evening while we ate I informed them that I would like to visit my cousin Elisabeth. They were rather surprised, as I had never been away from home for any length of time. But since my father made regular trips to Judea by caravan, they knew I would be in safe hands. So we made preparations for me to go with him on his next trip, which was the next day. I worried about not telling Joseph about this sudden decision, but my mother said that she would get a message to him. I would have to stay until my father came back for me, which would be in about three months. We left the next morning.

"We came to the town where Elisabeth and her husband, Zachariah, lived. The caravan could not stop there so my father gave me my bundles and let me walk the short distance to their home. As I came to the house, I saw Elisabeth tending the flowers and greeted her, and to my astonishment she gave out a loud cry and grabbed her abdomen as if there was pain.

"And she said to me, 'Of all women you are the most blessed, and blessed is the fruit of your womb. Why should I be honored with a visit from the mother of my Lord? In the moment your greeting reached my ears, the child in my womb leaped for joy. Yes, blessed is she who believed that the promise made her by the Lord would be fulfilled.' Elisa, I don't know why, but the words of Hannah in the book of Samuel sprang to my lips:

My soul proclaims the greatness of the Lord

And my spirit exults in God my savior,

because he has looked upon his lowly handmaid.

Yes, from this day forward all generations will call me
*   blessed,*

for the Almighty has done great things for me.

Holy is his name,

and his mercy reaches from age to age

for those who fear him.

He has shown the power of his arm,

he has routed the proud of heart.

He has pulled down princes from their thrones, and
*   exalted the lowly.*

The hungry he has filled with good things, the rich sent
*   empty away.*

He has come to the help of Israel his servant, mindful
*   of his mercy —*

according to the promise he made to our ancestors —

of his mercy to Abraham and to his descendants
*   for ever.*[1]

"Elisa and Joseph, I stayed with her for three months until the birth of her child. I wore a loose cloak and no one noticed that I was with child. My father stopped on his way home from Jerusalem and I came home with him in the caravan. During all of this time I was worried about what Joseph would do. I knew that the decision was in his hands. I knew him to be a man of honor. As his betrothed, I would abide by his decision. My mother met us and it was so good to be home again. 'Your betrothed, Joseph,' she said, 'wanted to be informed the moment that you returned. I will send a messenger to him.' My friends, I was torn between relief and fear, relief that Joseph was still interested and fear of what his decision would be.

"After our evening meal Joseph knocked at the door and my father let him into the room. It was so good to see him. He clasped and kissed my hand. It was such a pleasant feeling. After the usual greetings, my mother said, 'Come, Jacob, let us go for a walk.'

"That left Joseph and me alone. I suggested that we walk into the garden and he was agreeable. We sat on the bench and Joseph said, 'Mary, I missed you very much.' And I answered, 'I missed you too.' But I was worried what he would say next.

"'Mary,' he said, 'I had a very difficult time after you told me your story three months ago. I prayed and read the Scriptures. Finally, wanting to spare you disgrace, I decided to quietly end our relationship. But a few nights ago the angel of the Lord appeared to me in a dream and said, "Joseph, son of David, do not be afraid to take Mary home as your wife, because she has conceived by the Spirit of God. She will give birth to a son and you must name him Jesus, because he is the one who is to save his people from their sins."'

"The following morning Joseph went to see my mother and asked that he be notified as soon as I return. Elisa, you cannot imagine the joy that I felt as I held his hand and realized what this meant. I was so thankful to God that all this had happened. Then I told him of the experience when I first spoke to Elisabeth. Joseph said, 'I cannot understand this but it must be the will of God.'"

Mary paused and Elisa was moved to speak. "All of this fulfills the words spoken by the Lord through the prophet Isaiah: 'The virgin shall conceive and give birth to a son and they shall call him Immanuel,'[2] a name that means 'God be with us.'" .

Mary nodded. "We were soon married and Joseph took me into his home as his wife, and we had no relations. I was able to keep the house, cook, fetch water from the well, wash clothes and do everything that needed to be done. Joseph worked hard and we kept our secret. No one but the angel of God and the two of us knew about it, and later we told Jesus. Now both of you, Elisa and Joseph, know too. We could not understand it, but believed in God and in His messenger.

"Then one day, Joseph came home and said that a Roman officer had posted a decree from Caesar Augustus, the emperor of Rome, that a census of the Roman world would be taken and everyone was to go to his own town to be registered. The decree was also signed by Querinius, the governor of Syria, of which Judea was a protectorate. Joseph was very disturbed as he was of the family of David, and we must go to Bethlehem near Jerusalem, seven days' journey south of Nazareth. He sought permission to come after the child was born, but the pleas were to no avail. I packed a few belongings, some food and swaddling clothes in case the child would be born while we were gone.

"We followed the road along the Jordan. I would walk for a while and then ride the donkey. It was dusty. Finally on the afternoon of the eighth day, a few hours after skirting Jerusalem, we climbed the final hill and saw Bethlehem below us. I was tired and anxious to wash myself and our clothing. Joseph was very concerned about me. He had cooked the sparse meals and tried to make things easy on me the entire way.

"As we entered the village Joseph spied an inn. He tied the donkey to a stake, made certain that I was comfortable, and went to ask for a room. Shortly he returned with a disappointed look on his face. 'They have no room,' he told me. And on we went, from one inn to another. It was now near sunset, and we were tired and hungry. I started to have cramps in my abdomen. I knew that this signaled the child was coming.

"I had been in attendance at the birth of my cousins' children and knew what to expect. The last innkeeper, who was a kindly man, felt sorry for us, but every room that he had was occupied, some by two families. The only space that he could offer was a stall in the stable. Joseph was offended and refused to put his wife in a stable. But I said that it would be fine. Finally, Joseph allowed the innkeeper to show us to the stable.

"It was dark and Joseph lit a candle, making certain it would not fall and start a fire. He brought some fresh straw and made an area where I could lie down and rest. He left to find some food for our dinner. When he returned, I was having regular pains. I could not eat. Joseph wanted to find a midwife but I said, 'No, stay with me. I know what to do.'

"The pains of the first-born are always the worst. Joseph was frantic, feeling helpless, and all he could do was hold my hand. The innkeeper came, but he was of little help.

"Finally, about three hours later, a male child was born. I tied the cord and Joseph cut it. The child cried and we were overjoyed. Joseph bathed the child and I wrapped him in the swaddling clothes. The child and I fell asleep. Joseph, as exhausted as he was, cleaned everything up, brought in some fresh straw, and ate the meal that he had bought hours before. Exhausted, he too fell asleep.

"Some time later, Joseph was awakened by a loud noise outside, as if many people were coming. He rose quickly to protect the baby and me. The voices came closer, singing and making joyful sounds. Suddenly -

shepherds with lanterns burst in. They came over to me and the baby and knelt in adoration of the child. Joseph asked one of the men near him what brought them here, what this was all about.

"The stranger said that he and other shepherds lived in the fields near Bethlehem and took turns watching their flocks at night. That night, an angel of the Lord had appeared, surrounded by a light almost as bright as the sun. They were frightened, but the angel said, 'Do not be afraid. Listen, I bring you news of great joy, a joy to be shared by the whole people. Today in the town of David a savior has been born to you. He is Christ the Lord. And here is a sign for you. You will find a baby wrapped in swaddling clothes and lying in a manger.' And suddenly there was a great throng of angels praising God and singing, 'Glory to God in the highest heaven and peace to men who enjoy his favor.'

"Now when the angels had gone from them into heaven, the shepherds said to one another, 'Let us go to Bethlehem and see this thing that has happened which the Lord has made known to us.' So they hurried away and found Joseph and me, and the baby lying in the manger, just as the angel had said."

Mary paused for a few moments. "As the shepherds left, they were singing praises to God. And suddenly, it was quiet. Joseph seemed bewildered and came to me. I put my hand on his cheek and recalled the words the angel Gabriel had said to me nine months before. 'You are to conceive and bear a son, and you must name him Jesus.'

"'Am I worthy to raise the Son of God?' Joseph replied. I answered, 'The Lord God has selected you to raise His Son.' Joseph answered, 'And you, Mary, to be His mother.' We both smiled and fell asleep in each other's arms. And I kept in my heart the memory of the shepherds kneeling before my infant child."

Elisa and I had listened intently. Again Elisa was struck by how this story echoed the words of the Scriptures. "It was all done to fulfill the words of the prophet Micah:

> *But you, Bethlehem-Ephrathah,*
> *the least of the clans of Judah,*
> *out of you will be born for me*
> *the one who is to rule over Israel.*
> *His origin goes back to the distant past,*
> *to the days of old.*

God is therefore going to abandon them
till the time when she who is to give birth gives birth.
Then the remnant of his brothers will come back
to the sons of Israel.
He will stand and feed his flock
with the power of the Lord,
with the majesty of the name of his God.
They will live secure, for from then on he will extend
*   his power*
to the ends of the land.
He himself will be peace.[3]

Jesus approached at that point. "It is time for evening prayer. Let us leave the rest of the story for tomorrow night." He took his mother and led her in the early darkness to the camp. Elisa and I followed in silence, reflecting on her words.

"Elisa," I said, "what is most difficult to believe is how Jesus was conceived. Mary told us that she conceived by the Spirit of the Lord. But it takes the father's seed deposited into the womb of the mother to produce a child."

"I agree, Joseph, that this is beyond our understanding. But you and I have seen many things that are beyond our understanding. We have seen lepers healed, the dead arise, the blind see and the deaf hear. We know that the great God made everything on the earth, under the earth and above the earth. Therefore is it beyond belief that He can create life without the father's seed?"

Luke, I have seen all of these things that she described and I have no explanation for any of them. I have no explanation for this conception either. I believe that it did happen. Why do I believe? Because I have seen the unbelievable happen over and over again in my association with Jesus.

As we lay down to sleep, I said, "So Jesus is of the family of David and was born in Bethlehem of a virgin — as hard as that is to believe. But has he ever lived in Egypt?"

Elisa's voice was tired and faint as she answered. "Let us wait for the rest of the story tomorrow."

Joseph

1   1 Samuel 2:1-10

2   Isaiah 7:14

3   Micah 5:1-4

Letter 103

Luke, the morning we left Mount Tabor, Jesus informed us we would return to the usual road. It was much easier walking and we should prepare to walk at a fast pace. I loaded the donkey with the supplies and we took off. Elisa was walking with Mary, and I brought up the rear of the column, leading the donkey. Mary was obviously in good health and able to keep up the pace. By this time my muscles seemed to be in condition to walk. My only soreness was the wounds of my adventure the day before.

Some time later we approached an area where we would have to enter Samaria. The Samaritans often deny passage through their territory to Jews going to Jerusalem for the Passover.

Now Jesus does not harbor any of the ancient grievances against the Samaritans, but he was still cautious in their territory. He sent two disciples ahead to make preparations in the town. About the tenth hour they came back to us and told Jesus that the village would not receive us because we were on the way to Jerusalem. James and John heard this and both spoke. "Lord, do you want us to call down fire from heaven to burn them up?" But Jesus was sharp in rebuking them. Then he set our course across the Jordan River in order to stay out of Samaria. We arrived in a village in Decapolis and camped at the outskirts. I unpacked the donkey, we had a short rest, and the women prepared the evening meal. We all ate heartily.

It was cool and breezy as Jesus came to Elisa and me and led us off to a quiet place where his mother was sitting. "Now, Mother, tell them the rest of the story while I pray." And Mary resumed her tale.

"After the visit of the shepherds," she began, "the innkeeper came to the stable. He again apologized for not having a room in the inn but promised that as soon as he could he would arrange a place for us. Joseph prepared the meals and made the child and me as comfortable as possible. The innkeeper came back the next afternoon and brought news that he now had a choice room. It had been freshly washed and even smelled clean. Joseph said he did not have much money, but the innkeeper offered him work as caretaker and carpenter. That seemed fair to everyone. The baby nursed well and often. I soon regained my strength. The innkeeper did not tell anyone else about the shepherds, so things were quiet.

"The time for the circumcision arrived, and we took him for the ceremony. The innkeeper came with us. It was brief, the baby did not cry, and we gave him the name Jesus, the name that the angel Gabriel had given him."

Luke, in our faith every male must be circumcised. This is part of the covenant that God made with Abraham centuries ago.[1] You have read all about this in the first book of the Scriptures.

Then Mary continued her tale. "That same day Joseph fulfilled the Law and completed the registration for the census. On his return we discussed what we would do. We decided to remain in Bethlehem until the allotted time for my purification, when I should be able to travel the short distance to the Temple in Jerusalem, and later we would return to our home in Nazareth.

"When the day came for the purification, as laid down by the Law of Moses, we took Jesus up to Jerusalem to present him to the Lord. We did not have much money, so we purchased two young pigeons to offer in sacrifice."

Luke, you will find this in the Writings about one-third of the way through Exodus.[2] Since the first-born sons of the Egyptians were destroyed because of the stubbornness of the pharaoh, the Lord says that all first-born sons of Israel belong to him and must be redeemed. The rules for purification are found in Leviticus.[3] It says that if a woman has a male child he must be circumcised on the eighth day and the mother must be purified another thirty-three days later. In the case of a female child the mother must wait sixty-six days to be purified. It also states that she should take as an offering a lamb, but if she cannot afford one she is to take two turtle doves or young pigeons.

"Shortly after our arrival in Jerusalem we were standing in the beautiful Temple and, to my surprise, a man came up to us and took the child from my arms. He held him, looked up and blessed God. 'Now, Master, you can let your servant go in peace, just as you promised, because my eyes have seen the salvation which you have prepared for all the nations to see, a light to enlighten the pagans and the glory of your people Israel.'

"Now, Joseph and I stood there wondering at the things that were being said about the baby Jesus. Then the man blessed us and said, 'You see this child. He is destined for the fall and for the rising of many in Israel, destined to be a sign that is rejected, and a sword will pierce your own soul, too, so that the secret thoughts of many may be laid bare.'

"As he finished, he placed the child back into my arms. Just then I felt some movement behind me. It was an elderly woman, and I thought that she was going to admire the baby, but she touched him in some wonder and then began to praise God. She spoke in a loud voice of the day to come when the Lord would set Jerusalem free. Then she left and we were there alone.

"Joseph went through the ceremony with the pigeons, and as we were preparing to leave he asked a Temple guard about these two people who had given praise to the Lord for our child. He said that the man was Simeon, a devout man who looked forward to the comforting of Israel. The Spirit of the Lord had told him he would not die until he saw the Christ of the Lord, the Messiah.

"'And the woman?' he asked.

"She was Anna the daughter of Phaneul, of the tribe of Asher. Anna was eighty-four years old and had been widowed seven years after her marriage. She worshipped daily in the Temple, fasting and praying.

"As we left the Temple, Joseph said, 'This is beyond all comprehension. What do you make of it, Mary?' And I replied, 'I do not know, but let us trust in God. We know that He will guide us and direct us to do the right thing for this infant.' And we kept this in our hearts as we returned to the inn in Bethlehem. Elisa, I was exhausted by the time that we returned to the room. Joseph told me to rest while he took care of Jesus."

Mary paused only a few moments. "A few days later, as we were preparing to return to Nazareth, another strange thing happened.

"That evening Joseph came in and said that a caravan had just arrived at the inn from the East, and among the group were three magnificently robed men, each with his own entourage. He did not know who they were or where they were going.

"Just then there was a knock on the door and the innkeeper ushered in these same three men, each carrying gifts. They walked to the crib, knelt down before the baby and offered gifts of gold, of frankincense and of myrrh.

"Elisa and Joseph, I had never seen so much treasure in my life. They bowed to the child and conducted themselves as if they were in the presence of a king. They stayed only a short while, bowed and left. The innkeeper closed the door and we were left alone with the child and the gifts. We looked at each other and sat there in wonder, looking at the sleeping Jesus. Then the innkeeper came and told us the story.

"These men were very wise men, astrologers by profession, who live many days' journey over the desert to the east. They had seen a great star and realized that a king had been born. They set out to worship him. As they traveled the star preceded them and guided them. After long days they finally came to Judea and sent messengers to King Herod, inquiring where this infant was born. From what they had said the king was astounded. Herod said that he was king and that no one would take his place. But the messengers insisted, asking, 'Where is this infant king of the Jews? We saw his star as it rose and have come to do him homage.'

"The knowledge of their visit soon spread all over Jerusalem. King Herod was perturbed. He called his chief priests and scribes and inquired from them where this king was to be born. 'At Bethlehem of Judea,' they told him. 'For this is what the prophet wrote: And you, Bethlehem, in the land of Judah, you are by no means least among the leaders of Judah, for out of you will come a leader who will shepherd my people.'[4] When Herod heard this, he turned red with anger. He was almost violent, his servants said. 'No one is going to replace me,' he continued to repeat. But we were told that he soon calmed down.'

"He asked the scribes to invite the visiting astrologers to the palace so that he could direct them to the infant king. The caravan was approaching Jerusalem when the messenger found them. King Herod extended all honors to the visiting dignitaries and gave a banquet in their honor. At the banquet he inquired just when and where the star appeared to them. Then he told them that the prophet Micah stated the child was to be born in Bethlehem. And he told them, 'Go and find out all about the child, and when you have found him, let me know so that I, too, may go and do him homage.'

"So early that evening they set out. And the star appeared and went before them and halted over the room where we three were staying.

"After the innkeeper finished his story," Mary said, "Joseph carefully placed the gifts away where they would not be seen, and we went to sleep."

Luke, these gifts were meant to honor and worship a king. Gold is a rare and precious metal given to royalty. And frankincense is used for worship. But why these men would bring myrrh, Luke, I don't understand. It is used to embalm bodies.

Mary continued. "Several hours into the night, Joseph awakened me.

"'We must leave now,' he said. 'The same angel who told me to take you as my wife has appeared again and said that we must leave for Egypt immediately. He said that Herod would harm the child. These were the angel's words: "Get up, take the child and his mother with you, and escape into Egypt, and stay there until I tell you, because Herod intends to search for the child and do away with him.' And we prepared to leave."

Elisa and I looked at each other. "For Egypt?" I asked.

"Yes," Mary replied. "Can you imagine? We were to go to a strange land for an undetermined amount of time without any preparation. But we had placed our trust in the Lord and agreed to rely on His guidance. We had heard there were many Jews in the land of the Nile. In Leontopolis in the region of Heliopolis, Jews had even built a temple that rivaled the one in Jerusalem.

"Joseph went to awaken the innkeeper and pay him for the accommodation. He helped us pack our meager belongings, then brought our donkey. With the sleeping child in my arms, I left the inn for the last time. We thanked the innkeeper and asked God's blessings upon him and on our long trip to Egypt. I mounted the donkey, then Joseph handed the child to me and off we went in the darkness, away from Nazareth.

"Elisa, Joseph was strong-willed and brave. He guided the donkey over smooth portions of the path and by morning we were well on our way. On the road near Hebron we were able to join a caravan and travel more safely. It would be a journey of more than ten days."

Mary stopped her account, understanding we needed time to absorb all of this. We asked a few questions, then she resumed her story.

"The sun was hot and bore down mercilessly. We tried to protect the child from the sun, but he fussed and chafed in the heat. At night we slept in the open or on the grounds of an inn, as we did not have much money. We ate sparsely but made certain that Jesus was fed.

"We did have the gold that the wise men had given us, but Joseph and I had decided we would provide for Jesus ourselves. The treasure would be for his use when he grew to manhood.

"One morning a smiling woman named Adah approached us, admiring the baby. She asked to hold him, then took us to meet her husband, Josiah. They were Jews living in Thmuis, a town east of the River Nile, and were returning from a pilgrimage to Jerusalem. They were clearly prosperous, as each had a camel to ride and a canopy to protect them from the sun.

"Josiah was a man of spare frame but strong will. He insisted that the child and I ride his camel while he and Joseph walked. And for the rest of the journey we were their guests. When we arrived in Thmuis they took us into their home until Joseph could find employment. He did not like accepting their charity, but really we couldn't have made it without their kindness.

"Josiah enjoyed woodworking and had a shop with all the tools needed to make furniture. Within a week Joseph had made a handsome set of chairs for our hosts. Everyone who came to the house admired his work, and soon Joseph had many requests to build fine furniture. The customers paid handsomely and we tried to repay Josiah, but he refused.

We began to look for a home of our own. We purchased some new clothing, which we needed, and saved the rest of the money.

"In the meantime, the child grew and began to crawl. Josiah and Adah were like grandparents to him and like parents to us. They were sorry to see us go.

"We settled in a small house in the Jewish section and became part of the community. But one day Joseph came home with upsetting news about the three astrologers. They apparently had been warned in a dream not to return to Herod to tell him about the child Jesus but to go home another way. Herod had waited for the wise men to return. When they did not, he sent messengers and learned they had already left for their home countries. Herod was furious when he realized that he had been outwitted. He called for his scribes and issued an edict that all male children under the age of two years in the area around Bethlehem were to be killed."

Mary stopped and shed a few tears, and I recalled the story my mother had told me about the slaughter of so many infant boys. But Elisa was moved to speak. She recounted the prophecy of Jeremiah: "In Ramah is heard the sound of moaning, of bitter weeping. Rachel mourns her children. She refuses to be comforted because they are no more."[5]

Mary nodded, then continued her story. That night, she said, she and Joseph sat and held hands. They thanked God who through his guardian angel had saved Jesus, and they prayed for the infants who were massacred by Herod.

Jesus was a healthy baby. He learned to walk and talk under their guidance. Joseph did good work and they were able to live comfortably on the amount that he earned.

"One night, Joseph awoke me and told me that the angel had returned and spoken to him. 'Get up,' he said, 'take the child and his mother with you back to the land of Israel, for those who wanted to kill the child are dead.' So in the morning, we made plans to leave. We thanked Josiah and Adah for

---

their kindness, loaded the donkey and joined a caravan. This time we had adequate money to sleep in an inn and to eat well.

The road was hot and dusty, but we were full of joy because we were going back to our own people. As we approached Judea, we were told that Herod had died and his son Archelaus was now ruler. But that night in a dream Joseph was again warned of danger, so we traveled through Judea and on to Galilee, returning to Nazareth. Our parents were very happy to see us.

"Joseph purchased more tools with the money he had saved and made a good income as a carpenter. We did not live lavishly but we always had more than enough.

"Joseph taught young Jesus all that he knew about making furniture. As the boy grew into a man, he helped his father more and more until he took over most of the heavy work. Then," Mary said, her voice breaking, "Joseph died." It was a few moments before she could go on.

"Jesus continued to make furniture for the fine homes in Nazareth. We did not spend much. I wove our clothing and we put aside what we did not need.

"One day three years ago Jesus informed me that he must do what he came to do. I did not understand what he meant at that time, but he said there was enough in savings to support me. As he left Capernaum to begin his ministry, I insisted he take the gold given him at birth. Before long I began to hear of the wonders he was performing throughout Galilee as a healer and teacher."

Mary was tired by then, but she knew that Elisa and I had many questions. "Tomorrow I will tell you about Jesus' childhood," she promised.

At that time Jesus returned and we all walked back to the camp and sat around the fire with the others.

Later, when we were alone, I expressed one of my thoughts to Elisa. "This visit of the astrologers may have great significance. God may be using them to tell the world that Jesus came for all people and not just for the Jews. I remember a passage of the Psalms where it says, 'The kings of Tarshish and of the islands will pay him tribute. The kings of Sheba and Seba will offer gifts.'"[6]

"Joseph, you are starting to quote the Scriptures!"

"Yes, I have to keep up with you and with Luke. He continues to ask questions."

The more I learn about Jesus, Luke, the more I understand that the Messiah has come into this world to save us all and that the Gentiles are also God's people.

Joseph

1   Genesis 17:10-11

2   Exodus 13:11-16

3   Leviticus 12:1-8

4   Micah 5:1-2

5   Jeremiah 31:15

6   Psalms 72:10

Letter 104

By early morning, Luke, we had broken camp and were back on the road to Jerusalem. Our path leads us south from Decapolis through Perea, then we will recross the Jordan River and enter Judea.

Even this distance from Capernaum, people know of Jesus and his powers of healing, as we were soon to learn. But many of them want him to be a Messiah king, an insurgent who will liberate these lands from Roman rule.

As we approached one village we could see people keeping themselves at a distance but shouting for our attention. "Jesus, Master, have mercy on us. Jesus, Master, have mercy!" They were lepers, and as we walked closer I could see that several were in advanced stages of the disease. They were Jews, Gentiles and Samaritans.

Jesus spoke to them calmly. "Go. Show yourselves to the priests."[1] Then he walked on, with his followers, toward the well in the center of town. The ten lepers did not know what to do, but finally left in a group and headed toward the synagogue to see the priests. I told Elisa I would follow them.

As they arrived at the synagogue, I noticed the dry, scaly skin fall off the face of one man until his cheeks were as smooth as a baby's skin, his hands were whole and the sores were healed. As I watched, all of the ten were cured at once. They shouted and danced for joy. "I am cleansed, I am cleansed!"

But where before there was a group of ten, suddenly there were three distinct groups, one of Jews, one of Gentiles, and a single Samaritan. After a few moments of rejoicing, all but the Samaritan left to return to their wives and children and friends, to live in a house again and eat with the family. Their lives had been restored. They were no longer lepers. They were normal.

The Samaritan, however, praised God at the top of his voice and made his way toward the well. He went straight to Jesus, threw himself at his feet and thanked him.

Then Jesus said, "Were not all ten made clean? The other nine, where are they? It seems that no one has come back to give praise to God except this foreigner." Then he said to the man, "Stand up and go on your way. Your faith has cured you."

As I told all of this to Elisa she said, "The ten were not cleansed until they did what they were told to do, show themselves to the priests. It is like the commandment that Elisha gave to Naaman."[2]

Luke, you read the story in the Scriptures. Naaman was told to go and wash seven times in the River Jordan. He was cured only after he did so, on the basis of his faith in God.

As word spread of this cure, many of the townspeople came out to see Jesus. There was wonder in their eyes and there was clearly a hunger to know more about Jesus. Could this be the Christ, the king who would liberate the Jews from the Romans?

But Jesus did not linger. He turned to us and said, "We had better get on our way if we are to get to Jerusalem for the Passover."

The rest of the day's walk was uneventful and we camped for the night under a grove of sycamore trees. After the evening meal Mary, Elisa and I withdrew from the larger company and Mary resumed her story.

"I know that you are eager to learn about the childhood of Jesus. Really, it was not unusual. He played with the other children of Nazareth. He needed correcting like all children do, and he learned from our guidance. He went to the synagogue to learn Hebrew and the writings of the prophets.

"As he grew, he seemed a little taller than others his age. He was attractive and always had many friends. Several women selected Jesus as the spouse they wanted for their daughters." Then Mary stopped and sighed.

"When Jesus was twelve years old, we went to Jerusalem for the Passover, as we had done every year. As we set off on the return journey Joseph and I allowed him to walk with his friends in the caravan, but we expected him to join us as usual at the end of the day. That day he did not. We searched for Jesus among relatives and acquaintances, but no one had seen him.

"We were beside ourselves. Here God had given us His child to raise and we had lost him. We did not sleep much that night, and early the next morning we returned to Jerusalem to look for him."

Mary's voice broke several times as she described the next three days in Jerusalem. She and Joseph searched everywhere but no one had seen young Jesus. Neither one of them ate or slept much those three days.

"We finally decided to give up and go to the Temple the next morning, to pray and ask forgiveness for losing the child. We entered the Temple early and as we passed a room, we saw a group of doctors and other men learned in the Scriptures gathered in a circle listening to someone speaking.

It was a familiar voice, so we stopped to look inside. There was Jesus sitting in the midst of all of these men, listening to them and asking them questions. The learned men all shook their heads and remarked at the intelligence of the youth and of his replies.

"Jesus saw us, asked leave of the men and came to us. We were overcome when we saw him so happy and that he was alive. But we were angry, too. I said, 'My child, why have you done this to us? See how worried your father and I have been, looking for you?'

"Jesus replied, 'Why were you looking for me? Did you not know that I must be busy with my father's affairs?'

"We did not understand what he meant, but he left with us. Joseph was very angry but tried not to show it."

I asked, "Why didn't you whip him?"

"I felt like it. I know that Joseph did too, but we did not. Jesus knew that he had hurt us both badly. He continued his studies at the synagogue school and worked with Joseph in his spare time. Never again did he leave without telling us where he was going and when to expect his return.

"He grew up to be quite a good-looking young man. He began to spend much of his time in prayer and reading the Scriptures. Most of his friends became betrothed and married, but he showed no such inclination. One day a matchmaker came to Joseph to arrange a marriage for Jesus. That night Joseph raised the possibility of marriage. Jesus replied that he was not interested. He felt that what was planned for him was not fitting for a family life. He simply said, 'My work is yet to come.'

"We did not understand all of this, but I just kept all of these things in my heart. And Jesus increased in wisdom, in stature and in favor with God and man."

Elisa and I held hands and looked at each other in silence, trying to absorb all of this and relate it to what is happening now.

At this time Jesus joined us after an evening spent in prayer. "Now I am sure that you each have questions to ask of me."

"Jesus," Elisa was quick to ask, "Joseph and I have often wondered about the reason that you came to Jericho to be baptized by John."

"I had come all the way down the Jordan for that purpose. It was time to begin my public ministry."

"But you walked out of the river that day and disappeared into the woods. What happened then?"

"I was led by the Spirit of the Lord through the wilderness. There I was tempted by the devil for forty days. During that time I ate nothing and I was hungry. The devil appeared to me and said, 'If you are the Son of God, tell this stone to turn into a loaf.' But I replied, 'Scripture says, "Man does not live on bread alone."'[3]

"Then he led me to a height and showed me, in a moment of time, all of the kingdoms of the world, and said to me, 'I will give you all this power and the glory of these kingdoms, for it has been committed to me and I give to anyone I choose. Worship me then and it shall all be yours.'

"I answered, 'Scripture says, "You must worship the Lord your God, and serve Him alone."'[4]

"Then he led me to Jerusalem and stood me on the parapet of the Temple. 'If you are the Son of God,' he said, 'throw yourself down from here, for Scripture says, "He will bid his angels to watch over you." And again, "They will hold you up on their hands in case you hurt your foot against a stone."'[5]

"'But,' I answered him, 'it has been said, "You must not put the Lord your God to the test."'[6] Then the devil said, 'I have exhausted all of my means to tempt you. I will leave to return at the appropriate time.' As he left, angels came to comfort me."

"What did the devil look like?" I asked. Jesus smiled.

"Well, Joseph, the devil can take many forms. He once looked like a simple traveler, once like a very devout Levite, and once like a shepherd. But the voice was always the same, and there were always the temptations that proved who was really speaking."

"Do you mean," I asked, "that the devil can come to us in any disguise and even tempt us with things that we need but urge us to get them in the wrong way?"

"Joseph, you have stated it well. Of course, I was hungry after all of the fasting. I had dreamed of food for days. I knew that my body needed the food, but if I had asked my Father to turn the stones into bread I would have consented to the wishes of the devil and been under his power.

"Yes, I was tempted to jump off the parapet of the Temple and have the angels catch me and preserve me from harm, just to prove to the devil that I could do it. But then he would have found some other means to tempt me. Any submission to the will of the devil will only lead to more and more submissions. The Scriptures tell of those who did submit and perished.

The Scriptures are full of sayings the devil can turn to his use, to make what is bad seem good.

"With the power of the Spirit of the Lord, I made my way back to Galilee to begin my ministry."

I asked, "When are you going to reveal all of this clearly and not veil your mission in parables?"

"The time will come that it will all be properly revealed. In fact, the time is short. But now," he said as he got up, "it is time to get some sleep."

"I have one other question," I asked. "Why did you choose Capernaum, one of two hundred settlements in the area, as a base for your mission?"

"The people of Nazareth," he said, "did not believe me when I revealed who I was in the synagogue. Capernaum, however, is the crossroads of many caravans. Like you and Elisa, the people are known to be open to new ideas and also to have the courage to follow through on new ideas. That is well-known even in the land of Judea."

The sun had set by then and the stars were high above and we had not even noticed. Elisa and I felt deeper exhaustion tonight than any earlier night on the journey to Jerusalem.

Elisa has believed for some time that Jesus is the long-awaited Messiah and now I too am convinced. What an extraordinary blessing to be living in Capernaum and to have the Son of God as our close friend!

Joseph

[1] Leviticus 14:1-20

[2] 2 Kings 5

[3] Deuteronomy 8:3

[4] Deuteronomy 5:6-10

[5] Psalms 91:11-12

[6] Deuteronomy 6:16

Letter 105

Luke, we have walked steadily the last three days. We are following the Jordan River, with Jericho being our immediate destination.

As you know, Elisa and I carry a bag of essential surgical instruments when we travel: scalpel, needle, thread, dressings, healing balm and some medications. We are not equipped for much, but it has served the followers of Jesus, and occasionally some strangers who need us. Sometimes we meet a caravan in which some of the people need attention, and they often pay handsomely. We put this into the treasury of the followers, handled by Judas Iscariot.

As a Judean, Judas sometimes seems like an outsider in the group. His clothing and manner of speech are somewhat different from Galileans. But he seems to hold himself apart as well. He handles donations and purchases for the group, which causes him to be absent from the company much of the time.

Our company of travelers has been together for more than a week and it has given me an opportunity to know all the apostles better. The last few nights we have all lingered around the campfire to sing or tell stories. Jesus is a great storyteller and keeps us laughing. So does Matthew. He tells many stories of his experiences as a tax collector and they are funny.

Jude organizes the construction of every campground. He also enjoys singing, and his bass voice is distinctive. Thomas is plain-speaking and skeptical, always asking questions. Simon, the lawyer among us, is methodical in his thinking and deliberate in his actions.

Bartholomew, Philip's friend from Bethsaida, is rather scholarly and polished in his manner.

Jesus has spent time teaching the disciples every day. Luke, I am often able to sit with the disciples and hear what they hear. I grow stronger in my faith every day, but I worry how this journey will end.

Last night we made camp under the huge trees that grow in this well-watered river area. This morning Jesus called to his apostles before he withdrew to pray. "Now we are going up to Jerusalem," he said, "and everything that is written by the prophets about the Son of Man is to come true. For he will be handed over to the pagans and will be mocked, maltreated and spat on, and when they have scourged him they will put him to death, and on the third day he will rise again."

I could see that Peter, James, Thomas and all the others were confused. They could make nothing of this dire prophecy. The Twelve were quiet even after Jesus returned and the company shared a light morning meal.

On the road to Jericho we travel through areas where there are no settlements, but also through good-sized villages. Our company is clearly making a journey to Jerusalem for Passover and so does not draw much attention — until someone recognizes Jesus. Then the news spreads and crowds gather to see him.

As we near Jerusalem we hear people more often refer to Jesus as the Messiah who is to come. But Luke, I sense that many of these people are angry and seeking not a savior but a warrior, and this worries me. As word of Jesus spreads, he must represent an even greater threat to authorities. But he seems as determined as ever to reach Jerusalem and face whatever fate awaits him.

As we neared one town Jesus stopped in a tree-shaded area to allow the women to catch up and see how his mother was doing. I saw a gathering of people in the distance coming toward us, and in their path, a blind man sitting at the side of the road begging. They reached him before our group did.

"What is this all about?" he asked, and someone answered, "Jesus the Nazarene is passing by." Luke, I still do not understand how they know Jesus is coming before he arrives.

The beggar called out, "Jesus, Son of David, have pity on me." The people in front scolded him and told him to keep quiet, but he shouted all the louder, "Son of David, have pity on me."

Jesus stopped and ordered that the man be brought to him. "What do you want me to do for you?" Jesus asked.

"Sir," he replied, "let me see again."

Jesus said to him, "Receive your sight. Your faith has saved you."

Instantly his sight returned and he set eyes for the first time on Jesus. "Praise God," he said, and knelt in gratitude. Many of the townspeople sang their praises and attached themselves to our group as we walked through the village. But others stood to one side as we passed, their expressions grim.

Tomorrow we will reach Jericho and see what has changed since Elisa and I were there. This is where we saw and heard John and witnessed the baptism of Jesus. Knowing him has changed our lives profoundly.

Joseph

Letter 106

Greetings in the name of the God of Abraham, Moses and David.

As we entered Jericho, we stopped to rest in the shade of trees not far from the inn of Matthias. I had suggested to Jesus that many of us could stay at the inn. "That will be good for you and Elisa and the women in the group, but I have other plans," he said. Somehow word had arrived that Jesus was arriving, and men and women of all ages started to gather. Mary his mother, Joanna and other women in the company stayed seated, but Jesus and The Twelve rose and started to walk into town. With the curious drawing close and calling out to Jesus, they formed a dense throng.

Elisa nudged me and showed me that Matthias had emerged from the inn to see what was happening. Elisa and I went to him and were pleased that he remembered us. "What brings you here?" he asked.

Elisa answered, "We are on our way to Jerusalem for the Passover with Jesus of Nazareth. This is the man from Galilee we first saw here when John was baptizing at the River Jordan. He has been healing and teaching in Galilee since then."

"I have heard of him," Matthias replied as we walked to the crowd around Jesus. "Some say he works miracles. Others say he will overturn the Romans and become a new king."

Our attention was called to a small man running around from one side to the other. He was so short he would jump up to try to get a look at Jesus. It was rather comical. Matthias said, "That man is Zacchaeus, one of our senior tax collectors. Too bad he is so short."

I noticed that Matthias did not have a sneer in his voice as most Jews do when they talk about a tax collector. "You know, Zacchaeus is the most honest man I have ever met. He collects the necessary tax, takes his allotted percentage, and that is all. He does not overcharge nor cheat."

Finally Zacchaeus ran in front of the crowd and climbed a sycamore tree hoping to get a glimpse of Jesus as he walked past. But Jesus stopped below the tree, looked up and said, "Zacchaeus, come down. Hurry because I must stay at your home today."

Zacchaeus' mouth flew open in astonishment. Jesus, an itinerant rabbi or teacher, was to stay at the home of a tax collector. Zacchaeus hurried down the tree and pushed his way to Jesus. As he came by us I noticed that he had on plain clothes typical of the people of Jericho. He did not wear the rich fabrics of a tax collector.

Some of the crowd complained when they saw what was happening. They said, "He has gone to stay at a sinner's house." Zacchaeus heard these murmurs too, but he stood his ground and said to Jesus, "Look, sir, I give half of my property to the poor, and if I have unknowingly cheated anybody, I pay him back four times the amount."

Jesus said to him, "Today salvation has come to this house. Because this man too is a son of Abraham, for the Son of Man has come to seek out and save what has been lost."

At that Jesus and The Twelve followed Zacchaeus toward his home. The crowd gradually dispersed but not without some cutting remarks.

Matthias then turned to Elisa and me. "Now tell me about yourselves. You must stay with me tonight." Elisa spoke, "We appreciate that but there are more of us, including Mary the mother of Jesus." But Matthias answered, "Bring them in. We have room." We walked to the tree where we had left the women with Mary and introduced them all to their host, who was most gracious in his greetings.

We were taken to the inn, able to wash and change before dinner. We had not slept, eaten indoors or bathed for days. We all enjoyed the change. Matthias seated Jesus' mother at a place of honor. After introducing everyone to all of his guests he asked me to give the traditional Jewish blessing. Then the food was brought in and, Luke, we were famished. Matthias enjoyed watching us eat.

When things became quiet Matthias said, "Tell me about Jesus." We all started to talk at once. Mary his mother just smiled. Elisa and I spoke of the cures we had witnessed.

But all of this was difficult for Matthias to believe. He asked, "Does Abraham know of this?"

Elisa replied, "We have written everything to him and hope he will meet Jesus in Jerusalem." She continued, "The cures are of course amazing, but equally extraordinary are his teachings. He speaks of the kingdom of God, where justice and freedom will prevail, where there will be no slave or master, no conqueror."

We talked long into the night. Soon we were all nodding and retired to our rooms. "This will take most of the coins that we have brought along," I said, but Elisa was not concerned. "God will provide."

Joseph

Letter 107

It was a very restful night, Luke. Our company will spend the day here in Jericho before resuming our journey. By morning Jesus had come to the inn and drawn a huge crowd with him. He sat in the middle of the main portico and began teaching, with servants from the inn among those listening.

"A man of noble birth went to a distant country to be appointed king and afterward return. He summoned ten of his servants and gave them ten pounds. 'Do business with these,' he told them, 'until I get back.' But his compatriots detested him and sent a delegation to follow him with this message, 'We do not want this man to be our king.'

"Now on his return, having received his appointment as king, he sent for those servants to whom he had given the money, to find out what profit each had made. The first came in and said, 'Sir, your one pound has brought in ten.' 'Well done, my good servant!' he replied. 'Since you have proved yourself faithful in a very small thing, you shall have the government of ten cities.' Then came the second and said, 'Sir, your one pound has made five.' To this one also he said, 'And you shall be in charge of five cities.' Next came the other and said, 'Sir, here is your pound. I put it away safely in a piece of linen because I was afraid of you, for you are an exacting man. You pick up what you have not put down and reap what you have not sown.' 'You wicked servant!' he said. 'Out of your own mouth I condemn you. So you knew I was an exacting man, picking up what I have not put down and reaping what I have not sown. Then why did you not put my money in the bank? On my return I could have drawn it out with interest.' And he said to those standing by, 'Take the pound from him and give it to the man who has ten pounds.' And they said to him, 'But, sir, he has ten pounds.' 'I tell you,' he replied, 'to everyone who has will be given more, but from the man who has not, even what he has will be taken away. But as for my enemies who did not want me for their king, bring them here and execute them in my presence.'"

The parable addressed a matter Elisa said she had been pondering in her heart. "Those of us who have been given the privilege of learning more about the kingdom of God have a great responsibility to tell everyone about it," she said. "We should not keep the knowledge to ourselves, but we should live the teachings and spread that way of life to others."

This teaching also confirmed one of my growing convictions. "God has given each of us special talents, such as singing, writing or skilled carpentry," I said. "Yours and mine, Elisa, is the knowledge to restore people to good health. Jesus is telling us that we should use the talents we have been given to their fullest." She nodded her approval.

After the noon meal and rest Elisa and I walked in the garden of the inn as we had done on our previous stay. There we found Mary the mother of Jesus enjoying the flowers. Elisa said, "I hope that you like it here."

"Oh yes," she replied, "it is lovely," and she motioned for us to sit beside her. We told Mary about our earlier visit here and our experiences watching John baptizing in the Jordan. And then Mary told us the story of John's birth.

John's mother, as you may recall, was Mary's cousin Elisabeth, and Mary had been in attendance at the birth.

Elisabeth, who was old enough to be Mary's mother, was married to Zachariah, a priest from the Abijah section of the priesthood and a descendant of Aaron. Zachariah and Elisabeth were devout and tried to follow Jewish Law. They had prayed for a child, but remained childless. Elisabeth was then past the child-bearing age and she felt inadequate as she had not fulfilled her role as a woman to be a mother. Then an angel appeared to Zachariah.

It was Zachariah's turn as a priest to enter into the sanctuary of the Lord and to burn incense while the entire congregation prayed outside. When he entered he saw an angel on the right side of the altar. Zachariah became frightened. The angel spoke to him. "Zachariah, do not be afraid. Your prayer has been heard. Your wife Elisabeth is to bear a son and you must call him John. He will be your joy and delight and many will rejoice at his birth, for he will be great in the sight of the Lord. He must drink no wine, no strong drink. Even from his mother's womb, he will be filled with the Spirit of the Lord, and he will bring back many of the sons of Israel to the Lord their God.

"With the spirit and power of Elijah, he will go before him to turn the hearts of the fathers toward their children and the disobedient back to the wisdom of the virtuous, preparing for the Lord a people lost for him."

Zachariah could not believe this. "How can I be sure of this?" he said. "I am an old man and my wife is getting along in years."

The angel seemed offended. "I am Gabriel who stands in the Lord's presence. And I have been sent to speak to you and bring you this good news."

It was a bold thing for Zachariah to do, to challenge a messenger of the Lord, although Abraham, Moses and others of our ancestors had done similar things.

Gabriel then spoke harshly. "Listen! Since you have not believed my words, which will occur in their appointed time, you will be silenced and have no power of speech until this has happened." And the angel left.

Zachariah stood alone near the altar. He tried to praise God for the fact that their prayers would be answered, but no words could come out. He stayed in the sanctuary for a long time thanking God in quiet prayer.

When he finally came out, the congregation was restless. Then they realized that he could not speak and that something had happened while he was in the sanctuary. He used signs to speak to them.

In time Elisabeth conceived. She felt that whatever happened was the work of the Lord and said, "The Lord has done this for me. Now it has pleased him to take away the humiliation that I have suffered among men."

Mary continued the story. "When Elisabeth's time was completed she gave birth to a son. Every one of her friends and relatives was elated. Zachariah was beside himself with joy because he would have an heir. They all thanked God.

"The child was to be circumcised on the eighth day, and it was understood that they would name him after his father. His mother objected. 'No,' she said, 'he is to be called John.' But they all told her that no one in the family had that name. Finally someone decided to ask the father. Zachariah, using a writing tablet, wrote, 'His name is John.' And as he did his ability to speak returned. Everyone was overjoyed and they all praised God.

"All of those present wondered what the child would grow up to be. They felt that the Lord had something special for him.

"After Zachariah regained his speech, he was filled with the Spirit of the Lord and uttered his own prophecy, echoing the Psalms, Leviticus and Isaiah:

> *Blessed be the Lord God of Israel,*
> *for he has visited his people,*
> *he has come to their rescue*
> *and he has raised up for us a power for salvation*
> *in the House of his servant David,*
> *even as he proclaimed,*

by the mouth of his holy prophets from ancient times,
that he would save us from our enemies,
and from the hands of all who hate us.
Thus he shows mercy to our ancestors,
thus he remembers his holy covenant
the oath he swore to our father Abraham
that he would grant us, free from fear,
to be delivered from the hands of our enemies,
to serve him in holiness and virtue
in his presence, all our days.
And you, little child,
you shall be called Prophet of the Most High,
for you will go before the Lord
to prepare the way for him,
to give his people knowledge of salvation
through the forgiveness of their sins,
this by the tender mercy of our God
who from on high will bring the rising Sun to visit us,
to give light to those who live
in darkness and the shadow of death,
and to guide our feet into the way of peace.

When Mary had finished, Elisa asked, "What about his childhood and youth?"

"The child grew up and his spirit matured, and he lived out in the wilderness until the day he appeared openly to Israel."

Then we heard voices from the path outside the garden. It was Jesus teaching. As he entered and saw Mary, he stopped, went to his mother and embraced her. He asked, "And how did you sleep last night?" She replied, "We have the most wonderful host," and at that she saw Matthias in the crowd. "Come and meet him." Our host bowed before Jesus. "For many months," Matthias said, "I have been hearing of the man from Galilee who speaks with the authority of the Most High and has the power to sway hearts from a life of sin. Now I have had the privilege of hearing you speak.

You and your court would honor me with your presence at dinner tonight," and he took Jesus and The Twelve into the inn.

After all had eaten, Judas offered to pay but Matthias refused to accept any money. "It has been my privilege to have such a wonderful rabbi as my guest." Later I took Matthias aside myself to pay for our lodging, but he again refused. "It is through you that I have learned of Jesus and his teachings. I am indebted to you."

Elisa and I then retired early in order to leave at sunrise.

Joseph

Letter 108

Dear Luke, today after two days' travel we arrived in Bethany, outside Jerusalem. It was a warm day as the hot, dry season is beginning.

The closer we came to Jerusalem, the more somber became our band of travelers. Every day we encountered people who knew of Jesus, who clamored to see and touch him. But the man they sought out was not the man of peace we knew so well. They wanted a Messiah to lead an uprising against Herod and the authorities in Rome.

What's more, Jesus has spoken ominously of what lies ahead in Jerusalem. If his own words are fulfilled, he will face suffering, betrayal and even death. We heard Jesus being warned to turn back, but he brushed the warnings aside. He acted as if he were being drawn to Jerusalem, and his step became even more determined.

Jesus had sent a messenger ahead to Bethany to tell his friends Mary, Martha and Lazarus that we were coming. We were tired as we arrived in Bethany.

Mary and Lazarus came to meet us and were overjoyed to see Jesus and his mother. Of course the journey had been hard on his mother, and the lines on her face showed anxiety as well as fatigue. She and the other women were shown to rooms where they could rest for the afternoon out of the heat of the sun. Martha informed us that we would be guests that evening at a banquet in honor of Jesus. The host would be a man by the name of Gideon.

We left at sundown for the short walk to the house of Gideon. He was a leper whom Jesus had cured in the past. I looked at his exposed skin, his face and hands, and they were clean. There were no knots on his face, he had all of his fingers. Gideon was very gracious and ordered a servant to wash our feet, as is our custom. All of the guests were gathering. Of course, there were Jesus and The Twelve, his mother and all of the followers, including Elisa and me. There were about thirty other guests, all friends of Gideon. They were well-dressed and some even had rings on their fingers.

Many of them, I was told, were tax collectors. As you know, the Jewish people ostracize them but Jesus dines with them. Jesus has said, "The well have no need for a physician, only the sick do."

Soon, a servant sounded a trumpet and our host came into the banquet hall. He was dressed well but not ostentatiously. He went directly to Jesus and escorted him to the head of the table. As they passed the group of women, Jesus stopped, walked to his mother, took her by the hand and escorted her with him to his assigned place. I could see this bothered some of the other guests, as it is the custom to seat men and women separately at the table. But Jesus had changed this long ago among his followers, so it did not bother us. Soon, we were all in our places and Gideon recited the Jewish prayers. The servants came with fruit. There were grapes, plums, peaches and other fruits from the fertile banks of the Jordan. Then came the vegetables, cooked in spices and roast lamb. We ate slowly, all talking to each other. Jesus was carrying on a conversation with Gideon, his mother and Peter, who was nearby. I was seated next to Cleopas, a follower of Jesus in Jerusalem.

As we were finishing our wine and the servants were bringing water in which to wash our fingers, Mary of Bethany came into the banquet chamber carrying a heavy jar of aromatic oil. She went directly to where Jesus was reclining. He turned and looked at her. Then she poured the contents of the jar on his head and feet. The room was filled with the fragrance of flowers and oil. It was one of the most pleasant aromas I have ever smelled. "Ah!" said Cleopas, inhaling deeply. "So much pure nard." The term is used for precious ointment that only kings and the rich can afford.

The room fell silent. It is customary for women of Jerusalem, as one of their good works, to carry ointment around their necks in a container and anoint the body of any dead person on the street. But this anointing was done on a living person.

Suddenly, Judas spoke up loudly. "Why this waste? This could have been sold for three hundred denarii and the money given to the poor."

Momentarily, I thought that Judas was right. Here the equivalent of three hundred days wages for a workman in our culture had been poured out on Jesus. But these thoughts did not last long, for Jesus rebuked Judas.

"Leave her alone. Why are you upsetting her? What she has done for me is one of the good works. You have the poor with you always but you shall not always have me. She has done what was in her power to do. She has anointed my body beforehand for its burial.

"I tell you solemnly, wherever throughout the world the Good News is proclaimed, what she has done will be told also, in remembrance of her."

Jesus thanked Mary, who got up and left the room with her jar.

Later, when everyone was finished with dinner, Jesus rose slowly and, as was his custom, turned to the host and thanked him. His mother graciously rose, with Jesus' help, and also thanked the host. Then all of us in turn said our thanks and took our leave. We walked the short distance to the home of Lazarus in silence. I could see that Elisa was eager to talk and so was I. Jesus had spoken of his burial as if it were near.

Elisa reminded me that Jesus has prophesied that he would suffer and die in Jerusalem. Luke, it is only six days before the Passover. If danger threatens Jesus in Jerusalem, I shall do my best to protect him.

Joseph

Jerusalem

Letter 109

Luke, neither of us slept well last night. Elisa and I had a foreboding feeling, as if we are going to lose Jesus soon. It is the same feeling physicians get when they are about to lose a critically ill patient.

Jesus had indicated that he wanted to go to Jerusalem early in the morning, and both of us decided to go with his group. As apprehensive as we were, Elisa and I were eager to see once again the magnificent city where we had made our first home. We suggested Mary stay here to rest. We had a light breakfast and then walked the short distance into the high country outside Jerusalem. The walk was pleasant and Jesus seemed to be in a playful mood, as if unconcerned about what might lie ahead.

Soon we reached the top of the hill and there in front of us, across the valley of the Brook of Kidron, was Jerusalem. It was about 200 cubits down the hill to the brook and another 200 cubits up to the hill on which Jerusalem is built.

Jesus led us to an area called Bethphage. There were some terraces there and a clearing where we could rest. It was on the Mount of Olives, with the Garden of Gethsemane below. Then Jesus said to Simon and Jude, "Go off to the village opposite, and as you enter it you will find a tethered colt that no one has ridden. Untie it and bring it here. If someone asks, 'Why are you untying it?' you are to say, 'The Master needs it.'" Luke, that was a little unusual, Jesus taking something without the owner's permission.

In the meantime, word spread from Bethany that Jesus had arrived and was approaching Jerusalem. Someone must have sighted us at Bethphage because people streamed out of the gates of Jerusalem and came toward us. Just before they arrived, Simon and Jude came with the colt. They said they had found a tethered colt, just as Jesus had said, and the owner had come out of his house and objected. "The Master needs it," they said, and he let them lead it away, even though he had guards he could have called to stop them.

The disciples threw their garments over the back of the colt and helped Jesus to mount. We all expected the colt to buck and jump, trying to dislodge Jesus, but he just stood calmly. It was a rather humble steed but strong enough to carry Jesus.

Suddenly, the crowd was upon us, lining the road. Some of the people spread their cloaks along the path in front of Jesus so that it would not be so rough and to prevent the colt from slipping. Jesus proceeded along the road on the colt and we followed. I had never heard so much acclaim. The people were praising Jesus at the top of their voices and bowing before him.

"Blessings on the king who comes in the name of the Lord!"

"Peace in heaven and glory in the highest heavens!"

Jesus had received many plaudits in the past but never have I heard such praises. There were shouts and cries as many pushed their way forward through the crowd, trying to see him or touch his cloak. On we went along the road beside the Kidron, with the garden called Gethsemane to one side up a hill and the wall of Jerusalem on the other. People were lined all the way up the steep path leading to the Damascus Gate. They had cut branches from the olive trees in the Mount of Olives and long leaves from palms and they waved them in homage as Jesus approached.

"Hosanna to the Son of David! Blessings on him who comes in the name of the Lord!"

Elisa and I were unsettled by all the uproar, but then she recalled a prophecy of Zechariah.

> *Rejoice heart and soul, daughter of Zion!*
> *Shout with gladness, daughter Jerusalem!*
> *See now, your king comes to you.*
> *He is victorious, he is triumphant,*
> *humble and riding on a donkey,*
> *on a colt, the foal of a donkey.*
> *He will banish chariots from Ephraim*
> *and horses from Jerusalem.*
> *The bow of war will be banished.*
> *He will proclaim peace for the nations.*
> *His empire shall stretch from sea to sea,*
> *from the river to the ends of the earth.*[1]

As we entered the city, the din was deafening. Jerusalem was truly in turmoil.

"Who is this?" a few people asked. And the crowd answered.

"This is the prophet Jesus from Nazareth in Galilee."

"This is the king who will free us from the Romans."

On we went through streets lined with shouting people. But not all the Jews of Jerusalem were pleased at his coming. As we reached the top of the hill on which the city was built, a number of Pharisees approached and confronted Jesus. They were concerned the Romans would have to quell an uprising.

"Master, check your disciples."

Jesus shook his head. "I tell you, if these keep silence, the stones will cry out!"

Luke, here in Jerusalem Jesus seems willing to make it known that he is the Messiah. But he did seem annoyed at the tumult and the clamor for a civil ruler, for Jesus the King. He stopped at the Pool of Bethesda, near the sheep gate that leads to the great Temple, and the people gathered all around. The rustle of the olive branches and the cheers of the crowd were thunderous. Roman soldiers were stationed by the pool, and several homes surround the area. Pharisees, scribes and the chief priests of Jerusalem were standing by in small groups. Someone in the crowd shouted, "Let us crown him king now!"

Luke, I could see the troops become tense. The centurion shouted a command. The soldiers drew their swords and stood at attention, ready to charge into the crowd at further command.

But the people did not know this. They kept making preparations to crown Jesus their king. They arranged a chair that would serve as a throne and fashioned a crown from palm leaves.

Suddenly Jesus was gone. No one had seen him leave, but the man to be crowned king had disappeared. And the cry went out, "Where is the king? Where is the king?" The search went on for a long time, to no avail. Then the accusations started. "The Romans took him to destroy him. The Romans took him!"

The centurion shouted an order and the troops charged forward. It did not take long for the throng to disperse, and soon the area of the pool was empty. The only things left were the chair and the hastily made crown.

Dear Luke, I cannot express our feelings as Elisa and I started back to Bethany at late afternoon. We had become separated from the other followers of Jesus. Where had he gone? Did the Romans take him? Or did he slip away on his own as he has done so often in the past?

We were disturbed that so many people in Jerusalem seemed to want a king with a crown and royal robes, who would live in a palace with hundreds of servants, command an army and engage in war to free Judea. "Remember, Jesus said that his kingdom is not of this earth," said Elisa.

But these people seemed bitterly disappointed when Jesus ignored their pleas to take up arms. I was afraid that they would turn against Jesus as passionately as they had praised him.

Finally we reached Bethany and the home of Mary, Martha and Lazarus. Mary the mother of Jesus did not seem disturbed by her son's disappearance. She listened and said, "He will be all right." With this assurance, we felt better.

As we sat down for the evening meal, Jesus came in and took his place at the head of the table. He looked calm and smiled. No one asked him about the day. He laughed and teased his mother and The Twelve, and soon we all joined in, thankful that Jesus was safe.

Joseph

[1] Zechariah 9:9-10

Letter 110

We arose early, Luke, but Mary and Martha were already up. After morning prayers we all gathered for breakfast of the brew of herbs and bread. Elisa did not feel well and ate lightly.

After we ate Jesus said, "Today we go to the Temple where I will teach for several days. We will spend the nights on the Mount of Olives."

I felt that I should stay home with Elisa since she was not feeling well. "No! I want you to go," she said. "Make sure that nothing happens to Jesus. I can take care of myself," she said in the tone that meant there was no use to argue. So I also prepared to leave with the group.

The women packed provisions for several days. As I kissed Elisa farewell she said, "Now, take care of Jesus."

Jesus led the way and walked very rapidly. Soon we reached the Mount of Olives where we could see the Temple gleam in the morning sunlight. I recalled the time Elisa and I had seen the Temple at dawn while we were training under Abraham. Then I looked at Jesus. Luke, he was shedding tears.

He wiped his eyes and spoke as if Jerusalem were a person standing before him. "If you in your turn had only understood on this day the message of peace! But, alas, it is hidden from your eyes! Yes, the time is coming when your enemies will raise fortifications all around you, when they will encircle you and hem you in on every side. They will dash you and the children inside your walls to the ground. They will not leave one stone standing on another within you — all because you did not recognize your opportunity when God offered it!"

Jesus started to walk again and soon we were in the Temple grounds. There were hawkers and vendors selling lambs and doves. Jesus shook his head as we passed one after another. People began to recognize Jesus and a crowd started to gather around him, among them many pilgrims whose clothes bore the stains of a long journey. Some of them had seen Jesus before, teaching throughout Judea and Galilee. And some of them, surely, had been among those hailing Jesus as king the day before, only to be dispersed by the guards.

Jesus continued past the market place into the Temple and started to teach, and I was reminded of Mary's story of his youth, how Jesus first taught in the Temple of Jerusalem at the age of twelve.

There were many well-dressed men in the crowd also, priests, Pharisees and scribes. "They are unhappy with what they heard yesterday," Peter said to me. "I suspect they have already begun to plot how they can discredit Jesus and turn the people against him." I decided to mingle among them and see what I could learn.

Their remarks could be easily overheard. "We must stop this man." "He is teaching things that we do not like." "He will get these people to follow him and avoid us."

Luke, I did not like this.

Jesus taught only a short time today then left early to pray. I stayed in the crowd and followed the scribes and Pharisees as they gathered in small groups, hoping I could learn their plans. But the chief priest led them all into an inner chamber and the servant closed and barred the door. I found Peter, called him off to the side and told him all that I had just heard and that there was a secret meeting going on.

"Joseph," he said, "Jesus has had full knowledge of the threats of these people, but he still is determined to do the work for which he was sent by his Father in Heaven."

All I could say was "I hope his Father protects him."

In the late afternoon Jesus returned from his seclusion in prayer. We all went to the Mount of Olives to a cave where we had our meal and retired for the night.

Joseph

Letter III

It was cool in the early morning, Luke, as we set off for the Temple again. We walked down the valley, crossed the Kidron and then up the other side. Soon we were at the gate of the city. People were coming in and going out. Many were pilgrims gathering early for the Passover. Some had come a long way and had pitched their tents outside the walls of Jerusalem. During this period of the Passover the population of Jerusalem increases by thousands. Tents and animals are everywhere.

We made our way through the crowded narrow streets to the Temple, where Jesus started to preach. Then the chief priests and scribes approached with the elders of the Temple. They had been waiting for Jesus.

"Tell us," they said, "what authority have you for acting like this? Or who is it who gave you this authority?"

Jesus turned and looked at them. "And I will ask you a question. Tell me about John's baptism: Did it come from heaven or from man?"

Luke, I watched their faces as they argued amongst themselves. One said, "If we say, 'From heaven,' he will say, 'Why did you refuse to believe him?' and if we say, 'From man,' the people will all come and stone us, for they are convinced that John was a prophet." Finally one man was delegated to give the reply. He approached Jesus and said, "We do not know where it came from." The entire group nodded in approval.

I could see a smile come over the face of Jesus, the kind that I have seen many times when his accusers were caught in their own trap.

"Nor will I tell you my authority for acting like this." And he turned his back to them and faced the large group of people whom he had been teaching. He told the assembled group this parable.

"A man planted a vineyard and leased it to tenants, and went abroad for a long while. When the time came, he sent a servant to the tenants to get his share of the produce of the vineyard from them. But the tenants thrashed him, and sent him away empty-handed. But he persevered and sent a second servant. They thrashed him too and treated him shamefully and sent him away empty-handed. He still persevered and sent a third. They wounded this one also and threw him out. Then the owner of the vineyard said, 'What am I to do? I will send them my dear son. Perhaps they will respect him.' But when the tenants saw him they put their heads together. 'This is the heir,' they said. 'Let us kill him so that the inheritance will be ours.' So they threw him out of the vineyard and killed him.

"Now, what will the owner of the vineyard do to them? He will come and make an end of these tenants and give the vineyard to others."

"God forbid!" cried the Pharisees.

Jesus looked hard at them and said, "Then what does this passage in the Scriptures mean: 'It was the stone rejected by the builders that became the keystone.[1] Anyone who falls on that stone will be dashed to pieces. Anyone it falls on will be crushed.'"

The scribes and chief priests were now conferring again. I heard one say, "I would like to get my hands on him this very moment." But another said, "We cannot do that at this time because of the crowds around him."

"Let us wait for the opportunity and send agents to pose as men devoted to the Law. Let them fasten onto something that he might say and so enable us to hand him over to Pontius Pilate." This was a plan that would lead the Roman governor to get rid of Jesus for them.

Luke, this group is a determined lot and I know that they will cause trouble for Jesus. I ran to find Jesus to warn him but he was nowhere to be found. I searched all of the corridors and rooms of the Temple buildings. I walked out into the Temple grounds to look, where hawkers were trying to sell doves and lambs and other animals to the pilgrims to offer for sacrifice. It was more like a barnyard than sacred grounds of the Temple. Finally, I walked back into the Temple and found Jesus again surrounded by a crowd. It was too late to warn him.

"Master," said one of the Pharisees, "we know that you say and teach what is right. You favor no one but teach the way of God in all honesty.

"Is it permissible," he said, "for us to pay taxes to Caesar or not?"

Whichever way Jesus answered this question, they reasoned, they had him caught. If he said, "No," they would report him to the authorities as a seditionist. If he said, "Yes," they would say that he was not from God.

But Jesus was aware of their cunning. "Show me a denarius," he said.

One of the men found one in his coin purse and handed it to him. Jesus took it, looked at it and pointed to the figure on it.

"Whose head and name are on it?"

"Caesar's."

"Well, then," Jesus replied, "give back to Caesar what belongs to Caesar and to God what belongs to God."

That silenced them, for they could find no fault with his statement.

Then a group of Sadducees, those who say that there is no resurrection of the dead, approached and put a question to Jesus.

"Master, we have it from Moses in writing that if a man's married brother dies childless, the man must marry the widow to raise up children for his brother. Well then, there were seven brothers. The first, having married a wife, died childless. The second and then the third married the widow. And the same with all seven, they died leaving no children. Finally the woman herself died. Now, at the resurrection, to which of them will she be wife since she had been married to all seven?"

Now, Luke, in Deuteronomy it states that a man is to marry the widow of his childless brother and rear their children in his brother's name. The Book of Ruth also shows this.[2] Since the Sadducees do not believe the dead shall rise again, they object to this. Jesus waited until all was quiet and then spoke loud enough to be heard above the din of the hawkers outside.

"The children of this world take wives and husbands, but those who are judged worthy of a place in the other world and in the resurrection from the dead do not marry because they can no longer die, for they are the same as angels, and being children of the resurrection they are sons of God. And Moses himself implies that the dead rise again, in the passage about the bush where he calls the Lord the God of Abraham, the God of Isaac and the God of Jacob.

"Now he is God not of the dead, but of the living. For to him, all men are alive."

As he finished, a scribe shouted in approval, "Well put, Master. In heaven there will be no procreation and no marriage." The Sadducees all drew back and did not dare to ask him any more questions.

Then Jesus asked the same kind of question that Pharisees and scribes can argue about endlessly. "How can people maintain that the Messiah is son of David? Why, David himself says in the Book of Psalms:

The Lord said to my Lord:
Sit at my right hand
and I will make your enemies
a footstool for you.[3]

"David here calls him Lord. How then can he be his son?"

Jesus turned then to his disciples and spoke in a voice he knew would carry. "Beware of the scribes who like to walk about in long robes and love to take places of honor at banquets and who swallow the property of widows while making a show of lengthy prayers. The more severe will be the sentence they receive."

Then Jesus stepped away from the scribes and Pharisees toward the treasury, where the donations are kept. He watched several richly garbed people approach, take out their heavy purses and drop offerings into the treasury coin by coin so that everyone would notice them. Then his eyes followed an elderly woman in a frayed cloak as she made her way through the rich donors and deposited two small coins.

"I tell you truly," Jesus told the group, "this poor widow has put in more than any of them, for these have contributed money they had left over, but she has put in all she had to live on." The richly garbed paid no attention to his words, but the widow turned and smiled at Jesus.

We stayed in the Temple all day and after the evening prayers we left, went out of the gate, down the valley of the Kidron and up the other side to the Mount of Olives. We ate, and after evening prayers we prepared to spend another night in the cave.

Joseph

[1] Psalms 118:22

[2] Deuteronomy 25:5-10
Ruth 4:5-11

[3] Psalms 110:1

Letter 112

I had a restless night, Luke. Each time I woke up, I looked for Jesus and I could not find him. I finally went out of the cave and saw him kneeling in prayer. At daybreak Jesus was alert and I was sleepy.

We retraced our steps down the valley, across the stone bridge and through the gates into Jerusalem. Jesus made his way through the crowds and entered the Temple grounds. We passed some people who were in Jerusalem for the first time. They were talking about the fine stonework in the Temple and the votive offerings. Jesus stopped and addressed them.

"All these things you are staring at now — the time will come when not a single stone will be left on another. Everything will be destroyed."

They were disturbed when they heard these remarks. So were we. "Master," said Judas Iscariot, "when will this happen then, and what sign will there be that this is about to take place?"

"Take care not to be deceived," Jesus said to us, "because many will come using my name and saying 'I am he' and 'The time is near at hand.' Refuse to join them. And when you hear of wars and revolutions, do not be frightened, for this is something that must happen, but the end is not so soon."

By this time, there was a small crowd gathering around our group, and Jesus continued his prophecy.

"Nation shall fight against nation, and kingdom against kingdom. There will be great earthquakes and plagues and famines here and there. There will be fearful sights and great signs from heaven.

"But before all this happens, men will seize you and persecute you. They will hand you over to the synagogues and to imprisonment, and bring you before kings and governors because of my name, and that will be your opportunity to bear witness.

"Keep this carefully in mind. You are not to prepare your defense, because I myself shall give you eloquence and wisdom that none of your opponents will be able to resist or contradict.

"You will be betrayed even by parents and brothers, relations and friends, and some of you will be put to death.

"You will be hated by all men on account of my name, but not a hair of your head will be lost. Your endurance will win you your lives."

Then he looked at the entire crowd and raised his voice as he addressed them.

"When you see Jerusalem surrounded by armies, you must realize that she will soon be laid desolate. Then those in Judea must escape to the mountains, those inside the city must leave it, and those in country districts must not take refuge in it. For this is the time of vengeance that all the Scriptures say must be fulfilled. Alas for those with child, or with babies at the breast, when those days come!"

By this time all eyes were on Jesus.

"For great misery will descend on the land and wrath on this people. They will fall by the edge of the sword and be led captive to every pagan country, and Jerusalem will be trampled down by the pagans until the age of the pagans is completely over."

No one even asked when this would be.

"There will be signs in the sun and moon and stars, and on earth, nations of agony, bewildered by the clamor of the ocean and its waves, and men dying of fear as they await what menaces the world, for the powers of heaven will be shaken. And then they will see the Son of Man coming in a cloud with power and great glory.

"When these things begin to take place, stand erect, hold your heads high, because your liberation is near at hand."

Now, Luke, most of those in the crowd knew of the Son of Man only through their knowledge of the Scriptures and had never heard anyone speak like this. I am familiar with the teachings of Jesus and even I do not understand these prophecies.

"Think of the fig tree and indeed every tree," he continued. "As soon as you see them bud, you know that summer is now near. So with you when you see these things happening, know that the kingdom of God is near.

"I tell you solemnly, before this generation has passed away all will have taken place. Heaven and earth will pass away, but my words will never pass away."

Then Jesus warned us to live each day as if it is our last.

"Watch yourselves, or your hearts will be coarsened with debauchery and drunkenness and the cares of life, and that day will be sprung on you suddenly, like a trap. For it will come down on every living man on the face of the earth. Stay awake, praying at all times for the strength to survive all that is going to happen, and to stand with confidence before the Son of Man."

Those listening in the Temple had fallen silent. These faithful followers of the Law had not heard words like this before. I looked over the crowd and then back to the place where Jesus had been, but he was gone. He had slipped off to pray.

Knowing he wanted to be alone, I knelt and tried to pray like Jesus does. Perhaps I will learn in time.

Finally about the ninth hour Andrew found me and said, "Come, Joseph, we must get the others. Jesus wants to return to Bethany tonight." It did not take long to gather The Twelve and off we went.

Upon our return, Jesus spent the entire evening with his mother. I was pleased to find Elisa feeling better. She and I went out to the garden, and I spent a long time telling her everything that I had seen and heard during the past few days.

Joseph

Letter 113

Dear Luke, as we set forth for Jerusalem again this morning, Jesus had a determined look in his eyes. Mary the mother of Jesus seemed unusually sad this morning, and Elisa decided to stay with her.

Throngs of pilgrims were entering the gate of Jerusalem as we approached, many carrying their first-born son to be presented in the Temple. The families come for days, set up tents and stay a while.

The streets were crowded with hawkers and the din grew louder as we entered the Temple area. This, of course, is the time before the Passover when families select an unblemished lamb, taken from the goats or the sheep, have it approved and sacrificed at the Temple, and roast it on the feast of the Passover.

When we entered the gate it seemed as if we were entering a bazaar. There were booths everywhere, each with cages of doves and pigeons, and many lambs tied to stakes. Each booth had one or two hawkers who shouted to every passerby, "Buy my birds, buy my birds." "Buy my lambs, buy my lambs." It was bedlam. Jesus' face lost his smile and became stern. His muscles tensed and his hands opened and closed, making fists. I had never seen Jesus like this.

This is the Bazaar of the Sons of Annas, and it is a disgrace to the Temple area. Devout Jews bring their lambs for sacrifice or their doves for presentation of the first-born, but the vendors stop and examine their offerings and always say, "These are not good enough for the sacrifice. Buy ours." The pilgrims, who had made the long journey to the Temple, do as they are told for fear their journey will be in vain. They purchase the animal from them at exorbitant prices. The vendors take their lambs, saying they will dispose of them. I wonder if they do.

As we neared the Temple, we saw the tables of the moneychangers. Luke, this may be hard for you to believe, but the high priest and the priests of the Temple demand a shekel from all pilgrims who enter. They will not accept any other money except the local currency. There are Jews from Mesopotamia, Greece, Ephesus, Alexandria and elsewhere, and they have coins from their homeland. So the moneychangers exchange these for Judean coins and charge a commission. The amount seems to vary but may be substantial.

All this profit-seeking in the House of God enraged Jesus. He grabbed a cord hanging from a stake, which had held a lamb that had been sold, made a whip out of it and charged the tables of the moneychangers, overturning them and scattering coins all over.

"According to the Scriptures," he shouted, "my house is a house of prayer.[1] But you have made it a den of thieves."

The moneychangers were shocked. No one had ever interfered with their lucrative business. They started to gather up their coins, but he swung his whip at them and said again, "You are making my Father's house into a den of thieves!" He chased them out of the Temple grounds.

Then he started on the bazaar. He swung his whip and shouted. "Take all this out of here and stop turning my Father's house into a market." They ran to the gate and shouted that they would be back.

Next Jesus moved from stall to stall, untied the lambs and opened the bird cages. The animals he herded out of the gates while the birds flew into the sky. Jesus then threw down the whip and walked calmly to the Temple, though he was sweating profusely.

Luke, this happened so rapidly that no one had time to summon the Temple guards. But the sons of Annas ran off in a group to tell their father, the former high priest, and their sister's husband, Caiaphas, the present high priest.

The grounds were quiet as we followed Jesus into the Temple. Even the lambs in the arms of pilgrims were still as they were carried in. This was now really a house of prayer. As we walked up the Temple stairs, Peter remarked, "Scripture says, 'Zeal for your house devours me.'"[2] We followed Jesus into the Temple.

The chief priests stopped him and asked. "What sign can you show us to justify what you have done?"

Jesus answered in his fashion. "Destroy this sanctuary, and in three days, I will raise it up!"

"It has taken forty-six years to build this temple!" they replied. "Are you going to raise it up in three days?"

Jesus brushed past them, sat down, and soon was in deep meditation. We sat down as well but I could not concentrate on prayer. Jesus had said, 'Destroy this sanctuary, and in three days, I will raise it up.' I just could not understand this.

I recalled his words one by one. Suddenly it came to me. Our language has two words that are used for temple, Hieron, which means the building, and Naos, which is specific to the Holy of Holies, that special place in the

Temple where the scrolls are kept and the high priest can enter only once a year at the Feast of the Atonement.

The Holy of Holies is separated from the rest of the Temple by a heavy veil trimmed with gold.

After an hour of prayer, Jesus arose and went toward the massive door. We followed. There were people gathering around him saying, "There is Jesus, the man who cures." "There is Jesus, a man close to God." "This is Jesus, the miracle worker!"

I stayed behind a little, just to hear what the priests and scribes were saying. The fact that he had cleared out the Bazaar of the Sons of Annas infuriated them. Jesus and his teachings threatened their control of Jerusalem, and they finally decided to do away with Jesus by any possible means. Caiaphas the high priest said, "It is better for Jesus to die than for the entire nation to perish."

But this was not the only reason, Luke. Caiaphas believed that if Jesus was not destroyed, he would have so many followers that they would take over the Temple and displace the priests, the scribes and the Bazaar of the Sons of Annas. It was jealousy.

I had heard enough by then and hurried to catch up with Jesus. It was not difficult, since Jesus walked slowly, stopping to speak to the lame, embracing the children, and talking about the kingdom of God. The crowd following him grew wherever he went. Some were believers in his message, while others were curious about this preacher of whom they had heard.

I noticed that some of the Temple priests, the Pharisees and scribes had followed in order to trap him in his teachings. At one point they sent the Temple Guard to arrest him. However, after listening to him the guards refused to arrest him.

An arrest would have been difficult in any case. The people to whom Jesus spoke hung on to his words and could have become violent had Jesus been arrested in their presence. The priests, scribes and leading citizens did not want this to occur during the feast of the Passover since so many Roman soldiers were patrolling the streets.

As soon as I could, I spoke to Jesus and told him all that I had heard. Jesus smiled and thanked me and went on with his teaching. It seemed to me that he had known everything I would tell him before it was said.

Jesus continued out of the city gate to the Mount of Olives. Here he sat down and we all rested. Then he addressed our unspoken concerns.

"I will not walk openly among the Jews," he said, "because my time has not come."

No one asked when that time would come, as we were so relieved that he was going to be more careful.

After a short rest, we returned to the home of Martha, Mary and Lazarus in Bethany. It was good to see Elisa vibrant and well. There we washed off the day's dust and ate a special meal prepared for us. I told Elisa a little of what had happened.

As soon as Jesus had eaten, he motioned his mother to come with him so that they could talk alone. When they returned, Elisa and I noticed that Mary had been crying. Then Jesus asked The Twelve to come with him for a few days to Ephraim. I was sure that he would find a quiet place where he could teach the apostles.

All seemed eager to go except Judas Iscariot. He was hesitant and had a scowl on his face. Jesus also noticed it and went to Judas and put his arm around him and said, "We need you very much. Come, follow me."

I really was glad I was not asked to go. I wanted to spend time with Elisa and tell her about all the day's happenings. I was also glad that Jesus seemed to heed my warnings and would not go back to Jerusalem at this time.

Elisa followed Mary into a separate room to comfort her, and I joined them. Mary spoke first. "Tell me, Joseph, what happened today." I told the entire story. Elisa asked many questions, which I answered from what I had observed and heard. But Mary was quiet and did not say a word. She indicated that she wanted to be left alone, so Elisa and I left.

We went into the garden, sat on a log and held hands. Elisa was worried. She said Mary believed Jesus would meet with harm when he returned to Jerusalem. Three times, Elisa recalled, Jesus had predicted he would suffer at the hands of others and then be put to death.

On the shores of Lake Galilee, Jesus had said, "The Son of Man is destined to suffer grievously, to be rejected by the elders and chief priests and scribes and to be put to death and to be raised up on the third day."

Later he had told The Twelve, "For your part you must have these words constantly in your mind: The Son of Man is going to be handed over into the power of men."

Then Elisa recalled the third time, when we were nearing Jerusalem just a few days ago. "Now we are going up to Jerusalem," he had said, "and everything that is written by the prophets about the Son of Man is to come true. For he will be handed over to the pagans and will be mocked, maltreated and spat on, and when they have scourged him, they will put him to death, and on the third day, he will rise again."

We could not understand what Jesus meant about rising again, but we understood the dire predictions of suffering and death. We prayed to the Lord to protect Jesus, and we went to bed with heavy hearts.

Joseph

1   Isaiah 56:7

2   Psalms 69:9

Letter 114

Jesus and The Twelve left as the sun was rising. Elisa and I enjoyed the quiet and the fact that we were somewhat alone. The past few days I spent with Jesus in Jerusalem were the longest time we have been separated since I spent that week in Nazareth more than a year ago. As you see, Luke, we are together at our home, in our walks, in our work and in our studies. We do everything together and never seem to tire of each other's company.

Elisa said, "Let us walk in the garden." It was beautiful. Flowers were in bloom and their fragrance filled the air. We found a comfortable place and sat down. Elisa said, "As soon as Passover is over, we must return to Capernaum. Erasmus and John are carrying a heavy load. But we will enjoy this now since we may never have such an opportunity again." I agreed.

Luke, the morning passed quickly. We held hands, thanked the Lord for being so good to us and sang a few of the Psalms that we knew from memory. We have not had an opportunity to be together like this since we left Capernaum. As usual, when one spends time in prayer, the time passes rapidly.

Then we noticed some movement in the garden and got a glimpse of Mary, Jesus' mother. Elisa called to her and she came and joined us. She remarked, "I have been watching the two of you, just sitting there, and you seemed to be so content that I did not want to disturb you."

"It is not a disturbance anytime to be with you," Elisa replied. And we turned our thoughts to the happy times we had spent together in Jerusalem in training. Hearing about the first years of our marriage brought a smile to Mary's face. "Oh, you must go see Abraham while you are here," she said.

"Yes," said Elisa, "that has been our plan. Joseph, let us go tomorrow. Since this is the time just before the Passover, he may not be too busy. And just think of seeing all of the helpers in the clinic. I wonder how many assistants he has now. Oh! It will be a great day."

And so it will be. Elisa has been through a lot since we last saw Abraham, and it will be good to have him examine her.

Joseph

Letter 115

Dear Luke, we were eager to spend a day with Abraham at his clinic. We got up early, dressed in our physician's robes, and walked the distance to Jerusalem in high spirits. We passed the room where we had lived and stopped to visit some of the friends that we had made in the neighborhood. Things have not changed very much.

Then we arrived at the clinic. Abraham was surprised but glad to have us come. He asked us to help out with the morning patients, and we were happy to do so. It reminded us of the early years of our marriage and the challenging days of our apprenticeship. Luke, we had a great time.

Over the midday meal we talked with Abraham about our work. However, soon the conversation centered on Jesus. He knew of him from our letters and from his patients but he was eager to learn directly from us. He questioned us thoroughly about the many miracles. You must meet him yourself, we said, when he returns to Jerusalem.

"Well, children," Abraham said, "after Elisa rests you will spend the afternoon teaching the assistants and the students." That surprised us. But, Luke, it was a wonderful afternoon. We talked about all of the things we had learned in our practice. Elisa discussed the different approaches that she has to our patients, all of the surgery she has done and all about her herb garden. I talked about the experiences during the house calls, and Abraham had me mention the trip to Nazareth and the surgery that I performed.

Finally, the classes were over and Abraham wanted to check Elisa. He asked many questions and then examined her. We were so relieved that he did not find anything wrong.

Abraham thanked us for spending the time with him. "God bless you," he said as we left, "and keep me informed about this man Jesus."

We laughed and sang as we walked back to Bethany. In fact, we had a very pleasant day.

Joseph

Letter 116

This letter is so hard to write. I cannot sleep. Elisa is exhausted and is fitfully sleeping but there is no sleep in me.

So much has happened, Luke, that I must begin to write now but it will take more than one letter. I will start with the Day of the Passover, the feast that we came all the way to Jerusalem to celebrate at the Temple. Jesus and The Twelve were expected back from Ephraim that morning.

After breakfast Mary, Jesus' mother, wanted to hear about our visit with Abraham, but it was not long that we had to talk.

Mary the sister of Lazarus came shouting that Jesus and The Twelve were back. We rushed out to see them. Jesus went right to his mother, embraced her and kissed her on each cheek. Then he led her to the garden for a private talk. The disciples did not speak much of Ephraim except that they had spent time in praying and listening to Jesus teach.

When Jesus returned he said, "The Twelve and I are going to Jerusalem to celebrate the Passover. I am sorry that all of you cannot be with us, but I have much to do." I whispered to Elisa, "The priests and the Pharisees want Jesus arrested. If he returns to Jerusalem, even during the Passover, he will be in danger. This time I must go with The Twelve. Perhaps I can protect Jesus."

I approached Jesus and asked to go to Jerusalem with him for Passover. "Your mother is worried for your safety. So is Elisa. And perhaps I could be of help. I do not ask to be at the table with The Twelve. Instead I could supervise the Passover meal. I had much experience in serving at banquets in Athens, and I could direct the servants."

Jesus agreed, and none of The Twelve seemed surprised that I would join them. We have been together so much in the last two weeks that it seemed natural.

As I kissed Elisa farewell, I said, "This is the first Passover that we will not celebrate together since we have been married." She replied, "With the blessing of God, there will be many others. Go, take care of Jesus, and please be careful."

As we approached Jerusalem, Jesus took aside two of his apostles. "Peter and John, go and make preparations for us to eat the Passover. Joseph will help direct the meal."

They spoke almost simultaneously, "Where do you want us to prepare it?"

"Listen, as you go into the city, you will find a man carrying a pitcher of water. Follow him into the house he enters and tell the owner of the house the Master has this to say to you, 'Where is the dining room in which I can eat the Passover with my disciples?' The man will show you a large upper room furnished with couches. Make preparations there."

True enough, there ahead was a servant carrying a jar of water on his head — an unusual sight in Jerusalem. Carrying water in a pitcher or jar is considered a woman's work. Men carry water in leather containers. Peter spoke to the man and the rest of us walked along. We went down one street after another. I realized that Jesus did not want the Pharisees to know where he would eat the Passover meal.

Soon the servant arrived at the home of young Mark, who had become a follower of Jesus when he was last in Jerusalem. Mark's father recognized Peter and John, welcomed us and showed us to a large upper room. The three of us left to buy bread, bitter herbs and a spotless lamb with the money that Judas had given them. We had to take the lamb to the Temple to be sacrificed by the priests. There was a long line of worshippers having their lambs sacrificed.

Luke, I had never seen this before. As a child my father would do this, and when Elisa and I were in Jerusalem, Abraham would have a servant do it. But there were many priests and it was not such a long wait.

Back at the home of Mark's father, the lamb was carefully dressed and roasted. All of this had to be done in time for the Passover meal at sunset.

Finally we heard voices on the stairs. Jesus had arrived. It was dusk, and the lookout at the Temple gave the blast on his trumpet to signal that Passover had begun. We had placed the lentils, the bread and wine, and the bitter herbs all in place. The aroma of the roasted lamb filled the room.

Jesus took his place at the head of the table, asking Judas to sit at his right and John on his left. Peter, who was accustomed to the position of honor, found the only remaining seat at the other end of the table.

Then it was the time for servants to wash the feet of the guests. I brought a pitcher of water, a basin and a towel into the room. As I approached the group, Jesus got up and took the pan from my hands.

"Wait, Joseph, I will do it this time."

I was offended and almost grabbed the water back from him. But he stopped me with that look that I have seen many times before. It meant "Leave me alone. I know what I am doing." So I just stood there.

Jesus removed his outer garments, took the towel and wrapped it around himself, then approached the disciples. He set the basin on the floor, poured the water into it and started to remove the sandals of James the Lesser, holding his feet as James tried to pull away, then bathed the feet.

There was a great hush in the room. Here the host was doing the work of a slave. They all looked at me with dismay.

Jesus finished washing the feet of James, dried them, kissed them, and then went on to the next disciple.

I looked at Peter. He was shaking his head as Jesus just went from one to the other. I finally came to my senses and started to carry the basin and the pitcher for Jesus. "Thank you," he said.

Finally we came to Peter, who was trying to hide his feet under the cushions, still shaking his head. "Lord, are you going to wash my feet?" he asked.

Jesus stopped and answered, "At the moment, you do not know what I am doing. But later you will understand."

"Never," Peter shouted. "You shall never wash my feet!"

Jesus, who was on his knees in front of Peter, sat back on his heels, and looked Peter in the eyes. "If I do not wash your feet, you shall have nothing in common with me!"

Peter's expression softened. "Then, Lord, not only my feet but my hands and my head as well!"

Jesus answered, but no one got the meaning of his words. "No one who has taken a bath needs washing. He is clean all over. You, too, are clean, though not all of you."

After all of this was over, I poured water on his hands and Jesus allowed me to wash his feet. I dried them and started to kiss them. But he withdrew them.

It was now about one hour after sunset. The lamb was ready and I was preparing to cut and serve it. Jesus and the apostles shouted as one, "There is no God but one," and the ceremony of the Passover meal began.

According to tradition, the youngest at the meal asks the question "Why is this night different from the other nights?" John took that role, and Jesus responded as the host. He told the familiar story of the Hebrews living in captivity in Egypt, the return of Moses to free them, his appearance before

Pharaoh, and the plagues imposed on the Egyptians by God. The Pharaoh would not release the captives until the Angel of Death destroyed the firstborn of every Egyptian, while the blood of the lamb on their doors saved the Hebrews. Then Jesus told of the escape, the parting of the Red Sea and the forty years in the desert. It was there that the group of former slaves became the People of God.

Jesus concluded with an ancient blessing, "Blessed art thou, Oh Eternal who redeemed Israel.

"Blessed art thou, Oh Eternal, our God! King of the Universe, Creator of the fruit of the vine."

Jesus then stepped out of the role of host and addressed The Twelve. "I have longed to eat this Passover with you before I suffer, because, I tell you, I shall not eat again until it is fulfilled in the kingdom of God."

That concerned me a moment, but I had too much to do to spend time worrying over his words. When everyone was finished, Jesus stood up and caught the attention of The Twelve, who fell silent. A few moments passed as they waited for him to speak. Instead he held out his cup and I poured wine into it. He gave thanks and said, "Take this and share it among you.

"I shall not drink wine until the kingdom of God comes."

Peter, Matthew, Thomas and the others exchanged worried glances. What could he mean? Then Jesus passed around the Passover cup. Everyone drank from the cup, one at a time. The room was still quiet.

Then he took a small loaf of bread, and when he had again given thanks to the Lord, he broke it and gave it to The Twelve.

"This is my body which will be given for you. Do this as a memorial to me."

He had me fill the goblet with wine again, but this time he said, after giving thanks, "This cup is the new covenant in my blood, which will be poured out for you." He passed it on.

Each disciple in turn ate of the bread and drank of the wine, and all was consumed. This, Luke, was clearly a moment of great importance. I recalled the time Jesus had said, "Unless you eat my body and drink my blood, you will not have life everlasting." What could this mean? Surely this was not his flesh and his blood. I wished that Elisa were with me to witness this.

Each disciple seemed concerned but reverent when they shared in what Jesus called his body and blood. Luke, I cannot explain it, but I felt a change in the room, as if candles were burning a brighter flame. The very air we breathed was different somehow.

Jesus was starting to speak again. I was still near his side, to serve his needs.

"And yet," he said, "with me on the table is the hand of the man who betrays me." The apostles were shaken at this remark.

"The Son of Man does indeed go to his fate, even as it has been decreed, but alas for that man by whom he is betrayed!"

Each of The Twelve looked around the room. Who could it be? Who among them would betray Jesus, the preacher they had come to believe was the Son of Man, God himself in the form of man?

Peter motioned to John to ask Jesus, since he was close to him. He leaned back on his chest and turned to Jesus. "Who is it, Lord? Not I, surely."

Almost in unison the others said, "Not I, Lord, surely." "Not I."

But one voice, that of Judas, trailed the others. "Not I, Rabbi."

Jesus turned to Judas and said, "They are your own words."

Then Jesus turned from him and said in a voice scarcely more than a whisper, "It is the one to whom I give this piece of bread that I shall dip in the dish." He dipped the piece of bread in the sauce and gave it to Judas Iscariot, whose face had paled. I could see he was agitated, but he took the morsel of bread and sauce. Jesus then spoke to him tersely. "What you are going to do, do quickly." Judas grabbed his sack of money and left.

Luke, I firmly believe that no one besides Judas and me heard these last words of Jesus. Perhaps John did and really did not understand. He must have thought, as I did, that Jesus was sending Judas out to buy something, or to give some money to the poor.

With his departure the tension broke and the mood lifted. The apostles began to talk among themselves. I busied myself with the many things to do but kept near enough so that I could hear.

Suddenly the subdued voices became sharper and louder, and I found an excuse to come back to the table. The apostles were arguing among themselves, as they had done before, about which should be reckoned the greatest. I looked at Jesus and I knew the look on his face was not of anger but of disappointment. He rebuked them.

"Among pagans, it is the kings who lord it over them, and those who have authority over them are given the title of benefactor. This must not happen to you.

"No, the greatest among you must behave as if he were the youngest, the leader as if he were the one who serves. For who is the greater, the one at table or the one who serves? The one at table surely! Yet here am I among you as one who serves."

He looked around and I recalled that just a short time ago Jesus, the host, had washed the feet of the guests, the duty of the most menial servant. Then he continued.

"You are the men who have stood by me faithfully in my trials. And now I confer a kingdom on you, just as my Father conferred one on me.

"You will eat and drink at my table in my kingdom and you will sit on thrones to judge the twelve tribes of Israel."

No one uttered a sound. All sat in silence with their eyes focused on Jesus. I realized that I was just standing there with a pitcher of wine in one hand and a half-filled goblet in the other. No one noticed, so I finished filling the goblet and put it down beside Peter. It was his.

Just at that time, Jesus turned toward Peter and spoke. "Simon, Simon! Satan, you must know, has got his wish to sift you like wheat. But I have prayed for you, Simon, that your faith may not fail, and once you have recovered, you in your turn, must strengthen your brothers."

Peter was aghast! "Lord," he answered, "I would be ready to go to prison with you, and to death."

Jesus looked sad. "I tell you, Peter, by the time the cock crows today, you will have denied three times that you know me."

Peter's mouth dropped in amazement, and I almost dropped the pitcher of wine. The other disciples shook their heads — no, not Peter, of all the disciples. Peter to deny Jesus? But we had all heard this dire prediction of Jesus.

I noticed the two servants looking at me with impatience. There were more wine goblets to fill and then the sweets for dessert. But I heard Jesus speak again to his apostles.

"When I sent you out without purse, haversack or sandals, were you ever short of anything?" He looked from one face to the other. "No," they all replied.

"But now, if you have a purse, take it. If you have a haversack, do the same. If you have no sword, sell your cloak and buy one. Because I tell you, these words of Isaiah must be fulfilled in me: 'He let himself be taken for a criminal.'[1]

"Yes, what the Scriptures say about me is even now reaching fulfillment."

Luke, I still do not understand why Jesus said to sell a cloak and buy a sword. Jesus, who taught us to love our enemies and to turn the other cheek! This was a mystery to me.

"Lord," Andrew called from across the room, "there are two swords here now." Jesus answered, "That is enough. That is enough."

What would these men do with two swords, I mused, or even a dozen swords? None of them were soldiers. Four were fishermen, one a tax collector and another a lawyer. None had any training in swordsmanship. What threat would they be to a trained Roman legionnaire or even a guard of the Temple? They would probably cut themselves before they got the sword out of the scabbard.

Jesus rose just then and prepared to leave. The Passover meal was over. He graciously thanked Mark's father for use of his home and the disciples for obtaining the lentils, bread and lamb. And then he thanked those of us who had served the meal. As quickly as possible, I prepared to leave myself, thanking the host and the other servants.

The streets were quiet now. Most of the Passover meals were over and people were preparing to sleep. Jesus was just ahead, walking slowly and stopping often to speak to the apostles. The moon was full so it was easy for me to see the small group of men. They would stop when Jesus talked and then set out again. I could not hear, but it was obvious that Jesus was doing most of the talking. He led the group out the gates of Jerusalem, across the Kidron and to Gethsemane, to the cave where we had spent several nights when Jesus was teaching at the Temple.

It had been an eventful evening, but the night was not yet over.

But now I must try to get some rest.

Joseph

[1]   Isaiah 53:12

Letter 117

Luke, I have tried again to sleep but there is none in me. Perhaps if I write down the rest of this tragic story, the despair I feel may lift enough to allow me to sleep.

I had not caught up with Jesus and his apostles when they approached the Garden of Gethsemane. But I was close enough to see Jesus stop at the entrance to the cave. He waved on the disciples, who must have been as tired as I was. They had been up before dawn, walked from Ephraim to Bethany and then to Jerusalem. But Jesus motioned to Peter and to James and John the sons of Zebedee, and stepped back into the grove of trees I was just approaching. I heard him say, "Stay here while I go over there to pray."

I was tired myself, but Jesus had something else on his mind and I knew the evening was not over. My feeling of dread returned. Whatever danger Jerusalem presented to Jesus was still real, and I felt compelled to protect him.

I slipped into the woods myself to be sure it was a safe place for Jesus to pray. The moonlight broke through the trees enough to allow me to follow their progress into the woods. Jesus paused at one clearing and sighed. "My soul is sorrowful to the point of death," he said. "Wait here and keep awake with me." And he went on. Peter, James and John sat down and leaned against a tree.

Jesus went a short distance farther, only 10 cubits from the bushes where I was standing. He knelt beneath an olive tree, pressed his face to the ground and prayed. I had seen him pray many times before, usually silently or at a low murmur. But this time I could hear him distinctly.

"My Father, if it is possible, let this cup pass from me."

His voice was very different than at the Passover meal. It sounded as if he were heavily burdened. He lifted his head and looked up to heaven, his smooth brow furrowed in pain.

"Nevertheless," he said, each word distinct, "let it be as you, not I, would have it."

Some time later he rose from the ground and returned to the clearing. The three apostles were asleep. Peter awakened and Jesus reproached him. "So you had not the strength to stay awake with me?

"You should be awake and praying not to be put to the test. The spirit is willing, but the flesh is weak."

Then he stepped back into the woods and this time prostrated himself on the ground. His face was drawn, his muscles tense. His words were uttered in a barely audible gasp.

"My Father, if this cup cannot pass by without my drinking it, your will be done." He continued to lie there under the olive tree, in great distress.

Finally, he got up again and went back to the three and they were again asleep. This time he just shook his head. Jesus went back and again knelt down and prostrated himself in prayer. Again I heard his anguished plea and his resignation.

"Father, if you are willing, take this cup from me.

"Nevertheless, let your will be done, not mine."

Luke, I have seen the pain of childbirth, kidney stone, amputation, crucifixion and abdominal wounds, but never have I seen such agony as I saw in Jesus that night. Sweat poured out every pore of his body, soaking his robes. I was about to go to him, take his hand in mine and mop the perspiration from his brow. Then I saw something very strange. A spirit appeared. An angel came to hold his hand, mop his brow and comfort him. Jesus managed a faint smile of appreciation. He prayed all the more earnestly and cried out in his torment.

Then I saw the sweat on Jesus turn reddish. His robe was stained a slight pinkish color. I crept closer. Could it really be? Yes, the sweat was mixed with blood and it fell to the ground like drops of blood.

Luke, it was hematidrosis, a condition reported by Aristotle.[1] Dividimus in Athens and Abraham in Jerusalem had taught us it does occur, but neither one of them had seen a case.

I was so astonished that I stepped closer and touched the skin of his arm, wiping it with my finger. Believe me, this was real blood coming out of the unbroken skin! It was excreted from skin all over his body, from the face, arms, chest, back and legs. The sweat tinged with blood flowed down his face and neck as if a vein had been severed. His tunic was so soaked that the pink fluid was dripping from it.

Jesus did not move even when I came to him. The agony must have made him momentarily unconscious. When I looked up the angel was gone, and I stepped back into the shadows. Jesus wiped the blood off his face with his wide tunic sleeve. I could tell that his skin was tender. I do not know how much blood he lost.

He rose very slowly, seeming lightheaded. He shook his head as if to clear it and held onto a tree to steady himself. He stood for a short period of time. His face appeared pale, as if he were about to faint. He held on to each tree as he walked unsteadily to the three disciples. They were again asleep. My heart was pounding in sorrow for Jesus, from astonishment at how much he had suffered and from the certainty that I had seen a case of hematidrosis.

But suddenly there were shouts and cries, and through the trees I spotted the light of torches, headed for the cave where the other disciples were asleep. Jesus awakened the three disciples with a sharp cry. "Get up! Let us go! My betrayer is close at hand!" The three scrambled up and came to him. They were too sleepy to notice his blood-stained robe.

As Jesus and the three entered the clearing in front of the cave, a man with a lighted torch came down the path. It was Judas! He was leading Roman soldiers under the command of a tribune and Temple guards dispatched by the high priest. They had lanterns, torches and weapons. The soldiers were marching in precision and stopped as ordered by the tribune. The guards were backed up by a crowd of onlookers that had followed them from the Temple.

Judas came up to Jesus, embraced him and smothered him with kisses, even getting some of the bloody perspiration upon his garments. Jesus freed himself and asked, "Judas, are you betraying the Son of Man with a kiss?"

Then he addressed the armed gathering. "Who are you looking for?"

"Jesus the Nazarene."

"I am he."

The crowd fell back. By this time, the disturbance had awakened the rest of the disciples. They poured out of the cave in some distress, a few armed with clubs and swords.

Jesus asked a second time, "Who are you looking for?" and they replied, "Jesus the Nazarene."

"I have told you that I am he," Jesus replied. "If I am the one you are looking for, let these others go," and he pointed to the eleven disciples gathered around him. James the Greater cried out, "Lord, shall we use swords?"

Before Jesus could answer, another disciple drew a sword and struck the servant of the high priest, cutting off his ear. But this violent reaction upset Jesus.

"Put your sword back," he ordered, "for all who draw the sword will die by the sword. Or do you think that I cannot appeal to my Father, who would promptly send more than twelve legions of angels to my defense?

"But then, how would the Scriptures be fulfilled that say this is the way it must be?" And he touched the injured man's ear and healed it. All of this happened so rapidly that the Roman tribune did not order his soldiers to attack.

Jesus turned to his attackers. "Am I a brigand that you had to set out to capture me with swords and clubs? I sat teaching in the Temple day after day and you never laid hands on me.

"But this is your hour. This is the reign of darkness."

By now, the Roman tribune had regained his composure and ordered a guard to arrest Jesus. All of the eleven retreated toward the cave. I stayed in the shadows, my heart beating rapidly in fear.

A Roman soldier came up, grabbed Jesus' right arm, and twisted it behind his back until a look of pain came upon the face of Jesus. Another soldier stomped on the arch of the right foot. Luke, this is the maneuver the Romans use when they take a prisoner. They break no bones but tear the ligaments on the foot so that it makes walking and standing painful for days. Escape is thereby extremely difficult.

Then the soldiers treated Jesus with the same roughness with which they treat prisoners of war. Each one wanted to outdo the other. One hit Jesus in the face, another tied his hands behind his back and another fixed a rope around his neck. The tribune watched. Then he gave the order to march. The troops surrounded Jesus, and off they marched back toward Jerusalem. I could see that Jesus' right foot hurt whenever he took a step.

I stepped out of the shadows and mingled with the crowd. I could see Peter and John following at a distance, but the other disciples were nowhere to be seen.

The Temple guards rejoiced at how easy the capture of Jesus had been. Some of the soldiers seemed annoyed that their entire command had been marched out in full battle array in the middle of the night just to capture this unarmed man.

The soldiers led the procession down the steep bank to the Kidron, across the bridge and up the other bank. Finally we reached the top. The moon was bright and there was no one else on the streets. The entire city was asleep after the Passover meal. Caiaphas, the high priest, had counted on this in arranging the arrest of Jesus at this hour.

We marched into the gate of the wall of the city and continued in the direction of the finer homes of Jerusalem. The soldiers stopped at the large gate that led into the compound where the houses of Annas and Caiaphas were located. The tribune spoke to the captain of the Temple Guard and ordered his troops to turn over the prisoner. The Romans then marched off. The Temple guards were not any gentler with Jesus than the Romans had been.

As I watched Jesus, I could see that he was pale and noticeably weak. Profuse sweat had washed most of the blood off his skin, but the faint pink stains on his cloak could be seen in the light of flares.

The guards took Jesus to the home of Annas, formerly the high priest. He still had considerable power and apparently wanted to see Jesus first. I slipped in unnoticed. Annas sat in a large room and was surrounded by his attendants and admirers. Jesus was brought in, still tied. Annas seemed smug, pleased that he was able to question him first.

"So you are Jesus. I hear that you have quite a following. Tell me about your teaching."

Jesus answered calmly. "I have spoken openly for all the world to hear. I have always taught in the synagogue and in the Temple where all the Jews meet together. I have said nothing in secret.

"But why ask me? Ask my hearers what I taught. They know what I said."

Annas was visibly irked. One of the guards standing near gave Jesus a slap on the face. "Is that the way to answer the high priest?" Jesus reeled from the slap and almost fell. He regained his balance and spoke to the guard.

"If there is something wrong in what I said, point it out. But if there is no offense in it, why do you strike me?"

Annas just waved his hand, dismissing Jesus, the guards and everyone else. As Jesus passed by me, his eyes flickered in recognition. I hoped he knew how concerned I was about him. Surely Jesus would not be condemned. He could prove his innocence in any fair court.

The guards led Jesus, still bound, down the portico of Annas' home, across the spacious courtyard and up the steps of the place where Caiaphas lived. There were many others also arriving but somewhat in disarray, as if they had hurriedly dressed. I asked one of the attendants who they were and he said that Caiaphas had called into session the seventy members of the Sanhedrin, the highest court for the Jews in Judea.

The high priest moved quickly. He knew that Pilate held three other prisoners sentenced for crucifixion later in the day, two thieves and a seditionist called Barabbas whose actions had endangered citizens throughout Jerusalem.

I followed with the crowd as the Sanhedrin assembled. Then I slowly moved to the front so that I could hear everything.

Caiaphas called the Sanhedrin into session. He read a list of charges against Jesus, that he taught false doctrine, that he didn't follow the Sabbath rules and had threatened to destroy the Temple. With this, I heaved a sigh of relief. They could not prove any of this and if they did get some witnesses, Jesus could outargue anyone.

In our court a prisoner cannot testify in his own trial before the Sanhedrin. The charges have to be testified to and agreed upon by two separate witnesses.

Witness after witness was called to testify against Jesus. Clearly they had been told what to say, but their stories did not agree. Several stood up and submitted false evidence against Jesus, but their evidence conflicted with that of other witnesses. I was beginning to enjoy the confusion that was confronting the high priest and his advisors.

One accuser got up and said Jesus had threatened the Temple. "We heard him say he would destroy the Temple and in three days build another." I was tempted to get up and testify as to the exact word Jesus used, referring to the Holy of Holies not the Temple building itself, but I hesitated, afraid that I too would be arrested. This was a crime guilty of death.

The confusion among witnesses had created confusion among members of the Sanhedrin. Caiaphas pounded for order and addressed Jesus. "Have you no answer to any of this? What is this evidence that these men are bringing against you?"

To my amazement, Jesus said nothing. I could see a faint smile on his face. But this only offended the high priest. He challenged Jesus, his voice ringing through the council room. "If you are the Christ, tell us!"

This question, Luke, every adult male Jew is bound to answer. And if he claims to be the Christ, he could be found guilty of blasphemy and sentenced to death.

"If I tell you," Jesus answered boldly, looking directly in the eyes of the high priest, "you will not believe me. And if I question you, you will not answer. But from now on the Son of Man will be seated at the right hand of the Power of God."

Several members of the Sanhedrin shouted, "So you are the Son of God then?"

Jesus answered, "It is you who say I am."

Caiaphas tore his robes. "What need of witnesses have we now? You heard him blaspheme! What is your finding?" he demanded of the Sanhedrin.

They shouted, "He deserves to die!"

I was shocked. I had failed Jesus. I had not even tried to defend him. I withdrew with tears in my eyes. I was both angry at myself and ashamed.

The clerk than began to call the roll. One by one the members of the Sanhedrin were called, and each in his turn shouted "Guilty," and they spat at Jesus.

There were two who did not answer the roll call, Joseph of Arimathea and a man named Nicodemus. I remembered the first as a friend of Jeremiah. "He is known as an upright and virtuous man," said the man next to me. "He lives in the hope of seeing the kingdom of God." I had met Nicodemus and knew he was a secret follower of Jesus, wanting to learn more of Jesus' teachings. These were two men, surely, who would have spoken in defense of Jesus, but their seats were empty.

So the decision was made. Jesus was guilty of blasphemy, of claiming to be the Son of God. Jesus was to be executed as a common criminal, a prisoner of war or a traitor. I could not believe it. I must get word to Elisa and she must tell the other followers of Jesus. But I did not want to leave Jesus.

The verdict would not be final until certified by the Roman procurator, but I knew there would be no problem. Pontius Pilate approved all death sentences. It only meant fewer Jews to trouble the Romans.

So Jesus would be crucified. The thought of it made me shudder. I had seen men nailed to crosses in Galilee. I didn't even want to think of the kind, gentle Jesus, suffering the agonies of crucifixion. I must tell Elisa. But how?

Jesus was led out into the courtyard to await daylight and his appearance before Pilate. I followed close behind. It was early morning, and Sabbath would begin at sundown.

He was tied to a pole in the middle of the courtyard, and Temple guards were ordered to watch him. He looked exhausted. His cloak was bloodstained and torn in places. His lip was swollen and bleeding. His hair was disheveled. His face and cloak were covered with spittle.

Jesus looked pale. His eyes were sunken, his cheeks drawn and the skin dry. I realized that he had had no water or wine since the Passover feast last night. Furthermore he had perspired profusely in the garden with the sweating of blood. He was dry, very dry. Here was my chance to at least help him.

I picked up a sheepskin of wine from which the soldiers had been drinking. I approached Jesus. As I neared, I suddenly felt a swift movement behind me and was knocked to the ground with the flat part of a sword. The wineskin was knocked out of my hand. A Temple guard stood over me and shouted, "Don't you know prisoners must not be fed or given to drink! Do that again and I will use the blade."

I looked at him as I felt the blood run down the back of my head. Then I looked at Jesus and he shook his head, meaning that I should not try again.

I felt the injury to my scalp. It was just a small cut that would bleed a lot but heal.

Now the thing to do was to get a message to Elisa. In the corner of the garden I spotted one of the servants of the high priest who had just been relieved from duty. I knew that they were all poorly paid and were eager to earn a few extra coins. I approached him and asked if he would deliver a message to Bethany. I offered him three denarii. I paid him one and promised the others when he returned. He agreed. I took a piece of parchment and wrote: "Dearest Elisa, Jesus is to be crucified. He is to be taken to Pilate at dawn." I told the messenger that I would know if he delivered the message when he brought back her signature. Then I would complete the payment. As he left, I said, "Run, run, run!"

I returned to the center of the garden. It was a chilly morning. The guards had built a fire to warm themselves. Off to the side was Jesus, tied to the pole. I could see that he was shivering. If I could just give him my cloak, but the same guard who had struck me was there. I could see that Jesus' tongue was already starting to parch from dehydration. He was also shivering with the pre-dawn cold. His sweat-dampened robe added to the coolness. Yet I could not help.

The guards now decided to amuse themselves at Jesus' expense. They drank watered vinegar in front of him and taunted him, knowing full well that he was thirsty. Then they started to mock him and beat him, each taking his turn. After that one of them came up with a cloth and wrapped it over his eyes, blindfolding him. Then the torment really started. They picked up sticks from the firewood pile and started to hit him on the head and face and shouted, "Play the prophet. Who hit you then?" And this went on and on, each one heaping insult after insult on Jesus.

My heart pounded in anger at myself for not protecting Jesus, anger at Judas for his betrayal, anger at the unjust trial and anger at the guards. But the worst of these angers was at myself. I had promised Elisa and Mary that I would protect Jesus. Yet I had not even tried to defend him at the trial of the Sanhedrin. I had not said a word. I tried to console myself by thinking that the guilty verdict had been decided even before the trial had started. Why did God permit such cruelty to innocent people? And if Jesus is the Son of God, the Messiah, why did not God send legions of angels to free him? Yes, I was angry with myself and with God.

But in a moment there was a disturbance in the center of the garden near the fire, so I pushed over there. A small group had suddenly surrounded a dark-haired, bearded man who was warming himself. I recognized the man as Peter. A servant from the group was peering at him and said, "This person was with him too." Peter shook his head and denied it saying, "Woman, I do not know him." I looked at Peter and could say nothing. By not defending Jesus, I had denied him, too. Shortly afterward, someone else saw him and said, "You are another of them!" Peter replied, "I am not, my friend." Then he disappeared into the crowd. I knew exactly how he felt. Yes, to save one's hide one will even deny Jesus the Messiah.

I turned to Jesus. The guards got tired of playing with Jesus and most of them went off to sleep. But two muscular, heavily armed men were constantly on the alert and on guard.

I got close enough to look at Jesus closely. His temporal pulse was pounding and rapid, his respirations were short and fast, he had a crooked nose as if one of the blows had displaced the cartilage, and blood was trickling from each nostril onto his mustache and beard. There was a bruise under the left eye as if he had received a direct blow there with a blunt instrument, perhaps a fist. The upper part of the cheek and the lower eyelid were swollen, partially shutting the left eye. There were a few bruise marks on his forehead. He must have received blows on the bearded part of his face because blood was oozing from several areas. What cruelty! And I was not allowed to relieve my friend.

I had taken the Oath of Hippocrates to help all in need. Now I could not. I knew that any attempt would be my last. The guard with the broad sword would see to that. So I withdrew to the fire to warm up.

A short time later Peter came back. As I tried to approach him, I heard another man saying, "This fellow was certainly with him. Why, he is a Galilean." Peter was quick to reply, "My friend, I do not know what you are talking about." He turned on his heel and started to walk away.

At that instant there was the clear sound of a cock crowing, announcing the coming of dawn.

I saw Peter turning toward Jesus and their eyes met across the distance. The look in Jesus' eyes was that of understanding and forgiveness. But I could feel the agony that Peter had in his heart. His eyes and head dropped down as he shoved on. As he passed me, I reached out and put my arms around him and walked with him. We walked in silence to a corner of the garden, sat on a log and cried together.

It was now daybreak. The Romans started their workday early. I left Peter and went to see Jesus, to find out if I could help him. But he was now surrounded with Temple guards. He was still tied to the stake with his arms in back of him. He could not sit or lie down. Occasionally he would fall asleep and sag forward, and the pull of the ropes would wake him up. I could see the look of pain on his face. There was dried blood on the upper lip that came from the nasal injury and there were crusts of blood on the bruises on his forehead and cheeks. Oh, Jesus was in pain, in agony, and I, a physician, could not relieve him. My heart ached. But there was no way that I could get near him.

I felt a tug at my cloak. Lo and behold! The servant to whom I had given the message to Elisa had returned. He had obviously been running. He was perspiring through his clothes even in the chilly morning air and was breathing heavily. We went off to the side and he brought out the parchment with Elisa's signature. I paid the servant the two additional denarii that I had promised. Then I tore up the parchment and went back to where Jesus was being held.

Elisa, having been notified, would do what she thought best with the information. She would decide whether to tell Mary the mother of Jesus and whether to bring her here. I knew that Elisa would come. I needed her so very much. Although I did not want her to see Jesus suffer, I needed her support and her advice.

I was able to get near Jesus and I noticed that he appeared weaker. I knew that he was thirsty. He had stopped perspiring in the cold air. His skin was pale. I could see his pulse beating in the temples and I knew that his heart rate was rapid. He was also breathing rapidly. He staggered as he stood. And I could do nothing.

Then Caiaphas ordered the guards to take Jesus to Pilate, for approval of the sentence. But the haste of his removal was suddenly slowed. It seemed the high priest wanted everyone from the Sanhedrin to follow also. All the servants of the houses of Caiaphas and Annas and all of the guards were also to make the march. This seemed odd to me because, as a rule, the members of the Sanhedrin and every other good Jew wants to stay away as far as they can from Pilate.

Jesus stumbled along the path. Whenever a guard felt the urge, he would strike him with the flat of his sword or spit in his face. I had never seen such cruel treatment. The long walk to the Fortress of Antonia, where Pilate was quartered with his troops, was over irregular stone streets and up and down small hills. I could hear the members of the Sanhedrin urging passersby to join in. "Come, help us crucify this man." To my amazement, many joined the group and soon the number was doubled.

I followed as closely as I could. The guards were surrounding Jesus all of the time. I heard them say, "Watch out for his followers. They may attack." Some of the shopkeepers were amazed that there was such a group of guards with drawn swords surrounded by a large crowd escorting a man who seemed about to faint from weakness.

We were near the Temple grounds, which was full of worshippers. Many of the visitors had traveled a great distance so that they would spend the Passover, the next day and the Sabbath worshipping at the Temple. I wondered how many of the people in the crowd around Jesus had hailed him as king less than one week before.

We approached the vast steps of the fortress and Caiaphas ordered one of the guards to take the decision of the Sanhedrin, written in Latin, to Pilate.

The guard gave the parchment to the Roman guard who appeared within the massive gates of the fortress. We waited what seemed to be a long time. The sun had now fully risen. Jesus was standing alone, surrounded by guards. I could see the look of pain on his face.

Now, I had to get into the fortress with Jesus. Perhaps I could convince one of the Roman guards to allow me to help him. I stayed close in the group around the high priest. Everyone had their eyes on the prisoner and I was able to slip by the guards and onto the portico of the fortress.

In deference to the Jews, who would be defiled if they entered the house of a Gentile, Pilate came out onto the portico. He waved for the rabble to quiet down, and it did. Jesus was brought up before him. He was really a pathetic sight. His robes were dirty, bloody and torn. His face was battered, with crusted blood and bruises, and there was a swelling under the left eye, which was almost closed. I could almost see an expression of pity on the face of this seasoned soldier of Rome.

"What charges do you bring against this man?"

Caiaphas was eager to reply. "We found this man inciting our people to revolt, opposing payment of the tribute to Caesar, and claiming to be Christ, a king."

Pilate started the interrogation from the last of the accusations.

"Are you the king of the Jews?"

Pilate knew that Jews were looking for a Messiah to free them from the Romans, but he also knew that someone claiming to be the Messiah could be found guilty of blasphemy and sentenced to death.

However, Pilate had sworn not to involve himself in Jewish religious matters. And this pathetic man before him did not look like a soldier or a conqueror who would defeat Rome. So he turned to Jesus and repeated, "Are you the king of the Jews?"

Jesus replied in a parched voice, "It is you who say it.

"Mine is not a kingdom of this world. If my kingdom were of this world, my men would have fought my being surrendered to the Jews, but my kingdom is not of this kind."

"So you are a king then?"

Jesus answered, "Yes, I am a king. I was born for this.

"I came into the world for this, to bear witness to the truth. And all who are on the side of truth listen to my voice."

Pilate seemed confused and retorted, almost to himself, "What is truth?" He had heard enough. His decision was made and would be announced officially. He motioned to the guard, who came up and led Jesus back into the courtyard, and I followed.

Behind me, I heard a noise and as I looked, I bumped into one of the pillars. Pilate turned to look. I was embarrassed. Jesus was too far ahead to notice. The noise that had distracted me was a guard carrying the cobalt blue chair from which the procurator renders his decisions.

The courtyard was full of people. I could see the chief priests, other priests of the Temple, and the scribes in a group out in front. I wondered what they had plotted next. Just then they began to jeer and so did everyone else. The chair was put in place. Pilate appeared and angrily motioned for silence. He seated himself and made his pronouncement.

"I find no guilt in this man."

The priests could not believe what they had heard. They quickly got into a huddle and came out with a challenge to Pilate, who was about to get up from the chair. One of them approached the procurator and said, "He stirs up the nations by his teaching throughout the whole Jewish country. He began in Galilee and ended here."

The procurator was annoyed but he did listen, and suddenly the furrow on his brow disappeared. "From Galilee, you say? That is not my - jurisdiction. That is under Herod, who is tetrarch of Galilee." He got up from the chair, motioned to the guards to take Jesus to Herod and left to go back into the fortress.

Everyone was in a state of confusion. Here the highest Roman official of the region had rendered a judgment, then withdrew it and surrendered the case to a lower Jewish official, a vassal of Rome, who had no authority at all in Jerusalem.

I had never known Rome to turn over a case to a lower authority. But Pilate was gone and the soldiers were shoving Jesus out into the street. I followed.

Jesus looked weaker. The skin of his face was wrinkled and his lips were dry and cracked. He walked with an unsteady gait but the soldiers shoved him on. His hands were still tied behind his back.

The Temple guards and their prisoner led the sad procession through the streets of Jerusalem with the priests right behind. I could see them motioning to bystanders to follow. Men approached them for instructions and then joined the throng. The entire actions of the crowd seemed to be orchestrated by the chief priests.

Herod and Herodias were staying a few streets over in the palace of Herod the Great. The sun was bright and it was getting hot. There was no breeze and no cloud in the sky. As we left the gates of the fortress, I could see worshippers going to the Temple. Suddenly I saw a group of women with Mary the mother of Jesus and Elisa in the lead. I rushed to them and embraced Elisa. "Mary insisted on coming," she said, and I could read the sadness in her eyes. Among the other women were Mary of Magdala and Joanna. Elisa noticed blood on the back of my head and I had to explain how it had happened.

As we made our way to the palace of Herod I quickly recounted what had happened during the night and early morning. The streets were narrow and crowded, and we were too far behind to catch sight of Jesus. I did not want Mary to see him like this in any case.

Soon, we saw Herod's palace. I told Elisa and the women that I would somehow gain admission into the palace and return with news as soon as I could. I hurried ahead.

The soldiers and Jesus were now at the gates. Apparently Pilate had dispatched a runner to inform Herod, for the gates were open and Jesus and the guards were allowed in. The priests were permitted to enter but the crowd was stopped.

I recognized one of the guards at the gate as the son of one of our patients from Capernaum. He greeted me with a warm smile. I indicated that I wanted to get in and he let me enter the grounds. It really does help to be a physician, a member of a respected profession. It gets one into places easily.

The courtyard was full of chariots, portable chairs, and the slaves who carried or drove them. Apparently, there had been a celebration after the Passover meal involving some of the nobility under Herod's jurisdiction, and it had not yet ended.

I went up the steps into the royal palace. I have made house calls in the mansions of the rich in Capernaum but I have never seen such magnificence. Elisa would call it extravagant and wasteful. The walls were made of marble trimmed in gold.

I asked a servant where the group was gathered and he pointed me to a large assembly room just off the massive dining room. As I passed by the open doors, I saw servants still clearing the banquet tables of empty plates and wineglasses.

I opened the door and entered a room full of people. At one end was Herod, dressed in his finest raiments as a host, a wineglass in hand. I was disgusted. Here at the Passover season, everyone comes to Jerusalem to pray and to thank God for the freedom from Egypt. However, Herod came here for a party. Since the beheading of John the Baptist, Herod's behavior has been erratic and often cruel. It is said he drinks too much wine.

I moved along the back of the crowd. Herodias was not in sight, but Herod was perturbed that the festivities had been disrupted. Jesus was brought before him. His hands had been untied and he was rubbing them. His fingers were red and swollen from the ropes having been too tightly bound.

Herod motioned for quiet. Then he spoke to Jesus. "So, you are the miracle worker who raises the dead and cures the sick." Luke, he had a wicked grin on his face.

"Now, perform some miracle for me and my friends here."

All eyes were on Jesus. He did not move or utter a sound. Herod grew aggravated and repeated his order, but much louder.

Jesus did not move or speak. Several more moments passed in silence. Herod took great offense at this insult in front of his guests.

"As your king," he bellowed, "I command you to perform a miracle for me!"

Again, no response from Jesus. Herod turned red. "Work a miracle, you wretched creature!" But there was only an ominous stillness. Herod called some of his advisors into conference, and they sent a servant off on an errand. He returned with a robe, which they showed to Herod. He nodded in approval and motioned for him to put it on Jesus. It was the purple cloak of a prince.

"You claim to be a king!" Herod taunted. He started to laugh at the sight of this bloodied man in tatters wearing a royal cloak, and so did the entire assembly. They mocked him as a fool. Then Herod ordered Jesus to be removed from his presence and returned to Pilate.

Luke, again, I did not step up and defend Jesus. I did not laugh. I did nothing. I hung my head in shame and found my way to the door of the palace, onto the grounds, and past the gates. I even avoided my friend the guard. I was too ashamed to face him.

Soon the soldiers marched by with Jesus in the center of their formation. The priests followed. The rabble from the Temple was waiting and, at a signal, also started to laugh and jeer. I found Elisa and the women. Mary was distraught at even this distant sight of her son. I told them what had occurred in the palace of Herod, then hurried ahead to be with Jesus.

We went back along the same route that we had just traveled, the shortest route to the Fortress of Antonia. It was hot now, hotter than when we had first arrived at the fortress.

Pilate must have received a message from Herod, because he was waiting in the judgment seat, his face showing annoyance. I don't think that he had planned it to happen this way. The soldiers marched in with Jesus in their center. His walk was slower, his posture more stooped. He was unsteady and he could hardly make the steps up to Pilate.

Pilate looked at him again. By this time, the priests and much of the Sanhedrin had gathered around and the crowd was filling the courtyard. Many of the onlookers, Luke, must have hailed Jesus as a king, the Messiah, only days before. Now they were incensed that the man they had hoped would deliver them from the rule of the Romans was mocked by Herod and made to play the fool. Now he was back in the hands of Pilate. I felt somewhat better knowing that Pilate had already declared he found no crime deserving of death.

Jesus was pale, weak and short of breath. Yet he was forced to stand in front of Pilate with the jeering crowd at his back. Pilate motioned for silence, but the response was too slow. The centurion spoke a command, the soldiers drew their swords and advanced, and the unruly throng settled down. Pilate motioned and the centurion called the soldiers back.

Pilate spoke. "You brought this man to me. I have examined him and have found that he has not broken any Roman law. I sent him to Herod and he sent him back. Now I will chastise him and set him free."

The priests started to shout and so did the crowd. The clamor grew louder, and Pilate seemed more and more uncomfortable. When there was no lessening in the noise, he barked an order. "Silence!" But the crowd did not quiet until the soldiers again drew their swords.

Pilate had reached a decision. "It is customary for me to release a prisoner on this day. Therefore, I will give you a choice. Whom do you wish me to release to you, Barabbas the insurrectionist" — he paused for the crowd to remember the trouble Barabbas had caused all of Jerusalem — "or Jesus, who is called your king?"

The priests were taken aback but consulted quickly. There was no question in their minds who was the greater threat. They caught Pilate by surprise when they shouted in unison, "We want Barabbas. We want Barabbas." Then the crowd took up the chant. "We want Barabbas. We want Barabbas."

Pilate had given them a choice and they had made it. It appeared that he wanted to free Jesus and chose this means but it had failed. So he bowed to the will of the people, ordering Barabbas to be freed and Jesus to be scourged.

This did not satisfy the priests. They wanted Jesus to be crucified. Soon, under their direction, the rabble was shouting disapproval.

By this time I was concerned about Jesus being able to stand. I was about 20 cubits from him and could see his weakness, his rapid respiration and his marked dehydration.

The soldiers came and surrounded Jesus and moved him to the room where he was to be scourged. It was not difficult for me to enter the scourging chamber. I stayed by the door of the rather large room. It was bare except for a row of pillars about 4 cubits high embedded in the stone floor. There was a metal ring at the top of each.

Jesus was led to the first pillar. His hands were tied above his head to the metal ring, with his chest toward the pillar. All of his clothing was stripped off, allowing his buttocks, back, thighs and legs exposed to the scourging. I felt for Jesus in his nakedness. Even though there were no women in the room it must have been humiliating to be exposed naked in public.

Two soldiers were assigned to do the scourging. They were large men and very muscular. They had been especially trained to do the scourging. Each one carried a flagrum, a short piece of wood to which are attached leather straps about a cubit in length. A pair of metal balls was fastened at the end of each strap. By this time Jesus was sagging on the ropes, unable to stand on his own. He was already weak. What would the scourging do?

Jewish law prescribes a scourging of forty lashes and no more, so thirty-nine are given, thirteen on each shoulder and thirteen on the lower back. The Romans have no limit on the number of strokes. However, a centurion is always present to ensure that the scourging does not kill the victim.

Two soldiers now positioned themselves about 2 cubits behind Jesus, one on each side. At a signal from the centurion, the first took one step forward and put his entire weight into the swing of the flagrum. I could hear the leather singing in the air, then the metal balls embed themselves into the flesh of Jesus. His head snapped back and his mouth gaped open. This skin that had excreted bloody sweat now was enduring the pain of lashing. Oh, how unbearable!

As soon as one soldier struck his blow, the other soldier started his swing and delivered his blow. The muscles went into spasm with pain. The two soldiers vowed to make Jesus scream. But he did not even moan. Thereafter each blow became harder and the metal balls cut deeper into Jesus' skin and blood seeped out of the wounds. Blood covered the metal balls and leather straps and soon was splattered on the soldiers. There was no sound from Jesus.

Soon there was no more motion of Jesus' body, no reaction at all to the lash. The centurion stopped the soldiers and approached Jesus. He signaled a guard to cut the ropes, and as he did, Jesus fell limp upon the stone floor. I was afraid at first that he was dead. Then I noticed that he was breathing and so did the centurion. He motioned for some water and a guard splashed water in the face of Jesus. I saw some slow motion of the facial muscles. Jesus slowly opened his eyes and moved his hands. Oh, how I wished that I could help Jesus! Just to dress his wounds and comfort him! But no, that was not allowed.

After a couple of minutes, the guards were told by the centurion to clothe him and get him up. One guard grabbed Jesus by the arm and pulled him up. As soon as he let go, Jesus fell again. This time, he hit his head against a pillar. The centurion angrily ordered the guards to hold Jesus up until he could stand. It took several attempts, but then Jesus did stay on his feet, and they started back to see Pilate.

As we passed the door one guard covered him with the robe that Herod had used to mock him. Another Roman soldier had fashioned a crown of branches with long sharp thorns. He approached the prisoner in mockery, said, "I crown you Jesus, King of the Jews," and forced the cap of thorns on Jesus' head.

I could see, and almost feel, the thorns puncturing the scalp. First there was the pain, then the ooze of blood. In Athens, we used to remark on how richly the scalp is supplied with blood, causing it to bleed profusely when punctured or cut. Imagine, about twenty puncture wounds into the scalp, with the thorns left in place to keep the wounds open.

Soon the matted hair of Jesus was covered with blood. It flowed down his long dark hair and beard onto his chest, shoulders and down his back. More blood loss! How much more of this could Jesus stand!

Another soldier put a walking stick into his hand as a scepter and bowed to him as if he were a king. They laughed as they led him back into the presence of Pilate. The procurator seemed troubled at the sight of Jesus.

The priests and the crowd were also unsettled, but no less determined.

Luke, now that I have had a little time to think, I wonder why God would let Jesus suffer at the hands of these men.

Since the experience on the mountain when I heard the voice of God say, "This is my beloved Son," I have believed that Jesus is the Son of God. But would a merciful God, or even a vengeful God, let his innocent son suffer without helping him?

I fully expected a legion of angels to come and slaughter Pilate, the priests, guards, scribes and the crowd. And I wanted everyone destroyed who had jeered or laughed at Jesus.

Then I wondered if I had had a dream on the mountain and if Jesus really was the Son of God. Or if God was really listening! A thousand thoughts came to my mind in that moment and I doubted that he was the Son of God, or if there really was a God.

Jesus stood in front of Pilate, his head, face, and neck covered with blood, a stick in his hand and a cloak around his shoulder. It was a pitiable sight. My heart ached for him. Why did God not do something?

Pilate got up and addressed the people. "Behold the man!"

Really, Luke, Jesus did not even look human.

Pilate shouted louder, "Behold your king!" I should have shouted in response, "His kingdom is not of this world," echoing the words of Jesus himself, but I did not.

Then there was bedlam with cries and shouts, pushing and shoving. A third time, at the order of Pilate and the centurion, the guards drew their swords. Pilate could easily have called out his troops and massacred the entire crowd. But that would also reflect on his ability to handle a riot.

As the din quelled, Pilate looked at Jesus. "What is your origin?" he asked.

Jesus' lips were cracked and there was blood all over his face. He did not answer.

Pilate continued. "Do you know that I have power to set you free or to crucify you?"

This time Jesus did respond, though each labored word seemed to cause him pain.

"You have no power whatsoever to harm me unless it is granted to you from above.

"He who surrendered me to you has the greater offense."

I wondered if God really meant his Son to go through this suffering, and for what? Why didn't God do something to save him?

Pilate looked around as if for support, but none of his officers moved. Then an elder of the Temple stepped forward with a compelling argument. "If you release this man, you are not a friend of Caesar. Anyone who declares himself a king renounces allegiance to Caesar." One of the priests saw the chance to further incite the crowd. He shouted, "We have no king but Caesar!" then motioned to the crowd, which picked up his words in their own chant. "We have no king but Caesar. We have no king but Caesar."

Jesus had told Pilate that his kingdom was not of this world, but no one seemed to recall that statement now.

Pilate was in a quandary. If he let Jesus go, the chief priest would surely send a messenger to Rome to tell the emperor Tiberius that Pilate had freed a man who claimed to be king. The truth of this matter would be distorted, and Pilate could be called back to Rome and demoted. Even though Judea was a poor region, it had its advantages. His wife was allowed to accompany him. Furthermore, a land bordered by the sea is far better than a desert outpost in Africa.

Pilate really seemed uneasy. He motioned for quiet.

"Look! There is your king! Am I to crucify your king?"

The rabble continued to shout, "We have no king but Caesar."

Pilate again turned to his officers. They did not move. Then the priests stirred up the crowd with a new cry. "Crucify him! Crucify him!" I felt sick at the stomach. All was lost.

Whether Jesus was the Son of God or not did not matter now. He was innocent, yet he was the pawn between the chief priest and the procurator. Whose will would prevail? Pilate as the civil authority had made an official decision in a case presented to him, then withdrawn it and put the decision into the hands of a lesser official, who also could find no guilt and returned the prisoner. Then Pilate had offered to free Jesus and the crowd refused that. Then Pilate had sentenced him to scourging, hoping that would satisfy the people. Finally, the procurator had withdrawn all of the decisions, as if to let the angry rabble make the final call.

Pilate then asked for a basin of water. He dipped his hands in the water, held them up and looked at Caiaphas.

"I am innocent of the blood of this just man. The responsibility is yours."

It was done. The cloak was taken off Jesus as the soldiers prepared to lead him away to the hill of Calvary, or Golgotha, where criminals are taken for crucifixion. I could not believe it. Jesus was really going to be crucified! Many thoughts ran through my head. If only we had not come to Jerusalem for the Passover! What if he had kept silent at the trial of the Sanhedrin? Could not Jesus release himself from this fate? He had raised people from the dead. Why not save himself? Perhaps he yet will do something.

I went into the courtyard and there were the women, with Elisa keeping watch for me. They seemed to be keeping Mary in their center. I told them what had happened before Pilate. It was a shock to all of them. Mary the mother of Jesus wanted to follow her son to Golgotha. We tried to persuade her not to go, but she insisted. Elisa looked at me and said, "Nothing will keep her away. We will watch out for her. Go and see if you can help Jesus in any way." So I left.

In the courtyard, the centurion assigned four soldiers to the crucifixion. A condemned man has to carry his cross to the site of execution. They then placed the patibulum, the crossbeam with a mortised hole in the center, across his shoulders and tied it to his outstretched arm.

The two thieves who had also been condemned to crucifixion were then brought up and tied to their crossbeams. They were constantly cursing the guards. A sign indicating the crime for which each had been sentenced was hung around the neck of each prisoner.

The one placed on Jesus was written in Hebrew, Latin and Greek. It said "Jesus, the Nazarene, the King of the Jews."

The centurion ordered the march to Golgotha to begin.

I wished that I could help Jesus, but I knew that the Roman soldiers do not strike a warning blow with the flat of their swords. They strike with the sharp side always and that is lethal. So I just followed.

Suddenly I heard a thud. Jesus had fallen forward. His head and nose were on the stone pavement and the heavy patibulum was crushing his neck and shoulders. A soldier kicked him and shouted for him to get up. With difficulty, Jesus moved. It was painful for him to sit up and then struggle to stand. He wobbled and swayed as the centurion gave the order to move on.

Jesus could not get his feet to move. A soldier nudged him with a spear. He moved a few awkward steps and again fell. This time he hit the right side of his face, and the crossbeam dug deeper into the skin of his shoulders. A soldier again kicked him. I wished that I could help him but I did not dare.

This time one of the soldiers pulled him up. Again, the order was given to march and again the soldier prodded him with a spear. Jesus made a few rapid steps forward and again fell, hitting the right side of his face and forehead again. Blood gushed from his nose and more fresh blood from the scalp because the crossbeam drove the thorns deeper into his scalp as he fell.

This time, in spite of the prodding of the soldier, Jesus could not move. He was breathing very rapidly. Perspiration soaked his clothing. The centurion called a halt. He went over to Jesus, saw his condition, and ordered him to be untied. As the ropes were loosened, Jesus lay on his side and started to rub his hands. I knew that they must have been numb, because I noticed some swelling in them. He seemed unable to get up. I tried to get in to help him, but a soldier had a lance pointed at me so I withdrew.

The centurion looked around. He looked over the crowd of Pharisees, pilgrims, merchants and others drawn to the scene of this drama. He finally pointed to a tall, husky tiller of the soil. "What is your name?"

"Simon of Cyrene."

"Simon of Cyrene, carry the patibulum for this condemned man."

Simon tried to move away, but the lancers pointed their weapons at him, so he moved forward in disgruntled obedience and put the heavy beam on his right shoulder. I could hear him mumble, "Why did I have to be so inquisitive?"

The centurion was anxious to deliver the prisoners to Golgotha. He pulled Jesus up and told him to walk on his own. Jesus staggered but slowly moved forward. Progress was a little faster now.

It was a rocky, uphill climb, two thousand cubits in length. There were people all around, jeering at the approach of the convicted criminals. But as they caught sight of Jesus, they fell silent in dismay. Never had they seen such a pathetic figure led to execution.

Soon we came to a group of women who customarily bring soothing drinks and wine to numb the pain of victims of crucifixion. They were moved to tears by the sight of Jesus. He stopped and spoke to them in a weak but distinct voice.

"Daughters of Jerusalem, do not weep for me. Weep rather for yourselves and for your children.

"For the days will surely come when people will say, 'Happy are those who are barren, the wombs that have never borne, the breasts that have never been suckled!' Then they will say to the mountains, 'Fall on us' and to the hills, 'Cover us!' For if men use the green wood like this, what will happen to the dry?"

The women tried to touch him, but the centurion ordered the march onward. I drew closer to Jesus. His breathing was very labored and rapid. I could hear wheezing when he inhaled and exhaled. His lungs were becoming congested. I thought for a moment that the centurion would let me help him, but he could show no mercy in front of his soldiers.

I did not think that Jesus could go another step, but he did. His heart was beating rapidly. His lips were dry and parched. There was dried blood over his forehead, on his nostrils, mustache and all through his hair. Finally we reached the field of crucifixion.

Now the crucifixion squad took over. They first stripped Jesus of all his clothing. I hoped that he did not see Elisa and his mother and the other women who were there. That would make the humiliation even worse.

Then I saw Jesus' eyes roll, and he fell backward onto the stony ground. The executioners seemed pleased. They took the crossbeam from Simon, who soon disappeared into the crowd. They lifted Jesus' head and were careful not to prick their fingers on the thorns. They stretched his arms and laid him on the crossbeam. Then one of the soldiers held out his hand, and another felt for the soft spot near the center of his wrist, between the bones. There he placed a crude nail, and with one blow of the sledgehammer drove the nail through the wrist. The nail partially severed a nerve, causing the contraction of his thumb into the palm and bringing Jesus back to consciousness. I knew that he had severe pain in his wrist, hand and fingers, even up to the shoulder.

Two more blows and the wrist was securely fastened to the patibulum. The two soldiers then went to the left hand and repeated the procedure. This was more pain for Jesus. Oh, the agony! And he had committed no crime. I thought, what could I have done to prevent this? What could I have done?

Now, all four members of the squad came forward to lift Jesus onto the stipes, which was set permanently on the ground. I was about 30 cubits away. As they picked up the crossbeam, two on each side, the weight of his body hung from the two nails. They dragged his body into a semi-sitting position, and then paused. On command, they lifted the beam to which Jesus was nailed and fitted the mortised hole into the top of the stipes. It slid into place with a thump.

The pain in the wrists and arms of Jesus must have been excruciating. His mouth was open in agony, but he did not scream. How he could stand it, I do not know. Jesus' entire body sagged down and his chest expanded. He was trying to breathe with his abdominal muscles, but he could not. I knew that if they left him in this condition for just a few minutes, he would suffocate. But the soldiers knew this too.

One soldier grabbed his left foot, raised it about one third of a cubit by bending Jesus' knee, and placed the foot against the wooden stipes. Another soldier drove a nail through the bones into the stipes. Then the right foot was placed over the left and the nail driven through both feet, deep into the wood.

Thus Jesus was nailed to the cross.

A soldier attached over his head the mocking sign "Jesus, the Nazarene, the King of the Jews."

Jesus was gasping for breath. He slowly straightened his legs, pushed his body up on the nails in his feet, and raised himself about one-third of a cubit. Now he could breathe more easily, and the pain was relieved in his hands, but the pain in his feet must be unbearable. But there he stood and, it seemed, looked around. I don't know how he could see out of his blood-covered eyes, but he spotted the group of women about forty cubits away. He knew, I felt, that his mother Mary was among the women from our company. They were all crying and Elisa was trying to shield Mary from the awful sight.

John the Beloved Disciple had joined the women and was of great comfort to Mary. Other than Peter, I had not seen any apostles since the Romans had arrested Jesus.

Then his body sagged again. Jesus could no longer stand the pain in his feet and the cramping in his leg muscles. But now his arms and wrists again bore his weight and he could not lift his chest to breathe. Spasms rippled the biceps and triceps muscles in each arm.

I moved closer and could see the pectoral muscles go into spasm. Jesus could not breathe. I drew even closer and the soldiers did not seem to mind. I finally was able to get within 2 cubits of Jesus and there I was, watching the man whom I loved and admired, helpless and suffering such agony on the cross. And I could not help.

By this time the two thieves were also fastened to crosses, one on either side of Jesus. They groaned and cursed and shouted and screamed.

I could hear Jesus uttering low sounds. He seemed to be moving his lips. He wasn't moaning, he was praying.

For a moment the thought flashed through my mind that God would send down avenging angels to free Jesus and smite the chief priests and perpetrators of this hideous crime. But nothing happened.

People pushed and shoved to get a good look at Jesus. They did not pay any attention to the two thieves. They started to shout at Jesus in his suffering. Caiaphas and his priests had made their way to the foot of Jesus, and the high priest derided the scene.

"Aha! So he saved others, let him save himself if he is the Christ of God, the Chosen One."

I was ashamed that I'd had the same thought myself.

One of the soldiers stood in front of the cross, just a few paces from me. He put his hands on his hips and said, "If you are the King of the Jews, save yourself," and laughed.

Luke, I felt like slapping him and the others, but I knew that it would start a scuffle and that would be enough for the centurion to call it a riot and the Romans would slaughter everyone that they could.

It was awful to see and experience all of this. I turned away and there were soldiers drinking weakened vinegar wine. They had started to divide the clothing of Jesus. I saw them cast lots for a seamless garment Mary had woven for him. Jesus had treasured it.

And suddenly I remembered a psalm Elisa had recited to me some time ago: "They divide my garments among them and cast lots for my clothes."[2]

I looked at Jesus. He started to pull himself up so that he could breathe again. This is the agony of crucifixion, rising up to catch one's breath and then sagging again. I had never before stopped to watch one. Yet here, the first that I see is my friend Jesus being crucified in his innocence. Unbelievable!

The next time Jesus rose up to catch his breath, he moved more and looked around at all of the people shouting at him. He started to open his mouth. His tongue was dry and cracked. He then looked up into the sky and summoned the strength to speak. The rhythm was halting, but the timbre was surprisingly strong.

"Father, forgive them.

"They do not know what they do."

A hush fell over the crowd. Caiaphas was speechless.

Immediately, one of the others crucified with Jesus turned and spoke between curses. "Are you not the Christ? Save yourself and us as well."

Jesus turned toward him as if to answer, but the other thief shouted at the one who had just spoken. "Have you no fear of God at all? We got the same sentence as he did, but in our case, we deserved it. We are paying for what we did, but this man has done nothing wrong."

He turned to Jesus and said, "Jesus, remember me when you come into your kingdom."

Jesus looked at him and replied, "Indeed, I promise you, today you will be with me in paradise."

Then in exhaustion, Jesus sagged down again. So did the second thief, but I could see that his face had an appearance of peace. The first, on the other hand, continued to curse as he struggled to raise himself to take a breath, then screamed as he sagged down.

Jesus' muscles were cramped again and he could not breathe. He raised himself up and this time looked at the group of women who were shielding Mary. Elisa noticed and she brought Mary and John forward. The other women of Galilee were not far behind. The crowd made a path for them, and they approached to within two paces of the cross.

Jesus cleared his head, shook it a little, and focused his gaze on his mother and John.

"Woman," he said, looking at Mary, "this is your son." Then he turned his eyes toward John. "This is your mother," he said, and sagged down again in utter exhaustion.

Mary was overcome with sobs. This seemed to be a dying wish of Jesus. He had given up all hope. This was more than any of us could stand, but was hardest on Mary.

I started to leave the spot where I had been standing and join the women and the disciple John, but Elisa motioned to me to go back, implying that she could handle the situation.

Then darkness overcame us, and it was still midday. Luke, it was a frightening phenomenon such as I have never before experienced. It had begun so gradually we had not noticed the shadow fall across the sun. In moments, it seemed, the stars appeared against a sky ashen in color.

A deep hush came over the crowd. On order of the centurion, the soldiers drew their swords and stood in battle formation, in case trouble should start. Some people fled in fright, others prayed.

Jesus continued his struggle. I could hear him wheezing and coughing as he breathed. I do not know where all the sweat came from, but he was perspiring still. I could see his skin and I wondered if he was developing the cold sweat of terminal shock.

Jesus was failing rapidly. The periods of standing up on his nailed feet were shorter and the periods of sagging were so much longer. He did not seem to have the strength to rise up. How much longer could this last?

I could hear the labored breathing and knew how rapidly his heart must be beating. Finally he straightened up, shook his head and looked up in misery.

"Lord, Lord." The words were scarcely audible as he repeated a lament from the Psalms. "My God, my God, why have you deserted me?"[3]

Then he sagged down on the cross again.

Luke, Jesus felt that even God had forsaken him. How could that be?

The rabble that had clamored for his death had long since dispersed. Even most of the Sanhedrin and the priests of the Temple had left, unwilling to see the last breaths of this man they had condemned. Elisa, Mary and the others had come forward to stand with me at his feet. John held Mary and Elisa slipped into my arms. By now Jesus could barely lift his head. But he managed to utter in a loud whisper, "I am thirsty."

Of course he was thirsty. He had taken no fluids for twelve hours, yet he continued to perspire and bleed.

One of the soldiers, feeling compassion, dipped a sponge into some vinegar, put it on a hyssop and elevated it to his mouth. Jesus sucked at it for a moment. How good that moisture must have felt, but the vinegar must have burned the cracked places in his mouth, lips and tongue.

Jesus struggled once more to rise up and breathe. Then he spoke.

"It is consummated."

Elisa, pressed against my chest, seemed to be holding her own breath in these last moments.

Jesus took another sip of vinegar from the sponge and uttered his final words.

"Father, into thy hands I commend my spirit." His head bowed forward and he stopped breathing.

Suddenly the earth below us shuddered and rocks split open.

Then the sun broke through and light poured from the heavens.

The centurion was shaken by what he had witnessed. "In truth," he proclaimed, "this was the Son of God."

There we were on the hill at Calvary with three men on crosses. One had just died. One was prayerful and quiet, the other kept cursing and struggling. I wondered how long their suffering would go on. The usual period on a cross was a full day or more.

Elisa and I stepped back from the foot of the cross with tears running down our cheeks. She whispered, "Joseph, God will make it right." But I could not be comforted. I just shook my head and kept my despairing thoughts to myself. "There is no God! Why did he let Jesus suffer so? Jesus called him Abba." But Elisa knew what I was thinking and it hurt her just to know that I would think such things.

The day had grown warm again. The soldiers were restless with their vigil at the crosses, and the few onlookers left were talking in small groups.

Through my tears I saw two well-groomed men conferring to the side. One was Nicodemus. The other, I learned later, was Joseph of Arimathea. I felt some anger that they had not been in their places when the Sanhedrin met and condemned Jesus. Joseph turned and left in the direction of the Fortress of Antonia and Nicodemus in another direction. There was also activity among the remaining priests of the Temple. Two runners were dispatched in the direction of the fortress.

Elisa said, "It is nearing the Sabbath, and the bodies must not stay on the cross during the Sabbath. The priests must do something." In a few minutes, a messenger from Pilate came for the centurion and both left in a run for the fortress.

The struggle of the two thieves continued, but I could see that their strength was waning. Mary was still crying and so were the rest of us. My tears continued. This was brutal.

In a short time, the centurion returned and ordered the executioners to break the legs of the two remaining victims. This is a brutal process in which a wooden beam is placed between the legs, and with that leverage two soldiers breaks the victim's legs. The pain must be excruciating. The victim cannot push himself up to breathe and dies within a short time.

The soldiers began with the first thief. His screams were almost inhuman. Elisa said, "Thank God Jesus was spared that."

Then they stepped over to Jesus and I came forward as if to protect him. He was obviously dead so they looked to the centurion. He motioned for one of his lancers to come forward. The soldier raised his lance and drove it into the right side of the chest of Jesus, into his heart. As he withdrew the spear, out came a clear fluid that had accumulated around the heart and lungs, and then the dark red blood of the heart of Jesus.

As I stood beneath the cross of Jesus a few drops of the pleural fluid and more of his blood fell onto me. The blood of Jesus! The precious blood of my Jesus!

The soldiers used the wooden beam to break the legs of the remaining thief. Now their work was over. They collected the garments of Jesus that they had divided, and the robe for which they had cast lots. At command from the centurion, they formed ranks and marched back to the fortress.

I withdrew to Elisa, who was quoting the Scriptures under her breath. "'Not one bone of his will be broken.'[4]

"'When I was thirsty they gave me vinegar to drink.'[5]

And finally, "'They will look on the one whom they have pierced.'"[6]

Nicodemus returned with a servant, each carrying about fifty pounds of myrrh and aloes. Then Joseph of Arimathea arrived, carrying a long linen cloth he had purchased to cover the body of Jesus.

Elisa and I did not need any signals from them. We left Mary with John and the women and went to prepare Jesus for burial. It would be one of the most difficult tasks we had ever done, but it had to be done before sunset. We knew what to do, for often in Capernaum we were the only ones who would touch the bodies of the dead.

Joseph told us that he had gone to Pilate to ask for the body. Pilate did not believe that Jesus had died so soon and sent for the centurion, who confirmed the death of Jesus. As he returned to Calvary, Joseph had encountered young Mark, who told him the other apostles had begun to gather in his father's home, where they had shared their last meal with Jesus.

Our first task was removal of the body of Jesus from the cross. The nails would have to be removed from his feet. Nails are so scarce that Romans save the ones used in crucifixion. The servant of the centurion was on hand with a curved piece of metal with two prongs on the end, to pull out the nails. At least Jesus did not feel this pain now.

Then, with the body of Jesus hanging by the arms and the feet dangling free, Joseph of Arimathea and I took one end of the crossbeam and Nicodemus and his servant the other. We raised it about one-half cubit and disengaged it from the stipes. Elisa held the feet of Jesus and we carried his body to a grassy spot. There the nails were removed from his hands. I examined him carefully. There were no broken bones, only the stretched ligaments of his foot and displaced cartilage of his nose.

Then John and Mary and the other women came forward. John said, "She wants to hold him on her lap one more time." No one argued. Quickly they arranged some stones for Mary to sit on, and the four of us gently placed the body of Jesus across the lap of his mother, her right arm supporting his back.

His body was completely limp. His right arm dangled down, his face was turned away from her, and his left arm was against her abdomen with his hand on his left thigh. Both of the legs were flexed at the knees.

I do not know where Mary got the strength to hold him. I shall never forget the sight of her holding the battered body of the man she had suckled as a child.

It was nearing sundown and we hated to disturb Mary in her grief but we must hurry. We gently took Jesus to a new sepulcher nearby, which Joseph of Arimathea had just made for his family and in which no one had ever lain.

Near the tomb, we placed the body of Jesus on a stone slab. There was no time to wash and prepare the body for burial. We packed around it the myrrh and aloes and some flowers Salome and Mary the mother of James had gathered. Then we covered it with the linen cloth. It covered the entire front and back of the body. We tore off a narrow piece and wrapped it under Jesus' chin and tied it at the top of his head in order to keep the mouth closed. I took two coins and placed one over each eye. Then we carried the body of Jesus into the tomb. It was cold inside and we were hot.

At the entrance of the tomb there was a large stone. Elisa went in for one last look at Jesus, to be certain the shroud covered him completely. Then we all went out. It took four of us to roll the stone and seal the opening. It was about sunset. Mary the mother of Jesus and Mary of Magdala were sitting at the entrance of the tomb.

Soon a group of Temple guards arrived. I asked why they were there. The leader explained that the chief priests and scribes had marched in a body to Pilate.

"Your Excellency," they had said to him, "we recall that this imposter said, while he was still alive, 'After three days I shall rise again.' Therefore give the order to have the sepulcher kept secure until the third day, for fear his disciples come and steal him away and tell the people, 'He has risen from the dead.' This last piece of fraud would be worse than what went before."

"You have your guard," Pilate had told them. "Go and make all as secure as you know how." So they had left and sent this guard. We watched as the guards put seals on the stone and then took their assigned positions.

The leader ordered us to leave. Mary was reluctant, but the guards became gruff and did not want anyone near. We appealed to Mary to come to Bethany with us but she was still loathe to leave. It grew dark. Finally we started back to the home of Mary, Martha and Lazarus but without John, who left to find Peter and the other apostles and tell them how Jesus had died.

It was a quiet walk back. Salome was supporting the mother of Jesus, so Elisa and I walked together. I could not even talk. I was in a daze from all that had happened in the last day and a half. Elisa knew that I would need to talk, but this was not the time. So we all walked along in silence.

It was late when we got to Bethany. Martha prepared a light meal. None of us could eat. Her sister was distraught when she heard the news.

Finally, Martha took the mother of Jesus to her room and motioned us to go to ours. I was exhausted but once Elisa and I were alone, I felt compelled to voice my despair.

"How could God allow this to happen? Jesus was crucified. He is dead, He is dead."

Elisa's eyes were shadowed with grief as well. But she spoke with conviction. "He said that he will rise again on the third day."

"How? How can he? It just does not happen!"

"He said that he would rise on the third day. Jesus said that he would rise on the third day."

Luke, I am devastated. I have no hope.

Joseph

---

1   Bloody sweat coming through the unbroken skin is a medical condition.

2   Psalms 22:18

3   Psalms 22:1

4   Psalms 34:20

5   Psalms 69:21

6   Zechariah 12:10

Letter 118

Luke, I had a horrible night. I did go to sleep, but I awakened in about two hours and just lay there. Everything that had happened to Jesus passed through my mind, beginning with his suffering in the garden, the cruel treatment by the soldiers and guards, and the trial at the Sanhedrin. I did not even attempt to defend him, not then, not at the home of the high priest, not at the trials by Pilate and Herod, not at the terrible scourging. I did not even offer to carry the heavy beam for Jesus on the way to Calvary. Then I relived his hours of suffering beyond any human imagination on the cross. I could give him no comfort, nothing to drink while his blood dropped upon me under the cross. Why? Oh why? Oh why? Where was God his Father? Or was he the Son of God? Or is there a God? If there is, why did he let this happen to Jesus? Had I really heard a voice on the mountain say, "This is my beloved son, in whom I am well pleased"?

I wish I had the faith of Elisa. She slept soundly. She was convinced that Jesus would rise again. I even wondered if she really was in her right mind. She has always been so stable, but now, Luke, I just do not know.

I must have dozed a little because I heard a rooster crow. I awoke with a start, and in my thoughts I was back in the garden again hearing Peter's denials of knowing Jesus. I also had denied him.

Finally Elisa stirred. I told her of my sleepless night. She put her arms around me and spoke softly. "Joseph, we must trust in God. He will make it all right." But I was not sure that there was a God!

Elisa went to see Mary the mother of Jesus, who had been in the room of Martha and Mary. I waited outside of the room. I could hear the two Marys sobbing, but soon, with Elisa present, they stopped and all three of them came out of the room. Martha had prepared a light breakfast. I was not able to eat. My stomach just could not take any food. Elisa reached over to me, squeezed my hand and again said, "Joseph, it will come out all right."

Luke, I tried to believe but I did not. Elisa made sure that Martha would care for the two Marys and led me out to the garden where we sat. I poured my heart out to her. I told her about my loss of belief in God. Our leader was gone and had died under such punishment. I am disillusioned, disgusted and confused. We had followed Jesus for months and months. He had not taught me his secret of healing. We had listened to many of his teachings and they had sounded good. But really, Luke, they are so impractical. In our society, money brings success. All of the wealthy have the highest places in the synagogues. The poor are considered lazy and not worthy to come to the Temple. The prostitutes, if caught in the act, are stoned to death but the men who patronize them, usually the wealthy citizens of high rank, are not touched. But Jesus asked us to feed the poor, visit the prisoners and love our enemies. He ate with prostitutes and with tax collectors and forgave them their sins. It makes good sense to do what he did, but what it won for him was a death by crucifixion. I ranted like this for a long time.

Elisa listened quietly. "When you came down from the mountain, you told me that you heard the voice of God say, 'This is my beloved Son.' You were convinced then that he was the Son of God." She was right.

'But if he was the Son of God, why did not God send legions of angels to save him?"

"He said three times that he would rise after three days. Don't you believe that? I want to go to Jerusalem in the morning and see this." It sounded ridiculous to me. Then I reconsidered. I half-believed and I half-doubted. But she was right. This should settle the matter.

We told Mary the mother of Jesus about our plans. She decided that she would go too. Jesus had been buried in such a hurry, she said, that his body was unwashed. Therefore we would go to the grave and wash and perfume his body in the early morning.

By now it was time to go to the synagogue. Elisa insisted. I went in body, but my heart was not in it. I was back in my thoughts again. I do not even remember what the readings were or any of the teachings. As we returned Elisa suggested that we go back out to the garden. There she selected a bench under the shade of an olive tree and sat down. As I sat beside her, she reached out and held my hand and then she started to quote from the Scriptures. Luke, she has an incredible memory. I had heard these passages read at the synagogue, but she knew them by memory.

"Joseph, I remember what Isaiah said:
We had all gone astray like sheep,
each taking his own way,
and the Lord burdened him
with the sins of all of us.
Harshly dealt with, he bore it humbly,
he never opened his mouth,
like a lamb that is led to the slaughter-house,
like a sheep that is dumb before its shearers,

never opening its mouth.
By force and by law he was taken.
Would anyone plead his cause?
Yes, he was torn away from the land of the living,
for our faults struck down in death.
They gave him a grave with the wicked,
a tomb with the rich,
though he had done no wrong
and there had been no perjury in his mouth.
The Lord has been pleased to crush him with suffering.
If he offers his life in atonement,
he shall see his heirs, he shall have a long life
and through him what the Lord wishes will be done.[1]

When she finished she asked, "Do you not believe the prophet Isaiah had Jesus in mind? He has described his crucifixion."

Then Elisa got up and motioned to me to walk with her a while. I did.

"Joseph," she said, "there are sections of Holy Writ that are meaningful in the light of what had happened. Listen to these passages." She hesitated and then recited one after another.

"'Yet he was pierced through for our faults, crushed for our sins.'[2]

"'I offered my back to those who struck me, my cheeks to those who tore at my beard. I did not cover my face against insult and spittle.'[3]

"'They divide my garments among them, and cast lots for my clothes.'"[4]

Then she stopped, looked up at the clear sky and said, "Joseph, do you suppose that God, in His saving action throughout the centuries, had all of this in His almighty plan and used the prophets to give some hints of it? You know, Jesus said that he must fulfill the Scriptures. Don't you agree?"

Luke, I stood there and looked at her. She was so beautiful, there in the garden, so confident, so resolute, that I began to believe in God again.

It was time for a meal and Elisa said, "Joseph, please try to eat something. You have not had a good meal since Passover." This time I was able to eat. Elisa's calmness had finally affected me.

May God be with you, Luke. I am not so sure that He is here in Jerusalem.

Joseph

[1]   Isaiah 53:6-10

[2]   Isaiah 53:5

[3]   Isaiah 50:6

[4]   Psalms 22:18

Letter 119

Luke, I have news of such great joy to share.

We were up long before dawn, having planned to get to the tomb at sunrise. Martha planned to stay in Bethany with her brother and her sister, Mary, who was too upset to leave. Joanna, Salome and the other women of Galilee had decided to join us. Mary of Magdala collected some spices and Mary the mother of James the Lesser a jar of water and some cloths, to wash the body of Jesus, bind it and prepare it for burial. Everyone except Elisa agreed that it was necessary. Then we set out, each carrying something.

It was dark, so very dark. I did not talk much. There were few travelers along the road. In due time we came to the Mount of Olives. There were still many pilgrims camped along the roadside. They were packing their belongings for the long trek back home after the Passover. I recalled how many times I had done this with my mother and father and sister.

Gethsemane was in the distance. It was too dark to see the olive grove where Jesus had knelt, but I resolved to return and see if I could find spots on the ground where Jesus had sweated blood. We walked on quietly and rapidly. As we reached the city, people were already coming and going through the gate.

The quickest way to the tomb of Jesus was through a corner of the city, past the Temple and the Fortress of Antonia, and up the path to Calvary, the same route we had taken on the day before the Sabbath as we followed Jesus on his way to his death.

Temple guards were around, but they did not bother us. Roman guards stopped us as we approached the Fortress of Antonia, but when we told them where we were going, they let us go.

It was getting lighter now, so it was easier to see the way. We reached the top of the hill of Golgotha where several stipeses were still in place. Each of us turned our heads away from the sight quickly, not wanting to be reminded of the horrible death of Jesus. We turned down the path to the right to the family tomb of Joseph of Arimathea.

As we approached, Mary of Magdala asked, "Who will roll away the stone from the tomb?" We had no answer. We knew it took four men using all of their strength to roll it into place three days ago. We approached the tomb quietly. The Temple guards stationed at the tomb might drive us away if they heard us.

I went first, drawing as near as 20 cubits to the tomb, and could see the guards in position. They were moving their arms and legs to stay awake. I looked at the tomb, and the huge rock was still in place as we had left it.

But then, Luke, there was a violent earthquake. Stones rolled all around us, the shrubs shook and we became frightened. At that instant, a man in dazzling white clothing with a brilliant glow around his face came and rolled the stone away.

I looked at the guards and they were all lying on the ground. I stepped closer to one and saw he had a frightened look on his face. I felt his pulse and it was slow and regular. I observed his breathing and it, too, was regular. His eyes were open but he did not react when I waved my hand in front of his eyes. The other guards were in similar condition. I made this observation in a few moments and went back to the women. They were looking at the man who had rolled back the stone, who then spoke.

"There is no need for you to be afraid. I know that you are looking for Jesus, who was crucified. He is not here, for he has risen as he said that he would.

"Come and see the place where he lay, then go quickly to tell the disciples. He has risen from the dead and now he is going before you to Galilee. It is there that you will see him. Now, I have told you," and he disappeared.

We moved toward the sepulcher, past the guards who did not move. We came to the opening of the tomb. It was quiet. There was no odor, as one would expect at this time. We cautiously peeked, then stepped inside. Jesus' body was not there. We stood there not knowing what to think or do.

The linen cloth that Elisa had so carefully tucked around the body of Jesus was lying folded. The facial chin wrapping was also there. The cloth that had been over his head was rolled up in a place to itself. The coins that had covered his eyes lay where the head of Jesus had been placed.

Luke, if someone had taken his body to steal it, they would have taken the coins too.

But why would anyone want to steal the body of Jesus? No one wanted to touch the body of the dead. And few, other than Joseph of Arimathea, Nicodemus, the Temple guards and the chief priest, knew where Jesus was buried. I looked at the women and they appeared as confused as I was. We did not know what to do.

Suddenly two more men in bright clothing appeared, one on each side of our group. Where they came from I do not know. We had the entrance blocked. There was no other way into the tomb.

Who were they? Where were they from? What would they do to us? I was frightened, though Elisa remained calm. So did the mother of Jesus.

The two then spoke in unison. "Why look among the dead for someone who is alive? Remember what he told you when he was still in Galilee, that the Son of Man had to be handed over into the power of sinful men and be crucified and rise again on the third day."

Elisa spoke first. "He is risen!"

Suddenly, the angels disappeared and we were again standing at the empty tomb of Jesus. There was a look of absolute joy on the faces of Elisa and the mother of Jesus. But the rest of us were still confused and worried.

The sun had risen and it was bright outside. Mary of Magdala was uneasy and said that she needed to step outside the tomb, so I followed her.

She had walked but twenty steps when she encountered a man whom she took to be the caretaker. The man asked, "Woman, why are you weeping? Who are you looking for?" Mary replied, "Sir, if you have taken him away, tell me where you have put him and I will go and remove him."

The man spoke softly. "Mary," he said. And suddenly, Luke, I realized it was Jesus standing before us. He was fully clothed, his brow smooth, his hair and beard clean. There was no apparent sign of the bloody scourging he had endured.

"Rabboni! Master!" Mary of Magdala exclaimed.

His words calmed her. "Do not cling to me because I am not yet ascended to the Father. But go and find the brothers and tell them, 'I am ascending to my Father and your Father, to my God and to your God.'" And he was gone. I realized that I had not seen his hands or his feet. They were covered with his robes.

Mary of Magdala had not moved. I came to her and said, "I saw and heard it all. It was Jesus. Let us go and tell his mother and the others." We did and they cried out in joy, embracing one another with tears in their eyes.

"We must go and tell the disciples," Mary of Magdala said with a new sense of purpose.

"They are probably at the home of Mark's father where they had the Passover meal," I said.

We hurried through the streets of Jerusalem, bypassing the Temple where the morning worshippers were gathering and crowding the area.

Soon, we were at the home of Mark's father. I showed them to the entrance of the Upper Room where the Passover meal had taken place. There was no activity around the house. I knocked and heard someone walking to the door. Slowly and cautiously, the cover of the peephole in the door was opened.

"It is Joseph," I said, "one of the company. With me are Mary the mother of Jesus and other women of the company. We have much to tell you. Please let us in."

The door opened slowly and there was Peter. His hair and beard were uncombed, his clothing crumpled, and there was a look of fear on his face. He opened the door just enough to let us in and bolted it again. The room was full of the disciples, who were just waking up. John looked as if he hadn't slept at all.

Peter said, "Don't talk loud. We are afraid that they will come for us and crucify us for following Jesus." But Mary of Magdala could not restrain herself. She exclaimed, "Jesus has risen!"

Peter looked confused. "What did you just say?" The other disciples got up quickly and crowded around us.

We all shouted joyfully, "Jesus has risen!"

"I don't believe it," Peter said. "He could not. It isn't possible."

Mary of Magdala then related all that we had seen that morning. Peter and the others listened quietly, but I could tell by their faces they did not believe her. He turned to the mother of Jesus. "Mary, do you believe that foolish story?"

"Peter, I was there. I know that it is true."

Peter then questioned Joanna, Salome and Mary the mother of James. They also confirmed it.

He looked at Elisa, whom he respected as a physician and as a learned woman. "Elisa, do you believe that Jesus rose from the dead?"

Elisa repeated what we had just seen and heard at the tomb. Peter was visibly shocked at her answer. Then he turned to me. "Joseph, you are a learned man, you know more than any of us. You know this is not true, don't you?"

I directed my response to all of the disciples. "Brothers, for months and months we have been following Jesus and listening to his teachings. Do you not remember that he said several times, 'The Son of Man has to be handed over into the power of sinful men and be crucified and rise on the third day'? Well, that is exactly what happened. Come and see for yourselves."

John the Beloved Disciple stepped forward. "Come, Peter, let us run and see." As he pushed Peter to the door, Peter muttered, "I cannot believe it, but I will go." He unbolted the door and the two took off in a run.

John's brother James said, "Let's go too," and the rest took off at a fast gait. I turned to Elisa and said, "Come when you can but Mary needs to rest here." She nodded and I took off. It did not take me long to overtake the apostles.

The tomb was just as we had left it. The soldiers were lying down and were not moving. The stone was still rolled back and the tomb was open. John stopped at the entrance and stepped aside, allowing Peter to enter first. I followed.

The linen cloths were where we last had seen them, and the tomb was empty. John spoke first. "I believe!"

Peter said, "Jesus told us several times that he would die and rise the third day, but I did not understand what he was saying. Now I believe. Why was I so thickheaded when Jesus told us three times? I believe. I believe."

He then turned to me. "Joseph, is this what you found when you entered?" I answered, "Exactly as it is now."

Just then there was a commotion on the outside. As I looked out, the guards were coming out of their trance and were surrounded by the disciples. All but three took off in various directions. The leader and two others remained but were dazed and frightened. They did not know what to do.

I stepped out toward them and spoke. "Shalom. Do not be afraid. Jesus has risen. Come and see for yourselves."

The leader looked at me and smiled, which is unusual for a Temple guard. I looked at the others, and they also had lost their fear. Peter and John came out of the tomb and joined the others.

The officer addressed me. "I saw it all, the earthquake, the man in white garments rolling back the stone, you and the women entering the tomb, and now you returning. I saw and heard your confusion. It was as if I were paralyzed. I could see and hear but I could not move. But a moment ago, I came to."

Boldly I said, "Jesus has risen. Come see for yourself." We ushered the three into the tomb and they saw everything as we had found it. Two by two the other apostles also went in, looked around and came out. "He is risen!" each said in wonderment.

I described to the guards the two men who had suddenly appeared to us in the tomb earlier, and what they had said. The leader said, "Who was this man Jesus? I must learn more, but we must first report to the chief priests." Off they marched.

Now Elisa and Joanna were approaching. Elisa went directly to the place where we had laid Jesus and picked up the long linen cloth and the facial wrapping. Now, Luke, the Law forbids Jews to touch the clothing or wrappings used on one who has been buried. But Elisa said with determination, "This cloth was last wrapped around Jesus, and I shall keep it."

I could see that Peter was about to object, so I quickly signaled him not to do it. There was no use to argue or to remind her of the Law. She knew it as well or better than any of us did.

As we walked out of the tomb, I started to worry about what the guards would tell the chief priests. I asked Elisa to go back with Joanna and the disciples to the Upper Room. I would go to the Temple and see what I could learn. She nodded her approval.

I caught up to the Temple guards just as they approached the chief priests in the portico. The leader of the guards stepped forward to Caiaphas and described exactly what had happened in every detail. I knew now that he had heard and seen it all.

The priests looked at each other in dismay. One asked, "Where are the other guards?" The leader answered, "Three of my group ran away as soon as they recovered their strength, but two came here with me."

"Bring them here. We must question them," Caiaphas replied. The test of truth is that two witnesses agree in separate testimony.

The two were brought forward and each was interrogated alone. But their testimony confirmed everything that the leader had told them, and they could not be swayed from their stories. The chief priest spat in anger, dismissed the witnesses and told the guards to keep them separated. The priests conferred privately, then one left in a hurry.

Finally, Caiaphas asked for the return of the three tomb guards. He dismissed the other Temple guards and cleared the area, but I stepped behind a pillar and stayed behind. The priest who had left came back with a heavy sack, and he gave it to the high priest. As the three guards stood at attention, Caiaphas addressed them. "I will give two hundred gold coins to each one of the guards who was present and saw this. But you must say, 'His disciples came during the night and stole him while we were asleep.' Should the governor come to hear of this, we will undertake to put things right with him ourselves and to see that you do not get into trouble."

The leader stood quietly, but the other two soldiers eagerly agreed. The priest with the bag counted out six hundred gold coins and gave two hundred to each of the guards. The leader remained at attention and the priest replaced the last two hundred in the sack and attached it to the leader's leather belt. The chief priest then dismissed them. The two ran out but the leader saluted and walked slowly. As he passed he spotted me and motioned that I follow him. As he passed the box for donations to the Temple, he dropped into it the purse of gold coins. We walked together out of the Temple gate, and he told me where he lived and said that he wanted to learn more about Jesus. I promised to contact him. He saluted and went to the quarters of the Temple Guard.

Just then I heard the priests approaching, congratulating themselves on the deal they had made with the guards. "But are you sure," Caiaphas said, "that we have also silenced those in the Temple who repaired the curtain at the sanctuary?" Luke, the heavy curtain had been torn from top to bottom at the time of the earthquake.

"Yes" was the answer. "They too have been well-paid."

Then I rushed off to the house of Mark's father to tell the disciples, Elisa, and the other women of the deceit of the high priest.

As I arrived I could hear conversation coming from the Upper Room. I knocked on the door, for it was again bolted. Peter let me in and there were the disciples and the women. They had all been discussing their experiences of that morning. Peter asked what I had learned at the Temple. I described everything that I had seen and heard in the discussions of the chief priests and the leaders of the Temple guards, including the torn curtain at the Temple.

"So they still do not believe," Peter said. He had hoped that the chief priests would accept the truth about Jesus now. But it was obvious that they would not. "We must confront them with the truth. But we must not use violence. We must act as Jesus taught us and show love for those who do us harm." Luke, not two days before, Peter had denied Jesus three times, out of fear for his own life, and fled in tears and despair. Today, knowing that Jesus is risen, he has begun to put aside his own fears and assume a role of leadership.

"We must all have the courage that comes from our faith in Jesus," Peter said, "and stay in groups if we can. We do have the instructions that the angels gave to the women in the tomb, that he would go to Galilee and we are to meet him there. Let us wait a day or two until it is safe, then proceed to Galilee." No one disagreed.

It was about the noon hour and Mark's father offered the hospitality of the midday meal. I was famished. I had not eaten much for two days. I ate well but noticed that Elisa had eaten just a few bites. I assumed that she had lost her appetite because of all the excitement. But that would be unusual.

I asked her how she felt and she said that she was just tired and wanted to go to Bethany to rest for the afternoon. We thanked Mark's father, bid goodbye to the apostles and set out for Bethany. Most of the other women returned with us, but Mary of Magdala stayed with Peter and the others.

We spent some time telling Martha, Mary and Lazarus what had happened. By this time, Elisa was visibly tired. She folded the linen cloth that she had been carrying and laid it on a cushion in our room. She did not need any urging to lie down and was asleep in a moment.

I felt her pulse and it was steady. Her skin did not feel warm. Her color was good and her breathing was even. I sat there and held her hand. I must have dozed because about an hour later, she stirred and I awoke with a start. She smiled and said with a twinkle in her eye, "Joseph, you were sleepy too." We both laughed.

Then she said, "I wonder if Abraham knows all that happened. Joseph, please go and tell him everything. I am too tired to go and I will rest this afternoon and evening."

"It will be late when I come back. Are you sure that you will be all right?"

"All I need is some rest. But check on Mary the mother of Jesus before you go." I kissed her and left. Mary was peacefully sleeping, so I set out for Jerusalem.

When I arrived at the clinic, the last patient was being seen. Abraham was glad to see me. First, he inquired about Elisa and I told him of her present fatigue. He frowned and said, "Watch her carefully, Joseph. This may be an indication of some other condition." I said that I would.

Then I asked him if he had heard of the events of the past few days. He replied, "Who has not heard of the crucifixion of Jesus of Nazareth? I had such hopes that he was a prophet for our times. But he was crucified like a criminal and I am disappointed."

I began to tell him all that we had seen and heard that very morning. He could not accept the fact that Jesus had risen from the dead.

"Joseph, you know that is not possible."

"I know that it is beyond our scientific knowledge. But God can do unusual things."

Abraham thought a moment. "Does Elisa believe he has risen?" I knew that he had much more faith in her judgment than he had in mine. He should have. He had trained her more years than he had trained me. I answered, "Yes, completely." But I knew that he would not be satisfied until he had heard it from her.

Abraham invited me to share the evening meal with his family. It was a pleasant meal, but Abraham's wife, a very devout person, had difficulty accepting any change from the way things have been done since the time of Moses. I explained that Jesus came to fulfill the promises in the Scriptures. I told of the teachings of Jesus to love your enemy, to feed and clothe the poor, give shelter to the homeless.

Imagine, Luke, there I was boldly repeating what Jesus had taught and practiced. As I finished, I wondered to myself if I really followed these principles.

I recounted what had happened in Jerusalem in the last few days — the trial of Jesus, the scourging, the crucifixion, the burial, my day and two nights of depression, and then the events of this day. Abraham and his wife listened, she in disbelief. Abraham had many questions, especially about the bloody sweat. He had a look on his face as if he wanted to believe but just could not accept the risen Jesus.

It was now dark and I prepared to leave. Abraham put on his tunic, saying that he would accompany me a short way. He told his wife that he would be late in returning.

As we got outside, Abraham asked, "Could we stop by to see these men who were his disciples? I want to meet them." I was pleased that he was interested. I was also worried. He would meet several men with little or no education. Peter spoke in the simple words of a fisherman. I was afraid that he would be unimpressed with the apostles.

It was just a short distance to the home of Mark's father. I knocked on the door. Before it could be unbolted, there was a noise behind us and I flinched. I feared that a contingency of soldiers had arrived to arrest us.

I turned and saw two men running up to us. They were unarmed. As they came closer, I recognized Cleopas and another of the followers of

Jesus. Peter had recognized my voice and by now had unbolted the door. Cleopas and his companion ran past us and entered ahead of us. Before I could introduce Abraham, Cleopas exclaimed, "Wait until I tell you what we have just experienced! Listen! Listen!

"We were on our way to Emmaus and were talking about the events that had just happened to Jesus. Now, a man came suddenly and joined us walking and listened as we spoke. He asked, 'What matters are you discussing as you walk along?' We stopped short, our faces downcast. I answered him. 'You must be the only person staying in Jerusalem who does not know the things that have been happening there these last few days.'

"'What things?' he asked. 'All about Jesus of Nazareth,' we answered. 'He proved he was a great prophet by the things he said and did in the sight of God and the whole people and how the chief priests and our leaders handed him over to be sentenced to death and had him crucified. Our own hope had been that he would be the one who could set Israel free. And this is not all. Two days have gone by since it all happened, and some women from our group have astounded us. They went to the tomb in the early morning, and when they did not find the body, they came back to tell us they had seen a vision of angels who declared that Jesus was alive. Some of our friends went to the tomb and found everything exactly as the women had reported, but of him, they saw nothing.'

"Then the stranger said to us, 'You foolish men! So slow to believe the full message of the prophets. Was it not ordained that the Christ should suffer and so enter into his glory?' Then, starting with Moses and going through all of the prophets, he explained to us the passages throughout the Scriptures that were about the Messiah.

"At this time, we had come into the village of Emmaus, and our new companion acted as if he were going farther. We pressed him to stay with us. It is nearly evening, we said, and the day is almost over.

"He finally consented to stay with us. It had been a long day and we were hungry, so we reclined to eat, with our new friend as our guest. He took the bread and said the blessing. Then he broke it and handed it to us. At that point, our eyes were opened and we recognized our new friend as Jesus.

"Yes, it was Jesus all of the time, but we were kept from recognizing him. As soon as we recognized him, he vanished from our sight. We were suddenly alone. We rose instantly and returned to Jerusalem to tell all of you."

Every one in the room was amazed. All the apostles were there but one. Thomas had stepped out to help a widow gather firewood. We all questioned them and they went over the story again.

And then, Luke, Jesus appeared, there in the Upper Room with us!

"Peace be with you," he said. But we were all alarmed.

"Why are you so agitated and why are there these doubts rising in your hearts?" Jesus said. "Look at my hands and my feet. Yes, it is I, indeed. Touch me and see for yourselves. A ghost has no flesh and bones as you can see that I have." As he said this, he showed us his hands and his feet.

Luke, we all looked, but Abraham and I looked as only physicians would look. Jesus' wrists had large wounds. Now these wounds were three days old. You know that old wounds are crusted, drain pus and have a foul odor. There was no odor nor any pus. The wounds were clean, as if they were freshly made, but there was no bleeding. The foot wounds were like the wrist wounds, clean and with no infection.

He also showed us the chest wound. The skin was gaping open and the inner muscles were visible. But there was no bleeding, no crusty blood, no pus and no serum oozing. To the side of the exposed chest wound, there were lash marks and hemorrhaging beneath the skin. Jesus did not expose his back because of his modesty. Mary of Magdala was still there, standing to one side of the apostles, with Jesus in front of them. Abraham and I were behind him. Abraham looked very closely at his wounds. Then I could see that he was convinced that this was really Jesus.

Yet the rest still could not believe what they saw. So Jesus spoke again. "Have you anything here to eat?" And one of the disciples offered him some grilled fish. He took and ate it before our eyes.

Luke, spirits and visions do not eat as humans do. This proved beyond any doubt that Jesus was fully alive again. He had risen and was present in his human flesh with the marks of his scourging and crucifixion. He ate grilled fish in front of everyone in the room. Then Jesus spoke again.

"This is what I meant when I said, while I was still with you, that everything written about me in the Law of Moses, in the Prophets and in the Psalms has to be fulfilled." He then explained the Scriptures so that we understood them as we never had before.

"It is written that the Christ would suffer and on the third day, rise from the dead. And that in his name, repentance for the forgiveness of sins would be preached to all the nations, beginning from Jerusalem. You are witnesses to that. And now, I am sending to you what the Father has promised. Stay in the city then, until you are clothed in the power of the Most High."

We all listened very intently. I could not get the real meaning of the last statement. I would have to ponder that with Elisa.

Jesus continued. "Peace be with you. As the Father sent me, so I am sending you." Then he breathed on each of the ten men. "Receive the Holy Spirit. For those whose sins you forgive, they are forgiven. For those whose sins you retain, they are retained." What all of this really meant was not clear to us at that moment.

Jesus then vanished from our sight and we stood in silence for a long time. We had all seen the Lord ourselves, and he had given the ten a special power, to forgive or retain sins. They did not look any different, but they had received a commission from Jesus to continue his work on Earth.

"We will have to tell Thomas about this when he returns," Peter said. Andrew shook his head. "You know that Doubting Thomas won't believe it until he sees it for himself."

Finally, I had the opportunity to introduce Abraham to the group. They were pleased that a man of his education, knowledge and stature had experienced what they had seen and heard. Everyone began talking at once. I noticed that Abraham spent much time talking to Peter and Mary of Magdala.

It was very late and time to leave. Abraham took me aside at the door. "Joseph, thank you for bringing me.

"I know now that I have seen the Messiah. He is not the type of Messiah that the Jewish people had expected. He seems to be far better. I must return and tell my wife. Another thing, Joseph. Did you hear him state that in his name, repentance for the forgiveness of sins would be preached to all the nations beginning from Jerusalem? He did not come just for the Jews but for all nations. Greeks, Romans, Canaanites, Assyrians — all will hear the gospel of repentance for the forgiveness of sins."

Abraham fell silent in thought. Then he said, "I really wanted to see Elisa and examine her, but it is too late now. Check her over carefully. She has been very active and it may be consumption again. But she was so well when I examined her a few days ago. I doubt it is phthisis."

He smiled. "Perhaps she is with child.

"Take care of her and return to Capernaum. I want to hear more about Jesus. I will visit with Peter and the rest of the group here, but I want to bring my wife to visit you someday in Capernaum. God bless you." And he left.

My mind was in turmoil, my thoughts focused on one statement, "Perhaps she is with child." Finally it all made sense. Elisa had been nauseated for several days but had not vomited. She had not eaten much. She had no fever, cough, chest pain, rapid breathing or elevation of her pulse, all of which one would expect of phthisis. Oh, how dumb of me not to think of it. Here I have diagnosed pregnancy in many women and missed it in my wife.

I hardly listened to John as he told me that he would remain again in Jerusalem with the other apostles tonight, but leave for Bethany in the morning to care for the mother of Jesus as he had requested from the cross.

I found Mary of Magdala and the two of us left. I was in a hurry to see my beloved Elisa. As we left the disciples, they praised God and sang with joy. We hurried through the dark streets and soon were at the home of Martha, Mary and Lazarus. It was quiet. Everyone was asleep.

I went to the room where Elisa was sleeping peacefully. My dearest wife and mother of our child, I thought, I will never leave you again. I sat down and took her hand. I held it a long time.

I finally lay down beside her. She awakened and put her arms around me and said, "Welcome back." I said, "I love you, my darling!" She said, "I love you too." Off to sleep we went.

Joseph

Letter 120

Luke, I had a restless night wondering how Elisa would do with her pregnancy. Of course, many physicians believe that women with consumption who become pregnant should have the rod to have an abortion, even though the pelvic infections that develop are almost always fatal, and those women who survive often become sterile. But, Luke, the Oath of Hippocrates you and I took forbids inducing an abortion. That would be taking a human life. And Abraham never used or recommended using the rod. He believes that a woman with the disease can have children but she must rest more. Those were our plans.

It was a long night. I saw the sunrise but then I must have fallen asleep again. Elisa was awake at the usual time. It took me a moment to realize where I was. Elisa smiled. "Sorry I awakened you."

"Oh, I am glad," I replied. "How do you feel?"

"I'm fine," she said. "I have something to share with you, but you do not stay in one place long enough for me to talk to you.

"Joseph, we have a baby in my womb. I have missed my flow, my breasts are fuller, I am nauseated and, Joseph, it just has to be that." She reached out to me for an embrace and we held each other for a long time. Then I told her of Abraham's observations and his instructions to me. She said, "Let's send a messenger to him, telling him the good news. But first let's tell Mary the mother of Jesus."

We dressed and went to find her. She was in the garden. She could see the joy in our faces as we came up. "What makes you so happy?" Elisa said, "We have a baby in my womb." Mary got up and embraced her and tears came into her eyes. "And if the baby is a girl," Elisa continued, "we will name her Mary." Then we told Martha, Mary and Lazarus. Soon the household was jubilant.

At morning prayers we gave thanks that Jesus had risen, and Elisa and I added our prayer for a successful pregnancy and a healthy baby. Then we sat down to the morning meal and Elisa was able to eat more. Mary of Magdala and I finally had the opportunity to recount everything that had happened in the Upper Room, how Jesus had appeared and commissioned the apostles with the ability to forgive sins.

Then I told the group that Abraham had said we must return to Capernaum if Elisa is with child, and that she must rest more. They knew of the consumption and all understood. We must leave as soon as possible.

How fortunate that we had brought our donkey so that Elisa could ride.

The other women in our company were not yet ready to return to Galilee and planned to attach themselves later to other groups of pilgrims making the return journey north.

I wrote a note to Abraham and also one to Peter telling them of our plans. I gave them to a servant, with a coin to deliver them. Elisa was to rest in the afternoon while I obtained provisions. We would join a caravan on the morrow.

Late in the afternoon, after I had returned, Martha came and said there was someone to see me.

I went outside and there was Deborah of Ephraim, the physician who had trained with Elisa under Abraham. I had met her several times when Elisa and I were in Jerusalem.

I was thrilled to see her and said that I would awaken Elisa. Deborah shook her head. "I don't want to see her. I just came to see you, Joseph. I was visiting Abraham when your messenger brought him the note. Abraham was pleased. I was shocked! I decided to come see you."

She looked stern. "Joseph, you must use the rod. You cannot let her carry that child. She will die and it will be your fault.

"Joseph, I am surprised at you. She must not have that child!" Then she turned and left.

Martha came out. "That was a short visit," she said. "It surely was," I said, not trusting myself to explain at that moment. I went into the garden and sat. Deborah's voice continued to ring in my mind, saying "She will die. … She will die." Then I prayed to Jesus. I poured my heart out to him. Gradually my fears disappeared. I knew that everything would be all right because he would be with us.

I went inside and found Elisa awake. I sat down beside her and told her of Deborah's visit. She laughed and said, "I expected that from Deborah. She gets overly excited. She didn't mean it at all." Then she held my hands and spoke softly. "Joseph, I will be all right. I know that I will." Nothing more was said about this incident, Luke.

It was a joyful evening meal. We celebrated the new life and prayed for a safe trip. Later we finished packing our belongings, including instruments and medication. We retired early, the three of us.

Joseph

Capernaum

Letter 121

Greetings, dear Luke, from Capernaum. We arrived after a remarkably pleasant journey of six days. I wanted Elisa to ride, but she was determined to walk as much as she could. I had to remind myself that she is a physician and knows her limitations, so I should let her do what she feels that she can do. So part of the time we walked, holding hands and singing. Then she would ride a short time while I led the donkey. Then she walked. She was able to eat well.

During the journey we tried to recall everything that had happened to commit it to memory. I repeated the stories of the Passover meal, the agony Jesus suffered in the garden, the arrest, the trial, the appearance before Pilate and Herod so many times that Elisa knew them as well as I. She knew about the walk up Calvary Hill, the crucifixion and death only too well, for she had been with Mary, Jesus' mother. In the retelling, we would each have different observations, and so we were able to piece together one long story.

In the evening around the campfire we talked to everyone about Jesus, the Messiah. Many listened, sometimes one, sometimes ten. Most had heard of the trial and the crucifixion while they were in Jerusalem. None had heard that Jesus had come back to life and walked among us. I do not know how many believed.

On our arrival at Capernaum, we went to visit Erasmus and Sarah first and told them there are now three of us. I could tell that Erasmus was pleased and so was Sarah. Then we told them briefly how Jesus had died and risen. Sarah's face showed disbelief and shock that we would say such nonsense. Erasmus was more reserved. "Ach!" he exclaimed. "What kind of wine did they give you for the Passover meal?" We insisted that what we were saying was true and tried to explain how Jesus had fulfilled the scriptural promises. Erasmus seemed interested but Sarah was not. Elisa said, "Mother, tomorrow I will spend the day with you and discuss this further."

Then we went to see Joseph and Mary, my parents. When we told them about the baby they were very happy, but I knew my mother would fret every day for seven more months. Elisa said, "Please don't worry. Everything will be all right." We did not try to explain what had happened to Jesus.

Then to our home. We had been gone several weeks but Mary and Sarah had kept it clean. How we have changed since we left. We saw Jesus crucified, dead and buried, yet he rose and appeared to us. He lives! The Scriptures have been fulfilled.

And now there are three of us. God is good!

Joseph

Letter 122

Dear Luke, I arose early this morning to make my rounds. Erasmus had informed me of the patients he had been seeing in their homes. I planned to see them early and get to the clinic about midmorning. As I walked out on the portico I saw my parents working in the orchard. They stopped and came to me. My father had a stern look on his face. "Joseph, what is this I hear about Jesus? The other travelers in your caravan are saying he was crucified as a criminal and that the two of you are saying he came back to life."

The travelers had stayed in town overnight, and by morning rumors were spreading throughout Capernaum.

I sat down on a log and began to tell the entire story. I even quoted the Scriptures to show how in his death and resurrection Jesus had fulfilled the promises of God. After I completed my story my mother was quiet and thoughtful, but I knew that my father had doubts. He said, "We raised you not to do anything that would cause a black mark upon your name. Consider Elisa and your new child!"

"But this is all true," I replied. "It did occur." Then they left.

Elisa had come out on the portico and heard the end of the conversation. She said simply, "It is not easy to believe that a man can rise from the dead."

"Tomorrow is the Sabbath," I said. "Let us ask our friends to meet the following day and explain all of this in great detail then. Let us not discuss it in the meantime."

Elisa said that she would spend the day with her mother and mine. I mounted my horse and rode off to see the patients. They had not heard the rumors. One wanted to hear about the weather, another about the crops and the third all about the Temple.

I arrived at the clinic about the same time as Erasmus. I explained our strategy to him. He agreed. I sent messages to our friends that we would talk about Jesus when we met the day after Sabbath.

Jonathan came in. He also had heard the rumors and was eager to hear the story from me. So was Judith. I told them briefly what had happened, but I could see Jonathan had doubts. Judith seemed very interested.

It was good to get back to work and it did not take long for me to catch

---

up. The patients still seemed to trust me as a physician. Erasmus and Jonathan have been working very hard. I plan to have Erasmus take it a little easier. I hope that he can eventually retire. But he is very active for his age.

I had asked Elisa to rest for a few days before she started seeing patients, but they were all asking about her and were thrilled to learn she is with child. It was a long day when we finished. Elisa had a fine meal ready. She was joyful and singing.

Joseph

Letter 123

Luke, it is the day after the Sabbath, and Elisa and I are exhausted after a long meeting. So many people came to hear our account as witnesses to the last days of Jesus. Interest in our story had been building since our return.

On the Sabbath I made my usual morning calls and arrived at the synagogue as the service was about to start. When I entered, a hush came over those assembled and all looked at me. I went to sit with my father and Erasmus and could hear murmuring. I am sure that both my father and Erasmus were embarrassed. I was uncomfortable also.

I do not remember much of the service. As soon as it was over the murmuring and the strange looks at me started again. I tried not to be concerned but I was really annoyed. I found Elisa. Apparently the women in the synagogue had not treated her with the looks and whispers I had received. She was happy and her cheer did seem to be contagious. We walked to the home of my parents and had a delightful Sabbath meal. No mention was made of our experiences in Jerusalem. But I was already apprehensive about how our story would be received by our friends this evening.

Today we worked hard to get everyone treated and clear the clinic early. Elisa had an evening meal prepared. Neither of us ate much. I spoke of my concerns for the meeting that was to follow. Elisa reassured me. "Joseph, we will just tell the truth as it happened and let Jesus guide us."

When we opened the door of our home we could see that people seemed to be coming from all over Capernaum. As we approached the clinic we saw that people were gathered outside the building. We were overwhelmed at the crowd. Our dear friends came out to meet us and congratulate us about our expected child. There were Miriam, Ruth, Esther and John, Samson and Hannah, David and Rachel, Elisabeth and Jonathan, Abriam and Judith, Eliab and Naomi, Ana, and Daniel and Leah. Even Thalia was there. Their presence and confidence were encouraging. Abriam said, "The crowd was so large that we asked them all to sit on the grass."

We all went forward as a group. I could see that there were several hundred people present. It seemed that everyone in Capernaum had come, including Nathan, the chief rabbi, and Menahem, the leading Pharisee. My parents and Elisa's were seated in front with my sister, her husband and other brethren. I spoke to them as I took my place sitting on the ground.

David stood before us and formally welcomed everyone. Then Naomi and Eliab led the singing of the Psalms. After that I arose. Luke, I was nervous. You know the difficult time I had in Athens speaking even to a small group. I would stutter and everyone would laugh. But Elisa smiled encouragingly. I prayed. "Jesus, if you want me to do well, please help me." And Luke, I felt his presence right next to me. I cannot explain it but I knew that he was there guiding me.

I began by adding my welcome and thanking the people for coming. I explained that we and the others in our company had been witnesses to an extraordinary series of events in Jerusalem. The apostles and the other women of Galilee had stayed, but we had returned early because of the child, and now we wanted to share our news with the people of Capernaum. Elisa would speak first.

She rose and quoted Scripture passages that predicted the coming of the Messiah, that he is to be of the House of David, born of a virgin in Bethlehem, live in Egypt and come from Nazareth. Then she recounted what we had learned of the early life of Jesus, beginning with his conception, Mary's visit to Elisabeth, his birth in Bethlehem, the flight to Egypt, their return to Nazareth and his young life as a carpenter. She reviewed the genealogy that my mother and sister had researched. She told of the conception of John the Baptist and our experience on the Jordan, witnessing the baptism of Jesus and the voice from above. Then she reviewed all of the miracles that Jesus had performed and his teachings. She repeated the words of his Sermon on the Mount. She quoted scriptural passages that predicted these happenings. Luke, she was eloquent. Everyone was spellbound and no one moved during the long period that she was speaking. I saw Ana taking notes.

Then she came to the story of the journey to Jerusalem for Passover, and the transfiguration of Jesus on the mountain. She stopped and turned to me. I took her place before our friends, our families and most of the people of Capernaum. I described the occurrence on the mountain and the voice that I heard. Luke, my confidence grew as I shared the wonder and power of what I had witnessed. I asked Elisa to relate what happened later in Jericho, the banquet at Bethany and Jesus' entry in Jerusalem when he was hailed as a king. Then I spoke again and described his clearing of the Temple and the plotting of the chief priests.

I told of the Passover meal and the words Jesus said over the bread and wine, then the torment he felt at Gethsemane that caused him to actually sweat blood.

Throughout these accounts I quoted, as easily as if I had been reading them, the scriptural passages fulfilled by these events.

The people of Capernaum had been listening intently even to the most extraordinary aspects of our account. There was disbelief in the eyes of many, but there was no outcry. I had to believe it was because they knew and respected Elisa and me.

As I was speaking, Zebedee arrived with his wife, Salome, and Mary the mother of James. The women must have just returned from Jerusalem. My father seemed disturbed that a caravan had arrived without his attendance, but he made no move to leave. Salome and Mary motioned me to continue, and I grew in confidence as I knew there were two other eyewitnesses to these events among us.

There were audible cries and gasps as I recounted the final hours of the life of Jesus, the arrest, the trials, the scourging, the long walk up the hill to Golgotha. All this had happened to a man well-known in Capernaum, who had healed many among us and brought comfort to far more. Then the listeners grew quiet again as they heard how he was nailed to the cross, struggled for breath, forgave those who crucified him, and finally died and was buried.

Elisa recounted our experiences at the tomb three days later, and the presence of several women of Galilee, including Salome, the mother of the apostles James and John, and Mary, the mother of the other apostle James. She asked them to tell their own stories, but only Salome rose. She said, "It is all as they say. Jesus is risen!" and sat down again. Zebedee's rigid posture betrayed his own doubts and confusion, but his face was unreadable, for the sake of his wife and his sons.

I then told of the tearing of the curtain of the Holy of Holies and the vow of silence the high priest had purchased, then the appearance of Jesus in the Upper Room, how I had examined his wounds myself and Jesus had actually eaten with us.

There was complete silence. I suddenly realized how to further explain what I had struggled to understand myself, why Jesus had to die.

"We must remember that the covenants God made with our ancestor Moses were sealed with blood. You will find in Exodus where on Mount Sinai the Lord ratified the law and the covenant with Moses with a bloody sacrifice of a young bull.[1]

"In Leviticus a bullock is slaughtered as a sin offering,[2] and in Numbers the blood of a red heifer is so used.[3]

"And now we have the prophecy of David fulfilled, that no bone in his body is broken.[4] Jesus was the lamb offered in bloody sacrifice to God his Father for the sins of all mankind.

"He suffered the most cruel and degrading form of death so that we might live in the love and knowledge of God.

"Jesus was the fulfillment of the promise of God to send us a savior. We in Capernaum were privileged to have known him, to have had him live and teach among us. He taught us to feed the hungry, cherish our children, provide for orphans, widows and those in prison, to care for the ill. He taught us by example to love and forgive our enemies. And now He has died for us."

This is not a new religion, I told them. It is a fulfillment of the prophecies of the Lord God of Hosts. This is what our ancestors have been awaiting for centuries. Jesus was not the vengeful Messiah that John had predicted. He was a loving and forgiving Messiah. I concluded by saying that it was now up to us to do as he did.

Then I sat down on the grass by Elisa. She took my hand and kissed it, so proud was she.

There was no immediate response. There were no questions. I had expected argument from the Pharisees, but there was none. It was almost like the end of a synagogue service. The people were quiet and absorbed in thought.

Soon a few started to come up to thank us for the account. Others gathered around Mary and Salome to hear their stories. The rest just left, and soon the others followed, all but our faithful group.

As Erasmus and Sarah passed us, Erasmus patted each of us on the shoulder and said, "Well done!" Sarah smiled in approval. My mother and sister were in tears and embraced each of us. My father, more reserved, said, "I knew that you would redeem yourself and you did."

Our friends remained and we went into the clinic to have the refreshments that Esther and Miriam had prepared. Even then there were very few questions. As they left, Samson said, "We need to hear this over and over."

Elisa and I walked home quietly. "It may seem odd," I said, "but I felt the presence of Jesus all of the time that I was speaking."

"So did I," she replied. "I know that he was there."

And so Luke, Jesus is with us.

Joseph

[1]   Exodus 24:3-8

[2]   Leviticus 16:11-14

[3]   Numbers 19:1-4

[4]   Psalms 34 :20
       Exodus 12:47

Letter 124

Several weeks have passed, dear Luke, since the truth about Jesus has been known in Capernaum. People often stop us to ask questions and we answer patiently and completely. But the Pharisees seem to be avoiding us. When they come into the clinic for treatment they do not mention anything about Jesus. Perhaps we should start the conversation, but Elisa and I feel that it would only lead to an argument and we have no time for that at the clinic.

It is with joy that we read your letters, knowing that your study of the Scriptures is going well. You are now studying the Book of Maccabees, a relatively recent part of the Scriptures. You write that you now believe there is only one God, the Creator of all. That is a deduction from your studies and your practical reasoning. Rabbi David must be a very inspiring and patient teacher because I know that you are full of questions. Have you discussed with him the events of the Passover, crucifixion and resurrection of Jesus?

Elisa has started back to work at the clinic, but she only works mornings. Her patients are pleased she has returned. The ones she cannot see will come to me reluctantly, then when they meet Elisa on the street they ask her if my treatment is correct. I do not mind that. She knows more medicine than I do anyway. It is also good for my humility.

Our meetings continue the day after the Sabbath, with more people joining us every week. It seems that so many people have become interested in the Scriptures and the prophecies and want to learn more.

We have developed a form of service that we follow. It just seemed to evolve from one meeting to another. We start with a general confession of sin, following the teachings of John to repent and ask forgiveness from God. Then we read from Scriptures, as before, and take turns discussing the passages. We may read and reread a section several times, and each time we develop new insights. After that Naomi and Eliab lead us in the singing of an appropriate psalm or two.

Then we talk about Jesus or his teachings. Others who encountered him during his ministry share new reports of his teachings and healings. Ana records all these.

After this discussion we offer everyone the opportunity to pray for a special intention. Rachel suggested this addition. Miriam suggested that this be followed with the prayer that Jesus taught us. We call this The Disciples Prayer.

Father, may your name be held holy,

your kingdom come.

Give us each day our daily bread,

and forgive us our sins.

For we ourselves forgive each one who is in debt to us.

And do not put us to the test.

Then, before we end, we offer each other a kiss of peace. This is so valuable in bringing us together as a community of believers. We have so many people now, and the service lasts so long that we each bring food and have a community meal afterwards. This is a long evening. but it seems that there are many people who keep coming back to learn more.

Today we entered a new dimension in our faith. During the service we were discussing John and his use of baptism as a sign of repentance. Later, during our community meal Miriam said, "I once heard Jesus say, 'Unless you are born again of water and the spirit, you cannot enter into the kingdom of heaven.' This seems to be more than a baptism of repentance."

David said, "We know that Jesus was baptizing in Judea. He implied that it meant a new life, a new direction, to dedicate one's life to God."

Then Samson spoke. "It seems that when one accepts the baptism of Jesus, one accepts the claims of Jesus. It's the death of a life of sin, and the beginning of a new life in Jesus. One is washed and sanctified and, in the name of Jesus, reborn and regenerated."

Miriam interrupted. "We all believe in Jesus, we all have been following his teachings and his way of life. What is keeping us from being baptized? Let us go to the lake and be baptized!" And we did. We marched to the shore where there is a sandy area and shallow water. Then we stepped into the water and baptized each other. We each proclaimed our faith, saying, "I believe in the Lord Almighty and in Jesus His Son." Then David, Samson or another doing the baptizing would say, "I baptize you in the name of the Father and the Son." Some were totally immersed, and others had water poured over them while the words were said.

It was an uplifting experience. Elisa and I felt that this was different from the baptism of John. This was a rebirth in Jesus, the Messiah. As we all walked back to the clinic, we sang and praised God. I doubt that there has ever been such a joyful group on the streets of Capernaum.

So now, Luke, we are baptized followers of the way of Jesus. May the Lord guide us and help us to live up to this great responsibility.

Joseph

Letter 125

Greetings of the Lord God to you, dear Luke.

Peter has returned to Capernaum. This is his first visit since the death of Jesus and the commission of the apostles to carry on his work, and it was unexpected.

The day before the Sabbath, as we were preparing to close the clinic, the door opened and in walked Peter. Elisa and I rushed to welcome him. I had not seen him since the risen Christ had appeared in the Upper Room, breathed upon the apostles and given them the power to forgive sins. Peter spoke first.

"Elisa, how are you? You have been in the prayers of the community at Jerusalem since we heard that you are with child."

She smiled. "As you can see, thanks be to God, I am doing well. Tell everyone of the company that I thank them for their prayers. But Joseph and I are eager to hear what the followers of Jesus are doing in Jerusalem."

"I am here to learn from you," Peter said. "I have heard how the community of believers has grown here in Capernaum. I came to visit the brethren here in Galilee, and my own family, then report back to the other apostles in Jerusalem."

Then I spoke. "We are doing our best to live by and spread the teachings of Jesus here in Capernaum."

"That is how we see our mission," Peter said, "to start communities of believers to spread the Word of the Lord. We have already decided to dispatch disciples and other followers to Ephesus and other towns to spread the teachings of Jesus. There is much we can learn from you here in Capernaum."

Before I could answer, Elisa spoke up. "Please, Peter, tell us what has happened to Mary the mother of Jesus since we left."

"She is well. The Beloved Disciple has taken care of her, as Jesus asked him to do from the cross. John will take her with him when he leaves soon for Ephesus."

Elisa then explained to Peter how our meetings have developed into services and our community of followers is growing each week. Peter listened attentively.

"I can see that the prayers, the songs and the readings must make for meaningful services. Perhaps other communities can follow your lead. But there is another aspect to our services in Jerusalem that I have come to share with you.

"We receive life everlasting at each service. We partake of the very Body and Blood of Jesus the Christ."

"But how?" I asked.

"Jesus said many times, 'Unless you eat my body and drink my blood, you shall have no part of me.' Then in Jerusalem, in the Upper Room as the Passover meal ended, Jesus allowed us our first taste of everlasting life.

"He took bread, gave thanks, broke it and gave it to those of us at the table. He said, 'This is my body which will be given for you. Do this as a memorial to me.'

"He did the same with the cup of wine, saying, 'This cup is the new covenant in my blood, which will be poured out for you.'

"Now we, as the first apostles, grew to understand that Jesus did not mean this for us only at that one meal. Jesus meant that everyone everywhere should be able to partake of his Body and Blood, and he commissioned us to make that possible. Therefore we offer this communion with Jesus himself at our services, as part of our new covenant with God. We offer it as he commanded, in his memory."

Elisa and I had grown quiet as we listened to Peter's explanation. She spoke first. "But how can it happen here? You are in Jerusalem but we are in Capernaum!"

"It will happen here as often as you want it to happen."

"How?" I asked. "I cannot understand."

Suddenly the door opened again and a messenger burst into the room, clearly out of breath. I recognized him as a servant of the chief rabbi of our synagogue. He said, "Rabbi Nathan wishes you to come at once. His wife is desperately ill. Come quickly, please." I had to go. I asked Peter to excuse me, and I left with the servant.

The rabbi's wife had been ill for several days with a lung fever. She had a cough, pain in the chest and bloody sputum. I used poultices and medications to bring down the fever and suppress the cough.

I worked all night. Dawn was breaking before she had the crisis and the fever broke. She stopped coughing and went into a deep sleep. Certain now that she would recover, I walked out of her room to where the rabbi was at prayer. I joined him, and when we were finished, I told him it would take several weeks for her to fully regain her strength. He thanked the Lord and also thanked me. I must have looked both tired and hungry, as he offered something to break my fast, then suggested that I get a little rest since this was the Sabbath. I replied that I would try. I said that Peter was visiting us, and the rabbi asked to meet the first apostle. He had known Peter well when he was Simon the fisherman, and Rabbi Nathan was interested to see how he had changed since his call to the ministry of Jesus.

Luke, the followers of Jesus in Capernaum have very good relations with the rabbi and the synagogue. We attend the services regularly on the Sabbath just as we have always been doing. We hold our special services in addition to it. The rabbi considers us a sect within Judaism.

I went to check the patient again. She was in a deep sleep and would probably sleep all day. I prescribed fluids and rest. I promised to come back in the afternoon to check on her.

I arrived at home as Elisa was preparing breakfast for herself and Peter, who had just come from his home. I described the case to Elisa and Peter in detail and the rabbi's desire to see Peter again.

Peter was encouraged by the excellent relationship we have here with leaders of the synagogue. He said it is not that way in Jerusalem. There they feel in constant danger from the scribes and Pharisees.

Since I had no house calls today, I changed garments and bathed. We had a little time before we would go to the synagogue and I was able to rest. I do not miss a service, even when I get no sleep the night before. After a short time Elisa awakened me and the three of us left. Elisa is showing her pregnancy now and walks with what we call the "pride of pregnancy."

After the service, we walked to the home of Erasmus where Sarah and my mother had prepared a meal. Like the rabbi, my parents had known Peter as a fisherman but not in his new role as leader of the followers of Jesus. They were amazed at the conviction with which he spoke. After the meal, Elisa returned to our home to rest. I had promised to visit the sick wife of the rabbi and to take Peter with me. Erasmus asked to accompany us to the home of Rabbi Nathan. I was only too glad to have him come. I always welcomed his help and advice. Erasmus had known and treated most of the local disciples and followers of Jesus, so he was interested in our conversation.

"Peter," I asked as we left for Nathan's home, "what happened that night after Abraham and I left you and the other apostles in the Upper Room?"

"Well, for several days we stayed in continuous prayer. We were still afraid of arrest by the high priest, but more and more followers found their way to the Upper Room to join us. We learned what had happened to Judas, our brother apostle who had betrayed Jesus.

"When Judas saw that Jesus was to be crucified, he bitterly regretted his betrayal. He went to the Temple, told the authorities the Jesus was innocent and tried to return the thirty pieces of silver. They laughed at him and mocked him. He threw the coins on the floor, left The Temple in great despair and went off to hang himself.

"Because it was 'blood money,' the priests could not put the pieces of silver in the treasury. Instead they took the money and bought the potters' field and made it a burial place for strangers. Everybody in Jerusalem heard about it and the field came to be called the Bloody Acre.

"The day we heard of Judas' death, about a hundred and twenty of us were praying. I got up and spoke. The book of Psalms, I said, had predicted the fate of Judas: 'Let his camp be reduced to ruin. Let there be no one to live in it.'[1] And the Scriptures went on to say, 'Let someone else take his office.'[2] So we must choose someone to replace Judas as an apostle. This person, I said, must be someone who has been with us from the early days until Jesus died on the cross and rose on the third day.

"There were two men nominated, Matthias and Joseph, known as Barsabbas. We then spent time in prayer asking for guidance. Finally we drew lots, and that is how Matthias came to join us as one of the twelve apostles."

By this time we had arrived at Nathan's house and were welcomed at the door by the rabbi himself. We went to see the patient, who had just eaten her first food in days. Both Erasmus and I thumped on her chest with our fingers and listened to her chest. There were still bubbling sounds in the right lower chest, and we knew they would remain several days. But she would get well. I encouraged her to keep coughing to help clear her chest. I asked the opinion of Erasmus. He was pleased that I had asked him and so was the rabbi. He agreed with the diagnosis and treatment. I left her some of Erasmus' tonic, which he has developed over a period of thirty years, to give her an appetite. Luke, Elisa and I use a lot of the prescription for our patients. I shall enclose the ingredients.

Then the rabbi asked Peter to lead us in prayer, and he was magnificent. Both Nathan and Erasmus were surprised at his eloquence.

Nathan offered us some wine and asked Peter about his life in Jerusalem. Clearly and briefly, Peter explained many of the predictions about Jesus from the Scriptures. The rabbi listened attentively. There was no argument or animosity. It was just friends searching each other's minds. Oh Luke, I thought, if the chief priests, scribes and Pharisees of Jerusalem had just listened like this rabbi did, Jesus would still be with us.

It was getting late so we bid Nathan farewell. I promised to return in two days and urged him to send for me if his wife did not continue to improve.

Erasmus left us to go to his home but said that he and Sarah would come to the clinic the next day to hear Peter.

Then Peter departed to spend the evening with his mother-in-law. He will spend the morrow visiting the docks and his friends in Capernaum.

We are blessed to have Peter here.

Joseph

[1]   Psalms 69:25

[2]   Psalms 109:8

Letter 126

Luke, this day has brought wondrous gifts to our community of believers, and lifted a great burden from my soul.

Elisa came to the clinic today, but she worked only in the morning, leaving in the afternoon to rest. Jonathan and Erasmus helped at the clinic and we finished early. I came home to prepare the evening service.

As Elisa and I were eating the fish she had prepared for dinner, she told me she had encountered Peter at the pier and asked several questions of him.

"I patted our child in my abdomen and said that we will soon have some problems about baptism. Peter replied, 'I am eager to hear.' Then I started.

"'We have followed the teachings of Jesus when he said, "Unless one is born again of water, he will not enter the kingdom of heaven." We use the lake of Galilee or the River Jordan when we baptize the members of the Followers of Jesus in our community. This is after they become active believers.

"'This is fine for the young and healthy, but many of our believers are old and sick and cannot get to water. We feel that Jesus would not have denied them baptism. So we pour water over their heads as they say the words. There is nothing else that we can do.'

"Peter answered quickly, 'As long as it is flowing water, no matter the amount, that is sufficient for baptism. In Jerusalem we had three thousand baptisms at one time, so we also used the pouring method.

"'Elisa, in these first days as a growing community of believers there are many things that we will try. Some will work and others will not. The foundation of our movement will be small communities like yours, run by devoted people. We have much to learn from each other. I do hope that someday my home in Capernaum will become a house-church such as yours, a meeting place for prayer and the celebration of the Breaking of the Bread.'

"Then I replied, 'That would be fine. Our community will soon outgrow our clinic and we will have to form a second church, perhaps in the large home of Esther and John. We hope to have many small communities.

"'And now, Peter, another important question. So far, all of the baptisms have been of adults. But how about the children? Did not Jesus say, "Suffer the little children to come unto me"? Doesn't he have a place for them in heaven? Why do we not baptize them? What about our child who will be born in four months? Will our child have to wait until adulthood to be baptized in order to enter the kingdom of heaven? Death claims two of every three children before they become adults. Cannot we baptize infants now and let them profess their beliefs when they are old enough to reason?'

"Peter was obviously surprised by the question. He thought a while and then replied, 'Your argument is convincing. I must discuss this with our brothers in Jerusalem, but perhaps an adult could act as sponsor for the child at baptism. God bless you for bringing such concerns to our attention.'"

She had more to ask him, but it was time to return home so she thanked him and left.

People started to gather early for tonight's service, as word had spread that Peter the First Apostle would join us. The room was full well before the time we usually started. All brought their food and laid it on a table. A stand was placed in front at one side from which the readings were given. A table was brought in and placed at the center front.

Peter was amazed at the orderliness in which everything was done. I told him that Elisa had arranged it.

Elisa covered the table with a cloth. I looked closely and then I realized it was the fine cloth that had been used to cover the body of Jesus at his burial. There was no way I could remove it now. I just hoped that no one would notice the bloodstains on it.

At sunset we started the service. We welcomed all who had gathered, and I asked that Peter, the rock upon which Jesus had founded his church, stand and be recognized. Then we started with our regular service. The general confession was first. This was new to Peter and he marveled at how well it was done. All confessed to one another. Then we praised God in psalm and song.

Miriam, who is very dramatic in her readings, stood to read from a scroll of the Hebrew testament. She chose the section where Moses and Aaron were criticized by the Jewish nation for the dryness of the desert.[1] Moses had complained to the Lord and he was told to strike a rock with his staff, and out came water. But they were all punished for their rebellion and had to stay in the desert forty years. She then spoke about the significance of this passage of Scripture.

Peter was listening intently. I realized he may never have heard a woman speak in a worship service, but he appeared to like it. Then Miriam read a psalm. After that there was a moment of quiet and it was time for Peter to speak.

All were amazed at the clarity and conviction with which this former fisherman spoke. I looked at Elisa and we both realized how complete was the change that had come over him since assuming leadership of the believers. This was not the man who had been afraid to even acknowledge he knew Jesus. He argued theological points with logic and brilliance. He discussed how cures had occurred in the name of Jesus. He recounted his own sinfulness and weakness, and the times that he had denied Christ, but he ended with the joy of Jesus' forgiveness of sins.

Then he paused for a moment, looked around the large group and said, "You have all received baptism, but I have come to bring you the presence of God himself.

"I bring you the gift of the Holy Spirit, who will inspire and guide you in your faith.

"And I bring the gift of life everlasting, a share in the Body and Blood of Jesus himself, who died for our sins."

Then he drew a deep breath and prepared to tell us how he and the apostles received the Holy Spirit from Jesus himself.

"For forty days after the risen Jesus appeared to us, he continued to appear. At one time he told us to wait in Jerusalem for what the Father had promised. 'John baptized with water,' he said, 'but you, in not many days, will be baptized by the Holy Spirit.' We did not know what these words meant.

"One day we were at Bethany together when the Lord appeared to us. Andrew asked him, 'Lord, has the time come? Are you going to restore the kingdom to Israel?'

"He replied, 'It is not for you to know times or dates that the Father has decided by His own authority, but you will receive power when the Holy Spirit comes to you, and then you will be my witnesses, not only in Jerusalem but throughout Judea and Samaria and, indeed, to the ends of the earth.'

"When he had said this, he was raised up before our eyes, entered a cloud and disappeared from our sight. As we stood there, two men in white suddenly appeared among us. They said, 'Why are you men from Galilee looking into the sky? Jesus who has been taken up from you into heaven, this same Jesus will come back in the same way as you have seen him go there.'

"You can imagine that it took us a while to regain our composure. We returned as a group to Jerusalem and went to the Temple, praising God all the way.

"Ten days later we were all again in one room in continuous prayer," he said. "Mary the mother of Jesus and other women were among us.

"Suddenly a strong wind arose and filled the house with noise, then small flames appeared above us. They were bright but they did not burn. They settled over our heads, and each of us was filled with the Holy Spirit of God."

The disciples, he said, then left the home of Mark's father and went out into the street to preach among the people. But they preached eloquently in dialects and foreign tongues they could never have learned in Capernaum or Bethsaida.

"Now there were Jews staying in Jerusalem, devout men from every nation under heaven, and at this sound, all of those assembled, each one, bewildered, heard us speaking in his own language. 'Surely,' they said, 'all these men speaking are Galileans! How does it happen that each of us hears them in his own native language?' Parthians, Medes, Elamites, people from Mesopotamia, Judea and Cappodocia, Pontus and Asia, Phrygia and Pamphylia, Egypt and parts of Libya around Cyrene as well as visitors from Rome, Jews and proselytes alike, Cretans and Arabs — each heard us preaching in their own language about the marvels of God. No one was able to explain it. They asked one another what it all meant. Of course, there were some who laughed at it all, saying, 'They have been drinking too much new wine,' but we knew better. It was the power of the Holy Spirit, the Advocate that Jesus said he would send to us.

"Then I stood up and spoke to the people. I recounted prophecies that applied to Jesus, the miracles that he performed, the manner in which he was put to death, his rising from the dead and walking among us.

"Hearing this, they were cut to the heart, and said to me and the other disciples, 'What must we do, brothers?' I answered, 'You must repent and be baptized in the name of Jesus Christ for the forgiveness of sins, and you will receive the gift of the Holy Spirit.'

"That day," Peter concluded, "about three thousand were added to our number."

Luke, we were all astounded to hear this and to learn about the gifts of the Holy Spirit.

Peter looked around and then addressed us. "Those of you who have been baptized believe that Jesus is the Christ, the Son of God, that he was born of Mary, lived among us, was crucified under Pontius Pilate, died and was buried, and that on the third day, he rose from the dead and appeared to many. He ate with us. He ascended into heaven, and he shall come again to judge us all.

"Those who agree with this come forward."

The believers among us stood up and came forward as far as we could in the crowded room. Then Peter raised his hands to heaven and spoke.

"By the powers given to me by Jesus, I ask God to descend as the Holy Spirit upon each of you."

He went to each one of us and laid his hands upon our heads and repeated the prayer over us. Some fell to the ground as if they had been slain, but they soon recovered. He then approached Elisa, next to me. What was I to expect? Well, Luke, nothing dramatic happened to me. Peter went on to all of the Followers of The Way and did the same thing. There were no flames above us, but I could hear a few murmurs that were unintelligible to me.

Then Peter said, "The Holy Spirit came to each one of you and will remain with you for all time. Some of you will have the gift of preaching with wisdom, another the gift of preaching instruction, another the gift of faith, others healing, others miracles, others prophecy, others the gift of tongues, others the ability to interpret them, and others the gift of recognizing spirits.

"And above all you will receive strength to withstand the sufferings that are in store for you. All of this comes from the same Holy Spirit that you have just received.

"This is the greatest gift that you will ever receive. God Himself in the form of the Holy Spirit will be with you all of the time. The Holy Spirit produces joy, love, patience, peace, faith, generosity, kindness, mildness and chastity. Isaiah said, 'A spirit of wisdom and understanding, a spirit of counsel and of strength, a spirit of knowledge and fear of the Lord.'"[2]

Peter's face was flushed with joy. "You now have the Holy Spirit, who now dwells in you, to help you overcome all difficulties. Your lives will remain your own and the Spirit will act differently in each one of you, according to your heredity and the training from your parents."

Smiles and cries of excitement broke out among the members of the community who had just received the Holy Spirit. We hugged one another in a newfound sense of community in the Lord.

Finally I resumed the service and had Elisa read the prayers and petitions of the faithful. Today we included a prayer for the rabbi's wife. Almost every member of the community had some special prayer. I noticed that this impressed Peter, since it gave everyone a chance to take part.

After this Peter got up to speak again. "You have developed an excellent form of service, but it is not complete. Jesus said that unless we eat his body and drink his blood we will not have life everlasting.

"Today, with the authority given by Jesus at his last supper, I now offer you that gift. Today you will receive the Body and Blood of Christ. This is by the will of the Lord God and the command of Jesus, His son.

"Jesus told me, 'You are Peter and on this rock I found my Church,' and when we received the Holy Spirit he told us, 'Receive the Holy Spirit. For those whose sins you forgive, they are forgiven. For those whose sins you retain, they are retained.' Again he told us, 'All authority in heaven and on earth has been given to me. Go therefore, make disciples of all nations, baptizing them in the name of the Father and the Son and the Holy Spirit, and teach them to observe all the commands that I gave you. And know that I am with you always, yes, to the end of time.'

"Therefore, we apostles will act on the power he gave us. We will say the words that Christ said over the bread and wine, transforming them into his Body and Blood, as he did at the Passover meal, and make this available to everyone. We call this part of the service the Eucharist, which in Greek means thanksgiving."

Then Peter took bread, raised it up so that everyone could see, and recited the words Jesus spoke at the Passover meal.

"This is my body which will be given for you. Do this as a memorial of me."

Peter then took a chalice of wine and raised it in offering, again echoing the words of Jesus.

"This cup is the new covenant in my blood, which will be poured out for you."

Peter then turned to the gathering of followers. "And now this is the Body and Blood of Jesus, just like it was for us at the last Passover.

"But before we all partake, I would like Joseph to lead us in prayer."

Luke, I was so engrossed in what he had just said and done that Elisa had to nudge me. So we all held hands and said the prayer that Jesus taught to the apostles. Then Peter distributed the Body and Blood of Christ to everyone who would receive. It tasted just like bread and wine but we knew that it was Jesus that we were receiving. A great hush came over the entire community.

After all had partaken, Peter spoke. "Now, Jesus would want you to partake of the Body and Blood daily here in Capernaum if you wish. Therefore, I am authorized to commission one of you to say the words I just said.

"In time there should be several house-churches in Capernaum. Some of you may wish to organize one in your home, and an apostle or his representative will commission more of you."

Peter paused and turned his gaze to where I was sitting with Elisa.

"There is among you one who was with Jesus from the Passover meal through all of his suffering and was prevented from helping him by the guards. He was present at the trial, the scourging, the carrying of the cross and the crucifixion, while I was in hiding. His wife was present during part of the trials, the crucifixion and death of Jesus.

"Joseph and Elisa," Peter said, "please come forward."

When we hesitated, he stepped forward to get us. He put his hands on my head, said a prayer and breathed on me. "You are now commissioned to hold the service of the Breaking of the Bread as often as your community wishes you to do it. The giving of the Holy Spirit is reserved to the apostles or those whom they appoint." He placed his hands on Elisa's head and said, "You are commissioned to help Joseph in distributing the Body and Blood of Jesus. You are both to be leaders of the Followers of Jesus in Capernaum."

Luke, we had tears in our eyes.

"You may both feel unworthy," Peter said, sensing our feelings. "I assure you, no one is less worthy than I am, but the Lord selects all types of people to do His work."

Then Peter smiled. "Now it is time to celebrate and have a meal." And we did.

Luke, it was a night to remember, an exceptional night. There was great joy in the group because we could now receive the Body and Blood of Jesus every time that we met. We all thanked Peter.

Finally everyone left and Peter, Elisa and I closed the meeting room. Elisa had folded the linen cloth, placed it in a box and was carrying it carefully. Peter asked, "Elisa, what is so special about that linen cloth?"

"Peter, do you not remember? This is the cloth which wrapped the body of our Lord when he was buried." Peter was astounded. "His executioners cast lots for his garments," she continued. "This is all that we have left."

Peter recovered and said, "It does seem meaningful to have prayers said over a piece of cloth that has touched the body of Jesus. Suppose we divide it and give each community a piece?"

"No! I feel that it should be kept whole. It covered his entire body, back and front. I arranged it around him before I left the tomb. Please let us leave it as he left it when he rose. I will keep it for the communities. There may be a better use for it, but it must stay undivided."

Peter knew that Elisa was determined and also that her decision had excellent reasoning behind it. "I know of no better place for it than with you."

Then Peter looked at us and said, "Elisa and Joseph, you have a vibrant community here, and you have the services organized very well. You should continue in this capacity as leaders to oversee the group of Followers of Jesus. But I also see that you cannot devote much more of your time to this work, since you are both physicians. You must train others of your group to start communities of their own and conduct the Breaking of the Bread. One of the disciples, or someone appointed by us, will come often to oversee the entire area and appoint additional community leaders as more people become Followers of The Way of Jesus.

"I see that you have some helpers with the tasks of preparation of the service area. Your community should appoint people to do special tasks, such as distributing food to the poor and caring for widows and the elderly. We had that problem in Jerusalem." We had just reached our home. It was warm so we sat outside as Peter continued his story.

"As the number of disciples was increasing," he recalled, "the Greek-speaking Hellenists complained that in the daily distribution of food their own widows were being overlooked. So we twelve called a meeting of all of the disciples and addressed them. 'It would not be right for us to neglect the word of God so as to give out food. You brothers must select from among yourselves seven men of good reputation, filled with spirit and wisdom. We will hand over this duty to them and continue to devote ourselves to prayer and to the service of the Word.'

"The whole assembly approved this proposal and elected Stephen, a man full of faith and the Holy Spirit, together with Philip, Procorus, Nicanor, Timon, Parmenus and Nicolaus of Antioch, a convert from Judaism. They were presented to us apostles, who prayed and laid our hands on them.

"Your group can nominate members to proceed with these duties as needed. When an apostle or disciple assigned by one of us comes to this area, he will lay hands on them and pray over them."

Elisa and I looked at each other and both of us thought of the same question, so Elisa asked it. "We have many active women. Do these leaders have to be men?"

Peter again thought a while and replied, "The ones of your community will be accepted by our representatives. The Holy Spirit will guide us."

Then I asked Elisa to describe the program that she has started for young mothers. "Peter, it is so simple," she said, "I doubt if you would be interested." Peter urged, "Please tell me about it."

So Elisa answered, "Since this is my first pregnancy, there are many new feelings and changes in my body that I experience. Of course, being a physician, I understand them. But I noticed that some of my patients who are with child for the first time experience the same feelings and do not understand what is happening. Recently, I invited the women to meet with me at the clinic. I discuss what I know about the condition, what changes to expect and how to eat, and I try to make the months a period of joyful anticipation."

I interrupted. "The young women flock to these classes. The rabbi approves of them so much that he sends as many as he can to attend."

"My hope is that mothers and fathers learn to cherish the child from birth, as Jesus taught us here in Capernaum," Elisa added.

"Mary the mother of Jesus told us that the angel Gabriel came to her and told her she was to be with child and that he would be called the Son of God. I call my group the Gabriel Group."

Peter could not take all this in. He had not heard all the details of the birth of Jesus, so Elisa recounted what Mary had told us on the journey to Jerusalem. Then Elisa said that she was tired and would retire. The three of us gathered in prayer and she left. Peter obviously wanted to stay a little longer. He looked at me and said, "Joseph, I am amazed at how well your community is doing here in Capernaum. I pray that it can be the same everywhere.

"But Joseph, I know that you carry a special burden of knowledge. You were a witness to most of the events leading to the death of Jesus. You were even present at all the trials, when I was afraid to show my face ..."

I broke in. "A lot of good I did him. I never stood up to defend him."

"And I ran away. I denied him three times." We both sat in silence for a moment recalling how we had walked off together in our misery and cried.

"But it had to happen as it did," Peter said finally. "Jesus told us at least three times that he would suffer and die. And if it had not happened, there would have been no resurrection and we would not now be preaching the repentance of sins, and you would not be offering the Body and Blood of Christ.

"It is all as it has been predicted in the Scriptures. It is difficult for us to understand, but who can understand the mind of God?

"I have stayed up at night chastising myself for all of my shortcomings, but that is the way that God planned it. Do not blame yourself for what you wish you had done. The future is before you. Please, you and Elisa continue to do the work of the Lord with your medical care of the community and spiritual care of the believers."

Luke, I hadn't known until then how heavy my heart had been with its weight of guilt. But Peter knew and forgave me in the name of Jesus. What a blessed feeling it is to be forgiven.

It was late when Peter left for his home. Elisa was deeply asleep. I reached over and kissed her.

Joseph

[1]   Exodus 17:1-4

[2]   Isaiah 11:2

Letter 127

Luke, there has been new enthusiasm in our community of the Followers of The Way since Peter filled us with the Holy Spirit and brought us the Eucharist. There is no good word in Greek or Latin to describe the feeling. Luke, it is wondrous! The reality that we are taking the real Body and Blood of the Messiah has changed the entire community. It is rare for anyone to miss our service of the Breaking of the Bread. There is a greater sense of dignity, and the faithful even seem to take more care in the way they dress. It is like everyone is attending a special banquet. Luke, what could be more special than to dine in the House of the Lord and receive Him?

There is a special hush that comes on all of the gathering when I repeat the words that Jesus said over the bread and wine, making them his Body and Blood. Jesus is there with us not only in spirit but also in his Body and Blood.

And Luke, the Followers of Jesus are growing. We now have baptisms twice a month. Many of the seventy-two commissioned by Jesus have returned to Capernaum. They join our community church and share their experiences before departing again to spread his Word.

Tonight after the community meal Ruth said, "You know it is becoming known around here that the Followers of Jesus stand out because they love each other."

Of course, we all were pleased that we were known for that reason. Then Rachel raised a question. "Should we not love everyone, even sinners?"

"All are our brothers in the Law!" said her husband, David.

"But Jesus loved and ate with sinners, prostitutes and tax collectors," she said. "Do we love them as he did? And what about the Gentiles?"

We soon concluded that, as Followers of Christ, we must be willing to serve all of God's people, not just the Israelites. Luke, as followers of the Law of Moses we were taught to serve others of the chosen race of Israel. But Jesus did not discriminate in his teaching, his preaching or his cures.

Then I recalled one of the most difficult teachings of Jesus for me to accept: "Love your enemy." Brother Luke, that is a very hard thing to do. I can serve anyone who disagrees with me as his physician, but it is hard to change the feeling in my heart. I can outwardly be nice to them, but it hurts me inside.

But now, when I think that loving my enemy is more of a burden than I can bear, I think of that day on the hill of Calvary where I stood at the feet of Jesus as he was dying on the cross. He said, "Father, forgive them, they know not what they are doing."

If Jesus could forgive them at that time, why cannot I do it?

I realize, dear Luke, that we must be instruments of God's love to everyone. Sometimes it is harder than at other times. But Jesus said that the Holy Spirit would guide and strengthen us.

Finally, everyone left and, as we were walking home, Elisa looked up at me and said, "Joseph, if we are to love our neighbor as ourselves, we must first love ourselves and forgive ourselves. Certainly, if we hate ourselves, we cannot love our neighbor.

"Joseph, we have a great opportunity to serve Jesus all of the time, and this may be of great help to you if you still feel guilty about not protecting him at the trial and crucifixion."

Luke, once more, dear Elisa has looked directly into my heart. While I know the Lord and Peter have forgiven me for my cowardice, I still have not forgiven myself.

"Jesus said that whenever we do anything for the least of our brethren, we do it for him," Elisa said. "So when we treat the ill we are really treating Jesus. When we clothe the poor we are clothing Jesus. When we feed the hungry we are feeding Jesus, when we visit the prisoners we are visiting the imprisoned Jesus, and when we care for widows and children we are caring for Jesus.

"The Scriptures tell us that God made us in His image and likeness.[1] Therefore, since God is good, we are good. In spite of our faults, God loves us. So we must love God, and we should love ourselves."

Luke, she is right. If God can forgive us for our failures, we should be able to forgive ourselves. And love others, even our enemies.

Joseph

[1] Genesis 1:27

Letter 128

Acaravan arrived today, Luke, and brought some very disturbing news. Persecution has stepped up against the Followers of Jesus in Jerusalem. It had already been having an effect here in Capernaum.

As you know, we have been having excellent relations with the chief priest and rabbi of the synagogue here. But some Pharisees came up from Jerusalem and have stirred up a few people here against us. These Pharisees avoid us and treat us as they would Gentiles. They cannot keep us out of the synagogue, but they make it uncomfortable for us with cutting remarks. The rabbi has publicly criticized them and personally apologized to us, but it does not stop them. They even stand outside the clinic during our services and try to stop our members from entering. Now, it seems, the chief priests of Jerusalem have commissioned Saul of Tarsus to hunt down and imprison all the Followers of Jesus.

Luke, this is the same rigid young Pharisee Elisa and I encountered in Jerusalem when he was studying under Gamaliel the Elder.

We hear that Saul is very determined and won't stop with imprisonment. He vows to slay all Followers of Jesus.

Jesus told us that following him would not be easy. May he guide and protect us.

Joseph

Letter 129

Luke, may the blessing of the Lord God of all be with you.

I am pleased to see from your letter that you are looking up the references in the Scriptures fulfilled by the death of Jesus. You always have been thorough in your investigations of medical knowledge, and I know that you will pursue this with the same tenacity. Luke, it can only lead you to one conclusion. You will become a Follower of The Way of Jesus.

You have asked about Elisa. She is about six months with child now, and we are thankful to God she is doing so well. She walks slowly but with pride and cheer. It is getting a little uncomfortable for her to move around.

She does tire easily, but rests often and insists on caring for the sick at the clinic during the morning. Elisa's mother and my mother bring food so that she does not have to spend much time cooking. She does enjoy making garments for the child. Our mothers are talented in making these and also swaddling clothes. My father, Joseph, has built a cradle.

This afternoon when I came home, Elisa met me with a great smile. "Joseph, you can't imagine who has come to visit us!

"Mary the mother of Jesus and the Beloved Disciple!"

I was thrilled to see them. Mary looked a little weary from the trip but there was radiance in her face that I had never seen before. I remembered her anguish at watching her son be crucified.

She stepped close and put her arms around me. "Joseph, please take care of my dear Elisa." I replied, "I am trying as much as she lets me," and Mary nodded. "Yes, we women have a way of failing to take care of ourselves as we should."

"Elisa is very dear to all of us in Jerusalem," John said, stepping forward to embrace me. He seems to have matured very much since we had last seen him. "Peter and all of the brothers there send their kindest regards to you. Peter reported on his visit here and was very enthusiastic about the things you are doing in Capernaum."

John certainly seemed to be more confident of his actions and in his talk. He even stood up straighter. I had noticed this inner strength and self-assurance in Peter also. And I have noticed it to be true of many of those of our group who have received the Holy Spirit.

"Thank you," I said. "It seems our community is developing so rapidly that we ourselves don't have time to really comprehend it. The story of

Jesus and his resurrection continues to spread through this area, and we often have special meetings to talk about it."

Elisa broke in. "I sent messengers to our group of the Followers of The Way of Jesus telling them that Mary and John are here and that we will have a special Breaking of the Bread tonight. We will gather about sunset. And John, we want you to speak during the service."

The Beloved Disciple answered, "I would be pleased to speak, but I would like to listen, too."

I asked about Saul of Tarsus. John confirmed the rumors and told us that Saul is outfitting a group of Temple guards to go to Damascus to arrest Followers of The Way. That was more disturbing news.

At the service tonight, everyone welcomed Mary, who smiled graciously, and John, whom many had known from childhood as the younger son of Salome and Zebedee. His father was with Salome today to greet Mary and attend the service.

It soon was time to begin. Elisa placed the shroud of Jesus on the table. Peter had told Mary and John about it, but Mary seemed a bit shocked.

When it came time for the commentary on the Scriptures, I asked John to speak.

Luke, practically all of the discussions we have had so far have been about the life of Jesus, what he said and did, and what it means for us. But today we had a completely different presentation. The Beloved Disciple just talked about love. Over and over again he told us to love one another because God first loved us.

Luke, the Scriptures tell us the Israelites suffered for their sinfulness. But Jesus reminded us that God forgave them when they strayed. Ours is a God of love.

The entire community was moved by John's talk. It was as if a great yoke had been taken off their shoulders, the burden of fear. John showed them the God of patience, goodness, forgiveness and concern.

We continued with the service, and Mary's eyes filled with unshed tears as she partook of the Body and Blood of Jesus.

I pronounced the Thanksgiving and concluded the service. Then there came the sharing of the meal.

Mary and John were so impressed with the faith of our community, the dignity with which the service was carried out, and the enthusiasm of the

Followers of The Way that they could hardly contain their emotions. We all left with joy in our hearts.

Joseph

Letter 130

Our community is blessed and overjoyed, dear Luke, with the presence of Mary the mother of Jesus and the apostle John.

Elisa spends her time with Mary and took her this morning to visit our mothers, Sarah and Mary. It was the first time the women had met but they are already developing a warm relationship. This makes Elisa so happy.

We called for another special service of the Breaking of Bread this evening, and Elisa carried the shroud of Jesus in the box. Mary said, "I just want to touch the cloth that wrapped my son. I remember the first cloth I wrapped him in, his swaddling clothes, so many years ago in Bethlehem. Now I have touched the last cloth which wrapped him."

Of course, everyone in Capernaum knew about John's return and the special visit of the mother of Jesus, and therefore more people came to the service. They had assembled early and wanted to speak to both Mary and John. Both were very gracious, answering questions and trying to be available to everyone.

The mother of Jesus had made it very clear that she was not going to speak at the service, so we again called upon John. And again, his message was about the love of God. This time he emphasized how we must love others as God loves us. "The one who has no love for the brother he has seen can have no love for the God he has not seen," John said. After he finished and sat down, members of the community rose to speak.

"John, when you speak of love of our brother," said Miriam, "I recall the story Jesus told us about the good Samaritan. This man considered a stranger his brother, even a stranger who might otherwise be his enemy. What God wants, then, is that we love everyone, because everyone is begotten by God."

"So then," said Daniel, "we must love even the Pharisee who beats his slaves and the Romans who oppress and kill us."

"Yes," replied John, "even those who do harm to us and to others. God loves and forgives them as he loves and forgives us.

"That is the world that Jesus wants us to have. That is the kingdom of God that Jesus spoke about, and he lived by these principles."

Luke, it would be a wondrous world if we lived by these principles ourselves. But I can't help thinking about those in Jerusalem who put Jesus to death, and about Saul of Tarsus. Elisa will soon bear our first child, and it is difficult to summon love for someone who could bring harm to my beloved Elisa or our child.

Joseph

Letter 131

Greetings of the Lord God, dear Luke.

Today Elisa spent the day with Mary the mother of Jesus, Sarah and my mother, visiting the poor and several women whose husbands have died and left their families without means. The four women filled the places they visited with joy.

Luke, the Followers of The Way have become involved with all people in need. Most of us do not have any funds except what we earn, but we give what we have.

It is good for Capernaum. There are no people sleeping in the streets and there are no beggars. We have arranged a midday meal for all those without food.

In fact, I am told that the chief Pharisee boasts that the town is devoid of poverty. He never mentions the Followers of Jesus as the reason for it, but God knows. We are only following the teachings of Jesus.

For our part, Elisa, Erasmus, Jonathan and I provide medications for those without the means to pay. I know that you will ask, "How can you afford to do that?" Well, that is what I asked when Elisa suggested it. But it seems that the more we give, the more we get. I cannot explain it. Also, the food and coins given to us in payment seem to increase as we give more to the poor and elderly. Elisa said, "The Lord will provide." And He does.

The Followers of Jesus are so united in our common purpose that we have become known throughout Capernaum and the surrounding villages. Rabbi Nathan, who should not be seen associating with the outcasts of society, sends us people in need.

One night I was coming home late from a call and I saw a servant of the rabbi leading a donkey that was pulling a cart. He unloaded the cart, full of food and clothing, on our doorstep. Then he hid a coin purse in the clothing.

Now we often receive a cart full of goods and a bag of coins, but always without a sign of who provides them. God bless the rabbi and his servant.

This evening, after another service of the faithful, John told us of the community of believers in Jerusalem. They go as a body to the Temple every day but meet in their houses for the Breaking of Bread.

He told of how the faithful all live together. They sell all their possessions and share the proceeds. They share their food gladly and generously not just among themselves but also with others in need. They care for the aging, the ill and the dying, they take in children who have no parents, and they visit those in prison. Day by day the Lord adds to their community.

And the apostles continue to work miracles and other signs of God's love, John said.

"Once, when Peter and I were going up to the Temple for prayers, a man was carried past us. He had been lame from birth, we were told, and his family brought him every day to the Temple entrance called the Beautiful Gate so that he could beg from the people going in. When we approached, the man began to ask us for coins. But Peter stopped him and said, 'Look at me.' He raised his eyes expectantly.

"Peter said, 'I have neither silver nor gold, but I will give you what I have. In the name of Jesus Christ the Nazarene, walk!'

"Peter then took him by the hand and helped him to stand up. Instantly his feet and ankles became firm, he jumped up, stood, and began to walk, and he went with Peter onto the Temple grounds. Everyone could see him walking and praising God, and they recognized him as the man who used to sit at the gate begging. People came running in great excitement to the Portico of Solomon, where the man was still clinging to Peter and praising God. When Peter saw the people he addressed them.

"'You Israelites, why are you so surprised at this? Why are you staring at us as though we made this man walk by our own power or holiness?

"'It is the God of Abraham, Isaac and Jacob, the God of our ancestors, who has glorified his servant Jesus, the same Jesus you handed over and then disowned in the presence of Pilate after Pilate had decided to release him. It was you who accused him, the Holy One, the Just One, you who demanded the reprieve of a murderer while you killed the Prince of Life.

"'God, however, raised him from the dead, and to that fact we are the witnesses, and it is the name of Jesus, which, through our faith in it, has brought back the strength of this man whom you see here and who is well-known to you. It is faith in that name that has restored this man to health, as you can all see.

"'Now I know, brothers, that neither you nor your leaders had any idea what you were really doing. This was the way God carried out what he had foretold, when he said through all his prophets that his Christ would suffer. Now you must repent and turn to God, so that your sins may be wiped out, and so that the Lord may send the time of comfort.

"'Then he will send you the Christ he has predestined — that is, Jesus

— whom heaven must keep till the universal restoration comes which God proclaimed, speaking through His holy prophets. Moses said, "The Lord God will raise up a prophet like myself for you, from among your own brothers. You must listen to whatever he tells you. The man who does not listen to that prophet is to be cut off from the people."[1] In fact, all that the prophets have ever said of these days, from Samuel onward, was fulfilled through Jesus.

"'You are the heirs of the prophets, the heirs of the covenant God made with our ancestors when he told Abraham, "In your offspring all the families of the earth will be blessed. It was for you in the first place that God raised up his servant and sent him to bless you by turning every one of you from your wicked ways."' Then Peter and I turned from the people and went into the Temple with the man who had been lame by our side."

With this account, John concluded his talk and the service resumed.

Luke, several months ago I would have been jealous of Peter and the other apostles being able to do what I could not, to cure the incurable. You know that is why I originally followed Jesus. After the service I explained to John how I had joined the community to learn the method of healing and how I had seen that power be given to him and Peter and all the apostles and not to me. But that I was not jealous.

"To be jealous is human," John said, "but the Holy Spirit raises us above such feelings. When the twelve of us were with Jesus, we were always vying with each other about who would talk, sit or sleep closest to Jesus. Now, since we have all received the Holy Spirit, we are overjoyed at each other's successes. There is now no jealousy among us."

John then remarked how impressed he was with our community, our services and the work that we are doing. "I pray that the peace you have here continues."

Luke, that is my prayer as well. But we must not let fear of persecution stop us from doing what is the will of Jesus.

Joseph

[1]   Deuteronomy 18:18-19

Letter 132

Luke, the mother of Jesus and the Beloved Disciple will be with us only two more days. Today Elisa took John to my father to get provisions for their return journey to Jerusalem. John offered to pay my father but he was refused. "You have blessed us with your presence. You are family," my father said.

In the evening we had another service, and John told us how helping the lame beggar walk aroused the ire of the high priests at the Temple.

"All the people were giving glory to God for what had happened. Peter and I were speaking to them on the Portico of Solomon about the resurrection of Jesus when the high priests arrived, accompanied by the captain of the Temple Guard and the Sadducees. They had us arrested, but since it was already late, the authorities held us until the next day.

"Now many of those who heard us preach became believers, as many as five thousand, and their numbers aroused the rulers of the Temple. The next day the elders and scribes met with Caiaphas, Annas, Jonathan, Alexander and other high priests. They began to interrogate us and brought before us the man who had been lame. 'By what power, and by whose name have you men done this?'

"Then Peter, filled with the Holy Spirit, addressed them. 'Rulers of the people and elders! If you are questioning us today about an act of kindness to a cripple, and asking us how he was healed, then I am glad to tell you all, and would indeed be glad to tell the whole people of Israel, that it was by the name of Jesus Christ the Nazarene, the one you crucified, whom God raised from the dead.

"'By this name and by no other is this man able to stand up in your presence. This is the stone rejected by you the builders, but has proved to be the keystone. For of all the names in the world given to men, this is the only one by which we can be saved.'

"They were astonished at our assurance, considering we were uneducated fishermen. They ordered us to stand outside while the Sanhedrin had a private discussion. 'What are we going to do with these men?' they said. 'It is obvious to everybody in Jerusalem that a miracle has been worked through them, and we cannot deny it. But we must stop this heresy from spreading any further among the people.'

"So they called us in and warned us not to speak of Jesus again. But Peter stood firm. 'You must judge whether in God's eyes it is right to listen

---

to you and not to God. We cannot promise to stop proclaiming what we have seen and heard.'

"The court repeated the warnings and then released us as they could not think of any way to punish us. As soon as we were released we went to the community and told them everything the chief priests and elders had said to us. When they heard it they lifted up their voices to God and all together we prayed, led by Peter.

"'Master,' he said, 'it is you who made heaven and earth and sea, and everything in them, you who said, through the Holy Spirit and speaking through our ancestor David, your servant:

Why this arrogance among the nations,

these futile plots among the peoples?

Kings on earth setting out to war,

princes making an alliance,

against the Lord and against his Anointed.[1]

"'This is what has come true: In this very city Herod and Pontius Pilate made an alliance with the pagan nations and the people of Israel, against your holy servant Jesus whom you anointed, but only to bring about the very thing that you in your strength and your wisdom had predetermined should happen. And now, Lord, take note of their threats and help your servants to proclaim your message with all boldness, by stretching out your hand to heal and to work miracles and marvels through the name of your holy servant Jesus.'

"As we prayed, the house where we were assembled rocked. We were all filled with the Holy Spirit and boldly began to proclaim the word of God."

Everyone sat in silence. We felt privileged to have heard all of this from one of Jesus' own apostles.

Then I continued with the Breaking of the Bread, and this time John joined in saying the words of Jesus over the bread and the wine. Luke, this is the most important part of the service, the partaking of the Body and Blood of Jesus. Yes, he invites us to a banquet in which he himself is the host and the nourishment.

As we ended the service I told John I could see it was hard for him to speak about the sufferings that he, Peter and others had endured for the sake of Jesus. But he said he was not angry. He felt that they were privileged to suffer a little of what Jesus had suffered on the cross.

Elisa and I both admired his outlook, faith and endurance.

Joseph

[1] Psalms 2:1-2

Letter 133

Greetings, dear Luke, in the name of the great God of Israel and Jesus His Son.

The faithful in Capernaum learned more today from John about the persecution our brethren are facing in Jerusalem. But this only makes Elisa and me more determined to live our lives as Jesus taught us, in obedience to God and love of our neighbor.

John joined Mary and our families at my parents' home today for the Sabbath meal. The two guests were good company and there was much laughter. Then I asked John to tell us of his plans. He said the apostles in Jerusalem believe they must carry out the teachings and directions of Jesus and spread the gospel throughout the world. Philip went to Samaria and Peter is going to Rome. John said he and Mary will travel across the sea to Ephesus to start a community of followers of Jesus.

John told me later, "Since Jesus gave me the care of his mother, I must find a safe place for her to live."

We had planned a final service of the Breaking of the Bread tonight before Mary and John's departure. The faithful assembled early. Our parents were there, all of the benches at the clinic were full and men were standing in the doorway.

As Elisa opened the service, everyone became quiet. We sang. Then she asked Ana to read from the Psalms. After that Elisa turned the meeting over to John, who told us how the followers of Jesus began to grow in number even as opposition mounted.

"We all used to meet by common consent in the Portico of Solomon. No one else ever dared to join us, but we were loud in our praise, and the numbers of men and women who came to believe in the Lord increased steadily. So many signs and wonders were worked among the people at the hands of the apostles that the sick were even taken out into the streets and laid on beds and sleeping mats in the hope that at least the shadow of Peter might fall across some of them as he went past.

"People even came crowding in from the towns around Jerusalem, bringing with them their sick and those tormented by unclean spirits, and all of them were cured.

"Then the high priest intervened with all his supporters from the party of the Sadducees. Prompted by jealousy, they arrested the apostles and had us all put in the common jail. But at night the angel of the Lord opened the prison gates and said, as he led us out, 'Go and stand in the Temple and tell the people all about this new Life.' We did as we were told. We went into the Temple at dawn and began to preach.

"When the high priest arrived, he and his supporters convened the Sanhedrin and ordered that we be brought before them."

I cringed as I imagined this scene, recalling how Jesus had been brought before the Sanhedrin in the middle of the night.

"But when the officials arrived at the prison they found the cells empty and the doors still locked. Hearing that we were at The Temple, they sent the guards to stop us and bring us before the Sanhedrin.

"There the high priest demanded an explanation. 'We gave you a formal warning,' he said, 'not to preach in this name, and what have you done? You have filled Jerusalem with your teaching and seem determined to fix the guilt of this man's death on us.' Peter answered on our behalf.

"'Obedience to God before obedience to men. It was the God of our ancestors who raised up Jesus, but it was you who had him executed by hanging on a tree. By His own right hand God has now raised him up to be leader and savior, to give repentance and forgiveness of sins through him to Israel. We are witnesses to all this, we and the Holy Spirit whom God has given to those who obey Him.'

"This so infuriated them that they wanted to put us to death.

"One member of the Sanhedrin, however, the Pharisee called Gamaliel, who is a doctor of the Law and respected by the whole people, told them to let us go. Others have made false claims in the past, he said. 'If this enterprise, this movement of theirs, is of human origin, it will break up of its own accord, but if it does in fact come from God you will not only be unable to destroy them, but you might find yourselves fighting against God.'

"His advice was accepted. They called us in, gave orders for us to be flogged, warned us not to speak in the name of Jesus and released us. And we left the presence of the Sanhedrin, glad to have had the honor of suffering humiliation for the sake of the name of Jesus. The flogging was severe but we took it with joy.

"We preached every day both in the Temple and in private homes, and our proclamation of the Good News of Christ Jesus was never interrupted.

"The word of the Lord continued to spread. The number of disciples in Jerusalem greatly increased, and a large group of priests made their submission to the faith."

Luke, this was a surprise, as any priests who defied the authority of the high priest would surely be banished from the Temple in Jerusalem.

"Now I will tell you about Stephen, one of the seven men of good reputation elected to lead our service to the poor and widowed. Stephen, filled with grace and power, began to work miracles and great signs among the citizens of Jerusalem. But then certain people came forward to debate with Stephen, some from Cyrene and Alexandria who were members of the Synagogue of Freedmen, and others from Cilicia and Asia. They found they could not get the better of him because of his wisdom, and because it was the Spirit that prompted what he said. So they procured some men to say, 'We heard him using blasphemous language against Moses and against God.'

"Having in this way turned the people against him as well as the elders and scribes, they took Stephen by surprise, and arrested him and brought him before the Sanhedrin. There they put up false witnesses to say, 'This man is always making speeches against this holy place and the Law. We have heard him say that Jesus the Nazarene is going to destroy this place and alter the traditions that Moses handed down to us.'

"The members of the Sanhedrin all looked intently at Stephen, and his face appeared to them like the face of an angel. The high priest asked, 'Is this true?'

"Stephen started on a long discourse on the history of the people of Israel starting with Abraham, recounting the fate of its prophets. All in the courtroom knew this history, but he spoke with such elegance, such clarity and such conviction that they listened. Then he chided them.

"'You stubborn people, with your pagan hearts and pagan ears. You are always resisting the Holy Spirit, just as your ancestors used to do. Can you name a single prophet your ancestors never persecuted? In the past they killed those who foretold the coming of the Just One, and now you have become his betrayers, his murderers. You who had the Law brought to you by angels are the very ones who have not kept it.'

"They were infuriated when they heard this. But Stephen, filled with the Holy Spirit, gazed into heaven.

"'I can see heaven thrown open,' he said, 'and the Son of Man standing at the right hand of God.'

"At this all the members of the council shouted in anger. They rushed at Stephen and sent him out of the city to stone him, according to the Law.

The witnesses to the stoning set down their clothes at the feet of a young man called Saul so they might be ready for the task." Luke, this was Saul of Tarsus, who now threatens all the Followers of Jesus.

"As they were stoning him Stephen was calm. 'Lord Jesus,' he said, 'receive my spirit.' Then, as life began to slip from his body, he knelt down and said, 'Lord, do not hold this sin against them.'

"Saul entirely approved of the killing.

"That day a bitter persecution started against the church in Jerusalem, and everyone except the apostles fled the city, dispersing through Judea and Samaria. There were some devout people, however, who buried Stephen and made great mourning for him.

"Saul then began to work for the destruction of the Church. He went from town to town and house to house arresting both men and women.

"Many of those who had escaped the reach of Saul continued the work of the apostles, going from place to place preaching the Good News. One of them was Philip, who went to a Samaritan town. The people united in welcoming the message Philip preached, either because they had heard of the miracles he worked or because they had seen them for themselves. There were, for example, unclean spirits that came shrieking out of many who were possessed, and several paralytics and cripples were cured. As a result there was great rejoicing in that town.

"When the apostles in Jerusalem heard that Samaria had accepted the word of God, they sent Peter and me to them, and we went down there and prayed for the Samaritans to receive the Holy Spirit, for as yet he had not come down on any of them. They had only been baptized in the name of the Lord Jesus. Then we laid our hands on them, and they received the Holy Spirit.

"We then returned to Jerusalem, preaching the Good News along the way to a number of Samaritan villages. And we are preparing now to disperse to other more remote villages of Judea and Galilee, and even into other nations.

"Again, I must warn you about this man Saul," John said. "I pray that he never comes here. But should he do so, God will give you strength when you need it. Just continue to love one another.

"To follow Jesus," John concluded, "you are to be in this world but not of this world. Your lives should be lived differently from others who do not have your faith. Your way of thinking, habits, actions, the types of choices that you make and your methods of evaluating a situation must be different.

There may be times that your actions will arouse persecution.

"You call yourselves the Followers of Jesus. You must be Imitators of the Messiah. You must pattern your actions on what you think Jesus would do."

No one stirred for a few moments after John sat down. Then Elisa got up and offered a prayer to God that He give us strength to endure whatever trial He may have in store for us. And we all answered a loud "Amen!"

When the service ended, the women of our company embraced Mary and bid her farewell. My mother and the mother of Jesus were in tears at the parting.

Erasmus never likes to say goodbye and would do anything to avoid it. But this time, Sarah held on to him. They finally embraced John and Mary, then Erasmus turned on his heel and set off quickly in the lead before anyone saw the tear in his eye.

Finally John took his leave to return to the home of Zebedee, and Elisa and I walked Mary home in the dark.

Before retiring, Elisa had one final remark. "I thank God every day that so far we have been spared the terrible opposition of the Pharisees. We have been blessed."

And so we have, dear Luke. May God bless you, as well.

Joseph

Letter 134

Our days are passing rapidly, Luke. Elisa looks and acts healthy. I check her chest daily and there are no abnormal sounds. She seems to have boundless energy as she runs the clinic with Erasmus every morning. We eat together at noon and then she rests.

She is always up early and insists that we have morning prayers before breakfast. Of course, she always helps with the weekly Breaking of the Bread. She prepares the table with the cloth that covered Christ's body in the tomb. She treasures it and will not let anyone else care for it. Of course, others are reluctant to touch it as good followers of the Law, which forbids touching anything that has touched a dead body.

As we were eating our evening meal, Elisa said, "Joseph, I am concerned about the burial cloth of Jesus. I notice that no one wants to handle it. I do not want it to become soiled and would like to preserve it. Could we just substitute a plain linen cloth for the altar table?"

"A smaller cloth would be a lot simpler, and be more acceptable to the group." She was relieved that I approved. "But what will we do with the cloth of Jesus?"

"The Lord will work out something."

She picked up the box in which she keeps the cloth, took it out and unfolded it. As she held it open, the light of the setting sun passed through it. "Stop!" I shouted.

"Why? What has happened?"

I grabbed the cloth, raised it again to the sun and said, "Look."

Rays of light were passing through the cloth in the area that covered Jesus' face. There was the stain of blood but also the outline of a head, a pale image of a face framed by the bloodstains of the scalp, hair and beard.

"The face of Jesus!" Elisa exclaimed.

It was very faint but, yes, it was the image of the bruised and bloodied face we had seen suffering on the cross months before. As I spread out the cloth we saw impressions of the entire body, front and back, with the marks of the scourging, the blood from the chest wound, the blood from the nail holes in the hands and feet, even the outlines of the bones!

As the last rays of the sun shifted, the image faded.

"God has spoken," Elisa said. "Yes," I agreed. "What shall we do now?"

Capernaum   481

"Joseph, will you make a frame for this cloth so that just the face shows? I will create a border and attach the cloth to the frame with thread so that everyone can view the image without touching it."

So that was our project for the next few days. Elisa substituted a small linen cloth for the altar table at our next service. No one objected. In fact, everyone seemed relieved.

Luke, I told you in Athens how I missed working with wood. Well, I enjoyed making the frame, but it took three nights.

It was late one evening when I brought the frame to Elisa. She attached the border she had made and we folded the cloth lengthwise twice, then a third time. Then we folded the sides so that only the head would show. We placed it upon the shelf and stood there looking at the face of Jesus.

Finally, she put it in a covered basket for protection and said, "We will place this high above the altar table at every service."

Dear Luke, it will remind us of how Jesus suffered and died in sacrifice for our sins, even as we strengthen our souls with his Body and Blood.

The blessings of God be with you.

Joseph

Letter 135

Dear Luke, Elisa grows more beautiful every day. It is getting more difficult for her to get around. I ask her to work less, but she says that she stops when she starts to feel tired. And she usually does.

Today we received some disturbing news. My mother came over and told us what was relayed to my father by one of the caravan leaders arriving from Jerusalem. Saul of Tarsus has stepped up his threats to slaughter the Followers of Jesus. He has gone to the high priest and asked for letters addressed to the synagogue in Damascus that would authorize him to arrest and take to Jerusalem any of the Followers, men or women, that he finds there. He is now outfitting a group of soldiers from the Temple Guard and an entire caravan to go to Damascus. Mary my mother stopped to catch her breath. Her face had paled.

"Joseph," she said, putting my own thoughts into words, "Capernaum is on the way to Damascus, and he and his soldiers will pass through here and arrest those who follow the teachings of Jesus the Christ!"

This disturbed us as we were both thinking of the child. I knew that Elisa was in no condition to flee, and in any case, where would we go? There are Pharisees opposed to Jesus everywhere.

But Elisa was calm. "Our duty, as appointed leaders of the community of Followers, is to them. Our responsibility as practitioners of the healing art is to our patients. We have our obligations here. We can all pray that the Lord sees fit to spare us. But we may have to suffer for Him. We must remember that Jesus suffered for us."

It is the day after the Sabbath, so we decided to give the news to the community at the Breaking of the Bread.

Luke, it hit like a lightning bolt. There was much confusion, and as many suggestions as there were people present. When everyone had a chance to speak, I told them of the decision Elisa and I had reached.

"Sisters and brothers in the Lord, Jesus told us that we might have to suffer for his sake. He said that brother would turn against brother. Perhaps that is the way it will be. But we must remember Jesus suffered for us.

"If any of you wish to leave the community of Jesus, you are free to go. As for Elisa and me, our duty as authorized by Peter is to offer the Body and Blood of Jesus to the community, and we will stay. Further, our duty as physicians is to our patients and so we must stay. We must help take care of the hungry, the homeless and the outcasts here, so we will stay.

"We will ask God to give us the strength to take whatever is in store for us for the sake of Jesus the Christ. We will continue our service of the Breaking of Bread as usual and continue to serve the sick and the needy of the community of Capernaum. That is what Jesus would want us to do."

Luke, the silence held so long I could hear my own heart beating. Then one by one everyone in the room got up and voiced their agreement. "I shall stay." "So shall I." "We will too."

We continued with the singing and then with the service. Then after giving thanks for our blessings, we had our community meal. As we walked home Elisa spoke. "Joseph, you spoke with such determination. I was proud of you."

"I was surprised at myself," I answered. "It was the Holy Spirit guiding me." Luke, it must have been.

So we are a community that has faced its fears. We will continue to do the work of Jesus.

Joseph

Letter 136

Dear Luke, it has been a tense week. There has been no more news from Jerusalem about Saul. My father questions every caravan leader who stops at his place, but no one knows any more. All this is reported to the faithful Followers of The Way of Jesus. Several have been told by friends among the Pharisees that they will send word to us when Saul comes.

Yes, there is fear among all of us, but we sing the Psalms together and talk about the times when our ancestors went through similar periods of distress and remained faithful to the Lord God. We too have decided to remain faithful.

At our services we seem to be bound more tightly to each other. Most of us followed Jesus while he was alive, and those who have joined us since his death are as dedicated as we are. But not one of us yet has been put to the test. We pray every day for strength.

Joseph

Letter 137

My dear Luke, only by the grace of God and our Lord Jesus Christ am I able to write to you today. There is much to say and I do not know where to begin.

Two mornings ago a group of riders arrived at my father's station. They reported that the soldiers of the Temple Guard led by Saul were expected to arrive that day from Jerusalem. Elisa and I continued with our work but sent word to John the husband of Esther. Since he had been an officer in the Temple Guard, we thought he might be able to learn what was going on. Luke, it was an anxious day and time seemed to pass very slowly.

In the evening we met for a special Breaking of Bread because we all needed the strength that we receive from partaking of the Body and Blood of Jesus. Elisa, Esther and Ana had everything ready, and most of the Followers of The Way were there. We asked forgiveness for our own sins and prayed for the persecutors of the disciples of Jesus. Esther selected Job for the reading, and she spoke of his trust in the Lord in spite of all his afflictions.

At this time John arrived to give his report on Saul. "I spoke to one of the soldiers. There are about sixty, a few attendants, and about twenty horses and donkeys loaded with supplies. They are camped near the synagogue in a very crowded place. There is not much room for the animals, and the soldiers have their tents next to a poorly constructed corral. The only way the animals can be moved is through the campground of the soldiers. I talked to the captain and he is very unhappy about their camp. He told me that Saul insisted they stay near the synagogue. He plans to bring back a lot of prisoners from Damascus.

"Several Pharisees contacted Saul and requested a meeting on his arrival. I was unable to get in, but I saw David slip into the meeting."

With this news, we resumed the service. We sang a few Psalms and had our Breaking of the Bread. We knew that the Lord had suffered for us and we all asked for strength to endure whatever trials he had for us. The service ended with a song of thanksgiving, and then we shared the evening meal. But we were quiet and no one ate much.

Suddenly the door opened and David burst in. "The chief Pharisee and the chief rabbi pleaded with Saul to leave our community alone. I heard words of praise for all the good that we are doing — yes, even from certain Pharisees who have publicly uttered contempt of us. A group came from

Nazareth also, but Saul was unmoved. Finally Menahem the Pharisee asked Saul for his letter authorizing the arrests, and he reluctantly produced it.

"One of the scribes read it, and it started out, 'To the Synagogue of Damascus...' A Pharisee from Nazareth objected. He rose and said, 'This is addressed to the synagogue at Damascus. Saul, you have no authority here. Please move on and let this special community of the Followers of The Way alone. My only wish is that we had a community like this one in Nazareth. They do no harm. They feed the hungry, clothe the poor, they care for widows and orphans, outcasts and prisoners, which we cannot do according to the Law. Please move on and pass us by.'

"Saul was irate. 'You are one of them too! I will send a messenger to Jerusalem and get the letters needed, so that on my return from Damascus, no one can stop me from cleaning out this city of the vermin who call themselves the Followers of Jesus. I will come for you in Nazareth too!' And he pointed at the Pharisee who had just spoken.

"The meeting ended in an uproar. It seems that everyone wanted him to leave us alone. All parties left the meeting in anger."

No one spoke. We were all fearful. But at least there would be a short reprieve from persecution by Saul.

Then we heard cries and screams in the distance, which set us all on edge. I called upon Hannah to read the Psalms, and the room was silent except for the verses she recited. I am not sure how many of us were listening to the words because the unnerving clamor in the distance made it difficult to focus on anything else.

Suddenly the door was pushed open by one of the servants of Menahem, the leading Pharisee. "Come quickly," he shouted. "We need help! A fire broke out in the soldiers' camp. The horses have stampeded and injured many soldiers."

There was no question. We must go. I told Elisa and the women to prepare the room to receive the wounded. The men and I gathered dressings, poles and canvas and ran to the synagogue. People were already gathering in the streets.

Luke, I have never seen such a sight. Horses were running, jumping and kicking, and men were trying to drive them into an area to calm them. There were injured soldiers lying on the ground, most of them unable to get away from the horses. The fire was very small — a pile of hay had caught fire — but it had been enough to frighten the animals.

John took command, and when he shouted orders everyone

immediately obeyed, from the captain of the guard to the lowest armor-bearer. I had never heard him like this but it was effective. Order was restored.

I recalled what Dividimus had taught us for situations like this — to first attend the most severely wounded. The townspeople quieted the animals and took them to a makeshift corral away from the scene, allowing us to get to the injured. I scanned the scene in the light of the torches and checked each one of the injured. Abriam, Samson, David and others of our group followed me, putting bandages on wounds and arranging with the uninjured soldiers to carry the injured to the clinic.

As I was dressing a deep chest wound, I heard a man approach on horseback.

"Who are these people?" he demanded to know.

I heard a familiar voice say, "Leave them alone. They will treat the injured." I looked up and there was Jeremiah of Nazareth. He did not see me and I did not have time to talk to him. Was he the man who had pleaded with Saul to spare us? But now was not the time to ask. By my count, there were twenty-two soldiers injured, ten of them severely.

Abriam, Samson and David directed the litter bearers, and the torchbearers lighted the way. The procession moved to the clinic where the women had set up the room to receive the injured.

In a few minutes the room was full of soldiers, torchbearers and the entire company of the Followers of Jesus. Elisa had sent a messenger to arouse Erasmus and ask him to come. The men of our company politely asked all to wait outside while we cared for the injured. Only one man refused to comply. He was later joined by Menahem.

Elisa, Erasmus, Jonathan and I spent the night caring for the injured. We took the severely injured cases first.

Luke, this is the first catastrophe in which Elisa and I have been depended upon for treatment. Each case had to be treated carefully and completely, as we had been taught. We used everything that we had in the clinic.

Jonathan and I took the fractures. Elisa and Erasmus cleaned and sutured the wounds. We made certain there were no puncture wounds since that type of injury received in a barnyard is particularly dangerous.[1]

We had four crushing wounds of the lower legs with fractures. With the help of strong men, Jonathan and I set the broken bones in place as best as we could and then affixed them to splints. We soon ran out of the poppy extract used for pain and resorted to strong wine.

Thank God for the women in the group. Under Judith's direction, they brought food and drink, calmed the injured, washed their faces and their wounds.

Everyone in the room stayed busy except the two who were observers. All through this, Naomi and Eliab sang the Psalms while the rest of the company was at work.

At one point I approached a soldier who had suffered a broken upper leg. I needed help to pull his leg into proper place. I felt someone beside me and saw the robes of a Pharisee. I looked up and there was Jeremiah. "Joseph, may I help?" "You surely can!" From then on, he was one of the workers. His robes were soon as bloodstained as ours.

We went from one patient to another. A couple of soldiers had scalp wounds but we could find no signs of fracture of the skull. The uninjured soldiers in attendance were told to watch these patients for signs of drifting into unconsciousness. We stopped the administration of heavy wine to them, which would, as you know, confuse us as to their state of consciousness.

Finally, hours later, I could stop to rest and take nourishment. Ruth and Esther supplied food, weak wine and water to wash my hands. I looked for Elisa, who I knew must be exhausted. As I was about to go to her, Jeremiah came up to me. He washed his hands and we embraced.

"Come," I said, "you must greet Elisa." We walked to her table. She continued to suture until she was finished. Luke, her hair was in disarray and she had dried blood on her cloak. But she smiled and she looked beautiful, just beautiful. Jeremiah said, "How good to see you again. I have been so impressed today watching you work." Then someone called that I was needed, so I left.

As I looked around, there were Hannah, Rachel, Leah, Ana, Miriam and all of the other women of the Company of Jesus, each busy with caring for the wounded.

About the time that the first light of dawn came, everyone was cared for. The wounds were dressed and sutured, the fractures were in place and in splints, and everything was calm. We washed our hands and the women of the community brought in food for the morning meal. The two Pharisees continued to stand and watch. I asked a soldier to bang his shield loud enough to obtain quiet. Jeremiah led us in morning prayers.

Then I led a prayer of thanksgiving. "Thank you, God, for the opportunity to be of help to the wounded, and we pray for their recovery. We are thankful to everyone, our community, the soldiers, the other helpers and Jeremiah of Nazareth for their help. Dear Lord, we bless you and we thank you for giving us the opportunity to help those in need. Amen."

The food was served to the wounded first and then the soldiers, and to us the last. I asked one of the soldiers to ask Menahem and his companion to join us. They at first refused but later relented. As we ate it was whispered that the second Pharisee was Saul himself.

Finally we were done. I sent Elisa, big with child, home to bed for the day, and Hannah and Rachel to see that she did. Erasmus and Jonathan went home too. They all looked tired. I realized that something had to be done with the injured.

About that time, Jeremiah brought to me the two men who had been present all through the night. Menahem spoke to me warmly and identified the other only as the civilian commander of the troops. He did not give his name but I introduced myself.

"I am Joseph of Capernaum. My wife, Elisa, Erasmus her father, and Jonathan and I are practitioners of medicine in Capernaum. I am sorry that this catastrophe has happened in our city. We cared for your wounded, and within a few days, they will be well enough to return home.

"They will need a daily change of dressings until the wounds heal. In about ten to fourteen days the sutures must be removed. The fractures need to be followed. I suggest that you seek out Abraham of Jerusalem and his group when you return to Jerusalem."

The man listened intently but with some impatience. He turned to Menahem and spoke. "That will delay my mission unless you can arrange to transport my injured back to Jerusalem."

I said, "We can feed and care for them until they are ready to travel."

"So, the rest of us could travel to Damascus tomorrow." Then he looked directly at me. "Where did you get all of these people to help so quickly and to work all night?"

"We are Followers of The Way of Jesus. We were at our evening service of the Breaking of the Bread."

The commander looked at me directly and asked, "Do you know who I am?"

"I am told you are Saul of Tarsus."

He was surprised. "Do you know why I am here?"

"Yes," I replied. "You have a mandate to arrest the Followers of The Way in Damascus and bring them back to Jerusalem. You want to get a letter to arrest us on the way back."

"Do you mean, you knew this? How long ago?"

"We learned about it when you asked for the letters in Jerusalem. We learned last night about your determination to arrest us…"

"Do you mean to tell me that all of those people knew it?"

"Yes."

"I cannot believe it."

"Ask them."

He stopped Samson and asked, "Do you know who I am?"

"You are Saul of Tarsus."

"And do you know why I am here?"

"You are here to destroy us!"

Saul in turn questioned David and other men and got the same answers. But he did not speak to any of the women.

"I cannot believe that these people all knew my mission and yet did all of this for my men."

I replied, "It is simple. They needed our help and we gave it. They will still need our help and we will continue to give it."

Then Jeremiah spoke. "This is the group for whom we pleaded last night."

"How do I know that they did not start the fire to stampede the horses?" Saul retorted.

"Because they were all at their evening prayers," said Rabbi Nathan, who had just joined the group along with others who had waited outside. "But, most importantly, these people would not harm anyone. They just love everyone and do good works."

"That I cannot believe," growled Saul.

"Well," said the rabbi, "you have seen for yourself what they have just done. Again I beg you to accompany me for a tour of Capernaum to see how they care for those less fortunate. They are a blessing for the community."

"But we are not poor or unclothed. We are their enemies!"

"Jesus taught us to love our enemies," I answered and Saul scowled.

"Love your enemies? That's crazy! You should kill your enemies."

I spoke calmly. "We were taught to do good to those who cannot pay you back."

"Absurd! Senseless! You are all crazy! I should arrest all of you!"

Then Rabbi Nathan said, "We are here, Saul of Tarsus. Arrest us too." And the others nodded. That was all that Saul could take. He turned to me and said, "How much do I owe you?"

I replied, "We have no fee. We give our services to those in need. If you want to pay anything, it will be put in the common treasury and used for those who cannot afford it."

Saul reached for his purse. I said, "Don't give it to me. Give it to this woman." I pointed to Hannah. "She keeps the money for the community."

Saul felt insulted to be asked to deal with a woman. Rabbi Nathan, Menahem and Jeremiah turned their backs to let Saul know that they would not see him speaking to a woman.

He walked up to her and handed her several gold coins. Hannah smiled and said, "Thank you, Saul of Tarsus. I hope that we meet again under better circumstances." He did not smile but turned his back. Hannah winked at me.

"Thank you, Saul of Tarsus," I said.

Rabbi Nathan spoke. "In the name of the Synagogue of Capernaum and the people of Capernaum, I wish to thank all of the Followers of The Way for the good that you are doing in our community."

I answered. "There is much more that still needs to be done."

Esther was going around to each of the severely injured. Saul asked, "What is that woman doing?" I answered, "She is assigning patients to homes of the Followers, where they will be cared for until they are able to travel."

"Why?" he snapped.

"They need care and your tents are destroyed. They cannot sleep out in the open."

"They will find out why we're here and they will kill my soldiers."

Jeremiah spoke. "They all know. It makes no difference to them."

Saul seemed suddenly unsure of himself. "I cannot believe all of this. They all know our mission? I cannot believe it."

"Saul," softly spoke the rabbi, "your mind refuses to admit what your eyes see."

I said, "Well, I had better go home, change my garments, and get ready for my patients in the clinic."

Saul grabbed my arm and said, "But you worked all night!"

"Yes, and all day yesterday, and I must see my ill patients today. Every morning I visit the ill at home, and every week the lepers who cannot come to see us at the clinic."

Saul recoiled. "Do you mean to tell me that you treat the unclean?"

"Well, sir," I replied, "they are ill and hungry and need care."

"But the Law says they are sinners and outcasts."

"But, sir," I answered, "they are still children of God."

By this time, it was obvious that Saul wanted to change the subject. He looked at me and asked, "Who was that woman who was doing the suturing? She seemed far along with child."

"She is my wife, Elisa, a fellow practitioner of the healing art. She trained under Abraham of Jerusalem. She has been with child for seven and one-half months."

"But she is a woman and worked on my men."

"Sir," I answered, "she is probably the best trained physician who has ever treated your men."

"And you let her work all night while she is with child?"

"Sir, I ask her to rest often, but she insists on working when and where she is needed."

Saul spoke rather harshly. "You should not let her do it."

Luke, I don't often take the opportunity to reprove someone, but this time I did. "Saul of Tarsus, I can see that you have never had the occasion to argue with a woman on equal terms." The other men turned their heads to suppress a smile. Saul replied, "God forbid!"

The soldiers took each person to one of the assigned homes. As I started home, Jeremiah came to me and asked, "Joseph, may I accompany you this morning?" I was surprised. One of the leading Pharisees of Nazareth wanted to accompany me to care for the ill and the outcasts. "I would be delighted," I replied, "but we both need to clean up."

We agreed to meet at the home of Menahem.

At home, Elisa was asleep. I changed my garments and set off to the clinic to pack my bags. As I surveyed the place, I saw that we had used every available bandage, most of the sutures, all of the opiate and much of the strong wine. We would have to replace the supplies.

I mounted the horse that Jeremiah had given me months before and rode to the house of Menahem. Just as Jeremiah came out a servant came up to me, limping, and threw his arms about me.

"Thank you, thank you for saving my life and helping me after my injury." I recalled that he was the man injured while building the barn for the Pharisee Geru.

"It is good to see you again, but how is it that you are here?"

"I was discharged by Geru after my injury, but about a year ago the chief Pharisee heard of it, had his men find me, and gave me work that I can do, and now I can support my family again."

"God works in His own way. Praise the Lord!"

Jeremiah was riding his finest horse. He looked at me and spoke. "You are taking good care of your horse."

"You have no idea how much time this horse saves me on my rounds. The donkey was so slow. I am forever thankful to you, Jeremiah, for your generosity."

We rode on. "Joseph," Jeremiah asked, "tell me the story of the servant who just spoke to you." I repeated the entire story. Jeremiah mused, "Well, it seems that the Pharisees are softening a little. Do you suppose the work of your community has anything to do with it?"

"It is by the grace of God and the influence of the teachings of his Son," I answered.

"Joseph, you are as convinced as ever that Jesus of Nazareth was the Messiah."

"Yes, Jeremiah, we all are. His teachings have had a powerful influence on all of our lives here."

By this time, we had reached the place where the lepers stayed. There were Jews, Gentiles, Assyrians, Greeks, all together in the brotherhood of the unclean. As we approached we could hear them call the customary warning, "Unclean, unclean."

We continued and then we heard a shout. "It is Joseph, the physician!"

I asked Jeremiah to stay a short distance away to avoid having to be considered unclean at the synagogue. I treated the ill and told them their food would be a little late since all of the community had worked all night.

They had heard about Saul's mission and also about last night. They asked, "What will happen to us if Saul takes all of you?" I had no answer except "We must pray to God."

The Greeks and Assyrians asked, "You must teach us to pray to your God." "There is a simple prayer Jesus taught us to say," I replied.

> *Father, may your name be held holy.*
>
> *Your kingdom come.*
>
> *Give us each day our daily bread,*
>
> *and forgive us our sins,*
>
> *for we ourselves forgive each one who is in debt to us.*
>
> *And do not put us to the test.*

I cleaned my hands and equipment and went back to Jeremiah. As we left, they shouted to Jeremiah, "Don't let Saul take our friends. Don't let Saul take our friends." Jeremiah was visibly moved. "You do this every day?" he asked.

"I come here every week, and more often if needed," I answered.

"And the pay you receive?"

"Words of thanks, knowing their deep gratitude."

"Do you mean that is all?"

"That is more than the thanks most of us give to God for creating everything in the world — the earth, the sky, the stars, the flowers and plants and trees, the animals, the rain for our crops — and most of all for sending us the Messiah to show us The Way."

Jeremiah fell silent. I changed the subject. "Please, tell me how your brother is faring."

As we rode to the clinic he told me about Neri and all the news of Nazareth. I invited him to eat the midday meal with us, but he said that he had to meet Menahem. He thanked me and left.

The remainder of the day, having sent the others home early to rest, I was in the clinic alone with the patients and managed fairly well.

When I finally finished and arrived home, I found that Elisa had slept all day and was alert and cheerful. I was exhausted.

So now we have Saul in Capernaum. God protect us.

Joseph

---

[1] Tetanus organisms are commonly found in barnyards and produce "lockjaw" if they enter a puncture wound.

Letter 138

Luke, last night I did get a good sleep. I came from the clinic, ate the meal Elisa had prepared and went to bed. I do not think I have ever slept so hard and so long. And I felt really refreshed this morning. We are so thankful to the Lord that Elisa was able to withstand all of the work and she still is smiling.

Today as Elisa and I finished our work at the clinic, Jeremiah arrived.

"Joseph and Elisa, I have so much to say to you. Saul is leaving for Damascus with those soldiers who are able, but he will soon return. I have to leave for Nazareth tomorrow, and I beg you both to come with me. I will keep you safe from Saul."

Elisa and I looked at each other and said in unison, "Thank you, but we cannot leave."

"But you know that Saul will arrest you and drag you and the others to Jerusalem. You must come."

Elisa was quick to respond. "Jeremiah, we appreciate your concern, but we are here to accept the same fate as the other Followers of Jesus. Jesus died for us. We may have to die for him. It is all in his hands. But he promised us that we would have an afterlife with him in heaven."

Jeremiah stroked his beard and shook his head. "I am amazed at your faith in Jesus, the son of a carpenter.

"Joseph, you first told me about his teachings throughout Galilee, and now I see it in practice in your group of believers. But Jesus was crucified. He is dead.

"You must remember, I was there in Jerusalem at the time, with my brother Neri. We were quite disturbed by the people who knelt before Jesus and proclaimed him the Messiah. Then we were appalled that a Nazarene, a man we had recently honored in our home, was hauled before Pilate and Herod and sentenced to die as a common criminal.

"Joseph of Arimathea told us that he bought a linen shroud for the body and had Jesus laid in his own tomb. I could not understand why he would do this for a man who had been crucified because we know from the Scriptures that such men are cursed.[1]

"Now there are wild rumors that Jesus rose from the dead and walked among the people of Jerusalem. But this I cannot believe."

"Jeremiah, he did rise from the dead. I was there with the apostles when he appeared, just before Elisa and I left Jerusalem."

Then Elisa and I spent a long time recounting all we knew about the resurrection of Jesus, his appearances to disciples, his ascent into heaven and the descent of the Holy Spirit.

We explained how our group of believers in Capernaum had developed into a community church, and recounted the visits of Peter, John and Mary the mother of Jesus.

"Jeremiah, we will pray for you and the Jews of Nazareth. Perhaps, by the grace of God, you will come to understand that Jesus came to fulfill the promises of the prophets in the Scriptures.

"A deliverer was promised to David when the Lord said, 'Sit at my right hand and I will make your enemies a footstool for you.'[2]

"And all through Scriptures there are descriptions of the way he would die:

"'When I was thirsty they gave me vinegar to drink.'[3]

"'I offered my back to those who struck me, my cheeks to those who tore at my beard. I did not cover my face against insult and spittle.'[4]

"Jesus showed us all this and predicted three times the manner in which he would die and that on the third day he would rise again. And he did. We saw him and ate with him. After forty days, he ascended to the Father in heaven. Then he sent the Holy Spirit to strengthen and guide us. Peter and the apostles, with the descent of the Holy Spirit, became fearless men spreading the teachings of Jesus in spite of persecutions. In fact, one disciple, Stephen, has been stoned to death for his belief in The Way.

"Scriptures tell us that the Messiah will be of the House of David and will come from Bethlehem. Jesus fulfills these promises. We, as followers of Jesus, are the fulfillment of what God promised in Isaiah.

> *For there a child is born for us,*
> *a son given to us,*
> *and dominion is laid upon his shoulders,*
> *and this is the name they give him:*
> *Wonder-Counsellor, Mighty-God,*
> *Eternal-Father, Prince-of-Peace.*
> *Wide is his dominion*
> *in a peace that has no end,*
> *for the throne of David*

and for his royal power,
which he establishes and makes secure
in justice and integrity.
From this time onwards and for ever,
the jealous love of the Lord of Hosts will do this.[5]

"Joseph, that does sound convincing. But give me time to study these scriptural promises myself."

Elisa broke in. "And pray!"

"Yes," he replied, "perhaps I do not pray enough to God for guidance. Pray for me."

We both answered, "We will pray for you daily."

He bid us farewell and I said, "May the Lord bless and keep you. If it is the will of God, we will see each other again on earth. If not, we will meet in the place that our Father has prepared for us."

And he left. As we stood and watched him go down the road, Elisa said, "Jeremiah will become a Follower of The Way." I nodded.

Just then Ana came running up. "Saul has taken Abriam!" she cried. "His personal servant was injured and is at the home of Esther and John.

"Judith is very distressed," she said, "but seems to accept it as God's will."

We joined her in a prayer for Abriam's safety.

Elisa was not alarmed, however. "Abriam is strong in his faith. He can take care of himself. Perhaps in the providence of God, this will be a blessing."

This I could not understand.

But Luke, I am thankful the Lord has given us another day.

Joseph

---

[1]   Deuteronomy 21:22-23

[2]   Psalms 110:1

[3]   Psalms 69:21

[4]   Isaiah 50:6

[5]   Isaiah 9:5-6

Letter 139

It has been three days, Luke, since Saul and the remainder of his troops left for Damascus. I was not around when he broke camp but I heard that he vowed to return, taking all of the local Followers of The Way back to Jerusalem to stand trial. My only worry is about Elisa and the child. I have urged her to go to Nazareth but she will not hear of it. We pray we are ready for whatever God has in store for us.

I finally did get to read your last letters. I am not surprised that you write only of your study of the Scriptures. The more of them you read, the more you will want to know. Elisa says, "The more that I know about God, the more I want to know about Him and the more I love Him."

Elisa and I go to see the injured soldiers every morning. They are at the homes of Esther and John, Naomi and Eliab, Samson and Hannah, David and Rachel, Elisabeth and Jonathan, Daniel and Leah, and Thalia. All of the soldiers are appreciative. Each one says in wonder, "We came to arrest you and now you are caring for us."

The final count of serious injuries was three fractures of the thighs, one of the lower leg, four of the ribs with severe pain in the spine — probably fractures — and two head injuries. The last two worried us because the soldiers did not taken any nourishment or liquids for three days. Elisa and I searched for any way that we could get some liquids into them, and finally tried to put some water into the rectum through a hollow reed. I do not know if it helped but the patients did not expel it. It must have been absorbed. Right now anything is worth trying. We pray every day for their recovery because without the help of God, we could not do anything.

Luke, we are getting much help from the citizens of Capernaum. Members of the synagogue under the leadership of the chief rabbi bring food to various homes caring for soldiers. Such cooperation has never happened in this town. Imagine, even the Pharisee Hupham has sent over some food.

The increased number of house calls has not become a burden as yet. Thank God that Elisa, Erasmus and Jonathan have all been able to stand this increased pace. Erasmus has even given up his fishing for the time being and helps at the clinic every afternoon. Jonathan has to rest often but is doing far more than he had planned to be doing. Elisa is just blossoming. I do insist that she not work in the afternoons now, but I have trouble keeping her at home. She wants to go and help the members who are caring for the injured soldiers.

Luke, the Lord has spared us these days and we are thankful.

Joseph

Letter 140

Luke, the injured soldiers continue to improve, thanks be to God. Both of the soldiers who were unconscious have started to take fluids. They made swallowing movements, so Elisa gave them water and they drank. Their breathing is steady. Now we wait, as Abraham taught us, to see if they will be able to move all of their muscles. There were no signs of changes in the pupils or extremely slow breathing, so I did not consider using a trephine like I did with the brother of Jeremiah. But as Abraham said, "Rather do nothing than do something and injure the patient."

My dear Elisa has been exhausting herself in the care of all of the patients, and she is almost eight months with child. Members of our group often bring food over so that she does not have to cook at night.

There is a great deal of anxiety about Saul's return to Capernaum. I wonder how many of our group will deny that Jesus was the Messiah and save their lives. Some of the newer members seem to be wavering. Others have left for other cities, as did the apostles in Jerusalem, to spread the story of Jesus elsewhere.

We pray for Saul every day. We pray that God in His Providence will enlighten him to the truth about Jesus. A large part of our service is devoted to these prayers.

If Saul does take us to Jerusalem, we will be tried before the Sanhedrin. If we deny Christ, we will live. If we do not, we will be stoned as Stephen was.

Elisa and I pray every night that God will give us the strength to face our fate when the time comes.

Joseph

Letter 141

We were again blessed by the Lord to awaken to freedom today, dear Luke, but anxiety is constantly present. Our parents are saddened but do not fear for their own safety. They are not yet baptized and thereby are not considered Followers of Jesus. They attend many of our gatherings for the Breaking of Bread but yet are not completely convinced. Elisa and I pray that the Lord will help them see the truth soon.

I know that it is rather presumptuous to pray for new converts when we may all be taken and destroyed, but the more there are of us, the more will be left, and someone must continue to tell the story of Jesus the Messiah.

Luke, we have had twelve days of peace here since Saul left. Thalia has organized the followers so that someone is praying for Saul's conversion throughout the day and night. We quote the Scriptures, sing the Psalms, meditate on the teachings of Jesus, and of course say the prayer that he taught us to say. Elisa and I manage time to pray every day after our evening meal. Sometimes we are so exhausted that we fall asleep during the time, but we are sure that the Lord understands.

I worry about Elisa, Luke. She is getting heavy with child. She tires easily and acts fatigued and has to rest often. But she is always smiling and prays daily that the Lord will see her through this crucial time. She shows no signs that her phthisis is coming back. She does not cough. Her skin is no warmer than usual as if due to a fever, and when I put my ear to her chest and listen to her breathe I do not hear the telltale bubbles typical of the condition.

May the Lord bless you, Luke, and bring you to full knowledge of the Lord Jesus.

Joseph

Letter 142

Praise and thanks be to God, Luke. The Followers of Jesus are safe in Capernaum.

Late this morning, one of my father's workmen rushed into the clinic. He said, "Joseph sent me to warn all of you to leave Capernaum. A rider just came in and said that he saw Saul's soldiers marching toward Capernaum. Hurry, hurry, flee!"

Luke, now we knew that the time had come. We prayed for strength to withstand whatever was in store for us. I said, "Thank you, but we have decided not to flee. Please give our farewells to my father and mother." He stood there astounded and silent.

"Thank you for warning us and giving us time to prepare," Elisa said. Then we sent the messenger to warn the other Followers of Jesus. Erasmus and Jonathan had left before the messenger came. Only Judith was with us to help with patients, but we released her to go home.

Elisa said, "We had better work fast to get these patients cared for before we are taken by Saul."

In time the messenger came back. "I told them the news. They all said, 'Thank you,' and went on with what they were doing. I cannot understand you people. Why don't you leave?"

Elisa replied, "Perhaps, by the grace of God, some day you will understand and become a believer, too."

"I am leaving!" he announced. "They might take me, too."

Elisa and I worked hard and fast, and soon there were no more patients. We sat in silence awhile. Then Elisa said, "Let's clean up this place. We do not want to leave it in such a mess."

So we picked up the bandages that we had removed, cleaned the instruments, swept the floor and were neatly rearranging the chairs and benches in the outer room when we heard a disturbance outside. I went to the window, and there I could see soldiers marching toward the clinic. In the rear were the wagons for prisoners. My heart was beating rapidly, but I felt unusually calm.

"Elisa, they are coming for us."

I was not so worried about myself but for Elisa, with our child in her womb. I might never see the child. Elisa and I likely would be separated and not know of one another's fate. I prayed to Christ to spare her and let me bear whatever suffering lay ahead of us. As I was thinking this, I embraced her and we turned to face the door.

In marched an officer and four soldiers. We recognized the soldiers by the wounds we had sutured twelve days ago. The stitches were still in place. Luke, it seemed like it took a week for them to walk through the outer room, but I knew it seemed that long only because we were expecting the inevitable.

The captain came up to us, stopped and saluted. Elisa squeezed my hand to give me courage. Then the officer spoke. "Shalom."

We could not believe our ears. The captain had spoken the word that meant peace. He repeated himself. "Shalom."

We stopped shaking long enough to utter "Shalom" in return. The four soldiers stood at attention. The captain turned on his heel, and we expected him to order the soldiers to arrest us. Instead he called out, "At ease!" He turned again and faced us. "We come in peace. Do not be afraid.

"We want you to see the men whom you treated so kindly twelve days ago. Their wounds need dressing. And we came to inquire about the soldiers we left behind."

Elisa recovered first and said, "Bring them in." The captain left and returned with about twelve more men. Elisa and I then set to work, with the Lord restoring our reserves of strength. We removed sutures, changed bandages and dressed new bruises that they had received on the twelve-day march.

When all was finished, Elisa had to lie down on the pallet that we had in the back. Luke, the captain helped her to the room. I could not understand all of this. I sat down on the nearest chair. As I looked around, our clinic was a mess again, with bandages, sutures, and dressings strewn all over. I was too tired to even care.

The captain returned, looked around and then left. Now that we had treated all of his men, I was certain that he would arrest us. He knew that we would be too exhausted to run. Perhaps they would just take me and leave Elisa alone. The officer returned shortly with two unarmed soldiers and issued new orders.

"Clean up. Get it as neat as it was when we came." I could not believe what I had heard. He went to the back and opened the door to the room where Elisa was resting. I got up and rushed toward him. He turned and whispered, "Quiet! She is asleep.

"Come, sit and tell me about the other men whom we left here in your care. But first, let me see that my soldiers have some water and can rest."

"There is a well back of the clinic. They may use it."

He said, "Thank you," and left.

Soon there were voices in the area back of the clinic and as I walked to the back door, I could hear the soldiers rush toward the well. However, they were orderly. The captain was watching them. Then he ordered one of his subordinate officers to take over and walked toward me. I moved toward the back to take one last look at Elisa. I stopped at the door. He stopped, too, and put his hand on my shoulder. I peeked in. There was my Elisa sound asleep.

As I closed the door, I spoke softly. "May the Lord bless and keep you, my Elisa and our child." Tears were in my eyes as I turned toward the officer. "Take me with you but please leave my Elisa alone."

He protested. "I told you that I did not come to arrest you or harm any of your group. See, our prison carts are empty." To my astonishment, I saw that he was right.

The captain said softly, "Physician, I prescribe a good drink of wine for you, and then let us sit and talk."

My tears dried as I went to the storage cabinet and brought out some strong wine. The captain found some cups and we walked to the waiting room. I sat while the captain inspected the place. Luke, it was clean and in order. I knew Elisa would not believe this when she awakened. He dismissed the soldiers and I thanked them. They nodded to me, saluted the captain, and went to join their comrades at the well.

I looked out the window. People were hiding in the woods to see what was happening. But no one ventured out for fear of being arrested.

The captain opened the wineskin and poured two cups full. We gave the traditional toast and drank. Both of us gulped the cupful of wine.

"Tell me about my wounded men," he said again, "and when I can take them back to Jerusalem."

I was able to describe each one's condition. I had seen them just this morning. The captain listened intently.

"I believe that five of them can stand the return journey to Jerusalem, but the others need more care before they can travel. Can you come for them in four more weeks?"

"As you say, good physician."

"My name is Joseph."

He smiled. "Mine is Ezabil." He reached out his arms and said "Friends" and I answered "Friends" as we gave each other the kiss of peace. Luke, it was difficult to conceive that I was greeting as a friend the man I thought had come here to arrest me.

We sat down. Still uncertain of our fate, I asked, "When will Saul arrive?"

The captain smiled, "Saul is not coming. He left us. We are returning to our duties in Jerusalem.

"Joseph, you will not believe this, but I swear by Abraham, Isaac, Moses and David and all that is holy that it is true. Sit back and relax and I will tell you everything that happened since we left you."

I sat but my muscles were still tense.

"Sit back," he said again. "This will take a long time." I finally leaned back and relaxed. The wine helped.

"Saul was in a foul mood when we left here. He was abusive, cursing most of the time. He was annoyed by the delay of several days and losing several soldiers. He blamed the soldiers assigned to watch the horses. In fact, he blamed every one of us. He cursed me because it happened and said he would see that I was demoted when we got back to Jerusalem. When I mentioned how much we owe to you physicians and your entire group in Capernaum, he stopped his horse, looked at me and shouted, 'I will have you put in chains with the rest of them when we get back!'

"Saul tried to control us through intimidation. He knew he did not have the respect of my soldiers, as he has only temporary authority and no experience as a military commander.

"Many of the soldiers were thankful for what was done for them here in Capernaum, but Saul would shout threats and curses when he heard them talk about it. In fact, he once threatened to throw everyone in chains when we got back."

Ezabil hesitated, and then refilled his wine cup. "Joseph, that tall man, Abriam, whom Saul took to replace his attendant, was amazing. He withstood all of Saul's curses with a smile and continued to wait on Saul, polish his boots and serve his food. Saul cursed him in spite of the fact that he was the best servant he had ever had.

"At night, Abriam would slip out among the soldiers. They would ask him about your group, and he would tell them all about this man Jesus.

When Saul heard about this, he ordered Abriam never to leave his sight and kept him chained in his tent at night. But the man continued to be cheerful.

"Joseph, I almost had a riot among my soldiers the third day out. They were so appreciative of what you all had done and they did not want to go on and arrest people like you. In fact, they threatened to kill Saul.

"When I learned of this, I went to each one. I told them that they would have to kill me first. I had no idea what would happen. I slept in the door of Saul's tent so that they would have to step upon me to get to him. They knew I was fully armed.

"Joseph, one night when Saul was asleep, Abriam, chained to the end pole, started to hum the tune of a psalm. I knew it because I was raised in the synagogue and attend whenever my duties permit me to do it. Well, I crawled near him and asked in a whisper, 'Tell me about your people.'

"Joseph, long into the night while Saul snored, Abriam told me all about Jesus and his teachings. I will never forget that night. He explained how Jesus was the fulfillment of the prophecies of the Messiah. Joseph, I listened for several hours. I heard all about the resurrection of Jesus and now of the work of the apostles and this company of Followers. I had just experienced what you all had done for us. I asked, 'How can I become one of you?' The man replied, 'Believe and be baptized with water and the Holy Spirit.'

"I replied, 'There is no deep water here — and neither one of us can leave.'

"Abriam replied, 'I can do it here. We must have flowing water, as a symbol of washing away of our sins. I can pour water over your forehead from a cup and you will be baptized.'

"I replied, 'I do want to be baptized.'

"The man took a cup and asked, 'Do you believe that Jesus is the Christ?' I replied, 'I do.'

"'Do you believe that Jesus is the Son of God, that he was crucified, died and was buried, that he rose the third day and lived among us, and that in forty days he ascended into heaven, and that he will come again?'

"'I do.'

"'Do you believe in the Holy Spirit?'

"'I do.'

"Then Abriam said, as he poured water over my head, 'I baptize you in the name of the Father, and the Son and the Holy Spirit.' And then he put his arms around me and said, 'Ezabil, welcome to the Company of Jesus.'

"And Saul slept through it all.

"Joseph," he continued, looking at me, "I want to learn more about Jesus. Abriam told me the names of the apostles to look up in Jerusalem. And, Joseph, I will. In fact, my period of service will soon be over and I can work with them all of the time.

"I have had a very joyful outlook on life ever since Abriam said, 'There will be a resurrection.' And I believe there will be.

"Later that night Saul woke up, and we were silent. He looked around and then lay back and went to sleep again. And so did we, across the doorstep of the tent, so that if anyone came in he would have to awaken us."

The captain stopped to fill the cups of wine, took a couple of swallows and continued.

"Saul woke up early and cursed us for not being up before him. I must have been smiling and Saul noticed it. He roared, 'Captain, get that smile off your face! I don't want anyone to smile around me.' My answer was, 'Yes, Sir!' But I continued to smile inside, because, Joseph, I now belonged to the Company of Jesus."

"Where is Abriam now?" I asked.

"Just be patient. I will tell you about him.

"Joseph, the soldiers knew that by nightfall we would get to Damascus, and the next day Saul would order the followers of Jesus out of their homes — men, women, and children — and pack them into the prison carts to take them back to Jerusalem to be stoned to death. They had heard about Stephen.

"Joseph, maybe it was the Holy Spirit, but something seemed to inspire me, and I told my men that something would happen to prevent it. They seemed to believe me, perhaps because I had that believer's smile. Then Saul came up and I gave out his orders and they obeyed. Saul mounted his horse and off we marched.

"Now, Joseph, comes the part that is hard to believe but it is true. But let me first check on my men and you check on Elisa."

Luke, I was so engrossed in the captain's story that I had forgotten about her. I went to the room and she was just waking up. I brought her water and she drank heartily. Then she asked, "They have not arrested us yet?" I replied, "Darling, they did not come to arrest us. Come and hear the rest of the story. The captain is one of us."

She gasped. "Do you mean that he is a Follower of Jesus?"

"Yes," I replied. "He was baptized by Abriam a week ago."

"Thank the Lord that Abriam is safe. We must tell Judith."

I helped her up and we went to the outer room and sat down. Elisa looked around and asked, "Who cleaned up the mess?" I replied, "The soldiers." Then I told her all that the captain had told me. As I finished, he walked in, greeted Elisa and said he was sorry that he and his men had over-worked us. He continued with his story.

"Well, the day was cloudy and we could march faster. By about the ninth hour we had reached a hill and could see Damascus.

"I was riding a little behind Saul when suddenly there came a light from above that engulfed Saul. I saw it and so did the soldiers, for they stopped suddenly. I looked again and I could see Saul in the light. Suddenly, he fell off the horse. I dismounted quickly, signaled to two soldiers and we went to help him. The light was no more.

"Joseph and Elisa, he was breathing regularly and his eyes were open, but he could not see anything. Then we all heard a voice say, 'Saul, Saul, why are you persecuting me?'

"I don't know where the voice came from. I could see that the soldiers had heard it, too, because they were looking around to see where it came from.

"Saul spoke. 'Who are you, Lord?'"

The captain leaned toward me. As he spoke, his eyes seemed to shine with a lightness that I had never seen before.

"Joseph and Elisa, even the horses must have heard the voice because they looked around to see whence it came. And let me repeat, we all heard the voice say, 'Saul, Saul, why are you persecuting me?'

"We were shocked. It came from all around us but from nowhere in particular. Saul heard it too. There was a moment of complete silence. Saul looked around with his eyes open and he asked again, 'Who are you, Lord?'

"Immediately, the loud voice boomed out again from nowhere and everywhere. 'I am Jesus and you are persecuting me. Get up now and go into the city and you will be told what to do.'

"Joseph, we all heard those words. We were astounded, speechless, for though we heard the voice, we could see no one. The horses also were quiet.

"I looked at Saul and he seemed to be trying to get up. Abriam gently helped him up. Then it became obvious that Saul's eyes were open but he could not see. Joseph, Saul was blind!

"I have seen men blinded from a head injury, but they were unconscious for days. Saul did not hit his head. He never lost consciousness. He just could not see with open eyes.

"Abriam took control. He said, 'Come, Master, and I will lead you to the city, and Jesus will tell us what to do.'

"Joseph," the captain continued, "I had been with Saul for many, many days, and whenever he heard the word 'Jesus' he would fly into a violent rage. But this time, to my astonishment, he smiled. Just imagine Saul smiling. He replied, 'Whatever Jesus wants me to do.'

"He held onto Abriam's arm and they started to walk toward Damascus. We just stood there in wonder until the tall Abriam and the short Saul disappeared in the distance.

"Then I suddenly realized that here was a company of Temple guards on their way to Damascus to arrest Followers of Jesus, and now the man in charge had left them without even a word. And he went off with one of Jesus' followers. I realized that I was now in sole command.

"I looked around, and the entire company was stunned. I said, 'At ease, men.' They came out of their silence but they held their positions. It was midafternoon and I had great decisions to make. So I ordered a period of rest. Then, Joseph, my troops started to talk among themselves about what they had heard and seen, and I could see that, even though they were amazed, they were thankful that Saul was gone.

"I called the junior officers together. We went through Saul's satchel, which was still attached to his saddle. Mind you, he had left everything behind. He left with only the clothing that he wore. I found the letters that he was carrying. They were addressed to the leaders of the synagogue in Damascus. They authorized Saul to arrest the Followers of The Way and return them to Jerusalem. They did not contain any orders for soldiers. Therefore, I concluded, there was no further need for us to proceed. We were not under orders to do so.

"I called the troops together, explained the situation, and gave my decision. We would return to Jerusalem. And, Joseph, you should have heard the shouts of joy. I have never heard such cheering, even when we won a great military victory, as I heard on that hill overlooking Damascus. The troops did not want to take part in the arrests of the Followers of The Way. In a short time they had turned from a mutinous rage against Saul to cheering that their vengeful mission had been canceled.

"Soon, my own joy was tempered when the supply officer came up and said, 'Captain, we had enough supplies to get to Damascus. We used some extra food in the stay at Capernaum. We can make them last only four more days.'

"That was a problem, Joseph. I addressed the men and told them our rations would run out in four days. I handed my purse to the supply man to buy food. At that, the soldiers emptied their pockets and we had enough for another day."

I looked at Elisa and we said in one voice, "You have not eaten today?"

"Nothing but water and this wine."

We got up and nodded to each other. I left the clinic and called over one of the onlookers and sent him to take a message to Followers of The Way. "Tell them," I said, "that the soldiers are back without Saul. The captain is one of us. They need food now." We knew that the news would be surprising and welcome and that it would not take long for things to happen. I returned to the captain and informed him that food would soon arrive. He smiled in appreciation and went to inform the soldiers. A shout of joy was their answer. They filed into the clinic room, now as guests, not patients. They left two outside to care for the equipment and horses.

The captain said, "Elisa and Joseph, the road back from Damascus seemed short because it was a joyous march. All of my men had joy in their hearts. Look at them now!" And then he whispered to me, "It is like the joy I felt the night that Abriam baptized me into The Way. I wonder how many of them are secret followers of Jesus."

By that time, the first food had started to arrive. I have no idea where the Followers found it at this time at the end of the day, but it came. First Esther, then Judith, Ruth and Miriam came with food, and eventually nearly every woman and man in our company. Finally, a small cart rumbled up. Thalia had one of her servants bring a cart full of food. How she managed all of this so soon I do not know. She also sent ample wine. The soldiers all helped to unload the food and set it out on a table. I marveled at their discipline. None of them would eat until they were told to eat, even though they had had no food all day.

Elisa spotted Judith and called out to her. "Judith, Abriam is well. The captain will tell you all about him when he can." Judith was so overjoyed that a stream of tears fell down each cheek. She offered a prayer to God in thanksgiving and we joined her.

The captain asked the men to line up for the food. All of our members were busy with the arrangements. Suddenly, everyone stopped and looked around. There on one side of the room were the troops who had been ordered to arrest Followers of Jesus, while on the other side were those whom they had been ordered to arrest, now feeding them. None of our company had asked what had happened, but I could tell by their faces that they were all eager to know what Elisa and I knew.

"Dear Lord," I said, filling the silence with a prayer of thanksgiving, "by your grace, we are again privileged to share in the bounty that you have given to us and to share with others of your children. We thank you for all the blessings of the past, and we ask you to guide us and watch over us in the future. This we ask in the name of the risen Jesus." Everyone of our group said, "Amen," and so did the captain and several of the soldiers.

Then the food was served to the soldiers. Each one received a bountiful helping. The soldiers on duty outside were served next and the captain was served last. Members of The Way mingled in joy and relief with the soldiers of Saul.

When the captain finally sat down, Elisa motioned to Judith and introduced her to him. The captain said, "You must be the wonderful wife Abriam told me about the night he baptized me in Saul's tent." Then he proceeded to tell her all about Abriam and Saul. Judith was disappointed that Abriam would not be returning this day, but also was pleased that God was using him as an instrument to teach Saul The Way of Jesus.

The food disappeared quickly. Then the captain ordered the men to clean up, and soon the clinic was neat again. I had asked the captain to speak to our members. He dismissed the soldiers and they set up camp in the orchard and areas behind our home. This time the animals were cared for at a distance from the tents.

All of the members gathered in the clinic and I introduced the captain, and he addressed his new friends.

"Brothers and sisters of The Way of Jesus the Christ." It suddenly dawned upon them that the captain was also a believer. In unison, there were shouts of "Alleluia!" He then continued.

"Your brother Abriam baptized me in Saul's tent a week ago."

Again came "Alleluia!" "Alleluia! Sing praise to the Lord!" "Alleluia!"

He recounted for the entire group the story that he had told to Elisa and me. Everyone was astounded. Jesus had spoken to the great persecutor of his followers. Saul and Abriam are somewhere in Damascus doing what Jesus instructs them to do. Unbelievable, Luke, but true.

It was late and everyone needed to leave. Now we had a company of soldiers and many horses to feed. Arrangements were made for breakfast, one meal at a time. Elisa and I finally got to our home at about midnight. We were exhausted yet invigorated with the sudden turn of events.

The danger is over. Elisa and our child are safe, and Jesus has a new soldier for his army of faithful. Praise be to our Lord God.

Joseph

Letter 143

Luke, the night was too short. I got up early and prepared my own breakfast since I wanted Elisa to rest as much as she could. As I rode by the soldiers' camp I saw they had already had their morning meal. The captain came up and greeted me. He said that the soldiers would like to visit their recuperating comrades before continuing on to Jerusalem. "And some would like to know more about Jesus and The Way."

All I could think, Luke, was that Jesus is going to keep us busy, but I said, "That is wonderful. I can arrange for them to be instructed in The Way."

The captain replied, "It is now two days before the Sabbath. I have issued orders that we march the day after the Sabbath. In the meantime, the soldiers are free to do what they wish as long as they leave adequate guard for the equipment and the horses."

Luke, I told him that we would do what we could to help. They could visit their comrades in the daytime, and I would arrange for them to get instructions in The Way in the evenings.

I wondered what soldiers free in the town of Capernaum would do. They could get drunk and go on a rampage like many soldiers do on leave. But, Luke, I was not really worried. I knew that the Lord would take care of things. But He certainly had a job on His hands.

The soldiers spent the morning and afternoon visiting their comrades, then strolled around the town to see how they could repay the people of Capernaum. They cleaned up vacant areas, and one group helped move a large stone for the foundation of a building for the Pharisee Menahem. Then they walked on to find something else to do.

I sent messengers to David and Samson asking them to arrange instructions about The Way of Jesus. And they did. In the evening, members of our group talked to the soldiers about Jesus. The questions and discussions lasted long into the night. By torchlight they continued.

Luke, it has been a remarkable day.

Joseph

Letter 144

Dear Luke, Elisa and I slept restfully all night. What a blessing from God! We are ever so thankful.

After we finished our morning prayers, we went to the back of the house and looked over the orderly encampment of the soldiers in the yard and in the orchard. Elisa said, "Joseph, they will have no food for the journey to Jerusalem. Our group has been supplying them here, meal by meal." I replied, "It takes us six days to walk to Jerusalem. Soldiers can make it in four, but they will need food." Then with a twinkle in her eye, Elisa made this suggestion. "Do you suppose that we could get the people of Capernaum to help us obtain this amount of food?" So, Luke, we notified our company to let it be known around town that the soldiers need food to get back home.

I left to make my rounds and visited each one of the injured soldiers. After I found that they all could travel, some on pallets and others in a cart, I instructed the soldiers attending them how to care for them on the way.

As I came back to the clinic, I found Ezabil waiting to talk to me. Since it was the sixth hour, Elisa and the two of us went to our home to eat. I informed the captain about the injured men and urged him to take each one to Abraham as soon as they arrive in Jerusalem. But I could see that he was still troubled.

"What worries you, Ezabil?" I asked.

"Joseph and Elisa, in our campaigns we live off the land and take what we need from whomever we can, but since I have learned so much about Jesus, I feel that I cannot do that any more."

"You have learned well," Elisa said. "Let us place trust that the Lord will provide." And off she went to rest. Ezabil and I looked at each other and I remarked, "She has great faith. It seems to me that Jesus has things under control." We walked out to see the troops.

On arriving at the encampment, we saw many townspeople arriving with baskets and carts of food. A cart of freshly baked loaves of bread came from the baker and a cart of dried fish from Zebedee. Then I recognized the chief rabbi's servant pushing a cart filled with supplies, and some of the carts that belonged to the Pharisees were there too. The prison carts were being filled with food rather than prisoners.

Ezabil exclaimed, "We cannot use all of this food. It is too much."

And I heard Elisa's voice behind me. "Give what is left over to the poor of Jerusalem." The commotion had awakened her.

Ezabil replied, "I do not know any poor folks there."

I was quick to say, "That is easy. Find Peter and James and they will direct you to those who need it."

Just then I heard the rapid beating of the hooves of a horse and I recognized the sleek mount of Jeremiah coming through the trees. He reined up, dismounted, and we embraced. "Thank God! I am not too late!" he exclaimed. "I heard that Saul's soldiers were on the way back to Capernaum and I came with gold to ransom you both from them." The sweat was pouring off him and his horse.

"No, no, Jeremiah," I replied. "No need for that. We are friends." And then he looked and saw the joyful activity of the troops getting their gear ready to march, all being helped by our friends from Capernaum. "I don't understand!" said Jeremiah.

Then I introduced him to Ezabil, the captain of the troops, who ordered one of his men to care for the beautiful horse. We walked to our home and sat on the portico. I explained the occurrences of the past few days to him. Jeremiah listened very intently. "You mean that Saul just walked off blind with his servant to Damascus?" he asked.

Elisa spoke. "But he is a special servant. He is one of our group of Followers of The Way of Jesus." And Ezabil added, "Yes, Abriam taught me The Way of Jesus one night while Saul slept. And now I belong to them." All Jeremiah could say was "Amazing! Amazing!"

He looked at the pile of supplies and asked, "What is all this activity?" I explained to him that the troops had come here hungry, that the Followers of The Way had fed them and now the people of Capernaum were supplying food for their march to Jerusalem. Ezabil added, "And what is left we will give to the deacons to give to the poor in Jerusalem."

"The soldiers who came to arrest you are now instead returning with food to feed the poor of Jerusalem. Astounding!" Jeremiah said. Then he turned to Ezabil, "I brought gold to ransom my friends. Take it to help the poor in Jerusalem." He handed him a bag of coins. We all thanked him.

Then a soldier came up to the captain, saluted and said, "We are ready for the guests, Sir." The captain returned the salute and the soldier left. "Now the surprise!" he said as he looked at the three of us. "The soldiers have prepared a meal for Elisa and Joseph. Now I would like to invite my new friend Jeremiah to join us." I could see that Elisa was pleased. I know that she was tired yet she wanted to have Jeremiah for dinner. We all accepted and had a very pleasant meal with all the soldiers. I could see that Jeremiah was very surprised by their behavior.

"Captain," he asked finally, "I have been among other soldiers and they are always rowdy and cursing, but yours are orderly, courteous and singing. How did you do it?"

"Our friends have been telling us about the teachings of Jesus during the past two days, and everything has changed."

After all was cleaned up, the soldiers started to sing the Psalms. On and on they sang. It was an inspiration to hear them. Elisa and I held hands and listened and thanked God. Jeremiah was amazed to hear this from soldiers. I asked him to stay with us and he was too tired to refuse.

May the Lord God bless you, Luke, as He has blessed us.

Joseph

Letter 145

Dear Luke, as we awakened this Sabbath morning, Elisa remarked, "Joseph, did you ever believe that a group of soldiers camped on our ground would be so quiet?" We looked out and they were all lining up for the morning drill. As I passed through the camp of soldiers behind our home to begin my rounds, the sentry recognized me and I was able to get my horse and leave. Fortunately, I was able to return in time to take Elisa and Jeremiah to the synagogue. As I approached our home, I saw all the soldiers lined up and Elisa and Jeremiah talking to the captain. "All of the soldiers are going to the synagogue with us, Joseph." she called out. "Put your horse up in a hurry."

And off we all went to worship, the three of us following the soldiers. Imagine the surprise of the rabbis and all of the Pharisees when the entire troop came to the service. Jeremiah sat with us. He was dressed modestly compared to the other Pharisees.

All of the soldiers listened to the readings and sang the Psalms. In fact, it was a very inspiring service. At the conclusion, the rabbi asked the captain to make a few remarks. He thanked the Followers of The Way for the excellent treatment of his soldiers and all the people of Capernaum for their generosity in supplying the food that they received for their long journey home to Jerusalem. He also mentioned the gold coins that he had received from Jeremiah of Nazareth. He further stated that after they reach Jerusalem, they will distribute all that was left to the poor. I watched some of the Pharisees squirming. Then he invited everyone, especially families with children, to come visit with the troops in the afternoon. I learned later that he had cleared this with Elisa this morning.

We had Jeremiah as a guest at the home of Erasmus and Sarah. They were very gracious hosts, and there was much talk about Nazareth. Jeremiah questioned my father on the work he was doing and asked for information about some equipment. He and Erasmus talked a lot about the Scriptures. It was a very pleasant meal, but it was time for Elisa to rest so we left. I did not know what to expect at the camp of the soldiers in the afternoon.

What a pleasant surprise! Elisa, Jeremiah and I watched from our portico as people started to arrive. It appeared that every family in Capernaum brought their children for a picnic in our orchard. It was full of laughing children enjoying the green grass. The soldiers mingled with the crowd, and I was reminded of the day Jesus and The Twelve had played with the children of Capernaum in our orchard.

Then the soldiers put on an entertainment. They sang. A juggler performed with short swords. They did several dances. The captain, watching the entertainment with us, explained that having the soldiers use their talents to put on programs helps keep up their own morale.

Then the soldiers served everyone a drink made from water from our well flavored with the juice of apples and a biscuit made of wheat with some fruit of the mulberry tree, which their cook had made. After this the people left and each family thanked the captain and all of their new soldier friends. As soon as the last had gone, the soldiers cleaned up everything until the orchard was immaculate.

During all of this time Jeremiah stayed by my side and seemed to enjoy everything that was happening. He marveled at the joy and friendship of the soldiers. We explained to him that, since the soldiers were leaving tomorrow, they had asked that we have a special meeting of our group of the Followers of The Way of Jesus tonight. We asked him to attend as our guest. I explained to him just what to expect. He seemed relieved when I told him there are many, including our parents, who do not believe like we do but come and observe.

As we were assembling that evening, we heard heavy footsteps approaching and in walked the captain and his men. They took their places in an orderly way and were quiet. Jeremiah sat with our parents and seemed comfortable there.

Elisa brought out the framed blood-stained burial cloth of Jesus. The altar was prepared and I started the service. We proceeded with a song, then a pause to ask forgiveness of our sins. Then Ana read from the book of Deuteronomy. We followed with the Psalms. I watched Jeremiah and he continued to nod approval. Then Ruth, Esther and Hannah each got up and told of things Jesus had said and done. Jeremiah listened intensely. Then Miriam asked for special prayers, especially for the safe return of Abriam, for the conversion of Saul and for the safe journey of the soldiers to Jerusalem.

As we started preparations for the bread and wine, the captain got up. "When do you receive new followers in The Way of Jesus?" I replied, "Whenever someone believes in the Lord Jesus Christ, as the Son of God and the Messiah, and is ready to be baptized." Suddenly we heard a chorus of voices shouting loudly, "I believe!" "We are ready!"

David got up and said, "Samson and I and others have been teaching these men the past few days, and I vouch that they are ready to be baptized and become Followers of The Way."

Luke, he and Samson each left to bring a bucket of water from the well, and every one of the soldiers was baptized. "I believe in God the Father Almighty and in Jesus the Christ and wish to be baptized."

Luke, it was inspiring to see the look of peace that came over each soldier's face during this ceremony.

When it was completed, the entire community rose to its feet, shouted and clapped. I surely expected the roof to explode there was so much joy in the assembly. The soldiers sang and praised God in their joy.

After all of this, Rachel read the special prayers and thanked God for the new Followers of The Way. Then I echoed the words that Jesus said over the bread and wine at his last Passover meal. This was followed by the prayer that Jesus taught the apostles and the kiss of peace. This was an especially joyful occasion with so many new members among us. Then all who believed partook of the Body and Blood of Jesus. In concluding the service, I reminded those who had just been baptized that they still need to receive the Holy Spirit to complete their baptism. This they could receive only from one of the original apostles in Jerusalem or from those whom they commissioned.

Luke, Jeremiah observed everything closely but did not show any emotion. At least he did not openly oppose us.

Then we had the community meal. Luke, I have no idea where all that food came from, but there was plenty for all. David and Samson took it upon themselves to care for Jeremiah, and he seemed be enjoying their company and the discussions that they had. I did not interfere.

Finally, it was over. Everything was cleaned and prepared for the clinic in the morning. The captain and his men got ready to leave. Elisa gave them a final blessing. "May God the Father, Jesus His Son and the Holy Spirit bless and keep you." And they left.

Luke, the soldiers who came to Jerusalem two weeks ago to arrest the Followers of The Way of Jesus are now going back to Jerusalem themselves as Followers of The Way. What an extraordinary spiritual journey we have all taken the last few days, from fear to joy, from ignorance of the Lord to acceptance of his will and a commitment to further share his love.

Blessed be the Lord God.

Joseph

Letter 146

Dear Luke, this morning, the day after the Sabbath, we awakened early and walked out on our portico facing the orchard. The campground of the soldiers was empty. On the portico we found a bouquet of field flowers with a note that said, "May God protect you." It was signed "Ezabil and his men." Elisa said, "God shows his love and concern for us in many ways. Isn't life wondrous? Just to know that Jesus the Lord is with us." All I could say was "Amen."

As we turned around, Jeremiah came out of the door. After the usual greeting, we showed him the note.

"Elisa and Joseph," he said, "these past two days while I stayed with you have been among of the most memorable in my life. I have learned more about your way of life by observing your actions. Of course I was here in Capernaum when the soldiers first came with Saul and saw everyone involved in the care of the injured. Now I see the outcome of that unselfish love of others."

"It has become our way of life," I answered.

Then we had our morning prayers and added a special prayer for the safety of the soldiers. After we broke our fast Elisa prepared a meal for Jeremiah to eat on his return journey. As we walked out of the back door, we found the beautiful mount of Jeremiah tied to a post. The soldiers had cared for it for two days and now it was groomed and ready to go. Then he thanked us again, mounted and left for Nazareth in a gallop.

I packed my medical bags, took them to where I kept my horse, and rode off to make my rounds. As I rode by the area where the troops had camped, I noticed that it was immaculate. I imagined how surprised Peter, John and the other apostles would be when the captain and his troops appeared at their services in Jerusalem.

Luke, we had our regular Breaking of the Bread service on the day after the Sabbath. Everyone was thankful to the Lord for sparing us the wrath of Saul and calling so many new Followers to Christ. Yes, the Lord is good.

Joseph

Letter 147

Luke, may the blessings of the Lord God and His Son, Jesus the Messiah, be upon you.

Our community of Followers of The Way of Jesus is increasing. People come from all over this area to learn more about the teachings of Jesus. Many of them saw Jesus work miracles or sat at his feet as he preached on the shores of the Sea of Galilee. Our clinic is full at every service of the Breaking of the Bread. Most of our members are involved in teaching the newcomers.

In addition our community is devoting nine days to a constant prayer of thanksgiving to the Lord for the events that led to the safety of our group and the conversion of the soldiers.

Today, shortly before the sixth hour, my father sent a messenger to the clinic. He had a letter addressed to Judith, delivered by the leader of a caravan that had passed through Damascus. Elisa and I took it to her and sat there as she read this communication from Abriam. It was the first message she had received from him since he had left with Saul. She had been going to my father's place whenever a caravan came from Damascus and questioning the drivers for any word of Abriam, but this caravan had come unexpectedly. There were tears of joy in her eyes as she read it.

"Dearest Judith, this is the first time I have been able to write since I left Capernaum with Saul. You know that I was in the hands of Jesus. Praise him and thank him.

"The first few days were very difficult. Fortunately, all I suffered was verbal abuse from Saul. Then he learned that I was teaching the soldiers about Jesus, so he chained me to a pole in his tent every night.

"By the third day out from Capernaum, the troops were very upset about the mission, and it took all of the captain's authority to convince them not to rebel and slay Saul. The captain, whom they respected, made it obvious that they would have to kill him first, and he slept at the entrance of Saul's tent to protect him. One night while Saul was asleep I was able to instruct and baptize the captain.

"In the late part of the next day, we could see Damascus ahead of us. Saul spurred his horse faster and we almost had to run to keep up. Suddenly as I was watching him and praying to Jesus that his mission would be stopped, there appeared a bright light all around Saul. It was as bright as the sun, but it did not hurt the eyes as sunlight does.

"Everyone noticed it and the entire company suddenly stopped. Saul slipped off his horse and fell to the ground, although his horse was perfectly still. Then we all heard a voice saying, 'Saul, Saul, why are you persecuting me?'

"It was the voice of Jesus, the same voice that you and I heard teach and preach in Capernaum. I was the only one present who was familiar with the voice of Jesus.

"All of this passed through my mind in a moment, because Saul answered, 'Who are you, Lord?'

"The answer came immediately. 'I am Jesus, and you are persecuting me. Get up and go into the city and you will be told what to do.' Judith, I know that it was the voice of Jesus.

"Now I know why the Lord arranged it that I would leave Capernaum so abruptly to go with Saul. The Lord Jesus was my guide all of the time. I took Saul by the hand and raised him up and said, 'Come, Master, let us go into the city and do as Jesus told you to do.' Then I noticed that though Saul had his eyes open, he could not see. I led him.

"We walked away from the troops, leaving behind horse, equipment, papers, tent, everything, and walked to Damascus.

"Judith, I do not know what happened to the captain and the soldiers. All I know is that they were astounded by what they had seen and heard. I know they did not follow us into Damascus.

"Now I had Saul in my power totally. Before I had become a Follower of Jesus I would have been tempted to destroy him for the harm he had done to our brothers and sisters. But, Judith, the thought did not enter my mind. I carefully guided him to keep him from stumbling as we walked toward the city.

"Judith, I had never been to Damascus. Here was a great city with large stone buildings, streets filled with people, carts, caravans. And I was a stranger with a blind man on my hands and no money, no papers. But I realized that Jesus was with us so I was not afraid.

"We continued into the outskirts of the city along the main caravan route when suddenly I turned up a side street. It was a street called Straight. It was now about sunset, and we just continued to walk ahead. It seemed to me that we walked aimlessly, but I knew that Jesus was in charge.

"In time we came to a neat, small house and I stopped, turned Saul toward the house, walked up the steps and knocked on the door. An old man came to the door, opened it and with open arms said, 'Welcome, my brothers Saul and Abriam. Come stay in my home. My name is Judas.'

"Judith, I was astounded! How did this stranger know my name and Saul's? But I knew that somehow Jesus had informed him. Then he explained. 'I was told in a dream that you would be my guests,' and he brought us into his modest home. Judas was a tailor by trade, but obviously a Follower of The Way.

"I was hungry and thirsty. Judas gave us water but Saul did not touch his goblet. I put it in his hands and said, 'Brother Saul, our brother Judas has welcomed us and given us to drink. Here, you must be thirsty, too.'

"Then Saul finally spoke. 'My brother Abriam, thank you for guiding me to the house of Judas, but I must not eat or drink until someone comes to me and I recover my sight. Thank you.'

"Judith, I could not believe what I had heard. It was the voice of Saul, but it was tender and courteous, not like the Saul I had served on the way to Damascus.

"Judas then spoke. "Saul, Jesus will guide us. We will make you as comfortable as we can. Come and let me bathe the dust off your feet.' Then he took us to a room where we were to stay. As he shut the door, Saul said, 'Abriam, did you know this man Jesus?'

"I answered, 'My wife Judith and I knew him well when he was in Capernaum. We listened to him teach and now, as you know, we are Followers of The Way of Jesus.'

"Good,' Saul broke in. 'Tell me about him.'

"Judith, I talked about Jesus long into the night. Judas came in and motioned that I should come eat, but I was too busy talking about Jesus. Judas came in and listened also. Finally during the third watch of the night we all three fell asleep.

"Judith, that went on for three days. Saul did not eat or drink anything. I did. Judas and I spent all of our time telling Saul about Jesus.

"Saul is brilliant and he knows the Scriptures in detail. Truly, Judith, the Holy Spirit was helping me quote text after text of the sayings of the prophets about Jesus, where he was to be born, where he would live, how he would suffer and die, and how he would rise again. Saul was familiar with all of these passages but had never considered them in this light before. Of course, he knew about the crucifixion of Jesus, but much of the story was new to him — what Elisa and Joseph had told us of his birth, childhood, the

Passover, resurrection, about the disciples meeting Jesus on the way to Emmaus. Some of the story was even new to Judas. All of this came out of me as I sat in this small room with Saul and Judas for three days. Then I talked about how we, as a community, are living the teachings of Jesus and reliving the Last Supper, with the bread and wine becoming the Body and Blood of Jesus.

"Saul understood this very well. Judith, Saul's long schooling under Gamaliel had given him a deep understanding of the Scriptures and now, with his inquisitive mind, he finally found in Jesus the fulfillment of all the prophecies about the Messiah.

"Toward the end of the third day, I begged Saul to eat or at least to drink, but he would not. I was worried about his health. I know that Joseph had said one cannot go many days without water, particularly in the dryness of the desert.

"I was exhausted by the afternoon of the third day. However, Jesus gave me strength to keep on talking. Whenever I needed a rest, Judas took over. He had learned about the Followers of The Way of Jesus from Ananias, who had been commissioned by the apostle Peter to preach the Gospel in Damascus and to baptize. Through him, the Holy Spirit has descended upon the members of believers. He is a commissioned successor of the apostles. When I learned this, I was eager to meet Ananias. But now my duty was to Saul.

"At sunset on the third day of our stay at the home of Judas, there was a knock on the door. Judas went to the door and I could hear his greeting. 'Welcome to my home, Ananias.'

"I was thankful that I would get to meet this man. But my voice was hoarse from talking and I was exhausted from lack of sleep.

"Ananias went directly to Saul, laid his hands on him, and spoke. 'Brother Saul, I have been sent by the Lord Jesus who appeared to you on your way here, so that you may receive your sight and be filled with the Holy Spirit.'

"Judith, immediately, as though scales fell away from Saul's eyes, he looked around the room at all of us and spoke. 'Blessed be Jesus, the Messiah, the Lord.'

"He embraced Ananias, then Judas and then me. It was a moment that I will never forget. Here the great persecutor of the Followers of Jesus was now embracing the ones he had come to arrest. I thought how great the Lord was!

"Then Saul continued, 'What do I need to do to be baptized?' Ananias answered, 'Believe in the Lord Jesus the Christ.' Saul replied, 'I do believe.'

"Judas fetched a pitcher of water and Ananias took it, poured some over Saul's forehead and said, 'I baptize you in the name of the Father and the Son and the Holy Spirit.'

"Judith, Saul had become one of us. Impossible except for the Lord Jesus, the Christ.

"There was more embracing and joyful rejoicing. Judas finally said, 'Brother Saul, will you eat now? Saul answered, 'I surely will, Brother Judas.' The four of us ate and drank. It did not take long for Saul to regain his strength.

"After we had eaten, Ananias told us his story.

"He had heard by messenger that Saul was on his way to Damascus with letters to the synagogue to arrest and to return to Jerusalem all of the Followers of The Way. Some had left the city for safety. Others remained in fear. Then one night he had a vision. The Lord called to him. 'Ananias.' He answered, 'Here I am, Lord.' And the Lord said, 'You must go to Straight Street and ask at the house of Judas for someone called Saul who comes from Tarsus. At this moment he is praying, having had a vision of a man called Ananias coming in and laying hands on him to give him back his sight.'

"He could not grasp all of this. He answered, 'Lord, several people have told me about this man and the harm that he has been doing to your saints in Jerusalem. He has only come here because he holds a warrant from the chief priests to arrest everyone who invokes His name.' The Lord replied, 'You must go all the same, because this man is my chosen instrument to bring my name before pagans and pagan kings and before the people of Israel. I myself will show him how much he must suffer for my name.' Ananias arose and came here, to the home of Judas.

"Judith, we all rejoiced at the ways of the Lord.

"The next few days Saul and I spent meeting the other brothers and sisters in Damascus. All were amazed that the same Saul who set out to arrest us for proclaiming the name of Jesus was now one of us. Some were still cautious. But as they listened to Saul speak, proclaiming the name of Jesus, they were persuaded that this conversion was real.

"The next few days passed rapidly. On the Sabbath we all went into the synagogue. At the proper time to speak, Saul got up. None of the leaders of the synagogue knew who he was.

"'I am Saul of Tarsus,' he said in a harsh tone. 'I received a warrant from the chief priests of the Temple in Jerusalem to come to Damascus to arrest and to bring back everyone of your congregation who invokes the name of this Jesus, who called himself the Messiah.'

"Judith, it was the voice of the Saul that I had heard in Capernaum, with a harsh tone in his voice. I looked around at Ananias and Judas. I do not know what they thought, but I suddenly believed this was a trap Saul had set for us, and we were caught. I could see Pharisees nodding approval.

"Saul continued. 'I am here today to tell you that this man who claimed to be the Son of God, the man whom we had crucified in Jerusalem, this man named Jesus ... I tell you, he is the Son of God!' His words thundered throughout the synagogue.

"All were silent. Then he roared again, 'Jesus is the Son of God!'

"The entire synagogue was in confusion. But Saul continued, speaking eloquently about Jesus. Using the Scriptures, he proved, point by point, how Jesus was the long-awaited Messiah.

"The rabbi, pressured by Pharisees, called a sudden end to the service. But other members of the congregation came up to Saul and asked many questions about his change in attitude. And Saul recounted everything that happened as he was about to enter Damascus.

"We were shoved out of the synagogue, but a crowd gathered around him outside. Saul answered all their questions with clear and precise answers, and the discussion continued there for several hours.

"Finally, it was time to go to a service of the Breaking of the Bread at the home of Ananias. We walked to his home and there was quite a gathering there. The news of Saul's bold declaration at the synagogue had spread around the community of believers. Since there was not enough room in the house, we gathered on the portico. I said a silent prayer of thanks for the spacious room we have at the clinic of Elisa and Joseph.

"Ananias started the service. I had mentioned to Ananias that we recite the prayer that Jesus taught us just before we receive the Body and Blood of Christ. He seemed to think it was a good idea, so he asked me to lead it.

"Then Ananias introduced Saul of Tarsus by his Roman name as Brother Paul, a Follower of The Way. There was a hush over the entire group. There must have been about fifty believers and about an equal number of onlookers. Then Paul started. He recounted what had happened and outlined the Scriptures as pointing to Jesus as the Messiah. He spoke as convincingly as he did in the synagogue, but not quite as long this time.

"I watched him as he received the Body and Blood of our Lord Jesus. A radiance came to his face. It was an inspiring sight to behold. I wonder if anyone who looks at me can see the joy that I feel as I also receive the Body and Blood of Jesus.

"During the next few days, the power of Paul's testimony increased steadily, and the Jewish colony at Damascus was thrown into complete confusion by the convincing evidence he presented that Jesus was the Messiah, the Christ. On every corner, we could see Jews were arguing among themselves.

"Tonight we received a message from one of our members, a servant of the leading Pharisee. The leaders of the synagogue have worked out a plan to kill Paul. They are taking turns watching the gates of the city day and night. They do not want him to escape Damascus. They have spies watching the house of Judas to observe his movements so they can secretly kill Paul.

"Judith, we are in the hands of the Lord Jesus. We ask him to guide us out of here safely. You may not hear from me again until I am somewhere away from here with Paul.

"May the Lord Jesus guide you and watch over you. Ask the members of The Way in Capernaum to pray to the Lord Jesus for us. Abriam."

Judith wept for joy as she finished the letter. There was much good news, but there is still the uncertainty of what will happen to Abriam and Paul.

"Abriam has been an instrument of the Lord in Saul's conversion," Elisa said with assurance. "Jesus will take care of them."

Joseph

Letter 148

Greetings, dear Luke, in the name of the Lord God of Israel.

The news of Abriam's role in Saul's conversion spread over Capernaum. There was much rejoicing among the Followers of The Way and among those members of the synagogue who did not approve of Saul's threat to drag us off to Jerusalem. But still we awaited word on the fate of Abriam and Paul in Damascus.

As I left this morning to visit the leper colony, I met Geru as he was riding out to survey his lands with his overseer. Usually he passes by me, not even returning my usual greetings, but today he stopped. I stopped too, and he sneered. "You and your group have bewitched Saul. You will get what you deserve. Saul will come to his senses and return to take you all away."

I smiled. "As you say, sir. I hope the Lord blesses you and your family all of this day." That really annoyed him. He reined in his horse, turned and spurred him off at a gallop.

When I returned from the clinic, Elisa greeted me with the news we had awaited. "Abriam is back! Paul escaped from Damascus and went off into the desert alone to pray." I was so thankful.

This evening we had a special service of the Breaking of the Bread to welcome Abriam. He was thinner but looked full of joy.

After the singing of the Psalms we asked Abriam to tell his story. He said, "You have all shared my letter, so I will tell you of our escape from Damascus. It all happened so rapidly. Ananias came over and spoke to us. 'Brothers Paul and Abriam, you must leave tonight and flee Damascus. We have it all arranged.'

"A caravan was leaving that day. I was disguised as a camel driver and was able to leave through the gate with no problem. I had bidden Paul farewell before I left. The caravan camped about one mile outside of the gate for the night.

"It was a dark night. I tried to sleep but could not. I had cared for Paul for several weeks and here we were parted, and I did not know where he was. I was lonely and I prayed to Jesus that Paul would be safe.

"Sometime in the middle of the night I was awakened. It was Judas. I followed him to a clump of trees just outside the wall of Damascus. He motioned for silence, and I did not ask any questions. Soon we were at the wall. Judas pointed up, and in the darkness I could see nothing until something brushed against my head. A large and heavy basket was being let down over the wall. We helped steady it until it reached the ground and then carried it back to the caravan. We attached it to the baggage on the extra camel that I was leading behind mine. Judas then disappeared.

"So there I was with Paul again in my care. I did not sleep much that night. We left at dawn and no one noticed the extra basket containing Paul.

"It was a cloudy day. I knew that Paul was thirsty and hungry but I also knew that I should not reveal him, because there may have been spies in the caravan.

"We traveled late into the night until we reached a campground. When all was dark, I untied the covers of the basket and there was Paul, safe but quite sore from the cramped position for a night and day. I gave him a flask of wine and some food.

"As Paul straightened up, he picked up the food and wine and spoke to me. 'Abriam, you saved my life. I owe you everything. You have taught me about Jesus. May the Lord bless you. Now I must go into the desert alone and pray to find out what the Lord Jesus has in store for me.'

"And he walked off alone into the desert. That is the last that I saw of Paul. As he slipped off in the dark, I prayed under my breath, 'May the Lord Jesus be with you until we meet again.'

"I continued on with the caravan to Capernaum and brought the basket to our home."

Elisa spoke first. "In your letter to Judith, you wrote that the Lord had a special mission for Saul. 'This is my chosen instrument to bring my name before pagans and pagan kings,' He told Ananias.

"That brought to my mind what Jesus said at a banquet when Mary of Bethany poured precious perfume upon his head and feet. 'She has anointed my body beforehand for its burial,' he said. 'I tell you solemnly, wherever throughout the world the Good News is proclaimed, what she has done will be told also, in remembrance of her.'

"Jesus clearly meant that his teachings are to go to the pagans as well as the Jews." Luke, I could tell that Elisa had been thinking about this for some time. She drew a deep breath and concluded with certainty.

"This man Paul will spread those teachings throughout the Gentile world. In this way will the Good News be known among all peoples that Jesus has died for our sins, and that following The Way of Jesus will lead us to salvation in the next world."

We looked at each other with some wonder at our small role in what seems destined to become a worldwide awakening to the Truth.

Naomi and Eliab then led us in singing praises to God, and we continued with the service.

At the community meal that followed, David and Rachel, Samson and Hannah, Daniel and Leah, John and Esther, Ruth, Ana, Miriam and all the Followers gathered around Abriam and Judith, thanking the Lord that he had returned safely.

Dear Luke, our community of believers here in Capernaum is blessed. Our fears of persecution have subsided, and our numbers are growing. Saul is now Paul, an apostle for the Gentiles.

It is God's will.

I looked for Elisa, who had taken a seat on a bench against the wall. I took my place beside her and reached for her hand. She took my hand, smiled and placed it on her rounded abdomen. Our child was dancing in the womb.

Your friend in Christ,
Joseph

Epilogue

Two weeks after Abriam's return to Capernaum, a caravan arrived unexpectedly late one afternoon. A traveler dismounted and asked directions to the clinic of Joseph the physician.

Joseph was alone at the clinic, just completing the day's work. Elisa was not working but at home with his mother, Mary. Erasmus had left at midday, and Jonathan had completed his work and left early. Joseph was about to close the door when the stranger walked in. "Is there a physician available?" he asked.

As Joseph looked closer he recognized the man. "Luke, what are you doing here?" was all that he could say as they embraced.

"I came to meet Elisa and to learn more about the Followers of The Way," Luke replied.

Joseph showed him the clinic and they went arm in arm to surprise Elisa. And surprise it was because she had just started to have her labor pains. Joseph had been prepared for this event and sent Mary to inform Erasmus and Sarah and the Followers of The Way. In a short time Judith, Hannah, Rachel, Jonathan and Elisabeth, Sarah and Erasmus, Mary and Joseph began to gather. With all of the commotion no one seemed to notice the stranger until he started to direct Elisa through her labor. Joseph was praying outside the door. The stranger directed the delivery and a beautiful baby daughter was born. And the first thing Elisa said was, "We will call her Mary, as I promised the mother of Jesus."

As Elisa rested, the women cleaned the baby and placed her for the first time in the arms of her father, Joseph. All of the Followers of The Way of Jesus had now gathered in and around the home. Sarah, Erasmus, Mary and Joseph were overjoyed and thankful. Then Joseph placed the child in his mother's arms and led a prayer of thanksgiving to the Lord God for the safe birth of Mary and the apparent good health of Elisa. Many of the Followers had words of thanksgiving to add. It was only then that Joseph introduced his friend and colleague Luke, the physician of Antioch. All the members welcomed him. Then they left, singing praises of thanksgiving. As Erasmus left he reminded Elisa and Joseph that she must stay in bed for four weeks, and Sarah and Mary prepared to stay as many nights as they were needed.

Luke also stayed at the home of Joseph and Elisa. The women of Capernaum's community church came to care for Elisa and the baby and to cook the meals. Luke helped at the clinic and spent much time with the Followers of The Way as they went about Capernaum tending to the needs of those in hunger or distress. He attended all of the services of the group and studied the writings of Ana. He also studied the teachings of Jesus under David, Samson, Esther and Miriam.

After four weeks he asked to be baptized. It was a jubilant occasion when Luke, the physician of Antioch, and Mary, the infant daughter of Joseph and Elisa, were baptized at the River Jordan. Luke, Joseph and Elisa, with the baby in her arms, stood knee-deep in the waters. Joseph poured water over his daughter's head, then placed his hand over the head of his friend and immersed Luke in the river. "I baptize you," said Joseph, "in the name of the Father and the Son and the Holy Spirit."

At the Breaking of the Bread service that followed, Luke partook of the Body and Blood of Christ for the first time, and he bowed his head and was quiet for some time.

Later, as he was welcomed into the community of Followers, he made an announcement. "I will be going to Jerusalem to meet Peter and offer my services to the apostles." And he prepared to leave the next day.

Joseph helped carry his belongings to the station. One bag was especially heavy and he asked Luke if he was carrying his medical writings. "No," said Luke. "Those are the letters that you have written to me throughout the years.

"You know, Joseph, you described Elisa to me in your letters but you did not do justice to her. She is truly a gift from God."

The Followers of The Way of Jesus in Capernaum continued to grow. Joseph and Luke resumed their correspondence as Luke followed Peter with his work. He later became a companion of Paul, and they visited the community church in Capernaum several times in their travels.

Elisa and Joseph had three more children, two sons and another daughter.

Many years later Luke gathered all of the material in the letters from Joseph, added his experiences and, after carefully considering the whole story of Jesus from the beginning, wrote it all down in an orderly fashion for his friend Theophilus.

About the Author

Drs. Alice and Joe Holoubek met in 1937 during a summer fellowship in pathology at the Mayo Clinic in Rochester, Minn. They corresponded almost daily during their senior year of medical school and during their internships.

Joe Holoubek, son of Joseph and Mary Holoubek of Clarkson, Neb., attended the University of Nebraska College of Medicine in Omaha. His father had been a tenant farmer but moved his family to town, took up employment in a service station and within a few years became the owner. Joe worked with his father from the time he was twelve years of age until he graduated from medical school.

Alice Baker, the daughter of Dr. Erasmus Baker and his wife, Effie, attended LSU School of Medicine in New Orleans, La. Her father was trained in Indiana, had a small-town practice, served in World War I and joined the Veterans Administration medical service. There were several generations of physicians in the Baker family.

Dr. Alice developed pulmonary tuberculosis during her internship and spent four months at absolute bed rest. After her recovery Dr. Edgar Hull, the renowned professor of medicine at LSU School of Medicine, offered her the last remaining fellowship in his department. When he learned of her approaching marriage, he offered to take Dr. Joe and Dr. Alice for the salary of one fellowship. This they gladly accepted.

In the early years of their marriage Dr. Alice had several more months of bed rest and three years of pneumothorax therapy for her tuberculosis. At that time there were no antibiotics for the disease.

When she became pregnant she was advised to have an abortion. They disregarded this recommendation, and Dr. Hull successfully treated her through that and three more pregnancies. Her tuberculosis healed and became inactive.

After their specialty training and Dr. Joe's five years of service in the U.S. Army Medical Corps during World War II, they started their medical practice in Shreveport, La.

Drs. Alice and Joe practiced together for more than 45 years and became heavily involved in medical, civic and religious activities. Dr. Joe chaired the Medical School Development Committee of the Shreveport Medical Society, which founded LSU School of Medicine in Shreveport. It is now in its 35th year and has graduated more than 2,200 physicians. He and Dr. Alice share the Distinguished Service Award from the LSU Medical Center Alumni Association.

The good doctors were bestowed among the highest honors conferred by the pope on Catholic lay people: Knight Commander with Star and Lady of the Order of St. Gregory the Great. As members of the Equestrian Order of the Holy Sepulchre of Jerusalem, they dedicated themselves to preserving the Christian presence in the Holy Land. They were founding members of St. Joseph Catholic Church in Shreveport and jointly received citations from the National Conference of Christians and Jews.

Dr. Joe is a member of the Catholic Academy of Sciences USA. He was associate editor of the Linacre Quarterly. He served on the board of directors of the American Heart Association, and as president of the National Federation of Catholic Physicians Guilds, the Louisiana Heart Society and the Tri-State Medical Society. He has received distinguished service awards from the Shreveport Medical Society, National Federation of Catholic Physicians Guilds, the American Heart Association and the American College of Cardiology.

The Doctors Holoubek were married sixty-five years before Dr. Alice's death in January 2005. They were blessed with two sons, two daughters, six grandchildren and three great-grandchildren.

Like Elisa's father in *Letters to Luke*, Dr. Erasmus Baker, the father of Dr. Alice, spent much time fishing, particularly in his later years.

The incident in Letter 41 about the contaminated well actually occurred early in Dr. Baker's practice. An 1898 graduate of medical school, he had been taught the new finding that germs were the cause of infectious diseases, but when he entered practice his fellow physicians discounted it. He was health officer for the county when an epidemic of typhoid fever developed. With his microscope he was able to prove that the water supply contained the germs that caused the disease. He suggested that the well be closed and a new one dug. The city fathers were upset, but the state board of health confirmed the young doctor's findings. The well was ordered closed, a new well dug on higher ground, and the epidemic stopped.

Sources

The author and his wife have conducted extensive research on the crucifixion and studied seventy-eight cases of hematidrosis, or the sweating of blood, in medical literature. Their published articles on these and other aspects of the sufferings of Christ include the following:

Holoubek, Joe E. and Alice Baker Holoubek, February 1994. A Study of Crucifixion with Attempted Explanation of the Death of Jesus Christ. *Linacre Quarterly* 10-18.

Holoubek, Joe E. and Alice Baker Holoubek, 1995. Execution by Crucifixion. *Journal of Medicine* 24:1-16.

Holoubek, Joe E. and Alice Baker Holoubek, 1996. Blood, Sweat and Fear – A Classification of Hematidrosis. *Journal of Medicine* 27:115-133.

Holoubek, Joe E. and Alice Baker Holoubek, 1998. Hematidrosis – Bloody Sweat – A Study of Seventy-eight Cases. *Science and Religion in Dialogue*, ed. Charles DeCelles. Washington, D.C.: Catholic Academy of Sciences of the United States of America 67-89.

Holoubek, Joe. E. and Alice Baker Holoubek, 1998. The Passion and Crucifixion of Jesus as Seen by Two Physicians. *Science and Medicine in Dialogue* 91-118.

Numerous other research articles and books were consulted in development of this fictionalized account of the writings of St. Luke. Among them are the following:

BOOKS

Barbet, Pierre, 1953. *A Doctor at Calvary: The Passion of Our Lord Jesus Christ as Described by a Surgeon.* Translated by the Earl of Wicklow. New York: P.J. Kennedy & Sons.

Bishop, Jim, 1957, 1977. *The Day Christ Died.* San Francisco: Harper and Row.

Daniel-Rops, Henri, 1980. *Daily Life in the Time of Jesus.* Ann Arbor: Servant Publications.

Edersheim, Alfred, 1990. *Sketches of Jewish Social Life.* Grand Rapids, Mich.: Wm. R. Eerdmans Publishing.

LaVerdiere, Eugene, 1990. *Luke (New Testament Message, Vol. 5).* Collegeville, Minn.: Liturgical Press.

Lofts, Norah, 1965. *How Far to Bethlehem.* Greenwood, Conn. Fawcett Books.

Lyons, Albert S. and R. Joseph Petrucelli, 1978. *Medicine: An Illustrated History.* New York. Harry N. Abrams.

The author also highly recommends the works of the late Archbishop Fulton J. Sheen, available in writing and audio form through St. Joseph Communications, www.saintjoe.com.

ARTICLES

Dubovsky, H., 1989. The Jewish Contribution to Medicine. *South African Medical Journal* 76 (1):26-28

Maier, D.M., May 1983. The Physician as a Man – The Man as a Physician, A Jewish Viewpoint. *New York State Journal of Medicine* 83 (6): 813-816.

Massry, Shaul G., Miroslav Smogrozewski, Elizur Hazani and Shaul M. Shasha, 1997. Influence of Judaism and Jewish Physicians on Greek and Byzantine Medicine and Their Contribution to Nephrology. *American Journal of Nephrology* 17 (3-4): 233-240.

REFERENCE MATERIALS

Dictionary of the Bible, 1965. Ed. John L. McKenzie. Milwaukee: Bruce Publishing.

Encyclopaedia Judaica, 1971. Jerusalem: Keter Publishing House Ltd.

Holman Bible Dictionary, 1991. Ed. Trent C. Butler. Nashville: Holman Bible Publishers.

Bible Gateway, 1995-2003. Gospel Communications International. http://bible.gospelcom.net

Bible History Online, 2004. http://www.bible-history.com

The Catholic Encyclopedia, Online Edition, 2003. New Advent. http://www.newadvent.org/cathen/

Catholic Information Network, 1987-2003. http://www.cin.org

The Bible, King James Version, Old and New Testaments with the Apocrypha, The Electronic Text Center, University of Virginia, 1995-2004. http://etext.lib.virginia.edu/kjv.browse.html

Manna Bible Maps, 1999. http://www.biblemaps.com

New Testament
People and Places

Ananias of Damascus 527-532

Andrew the Apostle 90, 133, 140-145, 195, 199, 209, 244, 365, 379, 427, 454; Called by Jesus 163; Catch of fish 137-138; Commissioned by Jesus 205

Annas the high priest 23, 37, 367, 384, 390, 473

Apostles (The Twelve)
Andrew *See Andrew the Apostle*
Arrest of the Apostles 473, 476-477
Bartholomew *See Bartholomew the Apostle*
Calling of The Twelve 163
Descent of the Holy Spirit 427
James son of Alphaeus *See James the Lesser*
James son of Zebedee *See James the Greater*
John son of Zebedee *See John the Beloved Disciple*
Judas *See Judas Iscariot*
Jude son of James *See Jude the Apostle*
Last instructions of Jesus 426-427
Levi the tax collector *See Matthew the Apostle*
Mission of The Twelve 205
Philip *See Philip the Apostle*
Simon *See Simon the Apostle*
Simon Peter the First Apostle *See Peter*
Thomas *See Thomas the Apostle*
Last Supper 373-379
Upper Room, the 419-420, 422-423, 425-427, 449-450

Barabbas the insurgent 385, 395-396

Barsabbas the disciple 450

Bartholomew the Apostle 163, 205, 209, 220, 335

Caiaphas the high priest 37, 367-368, 473; Arrest, trial and death of Jesus 384-386, 390-399, 404-405, 421-422

Chuza, steward of Herod 185, 207, 217, 219, 268

Cleopas the disciple 346, 425-427

Elisabeth the mother of John the Baptist 54, 314-315, 341-342

Essenes community 25, 28, 48-49, 55

Gabriel the angel 319, 323, 460; Annunciation 314-315; Appears to Joseph 317, 325; Appears to Zachariah 341-342

Gamaliel the Elder 32, 161, 464, 477, 527

Garden of Gethsemane 23, 266, 353-354, 379-382, 416

Golgotha (Calvary) 400-401, 416

Herod tetrarch of Galilee 37, 83, 185, 219, 221, 257, 345; Arrest and trial of Jesus 392-395, 397, 474; Arrest of John the Baptist 207-208; Beheading of John the Baptist 217-218

Herod the Great 22, 128, 185, 325-328

Herodias 83, 207-208, 217-218, 221

Holy of Holies 22, 367-368, 385, 422, 441

James the Greater 90, 140-145, 161, 174-175, 209, 213, 322, 517; Called by Jesus 163; Catch of fish 138; Commissioned by Jesus 205; Cure of Jairus' daughter 203-204; Gethsemane 380-383; Transfiguration at Mount Tabor 309-311

James the Lesser 163-164, 194, 205, 232-233, 303, 375, 416

Jesus 90-92, 95, 110-112
    Agony in the garden 380-383
    Ancestry 96-97
    Anointing with oil 346, 532
    Appears to Apostles in Upper Room 426-427
    Arrest at Gethsemane 382
    Ascends to heaven 418
    Associates with sinners 153, 179, 276-277, 293
    Banquet at Bethany 345-347, 532
    Banquet at Levi's 153-155
    Baptism by John 58-59
    Before Herod 392-394
    Before Pilate 391-392, 394-396
    Before the Sanhedrin 385-386
    Birth in Bethlehem 127-128, 317-318
    Burial in the tomb 409-410
    Call of Gentiles 111, 173, 260, 267, 533
    Call of Levi 152
    Call of Simon, Andrew, James and John 137-139, 143-146
    Call of the seventy-two 235-236
    Call of The Twelve 163
    Carrying of the cross 400-402
    Children, with 199-200, 233, 238, 291
    Circumcision of Jesus 322-324
    Commissioning of Apostles 205
    Crowning of thorns 397
    Crucifixion 396, 402-407
    Emmaus, road to 425
    Enters Jerusalem 353-355
    Expels the moneychangers 367

Judas Iscariot 205, 209, 335; Banquet at Bethany 346; Betrayal of Jesus 382; Last Supper 374-377; Return of the silver 450

Judas of Damascus 526-532

Jude the Apostle (Thaddeus) 163-164, 194, 205, 209, 233, 266-267, 335, 353

Lazarus of Bethany 242-243, 345-347, 356, 369, 410, 416, 423, 428-429

Martha of Bethany 242-243, 345-347, 356-357, 369, 410, 412, 416, 423, 429-430

Mary of Bethany 242-243, 345-347, 356-357, 369, 373, 410, 412, 416, 423, 429

Mary of Magdala 185, 393, 409, 416, 418-419, 423, 426-427, 429

Mary the mother of James the Lesser 303, 409, 416, 419, 441

Mary the mother of Jesus 412-413, 429, 447, 465-470, 476, 480; Annunciation 314-315; At the crucifixion 403-410; At the resurrection 418-420; Betrothal to Joseph 314-316; Birth of Jesus 318; Descent of the Holy Spirit 455; Flight to Egypt 325-327; Visit of the shepherds 319; Visit of the wise men 324-325; Visit with Elisabeth her cousin 315-316

Matthew the Apostle (Levi the tax collector) 152-153, 161, 163, 205, 209, 335, 376

Matthias the Apostle 450

Miracles of Jesus
Blind man 336
Boy with seizure 230
Calming of the storm 196-198
Catch of fish 137-138
Centurion's servant 172-173
Five loaves and two fish 223
Jairus' daughter 201-204
Man with leprosy 141-142
Man with demons 198-200
Man with dropsy 270-271
Man with seizures 130-131
Man with withered hand 159-160
Paralyzed man 149-150
Simon's mother-in-law 132-133
Ten lepers 330
Widow's son 174
Woman with a hemorrhage 202

Nicodemus 386, 407, 409

Parables of Jesus
Crafty steward 282-283
Fig tree 257
Good Samaritan 240, 468
House built on rock 167

New Testament People and Places

Judge and widow 289
Lamp 188
Lost drachma 276-277
Lost sheep 276
Mustard seed 195, 260
Narrow door 266
New wine and old skins 154-155
Owner of the vineyard 359-360
Pharisee and tax collector 289
Pharisees and lawyers 249-251
Pounds 340
Prodigal son 278-280
Rich man and Lazarus 285
Salt loses its taste 274
Sower 187
Tribute to Caesar 360
Unclean spirit 248
Widow's offering 362
Yeast 260

Paul (Saul of Tarsus) 507-511, 533; At the stoning of Stephen 479; Conversion 525-528; Persecution of the early Christians 464, 466, 479, 483; 486-496, 509; Preaching in Damascus 528-530; Studying under Gamaliel 32, 464, 527

Peter (Simon Peter) 90, 140-145, 203, 209, 213, 256, 263, 294, 358, 425; Arrest of Jesus 383; Arrest with the Apostles 473-474, 476-477; At the tomb of Jesus 420-421; Baptism, speaking on 452-461; Before the Sanhedrin with John 473-474; Called by Jesus 138, 163; Calming of the storm 196-198; Catch of fish 137-138; Commissioned by Jesus 205; Denial foretold 378; Denial of Jesus 388-389; Descent of the Holy Spirit 454-456; Early church in Jerusalem 449-450, 455, 459-460, 470-473; Expelling of the moneychangers 367; Gethsemane 380; Keys of the kingdom 225; Last Supper 373-379; Luke joins Peter 536; Mother-in-law's healing 132-133; Resurrection of Jesus 419-423; Selection of the seven 459-460; Transfiguration at Mount Tabor 309-311; Upper Room, in the 419-423, 425-427, 449-450

Philip the Apostle 163, 209, 220-224, 422-427, 476, 479

Pontius Pilate 37, 185, 257, 360; Arrest and trial of Jesus 385-411

Salome the daughter of Herodias 217-218

Salome the mother of James and John 303, 409-410, 416, 419, 441, 466

Samaria and Samaritans 22, 185, 240, 322, 330-331, 454, 468, 476, 479

Sanhedrin, the 33, 385-386, 390-391, 395, 400, 406-407, 473, 477-478, 502

Saul of Tarsus *See Paul the Apostle*

Simon the Apostle 163, 205, 209, 242-243, 335, 353

Simon the Cyrene 401

Simon Peter *See Peter*

Simon the Pharisee 181-184

Stephen the disciple 478-479

Susanna, follower of Jesus 186

Teachings of Jesus
Almsgiving 255, 294
Apostles' Prayer (The Lord's Prayer) 244, 445, 495
Ask and it will be given 245
Beware of the scribes 361-362
Brotherly forgiveness 194-195
Casting out devils 247
Coming of the kingdom of God 235-237, 287, 364, 376
Compassion and generosity 166-167
Danger of riches 169, 293
Day of the Son of Man 287-288
Exalting oneself 271-272
Faith of a child 194
Fasting 154
Great commandment 239
Greatest among you 378
Healing on the Sabbath 160, 259-260, 271
Hoarding possessions 169
Household divided 256
Hypocrisy of the Pharisees 249-250, 253
Inheriting eternal life 239-240, 293-294
Inviting guests 272-273
Jerusalem will be destroyed 363-365
Kingdom divided against itself 247
Kingdom of God 135, 165, 187, 260, 267, 287, 291, 294, 378
Last days 364-365
Last will be first 266
Lilies of the field 303
Love of enemy 166
Marriage 283
Open and fearless speech 253-254
Place of honor 264, 271-272
Power of faith 172, 183, 195, 198, 202-203, 271, 330, 336, 471
Prayer 244-245
Preparing for Master's return 255-256, 364-365
Renouncing family 274
Renouncing possessions 254-255, 274
Resurrection of the dead 361
Scribes and Pharisees 149-150
Sermon on the Mount 165-167